Praise for The Netherfeld Trilogy

"Amber Elby crafts a world that invokes the best of Terry Pratchett, Ursula K. Le Guin, and Neil Gaiman, all rooted in the mythology of Shakespeare. The Netherfeld series is a must read for lovers of magic, the inexplicable, and especially the timeless wonder conjured by the plays of William Shakespeare."
~**Montgomery Sutton**, Shakespearean Actor, Director, and Playwright

"Reading Amber Elby's work is like walking down a pathway into my own childhood fairy land. All of the characters we love from Shakespeare come out to play, and we lose ourselves in her text as easily as one might get lost in the forest of Arden. Artists and readers will feel more seen with each turn of the page."
~**Victoria Rae Sook**, Artistic Director and Founder of *Food of Love* Productions

"Whip-smart, and I think would be just as much fun to read even if you had no knowledge of the Shakespeare characters it plays with – though if you do have this knowledge, you'll have some extra spice from seeing how Amber plays with it all... Five out of five cats!"
~**Asha & Tomte**, *A Cat, A Book, and A Cup of Tea Reviews*

"Like Shakespeare!? Like Percy Jackson? Imagine if you combine Rick Riordan's brilliance and Shakespeare's genius! What you get is the perfection that is Amber Elby's *Cauldron's Bubble* Series! All the adventure and heartbreak leaves you begging for more after each chapter. Well researched and thought out, and finally another non-toxic author! This series is what the world needs right now."
~**Alice D. Bloomer**, Actor and Producer of *Socially Distant Cymbeline*

"This series is almost impossible to put down. Elby truly captures Shakespeare's works with her adept writing... Similar to a puzzle, in my mind, that Elby pieces together beautifully."
~**Tiffany Salazar**, *Beyond the Stars Reviews*

"Artistically and very cleverly written. The author Amber Elby certainly studied hard to make the book as perfect as possible, especially when it came to the Shakespearean characters that make an appearance. It is also a great introduction to Shakespeare for young adults that are either studying the Bard's plays or will be soon."
~**Stacey Garrity**, *Whispering Stories Book Blog*

"I love Caliban the best. A man of opposites who speaks in riddles and lives in time. This is all I can safely tell you without spilling too many beans. Each book in this series has been better than the one before... A delight to read as I immersed myself into this fantastical world of Shakespearean plays."
~**Linda Lou Weaver Oliphant**, Bookstagrammer @lilus_library

"Part of the joy of this book is the excitement you feel when reading the name of a character you know so well... It's the book I never knew I needed until I read the first couple of pages."
~**Rosie Threakall**, *Rosie Freckle Reads*

The Netherfeld Trilogy

CAULDRON'S BUBBLE
DOUBLE DOUBLE TOIL
TROUBLE FIRES BURN

*inspired by the **magic** of William Shakespeare*

an original trio of novels by
Amber Elby

Verdopolis Press

Published by Verdopolis Press of Austin, Texas, United States of America.
Printed and bound in the United States of America.
ISBN – 978-1-7323142-8-3
First edition, August 2021.
Cover art by TypeJar Studio of Austin, Texas, United States of America.

Visit www.amberelby.com. Follow Amber Elby on Twitter @amberelby

TRIGGER WARNING   This text contains instances of abusive behavior, thoughts of self-harm, and suicidal tendencies that parallel events described in William Shakespeare's plays. If you or someone you know need help, please visit nimh.nih.gov or reach out to your local mental health services. You are loved.

This work is dedicated to...

my husband,
for believing in me,
and to my girls,
for believing in magic...

...and to teachers;
you deserve so much more...

...and to the authors who live
within these pages, especially
William,
Charlotte,
Thomas,
George,
Emily,
Jane,
Alfred,
Branwell,
and
Anne.

Rest in Power.

This trilogy edition is in celebration of...

The 70th birthday of my mother on May 23, 2021
and
the forthcoming nuptial ceremony of Victoria and Michael.

TABLE OF CONTENTS

Volume Two: DOUBLE DOUBLE TOIL

Introduction to CAULDRON'S BUBBLE (2017)

"There are no pirates in *Hamlet*," my colleague scoffed condescendingly. It was clear that he thought I was unfit to teach the revered Bard.

"Yes there are. In Act Four, Scene Six,* Horatio reads a letter about how Hamlet encountered pirates on the way to England." (*I had to look up the exact scene later.)

"That?" He laughed. "That's just *deus ex machina*." *God the machine.* A plot device for writers too lazy or hurried to bother with the constraints of reality.

I wondered if my colleague was right. Maybe Shakespeare was looking for an easy way to get Hamlet back to Denmark. A simple way to progress the plot. Throw-away information. Trivial.

But what if *Hamlet*'s pirates were important?

When we teach Shakespeare today, we often forget that his plays were never meant to be read. He did not publish them. He – and his troupe – performed them. They were interactive and immersive. They broke the fourth wall. They pushed the boundaries of fiction and created new words and new worlds. They turned the expectations of the day upside down: women were powerful; rulers were petty; and magic was real. Shakespeare's plays were experiences, not performances.

But today, in classrooms in this country and beyond, students are required to read *Macbeth* and *Hamlet* and *The Tempest* either alone, silently, or sitting still at desks, taking turns and fearing that they may be called to participate. There are exceptions, of course, but this is by and far the norm. Teenagers struggle with Elizabethan language and trip over unfamiliar metric feet. They despise the plays because they cannot appreciate what they do not understand; they are disengaged.

Shakespeare, to them, is dead.

But he is not, not truly.

I was fortunate to have a professor in graduate school who was a Shakespeare fanboy. His enthusiasm was contagious as he compared the Bard to modern filmmakers. The opening scene of *The Tempest,* with its chaotic shipwreck, parallels quite closely with the cold open of any J. J. Abrams film. The character arcs of Hamlet and Lady Macbeth align with the best of Alfred Hitchcock. Shakespeare was a storyteller, my professor said, first and foremost.

So let's make Shakespeare relatable by focusing on his stories. Instead of force-feeding archaic vocabulary down the throats of disinterested students, let's perform the plays and give life to the characters. Ask questions. Speculate. Encourage improvisation and "what ifs." Let's even use Shakespeare to tell new stories. Let's resurrect him and make him our own.

And don't dismiss those of us who love the pirates in *Hamlet* or the witches in *Macbeth* or the backstory of *The Tempest.* In many ways, the parts that occur offstage are the most interesting, the most compelling, and the most complicated. Those aspects were too advanced to actually produce when Shakespeare was alive. They were impossible then, but that does not mean that they were not and are not vital.

What if *Hamlet's* pirates are important? They are. And so is Shakespeare.

Introduction to THE NETHERFELD TRILOGY **Edition (2021)**

It is not an exaggeration to say that Shakespeare's plays saved lives during the pandemic. And before, perhaps thousands of times, not because of his words alone but because of the way his texts continue to touch our lives, of the feelings and memories his stories evoke, and the community built around the Bard.

When *Cauldron's Bubble* materialized in 2017, I had only seen one live production of Shakespeare in the previous fifteen years: *Julius Caesar* at The Globe in London in the summer of 2014. This was not due to lack of interest but rather with issues surrounding money and geography and time. I had read Shakespeare nearly constantly and taught his works annually, but attending a performance was not readily within my means.

Everything changed in the spring of 2018, when my family attended a free production of *A Midsummer Night's Dream* by En Route productions at an urban farm in East Austin. It was quick and clever and modern and everything that I knew Shakespeare could and should be. It was what I saw in my head, come to life.

So the following year, my family and I set out on something like a grand Shakespeare tour. We saw *Romeo and Juliet* at The Globe in London, *Much Ado About Nothing* in Dallas, a festival of seven plays in one day in a beer garden in New Hampshire by Seven Stages Shakespeare, and other productions by the Rude Grooms, Shakespeare Everywhere, Baron's Men, Past is Prologue, Rosedale Shakespeare, Shakespeare Dallas, and the enigmatic Hidden Room. In total, we attended over twenty productions in less than twelve months.

Then the pandemic hit, and Shakespeare was no more.

Or so it seemed. In the spring of 2020, new performance models emerged from behind closed doors by The Show Must Go Online, Shakespeare Happy Hours, Sofa Shakespeare, Socially Distant Cymbeline, Food of Love Productions, and many more revolutionary companies that used props from pantries and costumes from families' closets and shared kisses and crossed swords through Zoom screens.

Shakespeare performances were reborn. Virtually. And that alone would be enough for many artists to weather the pandemic.

But something else emerged from the darkness and isolation of 2020: friendship.

When I wrote *Cauldron's Bubble*, I told very few people of my endeavor. It was a lonely process, often met with criticism and doubt. As time passed, however, I found encouragement from new sources and planted the seeds of friendship on social media with people far beyond my personal sphere. And during the pandemic, these friendships bloomed into a different kind of company...

I have many times described our virtual Shakespeare reading group, Beers & Bard, as the best thing ever. It is. And more.

On the surface, the Beers & Bard crew is a motley group of actors, theatre-makers, educators, and Shakespeare Stans. We meet once a week or so, usually on Sunday evenings, and randomly assign parts from a play. Then we cold-read, which would be terrifying if not for the acceptance and support and encouragement of our team. There are no gates, no guards, no negativity. We each bring what we will. Some performers fall into accents. Some sing. Some struggle with archaic pronunciations, but none are excluded or ridiculed or made to feel "less than." We are a team.

#TeamShakespeare #TeamBeersandBard

Some of us in Beers & Bard, such as my husband, had never read Elizabethan drama before, while others have been performing or teaching Shakespeare for decades. We are vastly different and would never have met without the internet; we never would have Zoomed before the pandemic. The odds that the gods would put us all in one spot were slim to none. Yet we found each other, despite this long shot, and flourished together.

Now is when I must pause, take a deep breath, and wonder how anyone else could understand the unity that we have in Beers & Bard, how mere words could explain the myriad ways our friendship — our connection — has pulled us through the darkest year of our collective lifetimes.

Of course Shakespeare says it best: "I do love nothing in the world so well as you: is not that strange?"

Yes, strange. Strange that reading 400 year old dialogue on a screen across thousands of miles has brought us closer than the most intimate scene in the tangible world. Strange that the feelings these plays evoke are repeated again and again in our own lives, and strange that the tools we learn from fiction to process these powerful emotions give us strength and hope and unity in ways that simple conversations never could. Strange that the love I have for these people whom I have never seen outside of a monitor is as strong as any I have felt before.

Love is strange, but we are not strangers. Shakespeare ensured that we are friends.

And like all good friendships, the Beers & Bard crew is merry. We have a spreadsheet of "what, HO"s and sigh, "Awww, sh*t" whenever we see "alas" in a script. We lean into innuendos and land hard on "but" and force our cats, screaming, onto the screen. We wear tiaras and pirate hats and filters with rainbow eyebrows. We have shirts with "Yay, Hamlet" and "What, you egg" and take Shakespeare seriously, but not too seriously. He is one of us in a virtual pub, not an idol on a pedestal. We treat the Bard as an equal and, in turn, we become part of his family as well as our own.

As what we knew of social interaction crumbled this past year, Shakespeare brought us friendship in a new form. That is the point of plays, of storytelling: to bring people into the same space, both fictional and literal. To demonstrate love and loyalty overcoming hatred and deceit. To inspire smiles and tears. To raise our voices. To be heard. Seen. To feel. To love. To become a community, a collective, a cry.

We are all players in Shakespeare's world. Together.

Volume One: Cauldron's Bubble

Banquo: The Earth hath bubbles, as the Water ha's,
And these are of them: whither are they vanish'd?

Macbeth: Into the Ayre: and what seem'd corporall,
Melted, as breath into the Winde.
Would they had stay'd...

~William Shakespeare (1564-1616), *Macbeth*
Baquo's conversation with Macbeth, Act 1, Scene 3
First Folio, 1623

Chapter One: Midwinter Night's Dream

Alda hesitated on the bridge, alone for the first time, in the vast middle of the night. The witching time of night.

Snow hovered, forming fantastic shapes in the new electric lights that lined the street.

She did not notice the winter's chill, or the sharp shadows around her, or the static hum that echoed through the longest night of the year.

Instead, Alda focused on the water below as she leaned on the icy railings. The Grand River swirled beneath the bridge, as black and solemn as the skirt that slapped against her legs, as wild as her raven hair that waved in the wind and snow.

She should cry. She knew she *should* cry, and she always did as she should. Even though she was sick at heart, she was complacent. Compliant. And calm.

But that was all before she was alone on the bridge.

Even though she focused on the water, Alda did not see it, not truly. Instead, in her mind's eye, she saw the dark soil as it was dropped unceremoniously on her grandmother's grave. She saw how the earth separated her from the one person she had ever loved and trusted, the only soul she ever really knew. A world was now between her and her grandmother, and all seemed lost.

The streetlight atop the post next to her flickered and went out with a hiss and a fountain of sparks. The new electricity was unreliable and, as Alda had said before, terrifying in its novelty. Almost magical.

As she stood watching the river, wondering at her inability to cry, the other lights likewise flickered and went out.

Now Alda was alone and in near total darkness. It was a sign, perhaps, or an omen, that she should go elsewhere. Leave.

She crossed the bridge, away from the cemetery, carefully treading over the ice in her soft leather shoes. Down the bank toward the river. Onto the Ledge Path that skirted the sandstone cliffs on the riverbank. Past the carvings on the protruding rocks, the graffiti of the hordes of visitors who flocked to Grand Ledge every summer.

She could have perceived the wooden rollercoaster spanning the resort island, rising in the river like a sea monster, or the Folly Hotel silhouetted above like a fairytale tower. But she did not linger to look at these familiar sites as she tread reflexively toward the farthest, smallest island. Home.

She reached the mural of the three animals near Lion Head Rock, the mural inscribed, "When Shall We Three Meet Again?" To her right, a smaller path led directly to the river, to the rickety bridge that crossed to their cottage on the seventh island. *Her* cottage now, not *theirs*.

Once inside, she lit the oil lamp as she had so many times before. But now, its light fell on an empty chair next to the fireplace and the untouched stereoscope on the end table. She was not greeted with the clink of a spoon in a bowl or the bubbling of soup in a cast iron pot. There was no smile, no happy voice in the quaint, cold cottage. Not even a mouse stirred.

Yet the smell lingered. Lavender, thyme, sage, rosemary. *Rosemary, that's for remembrance*, her grandmother would say. Now the herbs were all bundled neatly with twine above the wooden kitchen table. The smells of her grandmother's cooking. Of feasts. Of happiness. Of Gramma. Gone.

Alda suddenly felt weak, exhausted, and lowered herself onto a creaking chair at the kitchen table. She remembered the previous Christmas, when she was thirteen. How her grandmother somehow negotiated with the butcher on Bridge Street for a Christmas ham. They had no money, at least not enough for a ham, but Gramma had a way with words and convinced the man to part with it as Alda watched, amazed, through the store window.

That night, despite their transitory happiness, was the beginning of the end. It was the start of her grandmother's lapses, her strange exclamations and questions. As the ham cooked in a Dutch oven, the older woman glanced at Alda and mumbled, almost to herself, "When I saw you the last time, your hair was longer, but not much." Alda, confused, touched her black hair, reassuring herself it was unchanged, "But I've never cut it." Gramma pressed her lips into a line and nodded absentmindedly, again looking into the fire.

Alda, her attention back in the present, felt an illogical, overwhelming sense of fury. It was not fair. None of it. Her grandmother's forgetfulness, madness, death. Her own responsibility, burden, and grief. Fury turned into rage, and Alda turned to destruction.

She grasped the herbs above her head and pulled the bundles down around her wildly, crushing them into thousands of pieces in her fists. And she cried, finally, as the overwhelming scent brought unwelcome emotions and overpowering memories. She tried to wipe her tears, but the herbs on her hands stung her eyes, so she collapsed onto the table and sobbed into her arms.

After some time, and many regrets and sorrows, she lifted her head, wiped the tears away with her black sleeve, and picked the crushed herbs from between her fingers. As her focus shifted from her fingertips to the tabletop, Alda let out a quiet scream and jumped back in fear and surprise.

She hesitated and leaned forward, studying what could not be explained. She looked away, far out the window at the river in the moonlight, and back again.

It was still there.

Written in perfect script on the kitchen table, in the tiny crumblings of the herbs mixed with the tears that had pooled beneath her eyes, was a single word: CLOAK.

The letters were too perfect, the lines too precise to be accidental. This was not by chance. This was not natural. This was something that Alda could not rationalize, but she inexplicably understood the single word, the message.

She turned to her grandmother's cloak that hung, unmoved, on a hook near the door. Instinctively, Alda buried her hand within its lining until she found a shallow, hidden pocket. She felt a small shock as her fingers enclosed something cold and smooth.

Carefully, gently, Alda removed the object and turned toward the lamplight as she uncurled her shaking fingers.

In her palm was a perfect, iridescent sphere. It was the size of a marble but transparent, almost like a bubble, a delicate bubble that was unexpectedly heavy and solid.

As she turned the mysterious object in the dimming light, a strange sensation engulfed her, a feeling like slipping into a warm bath after a trek in the snow. Alda smiled for the first time in weeks, calmed by the sensation washing over her. She squeezed the sphere in her fist.

And then she was gone, vanished into nothing.

The oil lamp flickered in the empty cottage and then went out, as a cold draft swept the herbs into the air. The smell of rosemary lingered.

*   *   *

The boy awoke suddenly, roused from his uneasy sleep not by a sound or a movement but by a scent. He could not explain the smell, but it was something that he vaguely remembered from many years ago, something he associated with cooking and feasts and family. Rosemary.

The boy, now fully awake, lingered on the coiled rope on the floor of the gun deck where he slept, not wanting to begin the labor of the day. As he delayed his duties, the ship, a galleon called *The Tempest*, rocked gently, so gently that he no longer noticed, as he traced constellations in the knots on the wooden ceiling.

Yet the scent of the rosemary was with him despite being fully awake, and he wondered where the smell could have come from on a ship in the middle of the North Sea on the shortest day of the year. Was the smell a memory, or a dream?

The boy was still wondering ten minutes later, when the too familiar footsteps indicated the end of his four-hour rest. His watch had begun.

"Boy, there's work to do!" It was Ernesto, the red-haired first mate from Naples.

The boy mechanically stood and buttoned his cuffs. There was no need to change his clothes because he had no others. There was no need to wash his face because he had no water.

There was no need for the first mate to call out his name because he had none.

"Boy, get a move on," the Neapolitan called impatiently, ducking under the ladder to give the boy a threatening stare.

Within a minute, the boy was out from his corner of the gun deck and shivering on the main. The sky was dark, and the crew on watch had moments earlier stumbled up from the relative warmth below. They scratched and stretched as they cursed and spit upon the deck. One bearded man vomited, and the boy fetched a bucket of water to clean the mess.

As the boy bent to do his work, the same man kicked him in the ribs and laughed as he rolled aft. Ernesto laughed, too, as the men set about their duties.

The boy shook his head as he stood, getting his bearings. He had forgotten about the mysterious smell already.

Hours later, the boy finished his morning chores, his hands and feet aching from scrubbing and braiding and mending. He found refuge sitting in a corner of the forecastle, perched slightly above the prow of the ship, watching the long-haired figurehead cut a path above the white water as he absentmindedly chewed his salted meat, listening to the crew sing as they worked below him on the deck.

The ship would change course soon and head east to return the prisoner. The boy knew this, but the crew did not. The boy often knew more than the crew because he did his best to be invisible, hiding wherever and whenever he could, listening through a knot to the plans made in the great cabin. Whenever he was not being given commands.

But he did not care if they sailed the galleon east or west or north or south. All compass points were the same to him. Someday, he imagined, he would have a destination and a longing to go there. Home. Home was a foreign idea to him, but it sounded appealing, from what he heard.

As the boy looked past the forecastle, watching the white foam swirl about the ship, he had a feeling that he was being watched. This was not an unusual feeling. After all, the ship was crowded, and it was difficult to be alone.

But this time the feeling was different. He did not hear heavy, uneven breathing or smell stale ale. He did not fear a swift kick or punch or worse. He felt a kind of dizzy excitement, not dread, a sensation that something was about to happen, about to begin.

Taking a sudden breath to steady his nerves, the boy whipped his head around. Balancing deftly on the slats of the beakhead was a girl with long, black hair. A real girl, appearing to be flesh and bone.

He had not seen a girl before, at least not that he remembered, but he knew what one was from the figurehead and the crew's stories of adventures at port. She wore an unusual black dress, the same shade as her hair, and her feet were covered in soft leather shoes.

Girls did not belong on ships. Women did not belong on ships. Maybe this was a siren or a mermaid or a ghost from the rigging.

The boy wondered whether he had lost his mind, like so many sailors before him.

He looked down at his bare feet, closed his eyes, and took steady breaths. Summoning courage, he looked up, expecting to see the empty beakhead, but the girl was still there. He studied her. She seemed familiar. No, she *felt* familiar, like he knew her, but without a memory of her acquaintance. Could he have known her, somehow, before?

She stared at him, likewise confused and shocked, and moved her mouth, trying to speak, looking strangely like a fish gasping for air. Before a sound came out, she clenched her right fist, and vanished.

The boy looked around him as if searching for a wayward seagull, glancing frantically past the foresail to the sky and to the seas and all around him. The girl was gone, like fog before the rising sun. He was alone, for now.

He looked over the prow again, wondering what the sudden appearance of the girl could mean and whether she was a vision or material, when his musings were interrupted.

"Dreng! Dreng!" The calls were muffled, the voice of the prisoner in the hold barely audible between the planks of the decks. "Dreng!" The last call was clearer, obviously the result of increasing effort from frustration or desperation. The crew laughed and shouted obscenities through the floor at their captive. "Put his majesty in the bilge if he can't hold his tongue," one suggested, much to the amusement of his mates.

The boy sighed and climbed down from the forecastle. He could think of the girl tonight. Now his duty, quite literally, called. As he crossed the main deck, he once again smelled the familiar, herby scent that broke his morning slumber. He smiled.

Chapter Two: Seeds of Time

Alda sat upright, like one jolted from a dream. She was outside in her cottage garden, sitting on a millstone that her grandmother propped under the kitchen window, next to the old, dry well and herb beds. She shivered, but not from cold.

Moments earlier, Alda had been on a ship. At least she thought she was on a ship. With a boy her own age. He saw her, as she had seen him, and she had thought for a moment that she recognized him. No, not recognized, *knew*, like they had shared something, some experience, in the distant past.

Immediately before that, she had been in her cottage, holding the mysterious sphere. But how could that be?

Time. The word jumped into her head. She remembered a strange conversation with her grandmother, not more than a week ago, one of the last conversations they had that was still somewhat lucid.

In the memory, Alda tended to the fire while her grandmother reclined in her armchair, covered with her black velvet cloak.

"It's about time."

Alda glanced up before quickly returning her attention to the fire, annoyed at her grandmother's apparent impatience. "The wood is wet. I'm doing the best I can."

Gramma waved her hand dismissively and shook her head. "It's *about* time."

"I don't know what you mean." Alda said this more to herself as she poked the fire, watching sparks leap toward the flue.

"Life." The old woman sighed, her breath shaking. "Time is all you need. And have. Time and..." She trailed off.

Before Alda could reply, the clock had struck eleven. She sat silently while it chimed. When she turned back toward the armchair, her grandmother was asleep.

Alda had thought little of this past conversation, this memory, until now. Until this.

Had she traveled through time?

Was the sphere some kind of time device, something that could change chronology and allow her to travel from one day to another, one year to another?

But the ship was another place entirely, not simply another time.

It could have been her imagination, perhaps, but Alda did not know how she could imagine such a place. She had never been anywhere else, apart from the neighboring villages, and all she knew of the farther-away world was from books and stereopticon cards. And the ship and the boy were too real, too material to be formed in her mind.

Curious and deep in thought, she studied the sphere's glistening surface and thought how it might work. Finally, somewhat apprehensively, she whispered, "June the twenty first, eighteen eighty-six." It was a reasonably close date, not as distant as the ship, so she hoped...

But nothing happened. She turned the sphere over in her palm, clenched it in her fist, and tried commanding it, "Go to June the twenty first, eighteen eighty-six." Still nothing.

She studied the sphere more skeptically. It was unusual, certainly, but not extraordinary. Some of the souvenir shops along Bridge Street sold dainty, crystal ornaments that looked similar. Some homes in town even hung glass witch-balls in their windows to deter evil spirits, so perhaps it was a smaller one of those.

Maybe it was ordinary after all. Maybe she hit her head in the cottage and dreamt about the ship and the boy, her imagination more vivid than she had anticipated. Then she could have sleepwalked into the garden or lost her memory or had a delusional episode of melancholia from the grief of her grandmother's death and burial.

After several minutes, Alda decided that any of those explanations were more likely and rational than some magical sphere that could bend time and place.

As she dismissed the sphere's magic, a shock ran from her toes to her fingertips. She realized that even though it was midwinter's night in a snowy garden, even though her fingers should have been aching from frost and her breath should have hovered in the air before her, she was not shivering.

Then she looked around and realized that although she was in her cottage garden, it was not the garden she had left. The ground was covered in white crocuses, and the scent of her grandmother's fresh herbs lingered in the air. The nearby vegetable patch sprouted in the sun that streamed dimly through a thin canopy of new, green leaves. It was morning. It was spring.

The world was not as she had left it.

The cottage window above her head was open, and she could hear the soft clink of a spoon in a bowl. Alda stood slowly, looking through the window as cautiously as possible.

Her grandmother met her gaze, and smiled.

Alda jumped back, nearly tripping over a raised bed of iris. Her grandmother lifted a finger to her lips, motioning her to silence, and then beckoned her closer to the open window. Inside, Alda could see herself, a self two years younger, peering through her stereoscope, her back to the window.

Alda stammered, trying to phrase a question. She had so many. She started to speak, but her grandmother shook her head, still grinning, and replaced her finger to her lips, mixing something in the bowl as if nothing unusual was happening.

After a moment for Alda to recover from her shock, the old woman glanced over her shoulder at the younger Alda and then back again. She mouthed the word "bubble" and raised her eyebrows questioningly. Alda understood and raised the iridescent sphere in her hand. Gramma smiled, looked intently at the sphere, and whispered, "Go to the moor."

Alda felt the warmth once again engulf her, and she disappeared.

Inside the cottage, the younger Alda looked up from a stereopticon card of an Amazonian butterfly. "What did you say, Gramma?"

As her grandmother stared out the window, she responded absentmindedly, "Only thinking of a poem and mumbling to myself. Again." She turned toward Alda and recited dramatically, "I never saw a moor, I never saw the sea, yet know I how the heather looks and what a billow be."

Young Alda frowned as she considered, "What is heather?"

"A hardy shrub, with purple flowers."

"What's a moor?"

"A wind-swept hill, far, far from here." The old woman's eyes grew distant. "And even though you have never seen it, it is nonetheless very real."

*   *   *

The rude laughter and jeering were still audible from the deck above as the boy approached the cell in the hold, carrying a bucket of water. The prisoner, wearing clothes much finer than any the boy had seen elsewhere on the ship, crouched in a corner, avoiding the putrid puddles on the floor.

The man looked far more wild than when he had been captured, more desperate. Crazed. Mad.

"What is it, sir?"

"Sir, now? Am I suddenly more than a pissant to you?" The man tried to stand straight but was kept crouching by the low ceiling.

The boy sighed, frustrated. The prisoner liked to play games with his words. "Why did you call, *prisoner*?" The boy lowered his voice on the last word.

The prisoner crossed the cell and pressed his face to the bars. "Do you have fish today? *Poisson*, as the French say."

"You know you won't get any if we do."

"Venison? Quail?" The boy shook his head angrily. The captive leaned in and whispered with sharp enunciation, "If not *poisson*, have you poison?"

The boy couldn't help but laugh. "Why would we give that to you?"

"Don't worry. I'm selfish, Dreng, and don't intend to share."

"Why do you call me that?"

"That is what they all call you." The prisoner looked to the ceiling, indicating the crew above.

"They call me boy. Or nothing."

The prisoner chortled, pacing absentmindedly. "You, Dreng, are no thing. You are not nothing. I know. I have experience with nothing." The man laughed, and the noise sounded out of place in the cramped quarters.

But the boy was frustrated. "What does *it* mean?"

"That is a good question, but not *the* question."

"Dreng!" The boy's voice cracked. "What does *Dreng* mean?"

The prisoner stared at him, considering whether or not to be serious or to continue his sarcastic equivocation. He finally sighed and relented, "It means 'boy.' In my language. Of the Danes. This language that we speak now, together, is a borrowed tongue." After a moment of hesitation, he continued to himself, "All tongues are borrowed. Time is borrowed. Or stolen. Time's a thief that dances toward eternity."

The boy interrupted his nonsense. "Do what you will. Call me Dreng, then." He added, under his breath, "It's probably the nicest thing I've ever been called."

"Dreng, the Nameless. It suits you. Better than Boy, the Nothing." The prisoner clasped his hands and stared at the boy for several seconds, considering his negotiation. "Do you have poison, Dreng?"

"No. If they let me have it, they know I would use it."

"On them or yourself?"

The boy didn't answer.

"Fine," the prisoner continued. "I suppose I could use a dagger. Or a knife. Or perhaps a rope. What have you?"

"Why do you want to cause injury to yourself, sir?"

The prisoner smiled at "sir" and answered, "Better at my own hands than those of my enemy. The thing is — the king's the thing..." He chuckled at a joke that Dreng did not understand and then fell into silence. After a moment, the silence was unbearable.

The boy studied his rippled reflection in the bucket that he still held in his hand and summoned the courage to ask, "Are you really a prince, like the men say, sir?"

The captive smiled weakly and considered before answering, "Now, I am a Dane."

"You did not answer the question." The boy glared.

The man relented, "Some call me prince, but all should call me king."

"You speak in circles, sir, but I think I glean your meaning. You will be king, someday. That is why you were so brave, when you boarded our ship."

"Brave? No, I was mad to lead the charge. I thought there were men at my back, but there was only wind." The prisoner turned away, hiding his expression.

Dreng shifted the bucket in his hands, considering. "Do you know about the ransom? That the captain is taking you back to Denmark to collect money from the king? You'll be safe then, assuming your father pays."

The boy was met with silence, so he continued, "There's no need to harm yourself, you see."

The prince frowned, "That is why I prefer death immediately. The king — so *excellent* a king — will buy me and kill me. Or save his gold altogether and kill you and kill me. He has blood on his hands already, much nobler blood than yours or mine, and won't mind another spot or twenty." He fell into a kind of despondent reverie as Dreng considered this. "Maybe a storm will end us instead. This is *The Tempest*, after all," the prince sneered.

Dreng wondered for a moment before asking, "Why are you so welcoming of death?"

"You have not seen what I have seen."

"What is that?

"There are more things in heaven and earth than are dreamt of in philosophy."

For the briefest moment, Dreng smelled the rosemary again, faint and distant but somehow overpowering the worst odors of the chamber. He felt emboldened and sloshed the water into the cell, forcing the prisoner into a corner as he avoided the tainted liquid at his feet. Dreng demanded, "How much do you have?"

"How much what? Life? I doubt very little."

Dreng moved closer to the bars and frowned. The prisoner crossed the narrow cell and crouched to the boy's level, their faces inches apart, and repeated, "How much what?"

"Gold, riches. What will you give me if I let you go?" The boy's heart pounded. In his mind, he saw the girl, the black haired girl, and he felt stirrings of courage. He had never done anything this brave. Or genius. Or reckless.

The prince sneered. "How old are you, Dreng?"

"Thirteen or thereabout."

"Thirteen? I think I was on my mother's hip then. She thinks I still am." The captive paused and added, "Where is your family?"

Dreng didn't answer.

The prince lowered his voice, "Were you sold?"

The boy took offense and snapped, "I nearly died, sir." He rolled up his sleeve to show intricate, interwoven red lines stretching from his shoulder to his wrist. They looked like the roots of a tree, growing down his arm. "We were on a ship called *The Tyger* near Aleppo. There was a storm, and St. Elmo's fire killed my father. They told me I was only seven. I don't remember that or anything before. The first mate kept me and let me survive."

The boy sucked in the musty air around him, amazed at having said more about his life in a single breath to a stranger than in all the remembered years of his existence.

The prince looked sympathetic and, for the first time, kind. "Can you read?"

Dreng shook his head. "No books out here."

"Let me teach you. I'll help you at night until we reach a friendly port, and then you can release me." The man glanced at the lock. "Do you have the key?"

"I can get the key, but I need gold."

After a brief hesitation, the man removed his tall leather boot. He twisted the bottom of the sole, and a golden ring fell into his hand. He held it up for Dreng to see but moved it back into the cell when the boy tried to grab it through the bars. "It's a signet ring. My father's. It bears his royal seal. 'Twas a gift to me from my *dear* mother." He placed a sarcastic weight on *dear.* "You remind me of her, pining for riches over truth. I'll give it to you at port. When you release me." The prince hesitated. "Do we have a deal, Dreng?"

The boy nodded. "Your release for the ring, sir."

The prince beamed, despite the sadness behind his eyes. "Don't call me 'sir' now, Dreng. We are partners in this crime together. Call me Hamlet."

The boy hesitated as if to speak but then turned toward the stairs. The prince called after him, loudly enough for the crew to hear above deck, "So, Dreng, can you get me any fish, at least?"

"I am not a fishmonger."

Later, in the relative silence of the night, alone in his corner of the gun deck, Dreng traced the knotty constellations on the ceiling above his coiled rope-bed. They were shapes with no meaning, bent and curved and mysterious. What if they could be more?

What if he could read the significance of the woodgrains? Could they tell of his future?

If he let the prince escape, how could he safely remain on the ship? Would he have to change vessels to find a new crew, or should he risk discovery by the captain and first mate and stay aboard?

What if he had to leave the sea altogether?

And what if he could read? Then what might his future hold?

Dreng had never thought this much about anything, and his thoughts now were both exhilarating and terrifying.

Amid these worries, he could almost smell the rosemary and see the mysterious, familiar girl.

Finally, he realized that the future was too incomprehensible to navigate alone. He needed guidance. So in the darkness, the boy who had been nameless and friendless that morning tiptoed past the guns and the sleeping crewmen, down into the darkness of the hold below, and stood silently at the bars of the prisoner's cell.

As he watched the sleeping captive shivering on the damp floor, the boy had a momentary sting of pride and reconsidered asking the strange man for help. As Dreng turned to retreat, Hamlet arose and whispered across his cell, "Are you awake, too, or am I again seeing visions?"

Dreng froze and slowly met the prince's gaze.

The Dane seemed to read his mind, "Do you want to renegotiate now? To learn? To read?"

The boy did not know how the prince's offer would play out, especially because the prince could be more dangerous than he seemed. He hesitated. Was there a catch? A price? Was the cost of reading worth the risk of consequences? The boy stammered, "How do I know you're a good man?"

Hamlet retorted, "Is any man good? Or bad?"

"I mean, if you teach me to read and I then release you, what will you do?"

"I'll kill the king, of course, ideally in public and in a way that will look enviable in the history books. I may kill my mother, too, but that is really up to her."

The boy looked shocked. "You would kill your own father?"

The prince scoffed. "My father is dead. The king is my uncle. They are two. One killed the other, and I will kill the killer."

Revenge. This seemed fair and just, at least from what Dreng had seen of the world. The crew often lived eye for an eye, so the prince was honorable by that measure.

Hamlet continued, "There's a girl, too, a nymph who misses me now, I'm quite sure. But that's, well, a dream for another day. Or a dream for sleep, or something like it."

"I saw a girl today." The words spewed out before Dreng could stop them.

The prince, somewhat aghast, asked, "On the ship or in the sea?"

Dreng explained how he had met the black-haired girl, and Hamlet was silent for some minutes. "There is something in this more than natural. It is the heart of mystery." He laughed awkwardly to himself and added, "I can offer no explanation of what transpires between worlds, but perhaps your fate with hers is intertwined. You may come to know her again, I suspect."

Surprisingly, this put Dreng at ease, to be in company in his confusion. And he found comfort in the thought of meeting the girl again, somehow.

With newfound courage, Dreng inhaled deeply and considered, "You seem honorable..."

"I love the name of honor more than I fear death."

"...And reading, you might say, is like freedom?"

"It is truth. Truth to the end of reckoning."

Dreng sighed, and his breath trembled. "Help me find truth. Please."

The prince smiled. "Let us begin." Hamlet wet his finger in a tepid puddle and wrote mysterious bends and curves on the creaking floorboards.

Dreng watched, dumbstruck, waiting for the shapes to take on new meaning.

Chapter Three: Through the Fog and Filthy Air

Alda was disoriented by the stinging on her face. She thought for a moment that she was drowning, her wet hair flapping in the wind, stifling her breath and blocking her eyes. Her ink-colored dress was quickly drenched by the freezing rain and hung on her arms and legs like moss on a rock.

She knew where she was, despite never before seeing the place. A moor, the place her grandmother had sent her.

She walked cautiously over the low hill on sponge-like soil, feeling her way in the murky darkness. At first it was difficult to progress in this strange environment, but she persisted, even though she knew not where to go.

A memory flashed into her mind: Alda, some years earlier, found herself in a strange place. She was trapped in the top of an oak tree along the Ledge Path and screamed for her grandmother. The old woman ran from her cottage but stopped on the bridge, crossing her arms angrily as she scolded, "If you got up there, you can get down."

"That branch is in the way!"

Her grandmother smiled and recited a verse, "Strike it down that other boughs may flourish where that perished sapling used to be."

"A poem? Poetry will *not* help me!"

"Then help yourself, child."

"I don't know how," Alda wailed, with tears forming in her eyes.

"Nonsense. Climbing trees, up or down, is like anything else. Always hold onto something, and don't be afraid to fall." Her grandmother returned to the cottage, her feet angrily clomping across the bridge.

And Alda did fall, her skirt tearing on the outstretched branch before she landed in a puddle below. But she had tried, by herself. And after she wiped off the mud, she climbed another tree.

Now, on the moor, Alda looked for something to hold, even something immaterial. She needed a goal, hope. At last, over a small rise, she saw the red glow of a fire shining beneath a purple cloud, which hovered like a dome above a ring of standing stones.

It took her a considerable time to cross the sticky heath, pulling her shoes carefully from the muck and dense shrubs with each step, avoiding rocks and sudden valleys eroded by hundreds of years of relentless rain.

Finally she was nearly upon the fire, steps outside the stone circle. She froze at the sight before her, a nightmarish scene, and crouched behind a stone as she watched in disbelief.

The fire rose high above the moor, even above the boulders encircling it. Around the flames sat three hunched figures, bending and shaking with each breath, their faces feminine but bearded, their eyes blank and sunken. They cackled and laughed at an apparent joke told by the shortest one that ended in the word "runion," which Alda did not fully hear or understand.

Within the fire, twirling on a spit, was an unnaturally large, charred bat, roasting on the flames. Surrounding all of these figures, purple fog protected the interior of the henge from the rain and wind that still pelted Alda.

Alda stood in the darkness, watching the figures for what felt like hours, unsure what to do or where to go, wondering how she got there. And why she was there.

Then, as a suddenly strong gust pelted the hilltop, one of the hooded women sniffed the air, crinkled her nose, and stared directly at the rock protecting the trembling girl. The other two strange women followed the lead of the first, rising and circling the stone from opposite sides.

"Where are you going, my sweet maid?"

Alda turned her face from the figure, trembling, only to come face to face with the second. They dragged Alda into their protective fog, out of the rain, forcing her nearer the tallest monolith in the center of the stone circle, poking their bony fingers at her dripping hair and soaked-through clothes.

"Looking to find some trouble, eh?"

"Or finding some trouble to see?"

"Should we stretch her tongue for her to talk, sister?"

"Loosen her teeth for it to wiggle!"

"Let's give her a spell to see if it fits to a tittle."

"Or give her some silence to let her talk a little."

They stopped circling as Alda gasped, almost gulped, for air. She did not know what to say, where to begin, or how any of it would make sense to these creatures on the moor. She stammered only, "What?"

"A question, then, a simple one."

"We'll pass that by and add our own."

"Where did you come from, little maiden?"

Alda spoke quickly as if fear itself was her engine, "I came here from far away. Very far. A town called Grand Ledge. And I'm not sure how I got here or why I'm here, but I have this thing, this thing that is maybe magical that brought me here. And it looks like a marble but it isn't. It's a sphere, like crystal —" It was the most Alda had said since her grandmother died.

The tallest woman held out her hand to stop her. "Show it to me, girl."

Alda held out her fist and unclenched her pale fingers. The three women gathered around, reaching out but not touching the iridescent sphere, finally withdrawing to the far side of the fog dome. They huddled together but spoke amongst themselves loudly and openly, as if Alda was not there.

"Is that not Hecate's bubble?"

"But how did the girl?"

"Who is the girl?"

"Not who, what?"

"A bearer?"

"A sister?"

"A knower or a seer?"

"Why here?"

"Why now?"

"Why not tomorrow?"

"Or tomorrow?"

"Or tomorrow?"

"Or the last syllable of recorded time?"

The three women spoke in questions, never answering one before asking another. Perhaps, to them, there were no answers. Or it was all simply intuition.

They finally turned their attention back to Alda.

"Where —?"

"How —?"

"Did you get this orb?"

"It was my grandmother's. She's dead now."

"Dead, you say?" They exchanged a knowing look. "Then it cannot be as it seems."

Alda's impatience overwhelmed her, "What do you mean?"

The women cackled in laughter. "Witches do not die, young waif."

Alda laughed, somewhat forcefully, an awkward sound that echoed through the hills despite the rain beyond the stones. "Gramma was not a witch, of course! She grew herbs and traded in town. She built her

cottage, our cottage, and we lived there together. After my mother —"
She hesitated. "After my mother left." This was the most she had ever
said about her mother. Maybe the witches had loosened her tongue,
somehow.

"And what was your mother's name?"

"I'm not entirely sure." Alda was frustrated at their question, and at
her inability to answer. "I never asked because... I don't know why."

"And what was your grandmother's name?"

"Able Reeding."

The first bearded woman shook her head. "To be or not to be? And
yet." She arched an eyebrow. "Our lost sister spoke of a place in a far
away country, a place in a time not our own."

The second woman added, "With an enchanted river and seven
islands."

The third pursued, "Do you know a place such as this?"

Alda did not know if she should feel relief or alarm, if she should
answer honestly or bite her tongue. As she furrowed her brow in
consideration, the first woman nodded as if to encourage her. Before
Alda could control herself, she blurted, "We live — lived — on the seventh
island."

"Hecate?"

"But how can that be?"

"Dead?"

"Is she even?"

"Perhaps a curse or a spell?"

"Or a deed or a need?"

"Our dear lost sister?"

"Or another?"

"Here, we have another!"

They stopped chattering and stared at Alda. "Tell us your story, little sister."

They hurried Alda closer to the fire, where she sat on a warm, dry rock. She wanted to ask them about Hecate, but her words were not her own. Almost against her will, she told them all that had happened since she found the sphere, about the boy on the ship, and her grandmother's directions through the window.

The three strange women whispered more questions together and turned all at once, as if on cue, to Alda.

"You are freely given three questions to ask of us. Choose your words, and ask."

Alda considered for some time, watching the bat spin on the spit. "Who are you?"

In turn, the three women introduced themselves: "Nona," "Decima," "Morta." Then the women were silent, waiting for a second question. Alda realized that she had wanted to know more than their names, but it was too late to change her question now.

"*What* are you?"

"We are the weyward sisters."

"The weird sisters."

"We are wayward and weird."

"Three of a coven of four."

"The final coven."

"The final coven of this world, but not the last."

"There is not an other."

"Not one other."

In unison, they added, "Witches."

Alda was less surprised than she expected. Then again, she had experienced more in this single day — if it could be called a day —

than in her entire lifetime.

One question remained. She should ask about Hecate? No, that could wait. She needed an answer to a more immediate dilemma. Finally, she held up the crystalline sphere.

"This thing, this..." She paused, waiting.

Nona, the mid-height witch, piped up, "A cauldron's bubble." Decima, the tallest witch, hit the back of her head, giving the shorter sister a reprimanding glance. "You gave an answer for a question unasked!"

Alda smiled, pleased with herself, and continued, "How does it work?"

"The earth has bubbles."

"As the water has."

"And this is one."

"It takes the maker where she wants to go."

"And all others where they need to go."

"It bends and twists and knots the yarns of time and the fabric of place."

"It is a witch's tool and a layman's curse."

Alda now realized she had another, desperate question. "Am I a witch, then?"

The weyward sisters smiled mischievously. "One, two, three, and all is done." The three bearded women rose as if to leave, but it was not clear where they could go in the desolate wilderness.

Alda stood as well, feeling suddenly faint and exhausted and indescribably older than she had felt the day before, the day before the cemetery and the boy and the cauldron's bubble.

In a panic, frantic, Alda begged, "Where should I go? What should I do? I'm lost and do not know —"

Morta held a finger to her lips, the same gesture Alda's grandmother had used to silence her so many times in the past. "Sleep here." Alda, having no apparent ability to refuse, did.

Chapter Four: Blanket of the Dark

Dreng awoke violently, as if clawing his way from under some unseen, suffocating force. He had slept, despite himself, and lashed out as he opened his eyes to focus on the reality surrounding him.

In the weeks since the day of his dream — his waking dream of the girl and the unfamiliar smell — the ceiling above his coiled rope-bed changed from simple woodgrained shapes to outlines of letters scribed in candle soot. His eyes traced the letters compulsively, reassuring himself with their simplicity and elegance and the promise they held of knowledge and more.

Reading lessons with the prince had proved fruitful, and Dreng's mind gulped his new understanding of phonics and phrases. The lessons were more difficult than knotting but less distant than navigating, and within such a short time, Dreng had conquered the alphabet and progressed to a rudimentary understanding beyond the simplest words of his native tongue. But he could progress no more.

In the darkness of the gun deck, Dreng replayed the earlier scene of the day, the scene that was both the end of his scheme and the start of a new plan:

As dawn broke that morning, a faint light glimmered through the fog to the east, a light more intense and precise than the rising sun. A beacon. Land. This was not the first port they had touched upon since the prince was captured, but Dreng knew this was different. He listened intently as he twisted rope on the main deck.

"Send word to shore," Ernesto whispered to a crewman with warty hands. "Tell them our demands."

Dreng slipped into the shadows, listening as his fists clenched anxiously around the length of rope.

"In tomorrow's morning, when the fog clears," Ernesto continued, "we'll take him ashore for the exchange."

The sailor raised an eyebrow, questioning the first mate. Ernesto growled, "For the ransom. We'll get it before —" He coughed and did not finish.

"What of the captain?" The warty-handed man was more witless than most.

Ernesto cleared his throat and spit on the planks. The men spoke in whispers, so Dreng heard nothing else. As the coarse fibers of the rope dug into his fingers, he formed a plan.

Now, hours later, in his corner beneath the constellations of letters, the boy listened intently into the silence of the anchored ship. Waves lapped. Planks creaked. Men made no commotion; only two were on watch above.

After Dreng slipped out of the gun deck, he followed the rats' path below to the prince's cell. The crew slept on the main deck, as they did most anchored nights, comfortable in the cool night and fresh air and unaware of the clandestine happenings below. The prince, too, was asleep in his cage, oblivious to Ernesto's mutinous scheme, unknowing that this was his last night before freedom.

As Dreng approached the iron bars, the prince stirred. Dreng shifted the coil of rope in his hands and whispered forcefully, "Sir." Hamlet jolted awake as if hit by lightning, his eyes falling first on the boy's face and then on the rope.

"I see you've gone to great lengths for me." He waited for Dreng to speak but was only met with stutters. "Is your tongue now tied?" He spoke in full voice, dangerously loud.

Dreng winced at the thought of waking those above and whispered, "Tomorrow you'll be someone else's prey if I don't release you now."

And with no explanation and little sound, the boy hoisted the rope over a low beam and tied one loose end to a sturdy bar on the metal door. The prison's cage-like cell, having no ceiling, had corners formed of hinges sunk inside rusted tubes. Each wall of the cell stopped several inches below the low ceiling.

Although Dreng's mechanical knowledge was limited, he had surmised through observations during his reading lessons that enough force from above could simply lift and remove one of the iron panels from its hinges, thus freeing the captive without the necessity and danger of procuring the captain's key. In theory, this plan was simple and straightforward.

As silently as possible, Dreng leaned into the loose end of the rope, using the beam as a pulley to raise the cage's panel out of place. He grunted despite himself, but within seconds it was clear that he lacked the strength and grip necessary to free the captive.

The boy caught his breath as he finally explained, "We're in a port called Killandberg —"

"Kalundborg?" the prince grunted as he tried to simply lift the cage wall.

"Yes, that's it. A small boat went to shore with the morning tide and returned before nightfall with supplies and a message."

"From whom?" The prince still struggled against the cell.

"I do not know, but the first mate was pleased with it. I think he plans to steal your ransom for himself. He is —" Dreng considered how much to reveal of his experience with Ernesto. "Not an honorable man."

"Pirates seldom are."

Dreng once again pulled on the rope, combining his strength with that of the prince. With a final grunt and clang, the door panel escaped its hinges and fell to the floor with an echoing thud, a thud Dreng felt in his teeth.

"Quick, sir, take the small boat. Or swim. Anything. You must get to shore as soon as possible, before the sun rises and —"

Hamlet crossed out of his cage and placed his hand reassuringly on the boy's shoulder. It was the first time they had faced each other unseparated by bars. "Join me, master Dreng. Come to Kalundborg, now. And come to my palace at Elsinore."

In a flash that felt like an eternity, Dreng considered. He knew his past, the beatings and worse, the death of his father by the fickle forces of nature, the uncertainty of the sea, and a lifetime at the hands of men like Ernesto. No one could navigate the future, yet his was likely to repeat his past.

But he did not know land, the customs or trappings of the mainlanders who lived there. He did not know people. And for some reason, as he weighed the coming uncertainty against the too-familiar horrors of his past, he thought only of the girl with the black hair blowing in the sea breeze.

The prince continued, not skipping a beat, "I need someone loyal, someone clever. Someone to help stop the injustice and tyranny bred in the court of my home." Despite the prince's tendency to equivocation and irony, he was now serious. Pleading. More human and coherent than in all the days Dreng had known him. "Come. Please."

And in the darkness below the ship, in the stagnant mildewed air and under the weight of the sleeping crew on the deck above, Dreng made the most courageous decision of his life.

He only nodded slightly, speechless.

But it was for naught. A candle shattered the darkness, its light breaking the spell of the prince's invitation. Dreng turned to face the light and saw, by the flickering flame, the figure of Ernesto, one hand on his unsheathed cutlass, his mouth agape in shock and wonder.

Hamlet stepped back into the perimeter of his cage, wincing at the sight of the larger man. Dreng wanted to shrink into the shadows, to escape as he had so many times before, but there were no more shadows in which to hide.

"Boy, after all the kindness I've shown to you, after all the years of, of kindness, you —" Ernesto was drunk. He tripped on his words. "You and this prisoner plan to, to what?"

Dreng and Hamlet stood in silence. Dreng surveyed the situation, not so much thinking of a plan as heightening his senses to act on instinct when necessary.

Ernesto raised his voice, "Well, boy? What about me? What about your crew?" His words caught in his throat, and he coughed.

Dreng seized the moment and the loose end of rope that had fallen along the cage's panel. Waving the rope in the air, the boy distracted his opponent and leaned toward him, charging. The prince backed up, in shock, lethargic from exertion and malnutrition. The drunk sailor swung his cutlass. The boy fell on him, snarling the rage of an uncaged beast. The cutlass flashed again as the candle fell to the ground. The light flickered, and all was silent and dark.

Then signs of life and death. Moaning. The smell of blood. The prince crouched toward the jumble of limbs on the floor and sighed as he pulled Dreng out of the heap, laughing quietly with hysterics of ecstasy as the boy coughed and wheezed and opened his eyes.

"I thought I heard the angels come for you, boy, but I see not yet." Hamlet smiled in a way that was more eerie than reassuring. Dreng tried to speak, but only coughed again. The prince continued in a hoarse whisper, "I cannot say the same for your opponent, but I doubt angels will take him to his end."

Dreng struggled to sit in the stagnant nothing that surrounded him, but he lacked the strength. His shirt was wet with blood, either his or Ernesto's, and he felt unnaturally heavy. The prince cradled the boy in his arms for a few heartbeats until scuffing and movement above deck forced him to action.

"Life is without reason, young Dreng. The future is a blank page." In his hand, Dreng felt something smooth and round and heavier than its size betrayed. Hamlet pressed the gold signet ring into the boy's palm and closed his bloody fingers around it. "We know what we are, but not what we may be." After a moment, Dreng heard a far-away whisper, "And thus, the curtain falls." Hamlet's footsteps ascended the ladder and crossed the deck above. The rest was silence.

The boy's eyes fluttered, heavy for the depth of sleep that had escaped him for so many years. The darkness was complete now. Dreng was alone.

Chapter Five: Undiscovered Country

Alda was stiff and cold the next morning as she sat hungrily watching the three sisters slurp raw moorhen eggs. Morta observed the girl's longing and tossed her an empty eggshell with gusto. Alda considered eating it but set it aside with disdain. She was not that hungry, yet.

But Alda felt empty, inside. She longed for her grandmother, their last breakfast together: rhubarb jam on fried bread. When they had made the jam the previous summer, her grandmother was fastidious, demanding more precision than with past recipes. "Are you certain the sugar is correct?"

Alda glanced at the handwritten card and confirmed, "Yes, six cups."

Her grandmother shook her head disapprovingly, "No, that is a five, not a six. So what must we do?"

Alda thought, moving numbers in her head. "Adjust the ratios. I'll get more rhubarb."

As Alda walked into the garden, she heard her grandmother through the open window, "One wrong measurement to lose an entire batch."

Now, amid the circular monoliths, Alda studied her surroundings silently in the muted light of dawn, trying not to think more of the past or future. Beneath the fog-dome, she could trace carvings in the henge stones. Mostly geometric shapes, spirals and squares, and more intricate designs and patterns. Some animals. They reminded her of the graffiti along the Ledge Path, but these were more weathered and worn. Ancient.

Beyond the circled stones were great mountains. The tops of several were white with snow, and all were treeless and jagged. Inhospitable. A small ruin dotted the side of one mountain, but there was no sign of other life, not even a wandering sheep or low flying pheasant.

The gray clouds moved slowly above, and the nearby, crooked grasses shuddered in the wind. Inside the stone circle, beneath the purple fog, all was calm and protected.

Alda removed the cauldron's bubble from the fold in her sleeve and studied it in the yellow rays of dawn. How could something so small and insignificant hold such power?

"My sisters talked of you last night."

The witch's words broke Alda's reverie. She closed the bubble in her fist, trying to hide it.

"We walked and talked about you."

"And now we have a plan."

"A plan for a test."

"To get a familiar."

Alda furrowed her brow. "Familiar with what?"

"Not with. For."

"I don't understand. What —?"

Before Alda could finish her thought, Morta whispered, "Go to the canyon."

Alda felt suffocated by warmth enveloping her. The last thing she heard was the witches' laughter.

Within half a heartbeat, she found herself elsewhere. Taken by the cauldron's bubble. Disappeared and reappeared, now under a sun so bright that she was blinded.

The witch had commanded her bubble, as her grandmother had. But how?

Alda squinted down toward the sandy soil and lifted her hand to shield her eyes. But it was not her hand. It was long and thin, its nails and fingertips worn with use. It was an old hand, older at least.

Nearly an adult hand. How could this be?

Blinking, her eyes finally adjusted, she saw she was in a long canyon, surrounded by sand and cacti and, farther away, steep, rocky walls. The place was as desolate as the moor, as inhospitable, but opposite in its heat and drought. Where was she?

Her black dress was tight, so she tore its buttoned front and let it hang around her shoulders, her exposed white shift glowing liked scorched bones in the searing sunlight. She knew that her grandmother would not have approved of her immodesty. But it seemed to be a matter of survival.

As she stood, disoriented and gasping in the oppression of the blazing air, she finished her question that she began with the witches: "What is a familiar?"

A dark shape flew overhead. It looked down at her, cawing, and soared toward the rising ridges in the distance. It was the only living being in sight, so she followed its shadow. Her feet ached as she walked, burning and sweating in shoes that felt suddenly too small, and when she reached the cliffs at the edge of the canyon, she could barely stand from the forming blisters.

The black bird landed on a thick ledge halfway up the canyon wall, staring down at her.

"Do you want me to climb up there?" Alda knew, logically, that it was silly to speak to a bird. She also knew that a magical bubble should not have transported her to a desert, so logic was apparently not in play.

The bird backed into the shadows of the cliff-ledge. It was silent for a beat and then cawed again. Alda took the sound to be an answer to her question.

Carefully, slowly, painfully, Alda climbed to the protruding stone onto which the bird had disappeared, picking holds for her hands and feet with relative ease in the many pores of the stone, as she had so many times before on the ledges at home.

As she pulled herself up the final few feet, she discovered that the outcropping was deeper than she could see from below. Brick-like stones formed a kind of low wall, and the exposed rocks of the canyon face were almost polished, covered in intricate geometric designs like those on the witches' henge stones, but more varied: spirals, triangles, fish, turtles, people, handprints, even a large bird with outstretched wings.

Alda recognized these images from one of her stereopticon cards: petroglyphs. Before, in her cottage, she was always amazed by the detail of the three-dimensional images of her stereoscope. But now, in the reality of the desert, she understood how much the card's image was lacking.

She stared around her, breathless before this oasis of art in the rough of the wilderness, and only stopped her wonderment when she again saw the black bird, sitting in a far corner of the outcropping. It cawed three times in rapid succession.

With some hesitation and embarrassment, Alda asked, "Can you understand me?"

It lowered its head, almost nodding.

Alda crouched, inching closer to it. The bird tilted its head, watching her, its black eyes glinting.

Hesitantly, Alda wondered aloud, "Can you talk?" She was nearly to it now, unaware of everything else around her.

"Yes."

Alda jumped back, stumbled to the ground, and scuffed her feet against the stone until her back hit the cold wall. The bird, its beak not moving, spoke with a clear, somewhat hoarse voice.

"And I can also fly." And it did, off the outcropping and into the void above the canyon, where it hovered on a wind, watching her.

Alda, frustrated, started to stand. But she could not move from the wall. She shifted and wiggled, but her back would not budge. She was unnaturally stuck. Powerfully stuck.

The bird waited, suspended in the air, as Alda struggled. When Alda finally gave up and remained still, it flew toward the far horizon. Alda watched it disappear. She was alone, again.

For the next hour, Alda tried in vain to escape. Her spine felt fused to its spot, so she could not remove her dress. She hoped to chip away the wall behind her but could find no loose stones to use as tools. Instead, she clawed at whatever held her, but her nails were too brittle and the angle of her arms too awkward to seize or destroy whatever held her in place.

The sun edged toward her small refuge in the shade of the ledge. Alda was thirsty, tired, disoriented. It would not take long to die in a place like this.

Alda might have given up, or cried, but she finally resorted to begging instead.

"Bird! If you can hear me, please help! I mean you no harm, bird!" She searched the skies but saw no movement. After too long, she desperately tried a different approach. "If you're a familiar, I need your help. I met some witches, and they might, they might kill me, or something, if I don't get a familiar. I'm not sure what to do, bird. Please, can you help?"

After a moment, the bird flew down and hovered near the cliff-ledge, tilting its head as it examined the trapped girl. The bird had apparently been sitting on the outcropping above the entire time, unseen. "Are *you* a witch?"

"No." Alda considered, biting her cracking lip. "Possibly. I don't know. Can you tell if I am?"

The bird landed and hopped around her, inspecting where her back met the wall. "Well, does it hurt?"

Alda shifted as much as possible. She was uncomfortable, certainly, but, "No."

"Witch-traps will only catch witches, but they keep witches in immeasurable pain. You are trapped, yet..." The bird spoke this more to itself than to Alda as it scratched its sharp beak against the stone, setting Alda free.

Alda collapsed forward. As she bent her spine and adjusted her shoulders, she saw a spiral carved into the wall, its shape broken by the scratch of the bird's beak. She had been held in place by a petroglyph. But how?

"My name is Leana." Alda turned away from the spiral — the trap — behind her. The bird lowered its head slightly, like a human bowing. "And if I had left you in the witch-trap longer, you might have been trapped forever. Well, your soul at least. Your body would have died." The bird's tone was dry, condescending.

Alda smiled her appreciation and asked, "Are you a crow, or —" She considered. "Something else?"

Leana scoffed, "I'm a raven, of course. And you, Alda Reeding, have no manners."

Alda started. "How do you know my name?"

"Ravens are the observers of the observed. We know everything. Rather, if you need to know something, some raven somewhere knows it." The bird cackled. Was it laughter? "You simply have to ask the right raven. I have talked to many, many ravens, so I know more than most, but only second-wing."

"I'm sorry I was not more," Alda paused. "Polite." She did not know that ravens or crows or any bird had an expectation of civility or a tendency to gossip. "Please forgive my —" Alda struggled for the proper word, "importunity." She pronounced the syllables with some difficulty and did her best to bow as the bird had done. "But how can you talk?"

"I'm from Netherfeld, so naturally. I see you have been there lately. Did you see my cousin Celia?"

"No, only the three witches. And a dead bat. And rain and mud."

Leana stared at her. "There is no mud in Netherfeld. There is, most literally, no *thing* in Netherfeld."

"I have not been to a place with nothing." Such a place seemed impossible.

"You are mistaken."

Alda did not want to argue with a magical bird, so she held her tongue.

After an uncomfortable silence that lasted too long, Alda asked, "Where am I now?"

"This is the Canyon."

"Is it magical?" The question felt strange as she asked, almost silly.

But the raven replied seriously. "There is old magic here, in the stones, older than anywhere on this sphere. The Canyon is connected, like so many other places, to ancient people who left centuries ago to go to —" The bird clicked her beak, "Elsewhere. They took their magic with them, traveling through time and place. As you did."

Alda felt her brows furrow involuntarily. She was not angry, merely confused. What did the bird mean? But it might be rude to ask for clarification.

She felt Leana study her. If Alda had been conversing with a human, her companion might have a raised eyebrow and a curled lip. Instead, the raven cocked her head and stared at Alda with one eye. "How did you get here?"

Alda could answer that question. "With a cauldron's bubble."

Leana squawked. "Of course, that is why you do not remember Netherfeld. But I assure you that you did pass through that realm when you travelled in the bubble's sphere. That is how it works when one journeys as you have."

Alda must have leaned closer because the bird hopped back, keeping a polite distance between them, before she continued, "Netherfeld is the between space. A kind of void. It is between worlds, between lands, between time. Like the air between my feathers."

It was refreshing to get answers to unasked questions, unlike at the moor, even if these answers created more confusion than clarity. Alda considered for a moment. "If there's nothing in Netherfeld, then how can you be from there?"

"It is the realm of spirits and the immaterial, so there is existing without existence. Beings without form or substance." The raven paused, allowing Alda to absorb this, before continuing, "Some spirits are summoned elsewhere and then lose their material form, so they return to Netherfeld to exist when they are freed. Some spirits are born there, like me, and escape to worlds beyond. Some get trapped there accidentally as they travel between world-times, between yarns. It is a place of the unreal, the intangible. A place to be without being. A place of shadows seemingly come to life."

"But how do you know that I was there?"

"The bubble works —" The bird stopped, either simplifying her explanation or withholding information. "You are satiated. Your body coverings feel tighter, I suppose, and your feet coverings too small. You were there long enough to age. To grow. I can tell."

Alda looked at her older hands again, turning them over as she also realized that she had been hungry when she left the moor and was not when she arrived in the desert. She remembered the feeling of being older, too, when she appeared at the moor the first time. She must have looked worried as she thought.

"Oh, you did not age much." The raven eyed her up and down. "You are yet sixteen in human years. Perhaps more."

"Sixteen, or older? But I was fourteen, when — Did I lose those years?"

"You do not know what you cannot remember, so in a way they are lost."

Alda's breath came faster. She felt faint, not from the heat but from the shock of missing part of her life. It was like she had been dead for that time, or in a deep, enchanted sleep. "Years, gone?"

"But you have gained experience, too, in Netherfeld. Yet you will not know what you have learned until you are forced to use that knowledge. Then, it will come to you as a kind of skill, an instinct." The raven narrowed her eyes. "Magic."

Alda doubted this. Magic? She was more concerned about forgetting part of her life. Years of her life. "Could I ever remember Netherfeld, fully?"

"Some travelers have talismans that help them remember. There are spells to do it, but they are complex. Some are born with a natural way to remember." The bird tilted her head, looking out of one eye. "Some are born to remember but still choose to forget."

Alda thought that Leana started to sound like the witches, speaking in circles.

The witches. Alda had lost track of her goal. "Are you a familiar?"

"I could be, but then I would not be free."

Alda realized that she should have asked a different question first, "What is a familiar?"

The bird lowered her voice, "Familiars are companions, like servants to those who bind them. To their witches."

"Do familiars have magic, too?"

"Familiars do have increased powers, but not freedom." The raven flapped her wings and hopped a few inches into the air. "I prefer freedom to power."

Alda considered. She looked into the distance, at the opposite side of the canyon, the clouds moving over the western sky, the whirling dervish circling in the dry riverbed below. Certainly this place, this desolate place, was more free than the witches' dome of purple fog. She could not capture or convince any creature to leave here.

Alda worried out loud: "What do I do now? The witches told me to get a familiar. If I return without one, they might —" With a start, she realized her situation. Even free from the petroglyph, she was still trapped in the canyon, far from the moor, with no way to leave. "*If* I could return —"

"Witches seldom speak the truth. They speak anything but. Their true test was most probably not for you to ensnare a familiar but to use this witch-trap, the first one created, to determine if you are a witch."

"Are the witches good, then? Or are they —" She paused and whispered, "Evil?"

"There is nothing that is either good or bad. Our thinking makes it so. The world is never simple or straightforward." Leana stared at the girl for a heartbeat, and then ran her beak through her wing feathers.

Alda thought in silence. For a moment that held an eternity, she measured what was before her. She remembered the witches' words, their explanation of the cauldron's bubble: *It will take all others where they need to go.*

Leana watched her inquisitively, almost reading her thoughts, and explained, "If you need to go back to the moor, there above any other place, the bubble will take you."

Alda thought she understood.

The raven urged, "Try it. Do not fear."

Alda nodded and tightened her fist around the iridescent sphere, as she had in the cottage. And vanished.

Chapter Six: Come Like Shadows, So Depart

In the damp darkness of the hold, Dreng could only wait, his voice too weak to yell, his body barely strong enough to hold the golden signet ring in his hand. The prince was gone, escaped no doubt. The men were still asleep above. The only sounds around him were water and creaks. So Dreng waited, feeling faint and listening to the ringing in his ears.

He waited for help or for death.

Time continued to pass, slowly. As Dreng counted the waves that lapped the ship, the pain in his chest turned to ache and then nothing. He was almost weightless, floating above the planks like a ship above the seafloor.

As the longest minutes of his life slipped by, the longest in a lifetime of moments the length of eternity, his eyes fluttered. He wanted, more than anything, to sleep. To escape. To dream. Nothing was anchoring him to this place.

Then through the cloak of darkness, he suddenly smelled the scent: rosemary. From the corner of his eye, he saw movement in the far side of the room, and a figure emerged from the gloom. A female figure, clad in black and glowing white. Was she a ghost or an angel?

No, the girl from the beakhead, but older and fuller.

The figure crept closer to Dreng, either scared or cautious. She bit her lip as she knelt beside him, hands shaking, and cradled his head. The girl stuttered whispers as she struggled for words. She felt solid, warm, mortal. Real. Present.

"You disappeared," he barely breathed the words, too weak to enunciate.

"You're injured." The girl pulled aside his shirt and examined his wound. Then she gasped, "What happened?"

"What —?" He was too faint to finish, *What are you?*

The mysterious girl hesitated as she studied his face. "What is your name?"

"Dreng."

"Dreng," as she said it, he felt for the first time that it was truly his name. His. "What should I do? Should I —" He could feel her body tighten as her breath became uneven, frantic.

"Nothing," he sighed.

"No, Dreng, you need help." He looked away, toward Ernesto's corpse in the puddle of blood. The girl did not follow his gaze and only studied his eyes. She smoothed his dark, matted hair away from his forehead and caressed his cheek with her fingers, down his shoulder to the intertwined red scars on his arm.

It was the kindest touch the dying boy had ever received, and it felt like an electric shock that permeated his prone form. A force of nature. Kindness.

"Nothing," he repeated with conviction. He had asked for naught his entire life. Death should be no different.

But it was. Everything was different. He had her. And Dreng realized, for perhaps the first time in his life, that he truly and entirely wanted something. And he finally had the courage to ask aloud.

With what should have been his last breath, the dying boy pleaded, "No, I want — Take me with you —" The words were broken. He sputtered as warm liquid poured from his mouth. He lifted his head to cough, and when he lowered it again, he felt the hard planks of the floor.

The girl was no longer holding him. Vanished.

And in the darkness, he heard the thud of men's boots finally descend the stairs.

*   *   *

Alda was suddenly back on the moor in the witches' fog. For an instant, she doubted the raven's explanation of the cauldron's bubble. The iridescent sphere seemed to have a mind of its own, taking her twice now to a ship that held no connection to her, instead of where she needed to go. To a boy in tattered clothes. A boy who now was —

Alda stopped herself from thinking about Dreng. She felt a danger in his memory.

Somewhat disoriented, she looked down at herself. Leana was right, at least somewhat: she was older, taller, aged. Satiated. Her shoes now had holes cut in the toes to make them fit. Her torn black gown was gone. Her arms were clean, and her white shift underdress was spotted with old stains of brown. It felt stiff, worn for too long. But where was the boy's blood?

How long had she spent in Netherfeld this time? Months? Years? How much time had she lost in the place she could not remember?

Her throat wanted to close, to sob, but she did not have time to consider further. No time had passed here, in the stone henge. The remains of the bat still clung to the spit. The witches stood, gathered, as they were when she had left.

"What familiar have you brought?"

"Show!"

"Show us!"

"I — I didn't get one. But I met one." Alda carefully explained the witch-trap and her meeting with Leana the raven. She did not mention the boy on the ship.

The witches nodded knowingly to one another. "Then she has passed."

"This was not about the familiar?" Alda was angry. "Why did you test me?" She felt slightly empowered, no longer entirely helpless to the witches' wills.

Despite her tone, the witches gave her no heed and conversed in circular questions, speaking only to each other. Excluding her. Alda wrung her hands impatiently, doing her best to ward off the cold and keep her temper at bay. She realized she was still like an insect to them, easily swatted away or crushed underfoot.

After what seemed like hours contained in minutes, Nona finally asked, "Will she work?"

"She will do."

"We will make do."

"Make me do what?" Alda could more clearly understand their equivocation now.

Morta, the shortest and quietest weyward sister, started to adjust twigs near the fire as Nona pulled a large cauldron from a crevice under a stone. Decima examined Alda, prodding her hair with her bony finger and poking at her ribs. They spoke as they worked.

"There is another, girl."

"Another chance."

"Another way."

"Another test."

"An old familiar is trapped."

"On an island."

"An enchanted island that witches cannot reach."

"And so, *you* must go."

Alda stepped away, backing toward the ring of stones. "No."

The witches froze, staring, and said in unison, "What?"

"I will not."

"Your grandmother would want you —"

"No, she would not, not —" Alda stopped mid-sentence. She could not explain her grandmother, or grandmother's love, to the witches, but she knew beyond doubt that Gramma would not want her harmed or endangered.

Decima interrupted, "She would want *you*."

"You can see her."

"Speak to her."

"But she's dead." Alda spoke condescendingly, as if scolding misbehaving children. She could not remember ever speaking thus, especially not to an elder.

"Not always."

"Time is not linear or rigid."

"Not like a shaft of a spear."

"Not like the blade of a sword."

"More like yarn."

"To tie."

"To twist."

"To cut."

Alda considered. Her interaction with her grandmother through the cottage window. Her vision of her younger self. The boy on the ship. Somehow, she understood.

She also remembered Leana's warning about the witches' deceits and wanted to be as precise as possible: "How could I speak to her — to Gramma — to Able Reeding?"

"We have spells, girl."

"Caches of spells."

"Troves of spells."

"Spells to do anything."

"Or nearly."

"Spells to do — *if you do*."

The three bearded women stopped, waiting. The fog-dome grew darker and obscured most of the surrounding sights and sounds as Alda thought in the gloom and silence.

For a brief moment, Alda imagined she smelled rosemary.

"*If* I help you, then," Alda wanted to be perfectly clear. "If I go to this island, this *enchanted* island, and get the familiar, and risk being maimed or cursed or, or worse, you will let me speak to my grandmother, even though she's dead?"

The weyward sisters nodded.

"Could I die?"

Silence.

"What will happen if I die?"

Silence for what felt like an eternity.

Alda realized they would give no answer. Or there was no answer. So she weighed her options.

A few days before — was it mere days — she watched the singing gravedigger lower her grandmother's coffin into the frosted earth. There, alone in the cemetery at the top of the north hill above the river, above their cottage, she would have gone to any length to see her grandmother alive again. To laugh. To embrace.

And now, to ask the questions she had never known to ask before. More than anything, she wanted to see her grandmother. She needed to. She needed to know who — no, *what* she was.

"Fine. Send me to the island." She held out the cauldron's bubble.

"The island has enchantments."

"Protection."

"Against witches and their instruments."

"A cauldron's bubble will not get you there."

"Or bring you back."

"Not on the island."

"You need an elixir."

"A potion."

"A spell."

"Now you must sleep while the spell is done."

"Sleep, to say."

"Sleep for a spell."

The bearded women cackled in laughter. Nona snapped her fingers, and Alda's world turned black.

She felt heavy, like the fog had turned material and held her down with suffocating strength. Her limbs felt anchored, and the sounds around her echoed as if bouncing from the walls of a cave. She could hear the witches, distant, distorted:

"Does she remember?"

"Will she remember?"

"Will she be remembered?"

"Not now, sister."

"Bring the cauldron."

"But will she know?"

"Or hear?"

"I have the book."

"Bring it here."

"I will read it."

"I will do it."

"No, sister, not since the time past."

"With the tiger and Aleppo."

"Not without the four."

"Then let me do't, sister."

"No. She hears."

"Then once more."

Alda heard another snap, louder this time and reverberating like a bell. And she slept, unfeeling.

Chapter Seven: Sea of Troubles

Water poured over the deck of *The Tempest* as waves beat against the beakhead.

The young man, the man who after seven years still called himself Dreng, held fast to the ropes, forcing them into comparatively calm obedience against the forces around him.

His calloused hands did not bleed against the coarse fibers. His breath was not lost in the spray and salty mist. Dreng was not afraid. He was too timeworn to be afraid, too experienced. He was alert. This was not his first storm, and, Fates willing, it would not be his last. But this was different, somehow.

In the chaos, a thin crewman was washed overboard, screaming. An aged sailor rushed to the starboard side of the ship, peering precariously into the sea below. "Boatswain!" The old sailor called to the young man. "Man ov—"

"No need. He's swallowed," Dreng replied as he surrendered his hold on the rope and wiped his long brown hair from his eyes. "Down with the top sail," he ordered, his words fighting the swooping gush of wind. "Lower! Lower!"

The crew obliged, some cursing and some praying as they fought the breathtaking wind and swaying deck. Dreng joined their efforts and continued his commands, "Bring her to try with main-course!" The ship was in chaos, his words lost to the wind.

This may not have been the boatswain's first storm, but it was his worst. It was sudden, unexpected. A calm day giving way to darkness. Colored lights flashing above and around. It felt almost artificial, like one of the ancient gods blew a gale against a child's play-ship. An angry god.

Dreng heard a crash. A crack. And then silence. Full silence. A silence not of emptiness but of deafening sound obscuring all other noise. Rushing silence. Suffocating.

Too late, Dreng realized that he was no longer on the ship. He was surrounded by shades of white and gray and the smooth sensations of water mixed with foamy velvet. He was washed overboard, fighting the sea.

He kicked skyward, reaching, and for the second time in his life, he felt unnaturally weightless.

He could think only of breath. Of air. As he struggled through the current and the waves, he gasped above a crest. Again. On his third breath, he opened his eyes and saw land, distant land.

But not too distant.

With the same strength that willed him to survive his near-mortal wound from Ernesto so many years earlier, and the same determination that buoyed him on the ocean for his entire remembered life, Dreng swam toward the island.

He resolved that he would not die wet, consumed, and forgotten. His last breath, he willed, would be dry.

And as he turned toward the island's cliff-lined shore, his arms pulled against the waves, and he smelled an herby scent that he remembered from when he was a boy, seven years before: rosemary.

*   *   *

Alda could not swim. She had told the witches she could not swim, but they paid her no regard. So she dragged herself through the waves to the island's rocky shore as best she could.

Her mouth still tasted of the bitter potion that she had been forced to drink on the moor, after her enchanted sleep. The magical elixir that sent her through time and across distance into the sea-shallows near the enchanted island.

Finally on the dry beach, Alda collapsed on the warm sand and stared at the too-white clouds. They formed shapes, some familiar and some mystical, as Alda pondered her journey to this place: the ship, the moor, the desert, and now an island. An island, like home, but so different.

On her own island in the Grand River, Alda had been protected. And she could leave, in a way, through the lens of her stereoscope. It was from this quaint device's images that she knew the sea and the desert and the flora and fauna of the world. Illusions on flat cards that appeared to have three dimensions.

Her world, too, had been an illusion.

And on this island, she was trapped. Until she found the familiar.

Alda thought back to the moor that she had so recently left. Recently? Time was no longer linear. After the witches made her sleep, they told her what to seek: a familiar called Ariel. Then they made her drink the potion. And then she traveled here.

But the witches did not tell her how to reach Ariel. The path, they said, was hers to find.

Alda had anticipated that the island would be smaller, her task more straightforward. But there was no path, no trail from the beach. Behind her, cliffs met the sand, preventing entry to the island's interior. The cliffs stretched in both directions, like a natural fortress. Before her, waves lapped calmly.

But in the line of the horizon, a storm churned, tossing a masted ship between flashes of lightning. Not lightning, lights. Colored lights, unlike any she had ever seen.

As she watched, the ship rocked, fading into the gloom and reappearing again beneath each flash and swirl. The scene was unreal, fictional, as if painted. Fantastical. Alda pulled her blowing hair from her face, transfixed by the disaster. And helpless.

Then a sudden streak of red flashed on the horizon. There was a plume of smoke, a white-capped wave, and nothing.

The ship was gone. The storm was gone. And the sea was calm and glassy. Sunlight shone on the horizon. As if all had been forever peaceful.

Another flash caught Alda's eye, a bright and sudden light to her right, high above the beach on a protruding cliff that stretched like a jetty into the sea.

At the top of the cliff, dressed in a glowing white robe, stood an old man with a beard. A rainbow of moving light beams swirled around him, dancing like bees above a flower. He was motionless yet active. Awful. Terrifying. Terrible.

Alda shuddered. She knew that he was evil, not simply from observation, but from her heart of hearts. He had magic, a kind different than the witches, different than she had before seen.

And his name was Prospero.

Alda knew this, despite not hearing Prospero's name. Despite not *remembering* hearing his name. She knew it from Netherfeld. And this knowledge came like an instinct, like the way a child knows to avoid flames, without the imagery of a true memory.

As she watched the old man, she thought she heard the beating of wings, like a bird circling overhead. But there were no gulls. What unseen thing was flying so near?

A sudden, closer movement drew her eyes away from the bearded man and his swirling, colored lights.

Alda turned and saw another girl, a girl maybe seventeen or eighteen years old, her same height but with a fairer complexion, golden hair, and jet-black eyes.

The girl stared at her, unmoving. Alda shivered, finally feeling the cold sea-wind break through her wet shift, its effect compounded by the girl's unblinking, icy gaze.

After several heartbeats, the other girl smiled slightly, a kind of half-mouth curl that could have been benevolent or otherwise.

"You are not one of them?" The girl spoke questioningly, tilting her head.

"One of who?"

The girl looked toward the horizon. Alda understood her meaning.

"From the ship? No, I am from — from much farther away."

"You look kind." The girl spoke this quietly, to herself.

Alda did not know how to respond to such a statement, so she did her best to smile.

"There is danger here. Beware the lights." The girl, silently, swiftly, removed her long, sapphire blue cloak. She let it fall onto the sand, never breaking her eyes away from Alda.

The girl smiled again, sincerely and gently this time. She opened her mouth to speak, but was interrupted by a loud snap.

Alda wheeled around at the noise and looked at the protruding cliff behind her. Prospero was gone.

Alda turned once more, spinning a full circle in all, and saw that the girl had also vanished, her cloak abandoned in a heap.

Alda shivered again and reached for the cloak.

Chapter Eight: A Brave New World

The beach was calm. Waves lapped against Dreng's bare feet.
Overhead, gulls dove curiously but were too apprehensive to land near a
motionless body that still might harbor life.

Finally, after immeasurable time, his body regained motion. He
coughed. He spat. He vomited seawater. He wallowed in the sand like a
fish aching for the sea. Then, he looked around.

A beach. Rocks. Cliffs between him and the interior of the island.
One cliff in the distance that jutted into the surf. No storm, only calm.
And no ship.

Dreng guessed its murky fate.

The ship was more than his home. It was his world. His entire
existence had been at sea. First a foundling subjected to the adversities of
the friendless crew. Then, after Ernesto's death and the prince's escape,
reviled as a traitor by all but the captain. But he could read, and he could
work. So finally, after years of suffering and labor, good fortune and
vaulting ambition, he was a leader of men. He became the boatswain,
overseer of the deck crew, the man responsible for their actions and their
safety.

But the crew was now lost at sea. Lost like the ship.

He was lost, too. Who was he, without a ship? No longer the
boatswain. Friendless. Worthless. He remembered the captive prince's
words, so many years before, "Boy, the Nothing." It was sarcastic then but
seemed fitting now.

After some minutes, the young man stood with some difficulty. His
limbs felt heavy with the exertion of swimming, and his skin burned from
the sand and the sun. His clothes torn and hanging, exposing the lines of
the scar on his shoulder and arm. Exhaustion was not a new sensation, so

the young man overcame his fatigue and set forth. But where would he go?

He hesitated. As the former boatswain searched the horizon once more for his lost vessel, hoping for a miracle, he heard a rustling behind him and turned to see a girl. No, a young woman, with yellow hair, inky black eyes, and a gray dress that blended with the cliffs from whence she emerged.

She was only the second female that the young man had seen so intimately. The first, the girl on the ship when he was a boy, had flooded him with an emotion he had not before known: hope.

The sight of this young woman, so many years later, inspired a feeling that he could name: love. The passion that he felt was instantaneous, powerful, like the sudden storm. And he was helpless in its net.

She appeared like the goddesses the Italian sailors worshipped in their superstitious songs. Her hair like spiraled strands of gold. Her features carved from marble. Her eyes like the night. Her bearing majestic and commanding. She was poetic.

He felt owned by her, subjected to her power, but unworthy. In her control. She was regal, and he was only a peasant in sea-torn clothes.

As he stared, taking in her perfect parts, she stared back as if weighing his worth in her mind. He whispered, under his breath, "You are celestial."

The young woman did not seem to hear him. When she spoke, the waves and gulls seemed to grow silent to listen, and her words echoed off the cliffs behind her.

"You are one of them?"

She spoke? Dreng was tongue-tied.

"Who are you?" Her tone was impatient, hurried.

"You speak my language?" His mind reeled. "My name is— is Ferdinand," he lied. The name of a great king. *Dreng* no longer fit him. After all, it meant "boy." Here on land, with her, he felt reborn, grown. So a new, nobler name was fitting, he reasoned.

"You should not be here, Ferdinand. You must leave before my father — before the lights —" The young woman stopped, set her jaw, and looked out to the empty sea.

He moved closer to her. She backed away, keeping the distance between them.

"Are you scared?"

"Yes."

"I mean you no harm." He moved closer again. She did not back away.

"Not of you. *For* you. You see — no, it does not matter."

The young man hesitated, considering her words.

"Then come with me." His heart raced. He was close enough to touch her now.

She laughed, despite her solemn air. "How?" She should have asked, *Why?*

He had never been without a ship, without a means of escape. His breathing increased. "Then let me speak to your father. Ask him for —"

He reached for her hand, and his fingers brushed against hers as she pulled away.

"You seem kind, but it is not safe here, with you," the girl choked, overcome with emotions, her voice cracking with fear. "I must hurry. Before they come." And she finally broke her dark eyes from his as she retreated toward the cliffs.

"Before who comes?"

She did not answer as her pace quickened.

"Who are you?"

Without turning or slowing, she answered simply, "Miranda."

"Where are you going?"

But she was gone, apparently swallowed into the cliff's base.

The young man exhaled as he realized he had been holding his breath in his aching chest. He had died briefly on the beach, perhaps not literally but in an internal sense, in his soul, and was reborn in her presence.

And Ferdinand knew that if he could not be with her, he could not live.

*   *   *

The cliffs appeared to be impenetrable. They were taller than the Canyon, which itself was higher than most of the ledges near Alda's home. The island's cliffs were colossal in comparison to all she had seen before. And Alda could find no trail around them, no route to reach the interior of the island, so she resigned herself to search for a rise that she could reasonably climb.

She noticed, disturbingly, that even the gulls did not cross the cliffs. When they came from the sea, they circled above the sand, unable or unwilling to fly inland. What kept them at bay?

As Alda stared at the vertical rock, the other girl's blue cloak blowing in the sea breeze, she repressed her concerns about the birds and examined a less steep rise that led to a small outcropping.

Her inspection of the cliff was interrupted by dry laughter.

Behind her, lurching from the waves, a group of five men approached menacingly. Timbers and white sails topped the waves behind them, obvious remnants of the ship that vanished with the storm.

The leader of the men, a dark-eyed ruffian with a red beard, snarled, "Look, boys, our welcome party has already arrived."

"'Tis ill-mannered to turn away what the beach offers," another added with a grin.

Alda saw a glint of metal in his hand, a knife or a sword, and backed to the cliff until her fingers gripped its crevices.

The farthest man, older with leathered skin, called to the leader, "We need aid, not enemies."

The bearded sailor turned to his more reasonable companion, "Who are you to contradict me, old man?" And the red-bearded man lunged into the waves to attack his elder.

Alda did not watch the altercation. She turned toward the steep cliff, carefully planted her feet and hands, and pulled with all her strength toward the outcropping above.

The rock face was not as neatly pitted as that of the desert, the one she scaled when she met Leana the raven, but she was taller now with greater reach.

And for a brief moment, she forgot that she was on the island. She remembered ascending the ledge-faces opposite Hemlock Point, the sandstone cliffs on the shore near her grandmother's island. She had climbed them dozens of times, and she was never scared, then. She willed herself to be brave now.

Behind her, a deep scream returned her to the present: a splash, a snarl, and "Have at her!" She knew that the old man, perhaps her sole ally, was dead.

Alda could only look up, only pull and stretch as quickly as she could.

Breathing grew closer behind her. She could feel the men within feet, then inches of her, each more easily scaling the wall with their years of shiphand experience.

If she could reach the outcropping, she thought, she might be able to defend herself. To fight or push them from the cliff. She could do it physically, she was certain, but could she bring herself to kill a man, even one like these? She did not know, so she climbed faster.

Then the earth shook. It was an unnatural, deep vibration, almost a reverberation like a giant stomping in subterranean caverns. An earthquake?

Alda tightened her grip and pressed her weight toward the cliff-face, ducking her head as pebbles and stones fell around her. The air whistled and screamed. Flashing lights dazzled through her closed eyelids. Her blue cloak flapped in the screaming wind.

She opened her eyes and dared to look down. Colored lights danced and swirled around the sailors, tying and untying illusionary knots.

The same lights that she saw encircling Prospero. But more wild, frantic. Alda remembered the girl with the cloak, her warning. This was danger.

The closest sailor attempted to climb down to the beach, but the lights swirled and darted until he lost his grip and fell below, knocking the bearded man with him.

The two remaining men held still, stunned, as they leaned into the cliff for protection. The lights grew brighter and faster, their pitch increasing into shrieking screams. And then they struck.

The lights shot through the men, piercing their chests. The sailors slouched and then tumbled to the ground far below, lifeless.

As Alda gasped and struggled toward the outcropping above, the lights continued to swirl, seeking a new victim. They twirled around her, catching her hair in their drafts and whistling past her ears. But they did not touch her. They did not harm her. They only seemed to examine her before falling away.

Alda climbed again, faster, propelled by her fear of the magical, deadly lights.

When she finally reached the relative safety of the outcropping, she peered below. The waves broke with the blood of the murdered, old man.

On the sand, the red-bearded man and his men lay prostrate, their bodies limp in death.

The colored lights shone softly at the farthest point of the beach before disappearing into the distance.

As the lights faded, Alda heard a high-pitched scream. A woman's scream, filled with terror. Was it the other girl?

Alda listened, and the world lapsed into silence. The gulls were gone. Even the waves were unnaturally still. Alda slumped onto the cold stone of the outcropping, her heart racing, her hands raw and shaking.

Her fear filled her head with doubt. Would she find Ariel? And if she found him, how would she leave the island? Would he take her back to the witches? Or would she become trapped in this place of deadly lights?

As Alda wiped her hair out of her face, she saw them, etched into the wall of the outcropping and continuing up the cliff-face for as high as a man could reach: petroglyphs of intricate geometric patterns, shapes, and designs of animals and people.

And a deeply carved spiral. The same symbol that had trapped her in the desert.

Alda was careful to avoid the witch-trap as she inched her way to the top of the cliff.

Chapter Nine: When Sorrows Come

Ferdinand sat in the surf with his forehead resting on his hands and realized that for the first time in his life, he was free. No ship. No captain. No crew. No responsibilities or burdens, apart from simple survival. He could make his own decisions. Choose his own way. Be his own ruler.

But what did he want?

Miranda. He wanted only Miranda. To help her, and more.

Logically, he guessed he could find a way to leave the island now, alone, and perhaps reach safety. He could build a raft and hope to find a passing ship and reach some distant shore. After all, the sea was his life.

But no, he should find the girl, Miranda, and rescue her from — from what? It was clear to him that she needed to be taken from the island, away from some unknown danger. He should save her.

But how?

Alone, sitting waist-deep in the waves lapping the beach, Ferdinand watched the sea push toward him. The tide showed him his direction: toward the island. Nature told him where to go.

But then the earth shook. It felt like the land had become unhitched from its berth and was tossed by white-capped waves. After a few heartbeats, the trembling subsided.

Ferdinand, himself shaking, turned with resolve toward the cliffs but froze ankle-deep in the surf as he saw fanciful, colored lights disappear into the distance.

Then he heard a sound: a woman's scream. Miranda?

Ferdinand did not think. He ran out of the waves toward the source of the sound. Down the beach, along the base of the cliffs, toward a place where the sea turned inland into a rocky cove. The air around him still felt on edge, electric. It was the remnants of a storm, like the one that took his ship.

He stopped and listened. Silence. No movement. No lights. Nothing. Only the rising tidewaters that led into the cove, toward a secluded cave. Its entrance was marked by hundreds of tiny pillars made of crystal, reflecting the sun and further contrasting with the darkness within its depths.

In the shadows on the bank of the cove, steps from the entrance to the cave, was a form on the sand.

A body.

Miranda.

Ferdinand knelt beside her, wiped her golden locks from her forehead, and held her hand. No movement.

He leaned his cheek against her lips. No breath.

He bit his lip as he listened for a heartbeat. No pulse.

No life.

What did this? Was it the colored lights? Were they the danger that she feared? And did they have something to do with her father?

Ferdinand was helpless. Lost again, more lost than when he was swept off his ship.

Now, love itself was gone.

Despite himself and despite what he had always been taught, Ferdinand cried. He wept not only for the dead girl but for all of the bleakness of his past. The beatings, starvation, abandonment, brutality, seclusion. For the tortures he could not name. And for the future, a future now hopeless and alone. He had known love for a glorious moment, the culmination of his entire life. That moment was over, and the future dissolved before him like a tear upon the sand.

He held Miranda's form to his chest, his heart beating so loudly that it pulsed through her lifeless skin. In a fairytale, his love would have resurrected her. But Ferdinand knew that life was not a fairytale.

"Step away from her, *man*." A harsh voice spit out the last word with disgust.

Ferdinand did not jump at the sudden sound. He did not move. He was not disobedient, simply despondent. He held Miranda closer to him, protecting her.

"I said to *move!*"

Ferdinand looked up, toward the cave entrance. A figure emerged, limping and hunched, from its shadows. It had arms and legs and a head as usual, but they all protruded at odd angles and bent against their owner's body. Its face was contorted and unhuman, like a body bloated by the sea.

The figure brandished a large rock menacingly, tilting it back, ready to heave it toward Ferdinand and his fallen love.

"I give final warning. Move away from her now, or die." As the figure approached, its appearance was even more disturbing in the bright sunlight of the cove.

Instinctively, Ferdinand stood and placed himself between the hideous thing and the perfect body of Miranda.

"Who are you?" it asked.

Ferdinand ignored its question. "What happened to her?"

The thing studied the girl for a moment and spat, "Spirits, no doubt. She had no protection from them." The being reached toward Miranda's body, and Ferdinand pushed its hand roughly away.

The figure snarled, "What is she to you? Be away, and leave her to me."

"No." Ferdinand stretched himself to his full height and felt somehow taller than when he was on the ship. "I will not leave the woman I love."

"Love?" The thing laughed condescendingly. "That's a curse. You are passion's slave." It studied the pair for a moment, and its eyes fell on Ferdinand's hand. The sun fully burst from the parting clouds, and its rays fell on the signet ring. The ring with Prince Hamlet's royal seal.

The creature's hideous eyes widened, questioningly. The deformed thing hesitated and lowered its rock, commanding, "Tell me, who are you?"

"I am Ferdinand, boatswain of the lost ship *The Tempest*," he hesitated. "And protector of the maiden Miranda."

The thing chortled before it spoke with gravity, "And I am Caliban, son of Sycorax. Rightful heir and ruler of this island." He paused, perhaps waiting for acknowledgement of his lofty status. When Ferdinand did not respond, he continued, "And betrothed of Miranda."

They stared at each other, unblinking, unflinching.

Finally, "She is dead." Ferdinand struggled with the words.

"Then help me save her."

"How?"

*   *   *

Alda did not expect to find herself in a forest. The rocky cliffs gave way not to rolling, grassy fields but to ancient woods and dense undergrowth. There was no way around the trees, no path through them. Within minutes, Alda was disoriented and lost.

Branches and roots tugged at her hair and blue cloak, holding her back. Rocks scuffed her exposed toes in the holes of her shoes. Leaves rustled above and around her, not from her own movements but from other *things*.

And in this sylvanian labyrinth, Alda did not seek a way out. She searched for a tree. A tree, she knew now, in a forest.

Alda thought back to the moor: when the witches told her of the island, their instructions were expectedly vague. The weyward sisters told her that the tree would be apparent. That Alda needed to rescue the old familiar named Ariel, who had been trapped in that tree, and bring him back to the moor. Then, they would enable her to speak to her grandmother, somehow.

Before Alda drank the witches' potion, she had imagined that there would be one tree on the island. Or a tree that was taller than the others, or colored differently. Or obviously magical in some way.

But Alda knew now that nothing was ever easy or apparent, especially when dealing with the witches.

Alda remembered her grandmother's advice, "Never trust a witch." In Alda's memory, the old woman was reading a tattered book borrowed from the Tabard Inn's small library, and she raised her eyebrows over the pages. Alda had laughed, thinking it was a joke, and returned her attention to her stereopticon card's image of a coral reef, an image of a fantastical world she could never visit. A world like this.

Thinking back on it now, Alda considered her grandmother's harsh gaze and serious tone. What had Gramma known? What was she truly trying to say?

"Witch!" Now, in the forest, it sounded like the surrounding trees had vocalized Alda's thoughts. "Witch!" The noise reverberated and multiplied in the treetops, repeated like a chant, gaining strength. "Witch, witch, witch!"

It was an alarm.

Alda ran. Through the branches clawing at her skin, over the roots and rocks trying to pull her to the ground. All around, the chanting grew louder, "Witch! Witch! WITCH!"

Then, a splash. And silence. Alda was suddenly immersed in water, a stream. She fought, but the blue cloak held her down. She was sinking. Drowning. Panicking. She tried to breathe but choked and swallowed a mouthful of water instead of air.

And, illogically, she was suddenly dry. She was on the Ledge Path, walking to Sandstone Creek, her grandmother younger and more spritely as she strolled next to the ledge faces. Alda was younger, too, with shorter hair. It was a memory. A good memory. But it was real. It was immediate. It was happening now.

"Tell me another, Gramma," Alda felt herself say, as she had many years ago.

"This one," her grandmother pointed to a rough carving in the stone: a cowboy in an oversized hat, half covered by more recent graffiti of names and dates. "This is from an outlaw who robbed a train." The old woman looked toward the railroad bridge, partially visible in the distance above the trees and river. "He hid his gold in a cave in the ledges and left this carving as a reminder of where to find it."

"Which cave?"

"No one knows."

"Maybe I'll find it one day!" Alda laughed, "Maybe today!" She studied the carving, looking for clues, and found another nearby, deeper and more worn.

It was a simple spiral. She knew now that it was a witch-trap.

In her memory, Alda felt herself ask, "Gramma, is this the cowboy's clue?"

"No, that is ancient. It is from the people who lived here long ago."

"Tell me the symbol's story."

Her grandmother hesitated. Seeing Alda's eager face, she continued, "Long ago, this river was like a road that connected people from the entire peninsula and beyond. Dangers came, brought by outsiders, and spread along the river from village to village. So wise women carved magical symbols to try to stop these dangers, to save their villages. That symbol is here for protection." Her grandmother nodded solemnly, turned away, and continued down the path.

"What were the dangers?" Alda remembered that her grandmother did not answer, and Alda did not pursue more questions.

In the memory, Alda knew what should come next: they continued silently toward Sandstone Creek to search for crayfish and petosky stones.

But Alda's memory changed. The colors around her were suddenly more vibrant and, somehow, new.

Her grandmother turned abruptly. As the old woman's eyes flashed, she took Alda's two hands, holding them tightly. "Stay with me for a moment because what I told you before is not complete. There is more. One of those wise women lost seven children. She cried seven tears into the river, and an island grew where each tear hit the water. That woman was connected to this place."

Alda's heart raced. Her breath came in gasps as the colors around her grew brighter, almost fluorescing. Was this a memory, still, or something else?

"What does that mean, Gramma?"

"There is magic in the islands. In the water. Here. Ancient magic," she whispered as she squeezed Alda's hands tighter. "And danger. Go, now!"

Alda coughed and spit. The scene disappeared around her. She was again in the stream, struggling to stay afloat and still unable to breathe.

But why struggle? Alda was happy on the Ledge Path, with her grandmother. She took another gulp of water and reentered her past, her memory.

"Why are you returned?" Her grandmother was frantic, pushing her away. This was not in her memory. This was certainly new.

"I want to stay. Please!"

"No, child, no. Up! Look up!"

She did, and above the Ledge Path, between two boulders, was another path, wild and obscured. Ferns grew around it, and the trees above bent into arches like a tunnel. She wondered briefly why she had never seen this path before. She thought she knew every route along the river. How could she have overlooked this one?

"No, look higher. Breathe!"

Now, Alda breached the surface of the stream. She inhaled as much air as her lungs could contain. And all went black.

Suddenly Alda was in a different memory, in the ship with the dying boy in her arms. The smell was suffocating, the rocking incessant. Nothing was sturdy or dry. She felt a warm wetness on her arms as the boy's blood soaked through her black sleeves.

In the memory, Alda was overwhelmed with helplessness. This was her worst moment, illogically even worse than losing her grandmother. She shook, shivering uncontrollably with grief and fear.

The boy, Dreng, looked into her eyes, pleading, begging. He was gaunt and weak, yet somehow beautiful.

Alda felt connected to him as they spoke in whispers, as if she had known him for years before, or had some intertwined fate that she could sense but not articulate.

"Take me with you." He coughed blood. She knew he would die and wanted only to help him, to save him. But how?

Another thought pierced her mind: why had the cauldron's bubble brought her here, to the ship, in the first place? What did she *need* here?

And why must she see this boy suffer again, in this memory?

There was no answer that could allay her misery. She gave up, and her muscles relaxed.

Now Alda could see the stream before she sunk beneath its surface. She gulped its water yet again, filling her stomach, breathing it in.

The memory of the Ledge Path returned. Her grandmother held Alda's face in her hands, caressing her cheeks, concern wrinkling her brow. "You are too strong for this, child."

"No, let me stay! I need you. I need this. Please, please!"

Her grandmother shook her head. "This is not real. I am a memory. You know this. Fight."

Alda fought to the stream's surface again. Her blue cloak held her down, but still she struggled for air. A deep breath.

The air returned Alda to a memory. She was on the ship again with the boy, hopeless. His eyes like solar orbs burning into hers.

Then she opened her eyes and could see the stream's shore before another gasp returned her in a flash to the ship and despair. She felt the boy's struggling breath on her face. His last breath.

She inhaled again above the waves and heaved her arms. Her fingers touched soil. She scratched and pulled and finally, exhausted, she was on the stream bank. Coughing, spitting, shaking, yet recovering with each heartbeat on dry land.

Her last memory, as she escaped from the stream, had been the light that left the boy's eyes as she vanished from the ship.

Before Alda could comprehend what had happened, she heard, "Is it her?" The voice was calm and commanding and airy, like distant whispers in the wind.

"It is not the one you think. It is another," a second voice soothed.

The voice was melodious and peaceful, almost a lullaby. Alda relaxed. Soon, her shaking subsided, and she watched flowers fall onto the stream, floating on its luminescent blue surface. The terror she felt escaping from its waters dissolved as she watched the blooms circle and weave amid its waves.

But as Alda stared at the water, she realized that it was shallow enough to stand with her shoulders and head exposed. She should have been able to simply walk out of the water, but something had held her down. Something invisible and powerful.

The voices in the trees whispered again, incoherently rustling, as two forms emerged from the stream. They were like women made of mist.

Naiads, Alda remembered. Spirits of water, ancient nymphs that held magic unattainable by witches. She knew this instinctively, from the forgotten reaches of her mind. From Netherfeld.

"This is not the one you seek," the naiads assured the trees.

"Quiet, sister, the escapee listens," a voice whispered.

"It has no comprehension." One of the trees shifted, its leaves and branches bending to the shape of a tall woman. It studied Alda.

A dryad, nymph of the oaks, Alda remembered. Another memory from Netherfeld.

The other trees transformed likewise as the first tree suggested, "I will speak to it." The oak bent her branches downward and rustled as she asked, slowly, "Do you understand these words?"

"Yes," Alda replied, her voice hoarse.

The tree lost several leaves, and the nymphs around it shivered. One of the naiads asked, "*What* are you?"

Alda spoke more boldly, "A person. A human." She paused and added defensively, "I am not a witch."

The dryads shook their leaves. "Who are you, person?"

Alda did not know if she could trust these creatures. But she was alone otherwise. And scared. The stream had disoriented and terrified her. Her grandmother would know what to do.

After several deep breaths, Alda found her resolve and did as she was taught; she told the truth, "My name is Alda Reeding. I am from — from far away."

"You are the first to escape the Stream of Consciousness. The others we have captured all drowned in their past."

"What — what do you mean?" Alda inched away from the stream, suddenly more fearful of its magic.

The dryad leaned closer and ignored her question. "What did it show you?"

A second asked, "What dreams did you have?" The naiads leaned toward her, tilting their heads as they studied her face.

"I saw my grandmother first. And then a boy who, who died in my arms."

"Your best and worst memories," the closest naiad explained. "Good memories in the water, terrifying images in the air above."

"How did you manage to reach the shore?" another nymph asked.

"I, I, I fought." Alda whispered, only to herself, "I overcame my misery."

The nymphs' forms softened, as if Alda had passed some trial. A naiad added, "Strength, not magic."

"Not strength, perseverance," another suggested.

"Why are you here?" The dryad shivered her branches.

Again, Alda told the truth, "I have come to free Ariel from a tree."

Her task seemed simple, now that she said it out loud for the first time.

Whispers. Rustling. The naiads' forms seemed to vibrate, shaking the surface of the water. The dryads loosed their leaves, which swirled into the air above the Stream of Consciousness. They were angry.

Finally, the closest dryad asked, "Free Ariel? Or take him?"

Alda hesitated. "Free him. And then leave." She was not ready to tell the rest, about the witches on the moor, not yet.

"Then you are too late."

The dryads rustled and whispered to one another. As Alda rested on the bank, fatigued from the stream, she listened carefully and tried to distinguish the nymphs' words, but they were too soft.

"Is Ariel dead?" Alda finally asked. She suspected, from the low pitches of the dryads' murmurs, that their conversation was bleak.

"Ariel's tree is no more, but he is still kept," the tallest dryad explained.

Across the stream, a shorter dryad added, "The tree was our sister."

"Murdered! Murdered! Murdered!" The trees chanted. Alda knew now that it was they who had cried "witch" earlier.

The taller dryad continued, "Yes, murdered by Sycorax, long ago."

The name, like a viper's bite, stung Alda's body to her core. Her soul ached upon hearing it, terrified. She swooned, lightheaded from her time in the stream or from something else, but was supported by a branch behind her.

"Do you know Sycorax?" The dryad's voice was deep with concern.

Alda furrowed her brow. "No — perhaps — I don't remember. You see, I have been to a place called Netherfeld, and —"

The dryads rustled, and the naiads shimmered, but none verbally responded to the name of the magical realm. Yet Alda saw that they understood.

As Alda held her tongue, the dryad continued, "Only the strongest witch can kill a nymph, and Sycorax was the strongest."

"Ariel weakened her, tricked her, so she punished him."

"Many years later, Prospero set Ariel free."

"And then *he* captured Ariel. To use," the shortest dryad explained.

"Ariel is kept now, in Prospero's palazzo."

Alda considered and then asked, "What of Sycorax? Where is she?"

Silence.

"Is she dead?"

Continued silence.

Alda wondered aloud, "Then I must go to the palazzo and rescue Ariel."

"We will help," the nymphs whispered.

Chapter Ten: Fate Cries Out

Ferdinand did not have time to marvel at the cave's interior. He did not admire the glistening water dripping from the sharp stalactites, the gemstones protruding from the rocky surfaces, or the geometric and intertwined carvings that covered the stony walls.

He paid no regard to the deeply carved spiral on the wall directly behind him. And he was too distraught to care that this symbol glowed as he approached it.

Miranda's body was heavy in his arms. His mind was elsewhere, disconnected. Lost in "what if?"

"There, against the wall," the malformed man, Caliban, directed, his voice cracking as if rarely used, his gaze distracted and flitting, looking first to the wall and then ceiling and floor.

Ferdinand dared a question as he lowered the girl's limp form, "Is there magic in this place?" His voice felt small in the majesty of the cave. He did not belong here.

Caliban shook his head and directed, "No, not there. Sit her up." He pointed, "There, there! Against the wall."

Ferdinand did as he was told and placed Miranda's drooping shoulders against the cave wall. Her body slumped but stayed upright, tight against the cold stone. "What now?"

Caliban did not answer. The crooked man was distracted, wringing his hands and pacing as he mumbled prayers or curses under his breath, a strange metric string of meaningless words. His eyes darted in all directions and never fully rested on any single object.

Ferdinand turned back to his love and tenderly felt for her pulse.

Still nothing. No heartbeat. No breath. He felt his throat close, as if being strangled. Or drowning again.

And then, a sensation of extreme heat. Not burning, but an enveloping warmth on his hand as it rested on her sternum. When he pulled his hand away from Miranda, the heat immediately dissipated.

Caliban stopped muttering and fidgeting. He hobbled toward them, listening carefully as he bent toward the girl.

A wail broke the silence. A cough echoed through the cave. Then a fluttering of eyelids. Miranda awoke, convulsing as she struggled to breathe with resurrected lungs.

Joy. Ecstasy. Ferdinand did not have words for his overwhelming emotions. Relief, yes, relief. And confusion.

Miranda stared at Ferdinand, her wide eyes like blue waves of the sea. For a brief flash, the young man thought he remembered that her eyes had been dark, but no. The beach's light had played tricks, he decided.

She blinked, focusing first on the young man next to her and then the cave around her. She was disoriented, fearful, panicked.

Ferdinand caressed her hand gently, doing his best to make her calm. She studied his face as if she had never seen him before. Did she not remember him?

Finally, Miranda's frantic eyes fell on Caliban. "You?" Her voice was hoarse with contempt or hatred. Or fear.

Caliban stooped to her side, attempting to take her hand as she feebly pulled it away. He hesitated a moment and stood angrily, hovering over her. "I have been ever faithful. Your servant." She scowled at him. He considered and added, more apologetically, "I did not know it would be this long, this difficult. I lacked the proper instrument. Please, please, forgive —"

"Where is Ariel?" Miranda interrupted as she pushed Ferdinand aside, directing her question at Caliban. Before he could answer, the girl's eyes narrowed, and a realization flashed across her face. "Prospero! It was him."

Caliban nodded, and Miranda relaxed against the wall, her breath rasping and hands shaking.

Ferdinand wanted nothing more than to help her, to ease her. All the happiness in the world was his now that Miranda was resurrected, but he was the only one in the cave experiencing such an emotion. The two others were agitated, on edge. Were they scared?

After calming somewhat, Miranda struggled to stand. Her feet gave way beneath her, and she fell into the young man's arms. His heart leapt.

"I need to find Ariel," she continued to Caliban as she tried to pull herself upright, disregarding Ferdinand as he did his best to provide her aid. "My grasp here —" she waved her free hand awkwardly before her, trying to stabilize herself, as Ferdinand held the other "— is tenuous. I need his magic. I must go to his tree. And then —" Miranda's words were lost as she struggled for balance.

As she finally steadied herself, her eyes connected with Ferdinand's, and his soul fluttered. She took his hand and ran her fingertips over his rough knuckles and golden ring. Miranda seemed to see him for the first time, to recognize him. Her features softened, and she smiled. The furrow between her brows, darkened by worry and death, eased.

Her sapphire eyes sparkled. She touched his cheek and ran her fingers down his neck, toward his shoulder and the scars only partially covered by his torn shirt.

Miranda asked, with an almost incredulous tone, "You love me, don't you?"

Ferdinand nodded. She brushed her still-cold fingers against his cheek.

"You love me, even now? Now that I have returned from death?"

She glanced at Caliban, and back. And she smiled weakly. "Am I no different now?"

"Even death could not stop my love, which is as boundless as the sea. Both are infinite."

"Then help me. Help me to live," she implored.

Yes, Ferdinand decided, he would. Anything. He would even die for her, if she asked.

*   *   *

Alda sat on a rock near the Stream of Consciousness, considering her conversation with the nymphs. A taller naiad emerged from the depths of the water and held out her hand, offering Alda an opalescent stone. "We call it a percepstone."

Another naiad explained, "It is a disguise."

The girl held the stone up to the fading light of dusk, wondering how such an item would work. Should she trust the nymphs?

Alda tried to think of a pointed question, but her mind was numb and working in circles. She was exhausted. After several moments of awkward silence, Alda brushed her hair out of her eyes and asked, "How will a stone disguise me?"

The tallest naiad laughed at the girl's confusion, splashing water droplets. "Look into the stream."

Alda knelt and peered over the bank into the Stream of Consciousness. The sun's long rays danced over its surface, creating a shifting mirror that revealed not Alda, but a young boy.

The boy had Alda's eyes and complexion, but his hair was short and unkempt. She blinked, he blinked. She reached up to touch the hair on her head, and watched speechlessly as the boy did the same. His clothes, too, were different: a torn white shirt and muddy, brown breeches. Only the blue cloak remained unchanged.

A floating flower fell onto Alda's head, and she dropped the percepstone in her distraction. The boy on the water was gone. She now appeared in the reflection, older than when she had last seen herself, yet recognizable.

For a few heartbeats, Alda studied herself. She had not seen a mirror since the cottage, before she first touched the cauldron's bubble. Before her years in Netherfeld. Now, her hair was much longer but well groomed. Her collarbone pronounced, and her face narrower. Her cheekbones raised. The skin under her eyes somewhat darkened. The corners of her mouth turned down slightly. Her face seemed the chiseled result of worry and strife.

She had aged in Netherfeld. Her time there, the time spent when she moved between time and place, was lost and forgotten. What had happened in that time?

Absentmindedly, Alda touched the fold inside her sleeve where she kept the cauldron's bubble secure. If the nymphs noticed, they did not reveal their curiosity.

A naiad broke the silence, "It must touch your skin."

Alda broke her reverie and met the nymph's gaze inquisitively.

"The percepstone must touch your skin for the disguise to work," a second naiad added.

Alda tucked the stone into her sock, and her reflection returned to that of the boy. But when she looked down, she still saw her usual self.

The percepstone's disguise was merely a projection for the benefit of others. Alda could not see when she was altered by its powers; she remained unchanged in her own eyes.

Even though Alda knew she should have been grateful for the nymphs' gift, she was confused. "Why must I have a disguise? No one here knows me."

The nymphs whispered amongst themselves. Alda thought she heard one whisper, "Netherfeld."

Finally, one explained, "The unknown, the unexpected are always dangerous."

Alda thought back to the sailors on the beach. Their intent was not entirely clear to her, but she suspected they would not have reacted as aggressively to a boy. Her gender could endanger her, she knew. Perhaps there was more danger that she did not know, as well.

"Before nightfall, you must reach Ariel's tree. Our dead sister still has magic that will help you, so take one of her branches," the tallest dryad explained firmly.

"After sunset, the island will change, so beware," another warned.

Alda considered the nymphs' words and did her best to thank them sincerely as she set off through the forest toward the rose-colored sky, with the percepstone tucked inside her sock, pressed into her skin.

Alda should have worried. She should have wondered. She should have thought about her past and future, and the present. But she did not. Alda was tired of thinking. She was tired of "what if?" and "what next?" and "what now?" She was simply, utterly tired.

Yet her thoughts returned to the Stream of Consciousness, despite herself: the carvings along the Ledge Path, the story of the ancient people, the witch-trap. For a flash, she saw a connection between her hometown and the Canyon, their origins, and the petroglyphs, with the standing stones on the moors and the cliffs here. Did they share a common history, a common magic? But she was too exhausted to think on it fully, now.

The trees seemed to part around her, providing a clear and straight path, but her feet felt leaden in her cut-up shoes. When she finally reached the forest's edge, her drooping eyes surveyed a field spotted with purple flowers before her, giving way to barren, rocky heath in the distance.

Before Alda could proceed, she thought she heard serene music, almost like a lullaby. She desperately needed to sleep. The setting sun's beams were somewhat brighter here, away from the gloom of the woods, and the grass was warm and welcoming. The sun still had time before it disappeared, some time at least, so Alda thought she could rest safely before continuing to Ariel's tree.

The mysterious music continued, and the island seemed to dissolve into nothing as Alda finally, deeply, slept.

Chapter Eleven: All is Not Well

Night fell suddenly as the trio — Miranda, Caliban, and the former boatswain — crossed rocky, heather-covered fields toward the center of the island. Ferdinand felt as if one blink turned the sky from dusk to black. It was unnerving.

Ferdinand had not feared darkness at sea, at least not after the prince had escaped, after he had met the mysterious girl. After he survived Ernesto's blade. It was strange, now, to feel apprehensive during the night. But, he realized, his fear was of the unknown, not the dark.

And so much was unknown.

Miranda's burst of energy had already left her frail body. She insisted on walking unaided when they first reached the fields, but she soon needed support. Ferdinand did not mind. It gave him an opportunity to encircle her waist with his arm, to hold her elbow as she leaned into him. Her touch made him feel complete, whole.

Their walk through the heather was silent. The two lovers leading, Caliban limping behind, loosing an occasional grunt as he forced his crooked body over some obstacle.

Ferdinand ignored Caliban, Miranda's supposed betrothed, as much as possible. He did not want to think of some other man, some other *thing*, possessing the woman he longed to claim as his own.

Suddenly, Miranda stumbled over a rock and moaned in pain.

"We should rest for the night," Ferdinand pleaded as he helped steady her shaking body.

His love hesitated, tilting her head. "No," she determined. "We must keep moving." She limped forward, disregarding Ferdinand's outstretched hand.

All was silent for several moments until a whistling caught Ferdinand's attention. He turned and saw lightning, coming not from the sky, but from the ground. Green lightning, yellow lightning, the colors of the aurora borealis. No, not lightning. Lights. The fanciful lights he had seen on the beach, but closer and moving quickly toward them.

Ferdinand was the only one alarmed. "What are those?"

Caliban snorted and scoffed, "Those are only Prospero's slaves, doing Ariel's bidding." As Caliban spoke, the lights shaped first into abstract images and then distinct forms. Birds, animals, geometric designs, like the figures that Ferdinand disregarded on the walls of the cave.

"What, what do you mean?" Ferdinand sputtered.

Miranda watched the lights with wonder, and a curled smile twisted her lips. "Something wicked this way comes."

The young man watched in awe, suppressing his fear, as Miranda raised a shaking finger, mumbled some words under her breath, and swirled her wrist.

The forms were almost upon them now, and Ferdinand raised a protective arm before his love, shielding her the coming harm.

Miranda did not move. She did not flinch or turn away. The young woman simply snapped. And nothing happened. There was no attack, no harm. The lighted figures moved past them, toward a nearby forest edge.

"That is an old spell." Caliban spat the words in disgust. "Sycorax's spell. I'm surprised it still works."

"True magic is timeless," Miranda cast an angry look at the other islander. After taking a long, ragged breath, she added, "You should have learned it when you had the chance." Her feet gave out from under her, and Ferdinand lowered her to the heather-covered ground.

"You taught me more than enough, my *dear*." Caliban crossed his arms and slumped angrily to a low rock, where he sat and brooded.

Miranda smiled weakly, but Ferdinand could not tell if the expression was to cover her fear or something else. "Yes, we should rest now," she said to herself. "The spell worked, but I am tired from it. We are safe." She paused and added, "I know we are *all* safe." She squeezed Ferdinand's hand, and he was loath to release his hold on her.

As Miranda turned from him and reclined — no, collapsed — into the heather, the colored forms moved toward the distance and glowed on the horizon.

Ferdinand knew he could not sleep without the rocking and lapping of the waves, so he kept watch as the lights retreated.

And then he saw the glowing figure of a man near the forest. Even without discerning his face, Ferdinand knew that the being was watching him. The others seemed unaware, so the young man held his tongue and let them rest peacefully.

Ferdinand should have been afraid, but he was not. Instead, he was alert.

Within seconds, the two islanders appeared to sleep soundly, almost unnaturally. Miranda's slight frame quivered with exhaustion. She was noticeably weaker now, after the protective spell, and slept deeply, her eyes moving beneath her lids as she dreamed.

The young man turned his attention back to the luminescent figure, waiting for it to leave, to follow the other lights, but still the figure remained, watching him from the edge of the forest. It seemed to only glow brighter as the minutes passed, its features becoming more solid and defined.

The being seemed familiar, too, and although it did not beckon him, Ferdinand knew that it called.

So the young man rose silently and crossed the rocky field, lit only by the moonlight. As Ferdinand grew closer, he could clearly discern a man with a weathered face and coarse beard, a man whom Ferdinand might know but could not clearly remember.

The figure moved its mouth, almost chewing words, before it finally forced out, "You look not like you did in life."

Ferdinand froze and felt unnaturally cornered, his mind racing, reaching. He remembered. Not all, but some. Something distant and fleeting. An emotion more than a vision. Yes, he knew this man.

"Father?" As Ferdinand uttered the word, a shot jolted through his arm, igniting the scar on his shoulder and chest. The wrath of nature that had killed his father — and nearly him — felt fresh, raw. "But you are, are dead," Ferdinand stuttered. "They told me you died."

"Murdered, most foully murdered."

"No, it was a storm." Ferdinand's head whirled and groped for details, facts. "A sudden storm, on the sea near Aleppo. St. Elmo's fire, they said, that burned us both."

"Unnatural flames," its voice lowered. "Believe me, for I have not much time." The ghost, as Ferdinand understood it to be, moved closer to him, close enough to touch. It flickered and then continued, "I need revenge. Help me."

Ferdinand stepped back, not in fear, but in surprise. Was this being actually his father? Or was it some trick of the island's spirits? Some dark magic?

"The creature that cursed me will soon be found," the thing explained. "You will know. And when you meet it, you must destroy it. Revenge. That will be my end as *this*, and then I will be released to beyond." The ghost looked pleadingly at Ferdinand. "Please, my son."

"Who — no, *what* is the creature?"

The figure flickered again, like a flame in the wind. It forced out, "A witch."

"What is its name?"

The ghost's form blinked to black and then reappeared briefly, its mouth moving soundlessly, until it finally and completely vanished. And all was still in the darkness.

Ferdinand stood alone at the edge of the forest, staring at emptiness and thinking of what might have been and what could be. In the silence, he could only whisper into the wilderness, "What is *my* name?"

And the young man stood alone, and wondering what was real or imaginary, as his eyes adjusted again to the moonlight.

For a moment, Ferdinand thought he saw a pulsating glow from Prince Hamlet's signet ring on his finger. But no, he decided, it was only a reflection of the stars above.

*   *   *

Alda awoke suddenly on the edge of the forest, with a feeling that she was being watched. No, stalked. Hunted. She covered her head with the cloak as she stood and whirled around, squinting across the rocky field in the moonlight. Movement to her right. A snapping branch. She pulled the cloak tightly around her, finding bravery in its folds, and walked toward the noise.

She saw a young man staring blankly into the darkness. He turned toward her, obviously startled. Out of place. But she felt at ease with him. Not safe, but less afraid.

"Are you lost, boy?" The mysterious young man posed the question, and Alda remembered the percepstone's disguise.

Of course, she still looked like the boy she saw reflected in the stream. She lowered her voice somewhat and responded, "Are you?"

"Not yet." He approached her with a forced smile spreading over his features. His eyes revealed sorrow, and they looked familiar. "I have friends nearby," he added awkwardly.

Alda considered the possible danger of her situation before responding, "As do I."

"This is no place for a boy, alone." The young man's tone was nurturing, kind, not commanding.

She straightened to her full height, yet was not as tall as her companion. "I agree. But I am not —" She started to say "a boy," but then lied, "Afraid."

"Nor, nor I," he stammered. He looked over his shoulder toward the field, perhaps wanting an excuse to leave. Or seeing if someone or something was watching them.

He turned back to Alda, "Who are you?"

"Alda."

"That is — an unusual name for a boy."

"I am unusual." She smiled, despite herself.

The young man laughed forcefully, sounding out of place in the still darkness. They stood silently for a moment, each awkward and unsure what to say next, before he started to turn away. "Good night, Alda," he said over his shoulder.

Alda wanted to say more to him. Her thoughts raced. Why did he seem familiar? Had they met, somewhere, before? But she could not articulate her questions, not to him. Not here and now.

Finally, Alda called after the young man, "What is your name?"

He stopped and looked down, not turning around, "Ferdinand."

"Oh," Alda replied, her voice revealing disappointment. She muttered as she realized, "I thought I knew you." He turned toward her, and she added lamely, "You remind me of someone, but he was far away. On a ship. And younger. And his name was —" She stopped herself and shook her head. That boy had died in her arms, so saying *Dreng* somehow felt unlucky or ill planned. Or impossible.

The young man hesitated and then quickly crossed the small distance between them. Alda thought for a moment that he meant her harm and stepped back, but the young man stopped at her side and squinted at her face as if trying to read a page in the dark.

Boldly, almost brazenly, he lowered her cloak's hood. "You remind me of someone, too." He studied her face.

She felt at once hopeful and apprehensive. Conflicted.

Could Ferdinand recognize her, see her through the disguise? She considered removing the percepstone from her skin to reveal her true self, but it felt dangerous. And she had no time to act.

A high-pitched whine suddenly filled the air, almost like the whistle of a boiling teapot. Alda remembered the sound from the beach and looked for the colored lights. She saw them approaching swiftly in the distance.

"You are not safe here," he warned. "Go home." There was panic in his voice, but he studied her for still another heartbeat before turning away.

"You will go home, as well?" Alda felt that she needed to protect this stranger.

"Yes, soon." Ferdinand's words were almost lost in the lights' noise.

Alda felt a strange twinge of regret as the young man disappeared into the rocky, heathered field. She felt like there was something she had lost or misplaced, something important.

Something was missing. But what?

Chapter Twelve: Rough Magic

Ferdinand. Dreng. The Nameless. Nothing. He did not know himself. He was lost. And now, the ghost. Murder? Revenge? It was too much. He did not want to comprehend it, to think about it.

The strange boy, too. Was he a ghost, or a spirit, or a mortal? He seemed familiar. Was he something else?

Even as the whistling lights approached again, Ferdinand only wanted to think ahead. His future, with Miranda, was so much clearer than his past.

Absentmindedly, Ferdinand twirled the gold signet ring on his finger as he approached the reclined, sleeping forms of Caliban and Miranda on the hill. But as Ferdinand grew nearer, he saw that Miranda was not asleep.

She sat upright as he approached. "Where were you?" Miranda's voice revealed her worry.

Ferdinand smiled, at ease in her presence. "This is my first night on land. I need waves to sleep." He sat down beside her, and she leaned into his arm. His heart fluttered.

"Who was that, near the forest?" She sounded more than curious. Concerned.

Ferdinand considered before answering, "Only a boy." Yes, merely a boy, he assured himself. A stranger. Nothing more.

"A boy? What was he doing here?" Miranda's voice was hoarse. Was it anger, or fear?

"Only walking. Going home, I suppose." Ferdinand considered telling Miranda that the boy seemed familiar, but he decided that doing so might worry her unnecessarily.

They sat in silence. The lights were closer, nearly to them, but

Ferdinand did not fear them now. He studied Miranda and felt her shoulders tense, her fists clench. He dared a question, one that he was almost too scared to speak, "What happened to you, before?"

"Before? Before the island?" She was defensive and looked at him questioningly.

Ferdinand shook his head and explained, "I mean on the beach. Did you truly die? Or was it like a sickness, or a trance?"

Miranda eased and whispered, "I was reborn, in a way, in the cave."

Despite her brevity, Ferdinand understood, even though she was not being literal. "So was I. On the beach." He told her of his shipwreck, the lost vessel, the drowned crew. She listened and rubbed his arm reassuringly.

After a moment of silence, Ferdinand realized he had another question. "Why did the lights not harm me?"

"I protected us," she took his hand and ran her small fingers over his rough knuckles.

"No, on the beach. When the lights — when the lights harmed you. They passed me by."

"Were you in the waves or on the sand?"

Ferdinand thought back, reforming the scene in his mind. "In the water, but barely."

Miranda was silent for a moment, her fingers still caressing his. "Those light-spirits were sentinels, sent to defend the island's shore from men who might land."

"What are the lights here?"

"These serve a different purpose." Her tone made it clear that she would not explain further.

After several heartbeats, Miranda inhaled sharply and asked, "Ferdinand, what did the boy near the forest look like?"

Ferdinand had never before been asked to describe anyone. "Ordinary, I suppose. Dirty, with worn clothes. And a blue cloak."

A moment of silence passed, and he felt Miranda's head nod forward as she started to fall asleep. She whispered, "I'll need your help tomorrow. You should sleep now, too."

Ferdinand was not even aware that he had closed his eyes, but he dreamed that he was back in *The Tempest*, sleeping on the coiled rope-bed he used as a child. With two voices whispering as they watched him sleep.

*   *   *

Alda's gaze followed Ferdinand as he left, not knowing whether she should go after him or forget him. She could not shake the feeling of familiarity that the young man evoked, even as the fantastic lights surrounded her and formed into more tangible shapes: animals, geometrics, garlands of leaves and flowers.

Despite the lights' potential for harm, Alda was not afraid. She had been safe on the beach, even when the lights killed the shipwrecked sailors, so she was certain that no harm would come to her now.

But the lights dissipated suddenly as the ground beneath her shook, gaping open with a crack like a splintering tree. This was not like the earthquake before. This was new. The fissure expanded beneath her feet, until she was swallowed by the earth.

Alda fell, her hair and clothes caught by thousands of tiny roots, her skin scraped by rocks and dirt. She slumped to a stop, panting for breath, in a sodden hollow too deep to escape.

For an instant, she thought she was in a grave.

The moonlight shone through a fissure at least twenty feet above her, and she examined herself as best as possible in the dim light. Her cloak was gone, tangled in the roots above, but the percepstone was still in place in her sock. The cauldron's bubble was secure in her sleeve, but useless on the island. Her skin was slippery with black mud, but she was not injured. She forced herself to be calm.

After several moments of silence, soil fell into her hair, and she saw movement above that briefly blocked the moon. Swift movement. A flash of darkness. More moonlight.

A silhouetted shape like a human, but malformed, looked down upon her. And then complete darkness.

The opening above her had collapsed. Or was filled.

Alda counted to thirty, calming herself while she formed a plan. Nothing. Then sixty. *One hundred.* Yet nothing changed. No movement. No light. No air.

She wiggled her fingers and could not see them. The air grew heavy and wet.

Two hundred.

Buried alive. Swallowed by the earth. Silent as the grave. The words popped into her head, and she forced them away.

She would have to dig her way out. But could she? What if the ceiling collapsed and buried her immovably?

Three hundred.

But what else could she do?

She stopped counting.

Desperately, she screamed for help. Maybe Ferdinand would find her? But her words were lost in the soil. Who else could save her?

"Gramma!" It was useless, she knew.

"Dreng!" Nothing, of course. Why had she thought to call him?

"Leana! Raven Leana!" The last syllable was lost in a whimpering sob.

Alda would die here, helpless. An accident. Forgotten. Her mind raced in single syllables, unable to form full thoughts.

Unable to keep her eyes open. She felt heavy, crushing and crushed. Tired. Her head swam and then dipped.

She started to dream. Of a place with no light, no sound, but still sensations. A place that she could barely remember. Distant. Forgotten. Was it Netherfeld? Or was it an hallucination?

Suddenly, light shone through her closed eyelids. No, not light. Heat. A sensation, not a vision. With her last strength, Alda opened her eyes.

Dirt fell. Cold air filled the hollow.

Alda gasped, and her spinning head slowed. The blackness of the world formed into dim focus around her.

Then the whistling lights churned in the space around her before materializing in a form like an owl.

"I've been looking for you. With my sisters."

"You have?" Again, Alda found herself talking to a bird.

"Since you left." The owl's voice was smooth, almost hollow.

"Left? Left where?"

The owl spun her head sideways. "Do you not remember?"

"Remember? Oh, Netherfeld?"

The owl lowered her head in a nod. "Follow me, Alda." Then the ethereal form glided up through the fissure into the moonlight beyond.

Alda called from below, "What happened in Netherfeld?"

"Remember," the owl responded as she disappeared from view.

Alda tried to climb after it, but the slick soil prevented progress. She gripped at roots, but they gave way.

She had air now, at least, and some moonlight, so she relented and sat, trying to remember.

Netherfeld was nothing. She had no clue, no distant recollection of what happened there. It was like a blank page.

Instead of focusing on the forgotten void, she remembered as far back as she could, back to her earliest memory: Yellow corn in murky water, scattered off the shore. It was a strange memory, but Alda could see it clearly. She was no more than three years old because the other islands were still wild. No resort or hotel or rollercoaster. A lonely vision, a fragmentary image of golden kernels sinking into the river near their cottage.

Alda knew, from later memories, that the corn was to lure fish close to her island, where she could more easily catch them with a net. They were too small to eat, so she buried them in the garden near the herbs, hoping to fertilize the soil.

The herbs. Herbs for meals like sage and thyme. Strong chives in the heat of summer. Lavender, gentler and calming as it dried for winter tea. *Rosemary, for remembrance.*

Rosemary. The smell was with her, somehow, in the emptiness beneath the earth. And she could remember, vaguely, something far away and dark and blurred. Out of focus yet very real. A sensation, a feeling in her arms and hands that she willed into being, that she materialized. It was an instinct. Something from Netherfeld.

In the darkness, Alda felt her hands glow. They exuded no perceptible light, but the air around her fingers pulsated with invisible energy, like heat.

Alda's newfound power shook the ground around her. The earth hurled her upward, and Alda stumbled to the soil above as the fissure closed beneath her feet. Not a single grain of dirt was out of place. All was as it had been before.

Astonished, Alda felt the ground. It was warm. Netherfeld was returning to her, not as memories, but as power. As instinct. As magic.

As Alda stared at her hands, wondering at their abilities, the owl glided down from a nearby tree, light streaming behind it as it circled her shoulders.

"Was that magic?" Alda's voice broke as she asked.

"Absence of." The owl landed on the ground, flickering in and out of form as its light continued to dance and change. "A spell was undone."

"What spell?"

"This island is beheld by the magic of Sycorax."

"Who is Sycorax?"

"The once and future queen."

"The nymphs said she was a witch."

"No, more." The bird paused awkwardly between her words, obscuring their meaning.

"Who are you?"

The owl tilted its head, as if confused by an obvious question. "Of course, I am Celia."

"Leana's cousin." Alda could remember that, at least. "I met her in the Canyon." She added, under her breath, "I think Leana had fuller answers."

"We, here, are chained. Our abilities diminished. Our tongues tied. Enslaved." She forced the last word out with some difficulty.

"By whom?" Alda whispered, fearing some unseen being might hear.

"Ariel."

"What is Ariel?"

"An ancient guardian of Netherfeld, himself bound to Prospero."

"The witches only told me that he was a familiar." The owl did not respond, so Alda tentatively asked, "Is Ariel evil?"

Celia paused, flitting her head to look behind her.

Again, "Is he dangerous?"

The owl's light flickered. "I am summoned. I hope we meet again." And the bird form evaporated, twirling into strands of light that shot across the hilly field and out of view.

Alda was alone, again. She shivered without the protection of her lost cloak.

Chapter Thirteen: Into Thin Air

Ferdinand had questions the next morning as they continued to cross the island's desolate landscape. About the shipwreck. The beach. The cave. Now, the lights. For some inexplicable reason, he did not ask about this apparent magic or how it worked. Even though he suspected Miranda had answers.

Instead he followed blindly, as he had on the sea when he was a boy. Like a ship on the tide, tossed by the forces at work around him.

Miranda, as he aided her up a rocky rise, put more weight on his arm. Her breathing became labored. Her energy was failing, as it had after she protected them from the lights, and she was somehow more exhausted this morning. But Ferdinand saw no reason for her to deteriorate so overnight. He was alarmed and concerned.

What had drained her strength?

Several paces ahead, Caliban led the way, limping in the gloomy light and shrouded in a blue cloak.

Ferdinand thought briefly that the cloak was like the one belonging to the boy near the forest. But he dismissed the thought as he held Miranda's hand, guiding her around a patch of mud. Surely all cloaks were similar on an island so small, he decided.

The trio traversed the treeless hills, up and down in rapid repetition. Miranda did not speak as Ferdinand held her elbow. Caliban mumbled curses and expletives under his breath as he limped in the dim light, filling the silence around them.

Finally, after what seemed like hours walking in the early morning twilight, Ferdinand saw a figure on the horizon. It stood like a sentinel, unmoving. As they grew closer, he saw that it was an ancient pine. The top split in two, splintered by some violent force, both sides drooping toward the ground.

Caliban stopped and muttered something unintelligible before adding, "This is Ariel's tree."

"A twain pine," Miranda whispered, her pale lips barely parting.

She released herself from Ferdinand's hold before Caliban added, almost to himself, "Ariel is not here, of course. The great usurper has him." Caliban spat and wiped his nose.

Miranda, careless of Caliban's brutish behavior, tried to walk to the tree but stumbled to the ground. Her eyes flashed with anger. "Damn this, this mortal coil!" Miranda forced herself up and wiped off the mud, refusing Ferdinand's aid, and stood unsteadily.

"A branch, a branch" she begged impatiently, holding out her hand.

Ferdinand easily broke a lower branch, dry and dead for some time. Miranda snatched it from him, twisted it in the air, and mumbled some metric words. Once she stopped, she stood unaided, her weakness gone.

"Some of Ariel's magic remains," she told Caliban. "Enough to help me, for a time." She studied the tree and then added, "Now we must burn it." Miranda stepped back, waiting. Ferdinand looked to her, confused, but she was glaring at Caliban. When the crooked man did not respond, Miranda lowered her voice and repeated slowly, "I said to burn it. Do as you are told, boy."

Caliban turned violently toward the girl and raised his hand as if to strike. "I am not a *boy*!" He lowered his hand and added, "Do not underestimate me."

Miranda stood her ground and hissed, "You owe me everything. I gave you freedom, a voice, words. I gave you all you have."

"I only wanted your love." Caliban waved his hands absentmindedly, avoiding her gaze. Flames shot from his misshapen fingers and engulfed the tree.

Ferdinand stumbled back, avoiding the hot sparks and snapping wood. And avoiding Caliban's fury.

"How could I love a thing that looks like you?" Miranda's voice broke
with a slight sob as she, too, backed away from the burning tree.

"You sound like Prospero, *dearest*," Caliban sneered at Miranda as
the flames grew higher. Sarcasm weighted his final word.

"I must be cruel to be kind," Miranda replied sadly, the last word
almost lost in a whisper.

Ferdinand moved to Miranda's side and attempted to take her hand,
to comfort her, but she turned her head, trying to cover the tears
streaming down her cheeks. It was clear that the pair had some history,
something in their past that Ferdinand did not understand. Something
that inspired this sudden fury.

Caliban turned to Ferdinand and explained, in a lower voice, "I was
not always — I did not always look like this, like —" Caliban did not
finish. Instead, he angrily kicked the ground and mumbled a series of
curses that would have shamed the crew of *The Tempest.*

What were these two, before? Lovers, or less? As Ferdinand
struggled with his worries, both of the islanders stared blankly at the fire
engulfing the tree, unmoving and unmoved. Miranda and Caliban seemed
to look beyond the flames, lost in their thoughts, or their past.

As Ferdinand watched the burning tree, his own thoughts turned to
his father. And his ghost. No, *the* ghost. Ferdinand had no way to know if
the two were one and the same. No way to know if the apparition was
benevolent or evil.

After the flames died down, Caliban walked away, past the tree and
down the far side of the hill.

Ferdinand hesitated, watching the tree crackle and its smaller
branches fall, the scent of pine heavy in the smoke.

"Come with me, love." Miranda was at his side, the branch upright in her hand. Her eyes were wet with tears, but Ferdinand could not tell if they were from pain or something more potent. She took his hand, covering his fingers and his ring with her dainty palm. And he forgot his questions, his worries, and felt love, simply and wholly.

As they turned away from the fire, Miranda twisted her branch toward the remains of the twain pine, and the flames grew higher again. Ferdinand thought he heard a distant, high-pitched whistle as they walked, together, down the hill.

*   *   *

Alda's thoughts kept returning to the young man as she walked across the expansive, rocky field. *Ferdinand.* He should mean nothing to her, except she knew she was not alone on the island. Well, not the only human on the island, at least. That was all, she reminded herself. Finding Ariel was all that mattered.

But Ferdinand had said there were others, his friends. Who were they? Alda shook her head, clearing her questions. She had to find Ariel. That was all.

But her mind still had questions, nagging. What of the magical lights? Ferdinand knew about the lights, too. He knew to warn her of their danger. The lights could kill, she knew, but they could also... what? Watch her? Warn her? Help her, like Celia?

As Alda crossed the heathered field, she did not notice the whistling at first. She was too focused on a fire in the distance, a fire that was both a beacon and a warning. Like a lighthouse above a dangerous, rocky cove. Or a candle in an isolated cottage. The fire burned, brighter than the rising sun, and smoke wisped into the sky above it.

But what was aflame? What thing burned, so mesmerizingly?

Alda grew closer to the flames and could smell burning pine. But by the time she noticed the whistling, it was too late. Her head pounded at her temples, and her teeth ached from the noise. And in her delirium, the whistles turned to voices. Whispers, terrible whispers, of threats and regrets. "You let *her* die. The boy, too." The sounds seemed to have no source. Alda could not escape them.

As she pulled herself up the final hill, almost to the fire, she struggled through the sea of whispers. *Step*, she told herself, *step again*. But she could only hear, "Die. Let her die." She knew, somehow, that the flames would make the voices stop. She only wanted silence. To be with the fire.

Over a rock, her shoes slipped. Past a thorny bush, her white shift-dress caught. Finally, she reached the fire. The smoke curled upward, darkening the sky. Embers flickered, and ash floated into the air. It was peaceful, inviting. The fire called her even closer, reminding her with its whispers, "They are all dead. Join them."

Alda knew that the fire would make the voices stop.

She reached out her hands. Her palms grew warmer. Too warm. Her fingertips ached with the heat. All she could see or feel or want was within the flames. They would silence the whispers, the heartache. If she could touch...

Suddenly the smoke blew toward her, and Alda was lost in a flurry of wind. The ground seemed to give way, and she fell backward. The hill was not steep, but she felt herself fall for several heartbeats without catching the soil beneath.

And then Alda realized that she was far above the ground. She flew. Or rather, she was flown, by something.

The whistling stopped, the voices stopped, as the air blew through her hair. Her smoke-filled lungs cleared, and Alda once again had control of her senses. She looked around. The early sun rose in the ocean, and the fire was like a spark in the distance.

Alda looked up but could see only clouds and sky. She felt unseen thorns dig into her arms, suspending her as she glided above the island. A great flapping beat a wind around her, but the wings that stirred the air were invisible. She could not see the thing that held her.

Alda wanted to fight. She wanted to scream or kick or lash out. But she knew it was useless.

So Alda only hung, like a mouse caught by an owl, and waited to be devoured.

Chapter Fourteen: Foul Play

"Where are we going?" Ferdinand had never walked so far in his life. The field seemed to stretch on for days. He was drained and falling farther behind his companions, who both had newfound strength since they left the burning pine.

When Miranda and Caliban did not answer, Ferdinand considered that their destination may not have a name. He rephrased his question, "What is our goal? Our mission?"

He thought that Miranda's steps quickened. But perhaps his exhaustion was holding him back. After a moment of listening to their footsteps, Ferdinand finally asked a question that had haunted him for some time. "Miranda, your father — is he dangerous or —"

"He is dead." Miranda did not turn to him as she walked.

Ferdinand frowned, confused. "On the beach, you spoke of him, and I, I wondered. I worried. And since then, since the cave, you have not said a word about him."

"Do not worry about him." Miranda's pace slowed.

Ferdinand reached her side and took her hand. "I only worry about you."

Caliban limped ahead, leaving the pair to talk in relative private.

Miranda watched the crooked man for a moment before she turned and faced Ferdinand. Her long, fair hair whipped in the breeze. Her dress blew tight against her hips. Her gaze pierced into his eyes, and Ferdinand's heart skipped a beat.

When she spoke, her tone was low, almost harsh, "Do you know what destroyed your ship?"

"Of course, I told you such last night. It was a storm." As he said the words, her expression revealed his mistake.

Miranda's blue eyes flashed. She shook her head solemnly, "No. It was a kind of magic."

"What do you mean?"

Miranda held both of Ferdinand's hands as she explained, "Spirits. Like those that passed in the night. They have destroyed hundreds of ships near this island."

Ferdinand's heart pounded as he thought of his crew, the lives lost. He could only mutter, "Why?"

Miranda tenderly brushed Ferdinand's brown hair from his eyes as she explained, "This is Prospero's island, his fortress. And he rules like a tyrant, with the help of his slave, Ariel." Miranda was silent as she studied Ferdinand's reaction.

Ferdinand considered his dead father's warning. No, the ghost's warning. As he thought, the scar on his shoulder ached. He thought now that perhaps the light-spirits were like the sailors' descriptions of St. Elmo's fire. Perhaps this Prospero was the witch.

"What, what are we going to do?" Ferdinand stammered.

"*Sic semper tyrannis*," Miranda whispered. "Death to tyrants, always."

Ferdinand was no longer exhausted.

*   *   *

Alda landed on her wrist when she fell — when she was dropped — and rubbed it tenderly as she took in her surroundings. The flapping sound disappeared into the air, and she was left alone in relative silence.

She was still on the enchanted island, in an ancient palazzo's courtyard. It looked like her stereopticon cards' images of Grecian ruins.

Water bubbled up from a marble fountain. A mosaic floor of geometric patterns covered the ground. Ionic columns created a kind of cloister around the perimeter. Frescos of dancing figures, both human and mythical, lined the walls. Open doors led into darkened hallways, invisible in the shadows created by the late morning sun.

Alda did not care for this spectacle. She was exhausted. Her arms ached, too, as red welts formed where the invisible thorns had held her in the air.

Alda was hungry as well, and thirsty. The fountain's sparkling water was beckoning, so she cupped her hands and readied a drink.

"Halt!"

The sound reverberated against the stony walls. Alda spread her hands in surprise, and the water splashed against her feet as she stepped away from the fountain.

"Why are you here?" The voice came from an unseen speaker, and she could not determine its location. Was the voice from the thing that carried her?

"My name is Alda Reeding, and —"

"Answer the question first, before I allow you to enter his home."

"Whose home?"

The voice did not respond. After a moment, it asked again, "*Why* are you here?"

Alda considered the possibilities. She could answer the question, of course, but could she trust the disembodied voice? She could flee, somehow, and go — where? Or she could stay and enter the palazzo, to meet — *whom*?

As Alda ran through her options, she clenched her fists and steadied her nerves. "I suppose it was you who brought me to this place, so you know I am here against my will. Now I'm tired. And thirsty."

Silence.

"If I am a prisoner, then hold me back. Otherwise, let me drink." And without waiting, she did, defiantly.

Then she was gone.

And there was nothing. Absence of light. Absence of sound. Absence of sensation. Yet somehow, Alda still existed.

Then voices, whispering unintelligibly. And soft lights, some distant and some closer. Then lighted forms, like Celia the owl, but somehow even more abstract.

Alda thought logically that she must be dead. But she did not feel dead. Rather, she still felt. Her heart beat rapidly. Her breathing came in successive gasps. Her eyes strained to focus on the few figures materializing in the emptiness.

Was this Netherfeld?

"Where am I?" Lights intensified around her, illuminating the darkness into dusky gray, a fog that enveloped her and obscured the swirling forms.

The whisperings became more audible, more defined. "Home," they whispered. "Home, home, HOME," they chanted a crescendo into the gloom.

Was the word a command, Alda wondered, or an explanation?

They stopped as a single voice calmly explained, "Home at last, after so long. We have been waiting."

Alda asked, "Waiting for what?"

"The return."

"Of me?"

Silence. Alda felt her head spin, her arms light. She was afloat, she thought, until she looked down and saw her hands disappearing. Growing translucent.

"The other, the other, the OTHER," the voices whispered.

"Fetch the other," the single voice cooed.

Alda could not tell if the voice commanded the other beings, or her. But she had no time to consider. Her legs were gone, and her torso.

The last thing she saw was a deep glow in the distance, a hazy green dome rising over a black horizon.

And then Alda was whole. And real.

And she remembered Netherfeld.

Before Alda could fully comprehend what had happened, she vomited, spitting up water onto a finely mosaicked floor. She choked on air, looking at her hands for reassurance that she did, in fact, exist.

As her nerves steadied, Alda realized that she was now inside the palazzo, in a room with tall windows revealing the light of an afternoon sun.

But she was not alone.

Kneeling over her, a bearded man. The man she inexplicably feared. Prospero.

"You are returned." The old man smiled, but Alda flinched away, recoiling as he wiped a cold cloth against her head. "The nausea will pass, Alda. It is a side effect of the fountain." He frowned, "Not the easiest way to reach Netherfeld."

Alda started at the word, and Prospero looked at her curiously before he continued, "But at least the fountain's waters allow you to remember what transpires there. For now and hereafter."

Alda wiped her hair out of her face, thinking back on the voices that she heard in the darkness, the green dome on Netherfeld's horizon.

The old man frowned and turned to the floor, wiping where she had spit. After a moment, he asked, "Are you better?" Prospero studied her face, and Alda nodded. He nodded in return and added, looking away, "I knew it was her."

"You should not have tasted from the fountain. I told you such. It is forbidden," hissed a second voice, higher pitched and more shrill. The voice from the courtyard.

In a corner of the room, pressed into shadows, a large figure recoiled as Alda squinted toward it. Wings. Feathers. A human torso and arms. A face with a serene expression. And talons on its scaly feet.

They were not thorns, Alda realized, that had carried her through the air. This was the creature that had brought her to the palazzo.

"She learned her lesson," the old man replied to his winged companion. "Besides, I guessed she would do as she did. The fountain calls to some, bids them to drink. She passed this trial." Prospero clasped his hands contentedly. "All's well that ends well, Ariel."

Alda started at the name, pushing herself up off the sofa where she reclined, trying to stand but failing to find her feet. She sunk down again, exhausted.

Prospero misunderstood her reaction. "You have no need to fear. He is a harpy, yes, but he is docile. I domesticated him."

Witches. Talking birds. Lights. Nymphs. Now, a harpy. Alda knew that she should be astonished by the magical menagerie. Yet she felt almost indifferent. Why was she not amazed?

Instead, Alda was confused. "Why am I here? Why did you capture me?"

"Captured?" Prospero chuckled. "No, Ariel rescued you. You are our guest. And there is much to tell. But first, rest. You look exhausted. The time will come when I tell you all you need to know." The old man smoothly glided across the room, toward an interior door.

Before crossing the threshold, Prospero hesitated. "Ariel, sing to her."

The room filled with the serene music that had enveloped Alda the previous evening, at the forest's edge. She could distinguish no words, but she felt a sudden exhaustion. It overtook her.

As she leaned into the sofa and closed her eyes, she felt safe, despite herself. Despite her inexplicable hatred of Prospero. Despite being essentially a captive.

Her last thought was that safety was an illusion.

Chapter Fifteen: Torrent of Passion

The hill was rocky, and the palace atop seemed out of place in the island's wilderness, its light stone contrasting with the dark boulders below.

Ferdinand realized that his mouth was open in awe as he stared at its majesty, and he closed it self-consciously.

Miranda beckoned them to stop. "We are close. Find it." She held the branch from the twain pine toward Caliban. "Please," she added, hesitantly. "It may drain me to do it." Her eyes looked pleading, so the crooked man took it reluctantly.

Caliban held the branch horizontal in his hand, and wandered aimlessly. Ferdinand watched for a moment before he asked, "Is that Prospero's palace?"

Miranda only nodded.

Ferdinand stood idly, wanting to help her but not knowing how. Restless, he admired Miranda as she reclined against a protruding boulder. She noticed his gaze and smiled sweetly, bewitchingly. He looked away, blushing despite himself.

After a few moments, Ferdinand turned his attention back to Caliban. The deformed creature crossed back and forth, walking in a kind of grid over the ground, his eyes studying the stick as if he expected it to suddenly change.

"What is he doing?" Ferdinand wondered aloud.

Miranda smiled, "Water witching."

Ferdinand only blinked in response, his confusion evident.

"Divining. Dowsing." Miranda laughed, entertained by Ferdinand's simplicity at something that was, to her, so evident. "The stick will point him to water."

"But we are surrounded by water." Ferdinand looked to the distant sea.

"This is different. A spring bubbles beneath the rocks."

Ferdinand thought he understood and nodded. "Fresh water." Of course.

Miranda did not reply. She furrowed her brow and, after a moment of contemplation, turned suddenly toward Ferdinand and asked directly, "Are you certain that you love me?"

The young man did not hesitate. "Of course. Completely. More than you could know."

"I know more than you think." She smiled, amused. "Then marry me."

"Yes!" He reached her side and took her hand. "When?" He was aware that immediacy was impossible, but he saw no reason to delay. After so many years on the ship, he only wanted stability. A home. A family. To love and be loved. He was tired of waiting. Tired of being alone.

"Not now. But soon." Miranda returned again to silence.

Ferdinand caressed her small fingers absentmindedly as he considered their future. Happiness. Safety. Certainty. He did not know how marriage was supposed to work, but he knew that, more than anything, he wanted absolute, real love. It was the ambition of his mythical heroes, the subject of the sailors' songs. A lofty goal, one he once thought unattainable, but now about to be his. And to have a partner so perfect. Someone who, inexplicably, could love him in return.

In his ecstasy, he did not notice that Miranda slipped her hand away until he heard her say to Caliban, "Your powers are too weak for this." She plucked the branch from his crooked fingers and added, "It takes a woman's touch, I suppose."

"I thought you too frail, *woman*," Caliban hissed as he slouched away.

Miranda held the branch lightly in her palm. After a few steps, the stick twisted upright in Miranda's fingers, moved by some unseen force, and then immediately shot downward, pointing at a nondescript patch of ground near her feet.

"Here. Now, dig." Miranda paused. "Please."

It was unclear if her command was directed at Caliban, but the creature did not respond and only turned his back to her, brooding. Ferdinand obliged, moving rocks and soil as best he could. He would move mountains for her, his fiancée.

As Ferdinand dug, Caliban lamented to himself, "Such is the lot of poor Caliban. Injustice. Malice. Exile. Theft. Abandonment. Replacement." He glared at Ferdinand and continued, "Caliban the forsaken. Caliban the insignificant. Caliban the —"

Water. The soil was damp, then wet, and then gurgling. Ferdinand jumped back as it pooled in the hole and then overflowed around his feet.

Miranda knelt next to the gurgling spring, her azure eyes beaming. She cupped her hands in the water, drank, and — there was nothing. She vanished.

Ferdinand looked around desperately, helplessly. Where was she? What could he do?

Instinctively, he turned toward the spring, ready to drink. Caliban grabbed his arm, stopping him with unanticipated force. "Do not follow her." His tone was different now, darker, serious. "The world she is in now — it is not made for mere mortals. Even a mortal such as you."

Ferdinand stood and watched the water, his heart racing. "What world?"

"Netherfeld."

*   *   *

Alda awoke, but she did not move. Instead, she pretended to sleep as she surveyed the room, her eyes slightly open but appearing to be closed.

She was still in Prospero's palazzo, unmoved from her place on the sofa, and she was not alone. Light permeated the room. The orange tint of the setting sun. The soft glow of candles.

And a rainbow of spirit-lights that formed abstract, animal figures dancing around a table set with exotic fruits and chalices of various colored liquids. Flowers hovered in the air above the merry party. It seemed out of place, inappropriate.

When Alda was certain that she was alone with only the spirits, unwatched by Ariel and Prospero, she sat up cautiously.

One light-figure emerged from the rest, the owl Celia, who hovered before Alda's face as she whispered, "I was unable to thank you before. Please accept my gratitude now."

Alda thought back to the fissure in the ground and shook her head, "I deserve no thanks. It was you who helped me."

"I meant for, for what you did, for us, in Netherfeld." As the owl spoke, some other forms swirled around Alda, forming a menagerie of flying animals made of flickering light.

Alda watched them, amazed. "For what? What did I do?"

Another form, a Luna moth, spoke, "There is no time."

"Tell me what happened in Netherfeld," Alda raised her voice, pleading.

"He is come," the moth whispered.

Alda's heart sank; she needed to know what happened in her lost years. But the winged harpy, Ariel, stepped through the doorway, and the lights dispersed toward the ceiling. Alda jumped at their sudden change but recovered as Ariel kneeled at her side, his face uncomfortably close to hers. "Prospero told me to amuse and feed you."

"I — I am not hungry." She made no effort to move.

Ariel stood and continued, "I feared you were a witch, when you were on the beach, so I watched you in the woods and helped you sleep near there. To know your dreams."

"You saw my dreams?" She felt violated, intruded upon.

He nodded.

"What did you see?"

"A time may come to tell your dreams, but the time is not now." The harpy tilted his head, paused for a moment, and abruptly changed the subject, "There are none who have escaped the Stream of Consciousness. Until —"

Alda interrupted, "Why could I escape?" The nymphs, too, had said it was impossible. But surely she could not be the first to break free from its current.

Ariel set his jaw and again turned the topic, "My master read your book. He saw your tale."

"My book?" Alda thought this might be a metaphor.

"Prospero reads many books. And that is how he knows."

"Knows what?"

"All."

Alda shook her head in disbelief.

"Well, all that is worth knowing," Ariel clarified.

"Then who am I? No — what am I?"

"To know and tell are incongruous."

"Then tell me who you are," Alda heard her pitch rise in frustration.

"But you already know."

"Ariel. A familiar." She leaned closer to him, overcoming her fear to whisper more discreetly, "I can help you escape."

"But, how?" The harpy raised his eyebrows questioningly.

Alda considered. She had no real plan for getting off of the island, but she could not admit that out loud.

Without waiting for a response, Ariel continued dryly, "With your cauldron's bubble?"

Alda's eyes revealed her surprise. She reached into her sleeve's fold. It was gone, taken in her sleep.

"It will not work here. You should know." Ariel added, under his breath, "And it is almost empty."

"We can leave together, then. You can carry me from the island."

The winged creature disregarded her words and continued, "Prospero took your percepstone, too, for his collection." Alda had not noticed it was missing because, even with its powers of disguise, she always saw her true self.

Did the percepstone disguise her from everyone, though? Had Prospero and Ariel been fooled by it?

Before she could ask about the workings of the percepstone, Ariel added, "Prospero collects utensils."

"Like silverware?"

"No, magic utensils. He did not have a cauldron's bubble and is quite pleased."

Alda had to talk to Prospero, to get her bubble back, but she had another question, "You took me away from the fire. What was it?"

"'Twas magic. Awful magic. A curse upon my twain pine, a trap, most likely meant for me. Or my master."

The nymphs must not have known about the curse when they sent her to the tree. Alda needed to know, "Who made the curse?"

Ariel did not respond. After a moment, Alda realized that he was watching the playful spirits intently.

Again, Alda pleaded, "Let me help you, Ariel. We can find a way to leave here, together."

The creature laughed, a kind of awkward cackle, and turned his back toward her. His shoulders hunched as his wings folded. After a moment, he turned back to Alda, "I saw you when you came upon the island. Alone with nothing. Now you say you want to rescue me. I do not understand."

"You are a slave. Prospero is your master. Do you not see that?"

Ariel's eyes sparkled. "I am indentured, yes, as Prospero's familiar. I owe a debt to him, and it is soon repaid. I will be free in several days, without your aid." The harpy added, sternly, "Who sent you here?"

Fear or something else prevented Alda from telling him of the witches. As she struggled for words, the lighted figures stopped dancing and instead flickered in and out of concrete forms.

"Tell me," Ariel demanded, his voice suddenly deep with anger.

The spirits were likewise no longer calming, beautiful. They were terrifying. Alda wanted to run, to hide, but she could not move. Rather, something prevented her from moving.

The light-spirits crowded around Ariel, either controlled by or supporting him, as he hissed, "You do not know the magic on this island. You can't control what you can't see, what you can't comprehend." His wings beat the air, his breathing heavy. Alda turned her head away and closed her eyes, waiting for an attack.

After several heartbeats, Ariel took a deep breath, stepped back, opened his human arms. Kindly, he invited, "Now eat. As Prospero commands."

Alda was fearful of his sudden change and hesitantly approached the adorned table. The spirits surrounded her, encouraging her steps, lifting delicacies into the air before her, and planting flowers into her hair. She consumed the spectacle but hesitated before the food, her hands trembling. It seemed too good, too easy, too inappropriate. A trap, perhaps, or a trick. She dared not eat. But she dared not disobey.

Then a crash sounded outside the darkened window. Flashes, and another boom. Lightning. A thunderstorm. Rain beat against the tiled roof, and the spirits above the table darted up and down frantically, wildly. Goblets toppled. Plates fell and shattered. Chaos.

Ariel froze and looked up, as if peering through the ceiling. Alda's breathing increased as she sensed the fear around her. Her heart pounded. She asked, tentatively, "What is happening?"

"A storm." Ariel looked at her, his eyes piercing. "It does not rain here, on the island."

                    *   *   *

Ferdinand could smell a change in the atmosphere. After so many hours waiting with his senses heightened, the smell of oxygen and the drop in pressure tingled his nerves. A storm was coming.

Caliban, who had been resting awkwardly on a protruding rock, covered contentedly with the blue cloak, rose. A smile twisted across his face. "She will return soon."

Wind gushed first. Then small raindrops pelted down. Lightning and almost instantaneous thunder followed. And, finally, a curtain of rain.

Ferdinand was calm and stoic in the downpour, a trait he had learned at sea. He looked to the sky and let the drops trickle down his neck.

Caliban, conversely, ducked, panicking, and tried to cover himself with the cloak before surrendering to the rain and watching the droplets fall on his arms, transfixed by the water.

More lightning, but no thunder this time. This flash was lower, like the light that darted around them on the hill in the night. But now it was entirely red.

Ferdinand watched the crimson light as it spread. Some beams formed shapes, and others appeared to be figures of animals, and even humans. Or something like humans.

A larger figure emerged from among them — no, appeared among them — closing the distance until it stood mere feet away from Ferdinand.

It was Miranda. Her hair longer. Her face leaner. Her clothes soaked through.

Despite this, the young woman smiled. But Ferdinand could not return her expression.

On the ship, before the last storm, Ferdinand was content. Collected. Even during times of hardship, he knew what to do. On occasion, he was startled or surprised. And, most often, sad. No, forlorn. But now, he felt something different. Love, of course, for Miranda. Always love. Jealousy, only slight, toward Caliban. And some other emotion, something foreign and alarming. Was it apprehension? Dread? He searched for the word.

Terror.

Miranda's smile grew, and she touched his cheek with her hand. "You're still here, after all this time."

Ferdinand stammered, "It, it was not long." An hour? Two? What did she mean?

And where had she been? Netherfeld? What happened in that place? But Ferdinand had no time to ask.

"I'm so glad." Miranda paused as she wiped her dripping hair from her eyes. "We will still be married?"

"Certainly." He had promised, and his word was binding.

A sudden gust of wind pushed Ferdinand back, and he stumbled. But Miranda caught his ragged shirt with unexpected strength and held him close. She was stronger than she looked.

"But first —" The rumble of thunder obscured her words.

Chapter Sixteen: Within the Book

Alda rushed to the window as the spirits flashed and shot around the room. Ariel was motionless, staring straight up, listening, before closing his eyes. His brow furrowed with the effort of concentration.

Through the window, beyond the torrent of rain, Alda saw what looked like distant fire at the base of the rocky hill. Red lights. But how could fire burn so brightly in a storm?

Ariel seemed to read her thoughts. "They aren't benevolent spirits."

Alda turned toward him. "What do you mean?"

"My spirits are benevolent. Mischievous, yes, but kind. To most. Those are not."

"What do you mean, *your* spirits?"

Ariel looked at her with the same confused expression that her grandmother used when she explained something that should be obvious. "I am a summoner. I take the spirits through divides of worlds to reach my island. They become mine and follow my commands."

Alda spoke her thoughts, "Who summoned the malevolent spirits?"

Ariel was silent for a heartbeat before he whispered, "I am the only summoner. Here."

"So what is Prospero?"

Ariel finally looked at her. "Prospero is of spells and charms and books. A sorcerer. Not this —" Ariel waved his human hand toward the window, indicating the red lights, as his wings spread slightly.

Alda again gazed through the glass, watching the fiery streaks move closer with unnatural speed, and whispered, "Who is doing this?"

Ariel had no time to respond.

"It is time, girl." Prospero stood on the doorway, resting his weight on a tall staff. Alda wondered how long he had been watching, but he made no indication that he had heard her discourse with Ariel.

The old man showed no reaction to the coming storm.

The spirits stopped moving, almost suspended in the air. Ariel remained silent, his face void of expression.

"Follow me, child," Prospero waved his arm invitingly.

As Alda followed the old man over the threshold, he added, "Ariel, fetch Miranda. See that she is safe."

Alda could not hear Ariel's response as she left the room.

The adjoining library was at once majestic and chaotic. Corinthian columns suspended a vaulted ceiling twenty feet above the marbled floor. Smooth shelves lined every wall and haphazardly criss-crossed the room, holding dusty scrolls and aged volumes. Books tilted sideways, and manuscripts hung from shelves. Ancient cobwebs draped below the ceiling. Nothing was clean. Nothing was organized. Alda marveled that anyone could make sense of the place.

Prospero led Alda to the center of the room, where an oversized oak table rested on the backs of four carved, wooden sphinxes. Their ebony eyes glinted blankly in the dim candlelight. As Alda studied the library in awe, Prospero leaned over a large volume, one of many open on the table, and began reading, seeming to disregard the visitor standing opposite him.

Alda walked around the table to his side, silently but boldly. Her eyes darted across the many pages, trying to make out the thin words of the texts. Even in passing, she could tell they were nonsense. The words were simply disconnected series of nouns and verbs, separated by spaces of various sizes and shapes. The lines were at all angles, and some words were even crosshatched and overlapping. Some passages were simply black squares and circles. Yet the sorcerer read, his eyes moving steadily from left to right across the page.

"What do you read?"

Prospero did not look up. "Words, words, words."

"I do not understand." Alda looked again, closer. They were still gibberish.

"I read what *you* cannot see."

Alda flinched as she realized that he was now studying her instead of his book. His head was bent intently over the page, yet his eyes pierced her own. She was inexplicably terrified but hid her emotions as best she could.

"Who is Miranda?" Her question was too sudden, awkward.

"My daughter."

Alda considered before she offered, "I may have seen her. On the beach. Yesterday." Was it only yesterday?

Prospero peered at her, skeptical. "What did she say to you?"

"She told me I looked kind and gave me her cloak."

The old man coughed. It may have been a laugh, or an attempt at a laugh from a throat that had forgotten the sound. He clutched his staff for support as he recovered. "You are mistaken. The cloak is her protection from my spirits, she would not —" He stopped himself. He raised an eyebrow and asked, "If she gave you her cloak, where is it now?"

"I —" Alda stammered. "I lost it. In a pit."

"Impossible." He laughed again, louder and deeper. "This is why I read. I discover truth in lies, meaning in absence." He pointed to a large space between two words. "This pause is pregnant. Only I can see what is missing. Only I can understand the absence, child."

"Then what do you *read* in me? In my book?" Alda was aware she was sarcastic. She felt hurt. Oppressed, almost. Perhaps she did not feel comfortable being called a child. Perhaps it was something else, something intangible. Something forgotten. From Netherfeld?

"You cannot know your own story. It is forbidden."

"By whom?"

"Me." The old man spoke this word with the emphasis of finality.

"Who are you to say what can be known?"

Silence. Then heavier rain, muffled by the vaults above. The storm's intensity was growing, quickly.

Alda clenched her jaw and ventured, "Then tell me of Sycorax instead." She spoke it as a command, not a question. The name had haunted her since she first heard it from the nymphs at the Stream of Consciousness. And Celia's cryptic description of her had only whetted Alda's curiosity.

The old man hesitated, studying her face. A crash of thunder interrupted his reverie, and he turned to a shelf. After a moment of searching, he retrieved a worn, nondescript volume and opened it to a marked page in the middle. The words were, like the others, nonsensical.

"I will show you."

Prospero waved his staff above the book, and a scene formed on the page. He explained what unfolded: "This island is formed of magic. In its core is a spring of Netherfeld." The island rose from the page, surrounded by sapphire-like waves. It was like a tiny doll-play, a miniature world come to life. Transparent and flickering.

Alda realized, "The spring feeds the fountain in the courtyard? Is that why it took me to Netherfeld?"

The old man nodded.

In the book, a tiny boat landed on the island, and two figures disembarked. Alda bent closer to watch. The characters moved and interacted but did not speak.

"Sycorax, a witch, knew of Netherfeld and came here to gain entry to its realm through the spring. She brought her son, Caliban, a deformed monster born from evil." Prospero's voice was angry, bitter.

Alda studied the two small figures. The woman's hair was dark and long. Her eyes clear, blue, and mesmerizing, unlike any Alda had seen before. The boy was crooked and grotesque. He did not appear human.

"Ariel was the guardian of the island, a being from Netherfeld sent to protect the spring from invaders." The, winged figure descended onto the page.

"He thwarted her attempt to gain the spring." The three fought, not with swords or weapons, but with rainbow lights. Spirits.

"Sycorax defeated Ariel and imprisoned him in a dead dryad, a magical tree." Alda saw a beautiful pine tree, first whole, and then split in two by the rainbow lights. Ariel disappeared into it.

"When I arrived on the island with my daughter, Miranda," his voice grew hoarse, "Sycorax had breached the spring and was struggling to overtake all of Netherfeld." A second boat landed, and two more figures entered the scene: an old man and a young girl. The girl from the beach.

"I was unaware of Sycorax's misdeeds initially and tried to help her. It was a mistake. She cared for naught but — but power. So I defeated her."

The image on the page turned first red, like a fire, and then grew into a black fog. Prospero watched it swirl above the book for a moment and then sighed.

Alda suspected there was more to the story, but the old man abruptly closed the volume and slouched in a wooden chair. He stroked his beard nervously as he considered something.

Then Prospero set his jaw and stared intensely at Alda for several breaths before he explained, "Sycorax is evil. She cursed Miranda, my only child. Now we are trapped here."

Alda turned questions over in her mind. She had many to ask, but anticipated that most would remain unanswered. Thunder clapped, and Alda asked, "What is Miranda's curse?"

Silence.

She tried again, "What made this storm?"

Prospero shook his head, so Alda guessed, "Is it another summoner?"

The old man considered, "I do not know who else it could be."

Alda persisted, "What are the red lights?"

"Spirits."

"From Netherfeld." Alda spoke it as a statement.

Prospero nodded.

"Is the other summoner dangerous? Will you stop him?"

Prospero looked away and rubbed his chin, thinking. He made no attempt to answer.

After a moment, Alda realized that she had another question and ventured, "Did Sycorax's magic — some kind of curse or the spirits— destroy the ship? The one that I saw from the beach?"

Prospero did not respond.

Again, Alda pressed, "I know that you saw it. You were on the clifftop. With your lights."

Prospero snapped, "Ariel destroyed the ship. Rather, I commanded him to destroy it. But I had to."

Alda stepped back, repulsed. How many men did he kill? She stammered, "Why? Why did you —"

Prospero waved his hand, dismissing her question. "Not now." He shook his head and suddenly appeared feeble. Weak. Tired. "There is more at play than you know."

More thunder. Heavier rain. The old man almost quaked in his chair.

Alda persisted, "Then tell me." More silence. She slapped her hand on the table, and its dull thud echoed in the chamber. "Tell me!"

The old man shuddered at the noise and finally relented. "Miranda's curse — My daughter is cursed. She cannot leave the island unless she is married." He ran his hand across his brow. "Sycorax wanted her to marry Caliban, but he is not — So Sycorax made the curse as a kind of vengeance. To trap her here. To trap us both here."

He had not answered Alda's question. "But why destroy the ship?"

Prospero paused and collected his thoughts. "After I defeated Sycorax, I tried to undo the curse. I cast a spell on Miranda. A kind of love spell. To undo Sycorax's curse." He looked at Alda as if she understood his logic. She did not.

Her brow furrowed. This was not right, immoral. "A love spell?"

"Yes, but it did not work properly. It was too rudimentary. I did not know magic then," Prospero explained defensively. "I had not yet freed Ariel, so I did not have his help. It went awry."

He smoothed his hand nervously over his beard and continued, "The spell did not work how I intended." He paused as he drew in a deep breath and added quietly, "It made all men fall in love with my Miranda. Any man who laid eyes on her. But she was young, too young. She still is. That is why I must destroy the ships. That is why I — I remove the men who set foot on the island. I cannot let men near her. To protect my daughter, you see."

Alda did not see, not like him.

"It is out of love."

"Killing is not love."

"But it is. At least this is. You do not understand yet. You are a child. Inexperienced. Unread. Unschooled. You do not know the world. Its ways. Its words. These books. You do not see clearly. Not like I."

Alda shook as she summoned enough courage to respond, "You do not know love. You do not know anything. You only know the words in your books, and they are nonsense."

She turned on her heel and walked away from the old man and his books, through the maze of shelves. As she left the library, she ran, not thinking where she might go.

Not remembering that the old man still had her cauldron's bubble.

Chapter Seventeen: Instruments of Darkness

Amid the storm, Miranda took Ferdinand's hand and told him simply, "You must secure the fountain." She had not told him what had happened in the other world, in Netherfeld, but Ferdinand could see that she had prepared for battle. They were to attack.

The trio were almost to Prospero's palace, the red lights streaming around them, whistling louder and higher. But Miranda's clear voice cut above the chaos, "Protect it."

"From what?" Ferdinand wanted to leave. To run. To escape from the rain and fiery lights. He was not a coward, but this suddenly all seemed too familiar. Like reliving an old nightmare, a waking dream.

"Harm."

He looked at Miranda. Her hair was wild, upswept by the lighted spirits. She almost glided in the lights' presence, swiftly ascending the hill. And she was more beautiful than ever.

Within a minute, they would reach the palace. Then what?

Miranda looked at him and, sensing his hesitation, stopped and took his shoulders. Her grip was commanding. "Prospero wants to harness the powers of another world, of Netherfeld." She paused as she studied Ferdinand's eyes. "He has destroyed scores of ships already, in addition to *The Tempest*, so what will he do if we do not stop him now?"

Ferdinand knew that, at sea, the punishment for such crimes would be death. "Let me fight him. Defeat him. For you."

"No, I must."

"Why?" Ferdinand was strong. And clever enough. And willing.

Miranda smiled at his eagerness, but there was sadness in her blue eyes. "He deserves to suffer. Not only for your ship and crew, but —" she hesitated.

A shadow seemed to fall across Miranda's face. She turned away and continued in broken tones, "He treated me unjustly, viciously. And he took someone from me. Long ago. Someone beautiful and perfect, and now—" She shook her head and inhaled deeply, her breath shaking. "Prospero has terrible magic, enough to destroy worlds, so he could easily destroy you." She took a deep breath and added, "I have magic, too. I have the power to kill Prospero." She wiped the rain from his cheek, "You must protect the fountain. Be safe."

Ferdinand pushed aside his fleeting jealousy of Miranda's lost lover and nodded. He looked up toward the whirling clouds, clearing his mind for the unknown ahead.

*   *   *

The world outside was chaos, and growing worse. Rain beat down violently. Colored lightning filled the sky. Wisps of red spirits wafted over the palazzo's roof and swirled around Alda in the courtyard.

She could escape, now. Immediately. Drink from the fountain and return to Netherfeld. And from there —?

It was clear, in hindsight, that the witches had deceived her. Ariel did not need to be released from the tree. He did not need to be freed or rescued because his indenture would soon be over. What did the witches truly want? What was their actual test? Their objective?

Or were the witches unaware of all that transpired here?

As Alda considered, she moved slowly toward the fountain. She was about to impulsively cup her hands into its waters when the rustle of feathers made her reconsider. "Did Prospero send you to fetch me?" Alda's voice betrayed her disgust.

"I came to protect the fountain."

"From whom?"

"The other summoner." Ariel paused. "And you."

"You think I would harm it?" She laughed, but the sound was obscured by the rain. "Or use it?"

"You know too little to act with reason."

Alda turned her back to him and walked toward the relative protection beneath the columns at the edge of the courtyard. She asked bitterly, "Where are your spirits?"

Ariel did not respond. He paced and watched the red lights swirl in the rain.

Alda pressed, "Surely your spirits, your lights can keep these at bay?" As Alda spoke, more red forms entered the courtyard, creating shapes and swirling between the walls.

Ariel explained, "They fled. At my direction. These beings are too strong. I cannot lead my spirits to destruction."

Alda felt no fear, until she remembered that before, she had worn the cloak when she had encountered the spirits. Now, she was unprotected, and realized, "If these can destroy other spirits, what will they do to us?" Ariel did not respond, and she understood his silence.

She thought for a heartbeat and added, "Why have the summoner's spirits not killed us yet?"

"They are watching. Observing. For the present."

"Why?"

Silence.

"What if they attack?" Alda's voice betrayed her panic.

Ariel did not answer.

Alda studied the air for a moment, until the red lights' speed increased. Then she swatted at the swirls like bothersome insects, annoyed at first. But soon she felt smothered.

Suddenly, they attacked.

Two beams of light separated from the others and barreled at her chest. Their whistling rose to a higher pitch, and their forms became more solid, almost like glowworms. Alda crossed her arms in front of her face and closed her eyes.

She felt her hands heat, as they had in the pit. The air around her grew heavy with a throbbing sensation. She smelled burning. And rosemary. Another instinct, from Netherfeld.

The light streams before her froze, suspended. She opened her eyes, blinked, and lowered her arms. The two attacking spirits dissipated completely.

Soon the other lights scattered and retreated above the surrounding columns and palazzo roof. Alda watched them vanish, and then her eyes met Ariel's. She expected him to look stunned, but he only nodded slightly.

Despite the danger around her, she smiled, pleased with herself.

The rain continued to fall. Thunder rumbled. The storm churned, but the red lights did not reappear. Alda waited and listened.

Soon, her thoughts turned to the fountain. To Netherfeld. She could return there and leave all of this, but then what? Use the cauldron's bubble to find the witches? Or, better, her island? Home.

Her heart sank. She remembered that she did not have the bubble.

Prospero still had it, and she had to get it back. Make him give it back. How?

Alda looked around, as if the courtyard itself would give her some direction. Rain puddled on the mosaicked floor. Ariel frowned as he paced. The storm flashed. Could Alda slip away, unobserved and unobstructed?

As Alda moved cautiously toward the outside of the courtyard, a tall figure rushed toward Ariel. Alda knew it could only be the summoner, the bringer of the red spirits.

Alda had relatively little magic or muscle, but she had courage. She charged the figure, ready to fight. To kill.

If that was what it took to get home.

Chapter Eighteen: A Deed Without a Name

Ferdinand saw no one in the palace. He slipped through a side window and navigated his way toward the center of the complex, his footsteps overpowered by the rain on the tiled roof.

He had left Miranda and Caliban to breach the main entrance, where he anticipated they would meet Prospero and face his magic.

Although he wanted revenge for his shipmates, he understood that the powers with which they would battle were beyond his capabilities. Protecting the fountain was a logical mission and, although he would prefer to kill the shipwrecker himself, he trusted Miranda to deliver his vengeance. And hers.

When Ferdinand finally reached the courtyard, he could barely distinguish the fountain through the dust and rain. A winged monster was there, some kind of guardian, pacing before the fountain.

Ferdinand did not expect anyone else nearby, not like this. Miranda had told him the palace would be deserted, the fountain only threatened with destruction if Prospero chose to destroy it upon retreat. Ferdinand was not prepared to fight now. He realized that he had no weapon, no plan.

So he did as he had learned on the ship: attack to survive. He charged the great beast, but before he could reach it, he was on the ground with a pain in his side and a weight on his chest.

He grabbed for the source of the weight and connected with white fabric. It tore in the scuffle.

Then he grabbed hair, which produced a slight scream.

He felt suffocated as a thin limb connected with his throat, pushing into his windpipe with uncomfortable, but not deadly, force.

Part of him wanted to relax, to give in to the pressure and sleep. But he thought of Miranda and reached out until his fist connected with a rib cage.

Ferdinand pushed, and the weight fell off his chest. He could breathe again.

Instinctively, he reached for something to use against his attacker. But he found nothing, so he held it down with his arm on its neck. Harder. It started to relax beneath his weight until he felt a blow and a sudden pain in his abdomen.

He rolled off his attacker and tried to stand, and his opponent shuffled away. He raised his fists and prepared for another assault. Instead, he heard a broken voice, "Dreng?"

He fully looked at the form opposite him: a wet face obscured by dark hair and trickling blood. A pair of dark eyes met his. His attacker pushed the hair from her face, and he recognized the girl from the ship.

His emotions were inexplicable, confused. The girl who saved him. The girl who abandoned him. Hope. Derision. Conflict. Contradiction. Guilt.

He backed away from her. Was this another spectre, like his dead father?

The girl straightened and stepped toward him, reaching out. "Dreng? Is it you?"

From the corner of his eye, Ferdinand saw the beating of monstrous wings.

"Ariel, no!"

*   *   *

"Ariel, no! I know him!" Alda stood between the harpy and the young man. Ariel hesitated as Alda asked again, "It is you? Dreng?"

He nodded and stood, checking his limbs for injury.

"How did you survive? In the ship, I thought —" Alda did not finish. She was certain he had died then. But he had lived, somehow. Instead, she asked, "Why are you here?"

The young man glanced first at her and then looked toward the door at the darkened interior of the palazzo. "She needs my help." He seemed evasive. Was he scared?

"Who?" Alda was confused. Did he mean Miranda?

"You cannot trust that woman," Ariel warned. He moved closer to the young man, studying him intently.

Alda considered for a beat. She was troubled by a different matter. "Why did you lie about your name before?"

Dreng looked at her, confused, his mouth trying to form words.

She persisted, "You told me your name was Ferdinand. When I spoke with you near the woods."

"No. I mean, yes — I said that. But not to you. I have not seen you since — in the hold —" He stared at her. Or rather, he gazed. She felt uncomfortable, as if he was trying to feel out her thoughts.

And she realized. Of course, with the percepstone, he did not know that he had told *her* a false name. "That was me, I, it was — a disguise," she stammered awkwardly, embarrassed at her mistake.

Dreng turned to her, ignoring Ariel's threatening stare, and tried to take her hand apologetically. She pulled it away. "Alda? I did not know that was you. I mean now. Or then. Or when I — I never would have." He reached out to touch the scrape on her forehead, and she took a step back. "I'm sorry. I didn't — I fought because you attacked me," he added as he looked down, and Alda thought he might have blushed.

After a moment, Dreng met her eyes and continued, "I searched for you, on the ship. And waited. For years, and —"

Alda had no time for sentiment, or for the past. She had to get home. So she asked again, "Why are you here, now?"

"She needs me to protect the fountain."

"Who is *she*?" Alda was frustrated with unanswered questions. And in pain. She had never fought before, never been punched or injured. She wiped the blood from her forehead as it stung her eyes.

"Miranda." Dreng looked at them both curiously, as if the name should have been apparent.

Alda glanced at Ariel. He did not react but continued to watch the pair intently.

Dreng continued, almost apologetically, "We are to be married, Miranda and I. It has been decided. I mean, I decided. No, we decided. Together."

Alda's heart sank. Prospero's love spell. She knew she ought to tell him, to warn him, but she did not know how. He would not believe her. Instead, she asked, "What does Miranda want?"

"To save Netherfeld." He looked first to Alda and then to Ariel, waiting for some reaction.

"What do you know of Netherfeld?" Alda was suspicious. And, she realized, protective. The place felt like hers, somehow.

"It is," Dreng hesitated. "An unmapped region."

Alda waited for him to continue, but it was clear that his understanding of the realm was even less than hers. "Have you been there?"

"No," he admitted.

Alda raised her eyebrows as she asked, "So why does it need to be saved?"

Dreng lowered his voice, as if revealing some great secret, "When Miranda returned from there, she told me of a great danger. Some kind of magic that threatens to destroy Netherfeld."

Alda was skeptical. Dreng was enchanted by Miranda, so it was impossible to tell what tricks she played on him. "What kind of magic?"

"Prospero's."

On hearing that word, Ariel spread his fearsome wings and lunged toward Dreng. Alda had no time to act. It was all too swift. The harpy connected violently with the young man, who collapsed in a heap, unconscious.

Ariel calmly walked away as Alda knelt anxiously at Dreng's side, feeling for a pulse. "I did not kill your friend, Alda."

"Why did you attack him?" She stood and glared at the harpy.

Ariel calmly explained, "He was a threat. We must protect the fountain."

"From Miranda? But she is Prospero's daughter. Surely this is all some confusion." She wiped sweat or water from her brow. "Dreng was enchanted. And confused. And with the summoner coming here —"

Alda could not finish. The ground shook, as it had when she climbed the cliff near the beach. An earthquake. The courtyard walls cracked, columns snapped, and part of the roof collapsed with a rumble.

Ariel looked toward the palazzo, glanced back at Alda, and said anxiously, "You, Alda, know not what is in play. Protect the fountain." The harpy turned to leave, but hesitated. "I wish I had more time with you. Your fate will call you soon."

Before Alda could respond, Ariel disappeared through a dark doorway into the palazzo's unstable interior.

Alda was alone with Dreng in the rain. His breathing was shallow, but he was safe. She could try to drag him toward the palazzo, but the weakened wall might crumble. No, he should stay here. They should wait for Ariel to return. Together. And then she could leave.

Besides, Ariel was correct, she should not try to help. There was too much unknown. Too much that she did not understand. She was too confused.

But as Alda waited, she thought. Why was this boy here, now, again? No, not boy, man. Time had passed for him, but not for her. Rather, she landed upon the island at a later time, his later time. But why had she met him again? Was it a great coincidence, or something more?

And what of Miranda? Was she safe? She would be, with Dreng. As her husband.

Alda felt a twinge of jealousy, despite herself. It was silly to think she could ever love someone whom she had met in flashes, someone so unlike herself, someone from another time. So mysterious and broken.

This was selfish, she thought. She should not worry about herself now. Or him. She had to protect the fountain. And Netherfeld.

But why? Because Ariel told her so?

Could she trust him, a harpy? Or, in fact, anyone?

It occurred to her, suddenly, that Netherfeld would be safe without the fountain, without the spring that led to it. Destroying the fountain would be like burning a bridge. No one would be able to access, or endanger, the world beyond.

But the fountain was her way to Netherfeld, perhaps her only way off of the island. She could go there through the fountain, and then use the bubble to return home. Or could she find another way? Could Dreng help her leave?

A great light erupted from inside the palazzo, interrupting her thoughts, and shining in streams through the narrow glass windows. It was a silent flash, like a blink of hot white. Then the ground shook again.

Another earthquake, stronger. Steam rose from fissures in the earth. It felt like the world was ending, being destroyed.

Whatever power was here, whatever was sending the red spirits and shaking the earth, was too dangerous to allow into Netherfeld. Even if Alda became trapped here, on the island, the spirit world would be safe. She knew what was right, so she raised her hands. The air pulsated, and heat shot out, instinctively, from her palms.

The fountain crumbled in a heap of blackened stone. Water trickled out for several heartbeats and then stopped.

The rumbling earth eased, and the rain lessened. Alda sat next to Dreng, silent and wondering what to do.

As she watched Dreng in his stupor, she knew that she could not help him here. He would be safe, in this dreamless sleep, in the rain of the open courtyard, away from any crumbling walls or spirit magic.

She had to find Prospero. And her cauldron's bubble.

Before she left Dreng's side, Alda wiped his brown hair from his forehead. And she paused as she saw him, truly looked upon him for the first time. His face was sun-worn. His brow perpetually furrowed. Dirt was caught in the stubble on his chin. Small, white scars protruded from his cheeks. A few drops of blood splattered near his lips. She hesitated briefly before she squeezed his hand, clasping it tightly enough to imprint her palm with his gold signet ring. He remained insensible.

As she rose to leave, his lips curled into an unconscious smile.

Once inside the palazzo, Alda heard a strange sound. Not a scream, exactly, but a series of wails and thuds. She followed the noise toward the library and, as she drew closer, she could hear cursing and tearing pages.

Alda ducked inside the room and hid behind a bookshelf, easily concealed amid the chaos of scattered papers and toppled furnishings. She peered carefully toward the center of the library and saw the girl from the beach, pulling books off the walls, tearing them apart, and throwing them carelessly in growing piles. It was clearly Miranda, and she was searching for something.

A second figure hunched over the sphinx table, running a crooked hand over the exposed pages on its wooden top. His body was angular and revolting. And he wore the blue cloak. Was he the one who tried to bury her alive in the pit?

Alda steadied her breathing as she watched. What should she do?

Where was Prospero, and her bubble?

"It is not here," the cloaked figure complained. "The usurper most likely destroyed it."

"No. It was too important." Miranda continued to search.

The crooked man laughed. Alda recognized him, finally. He was Caliban, the boy from Prospero's book, now fully grown. What was he doing here, with Miranda?

"He did not destroy it," the island girl said again, reassuring herself as she tore pages from another book and heaved it in anger. As she threw it, red lights shot from her fingertips. Red spirits.

Alda realized that this girl was the summoner. She was dangerous.

After another moment of searching, Miranda commanded, "Check him."

Then Alda saw, crumpled on the floor, a heap of robes, unmoving. Prospero. His staff shattered into splinters near his hand. His beard partially burned. Dead.

And before him, scattered on the floor, were feathers. Ariel's feathers, but not Ariel's body.

What had done this? Was it the great light, the light that flashed in the courtyard moments earlier?

Alda wanted to run. But she could not. She needed her cauldron's bubble. And, maybe, to find Ariel, if he was still alive, somewhere. She reminded herself that Prospero meant nothing to her and most likely deserved his fate. And Netherfeld was safe because the fountain was destroyed.

The rest was naught. Even Dreng.

None of this mattered, not really. Only her cauldron's bubble. To get home.

As Alda watched, trying to steady her breath, Miranda remained occupied with the books, and Caliban made little effort to search Prospero's body, sulking instead. Alda had to make them leave. Before they found her bubble. Or her.

Alda carefully picked up a fallen book and tossed it through the door from which she entered. Its thud echoed down the hallway. The pair turned to look, not seeing Alda stoop behind a different bookshelf.

"What was that?" Miranda's voice was shaking.

"Perhaps your beau has left his post," Caliban sneered sarcastically.

"Then go put him right. He need not see this." She waved her hand toward the old man's body. "It is safer for him outside."

Caliban rolled his eyes. "Ferdinand will be dead within a day, so why does it matter what he sees?"

Red lights shot again from Miranda's hands and swirled menacingly around the crooked man. She crossed the room and held her hand to his throat. "Do not say such things, boy. I need him. You evidently do not see his worth as I do."

Caliban hissed, "There are other ways to avoid the curse, to leave the island, surely." Miranda lowered her grip, and Caliban sputtered, sarcastically, "You could marry me instead." He laughed, a cruel chortle. The island girl turned her back to him, and he coughed and wiped his neck.

Miranda returned to her books and spoke more to herself than to her companion, "You know I cannot. Besides, the boy is special, somehow. I will tell in time."

Alda threw another book. A thud, and then silence. Miranda listened intently as her eyes scanned the room. Her gaze paused for too long near the place where Alda hid.

Miranda took several steps closer, and Alda sunk to the floor and closed her eyes, hiding behind the bookshelf. After a moment, Alda heard the other girl's footsteps retreat, back toward the center of the room.

After another moment of breath-held silence, Miranda told her companion, "Ferdinand's ring has worth, too. Powers. He does not know."

Alda barely heard Miranda's words over her own beating heart. Finally, fearfully, Alda ventured another glance out of her refuge. She peered around the toppled shelf as the rain stopped outside. Sunlight streamed through the long windows, instantly illuminating the room, sparkling off Caliban's stolen cloak and glistening in Miranda's eyes.

Blue eyes, Alda realized. Mesmerizing, like the woman in Prospero's book. Like Sycorax.

Sycorax? Could Miranda be — But, no, that was impossible.

This was clearly Miranda, the girl from the beach. But was it, still? The fair hair and dress were the same. But her eyes were too, too different. Dark before, and now bright, lustrous blue. The color of the sea before a storm.

Or was Alda mistaken? She shook her head to clear her thoughts and watched the pair again.

Through a gap in the shelf, Alda could see Caliban glare at the other girl. He retorted, "Of course, you know all. Always. And I know nothing. You think me a fool, an absolute knave" He laughed, but the sound was filled with anger. "What is there to love, here? Nothing." He paused and added, woefully, "And you care not, *mother*."

Alda's doubt dissolved. She heard the proof.

"Never call me that. Not anymore. Not ever." The summoner sent red lights from her fingers toward her companion, but he turned his back, and they sparked and fell harmlessly away from his cloak.

Alda grew dizzy with excitement. Prospero had told her that Sycorax was dead. But this was her. This was not Miranda. Something had happened. Something had changed. Some magic had occurred that Alda did not understand. Something wicked.

And what of black-eyed Miranda? Where was she now? Was she —

Alda held her hands over her mouth, trying to steady her breath. Trying to find courage to —

"You should be more grateful!" Caliban's voice was deep with rage. "I could have left you in that witch-trap, in the cave, locked away where Prospero left you. But I didn't. I released you. I even used her, whom I —" His voice cracked, and he looked away.

Alda listened for a response, but the other girl did not react to her apparent son.

Caliban waited in silence for a moment before he mumbled, "I will let you be, then, whoever you are. You never needed me, anyway, especially not after —" His final words were lost in a mumble. He slumped angrily toward the door, kicking loose books as he left the room.

Miranda — no, Sycorax, Alda reminded herself — paused and listened as Caliban's uneven footsteps disappeared down the hall. Alda also listened, waiting for her chance to flee. But she could not escape, not without her bubble.

The cauldron's bubble was truly all that mattered now. Not the girl with two identities or the mystery of her apparent transformation. Not the ugly son or the dead sorcerer or the harpy or anyone else. Not *anyone*. Alda could not fight them all, or even fully make sense of their chaos. She only had to find her bubble, and she had to get the other girl out of the library to do so.

Alda could throw another book, yes, but that had not worked before. What else did she have? She scanned the room: books, torn paper, some furniture. And the windows.

Alda stared at them, their glass wavy with age. Fragile. Alda remembered something, some feeling of magic that she had known in the past. In Netherfeld. An instinct.

Alda's gaze intensified, and she positioned her hands slightly above her head and angled her wrists upward. She did not think; she sensed. She felt heat, and a kind of invisible wind moved from her fingertips across the room. It smelled of rosemary.

The windows' glass shattered, and Alda hugged her knees for protection. Shards burst and fell but did not cut her. Alda glanced around her barrier and saw Sycorax, untouched, surrounded by a circle of broken glass. The summoner had been protected, somehow, and was unharmed. But harm had not been Alda's intent.

Sycorax looked around, almost fearfully. A frown clouded her face, but then she smiled. She hesitated for too long as her eyes scanned the library.

Alda held her breath and sunk cautiously to the floor as she waited, expecting an attack.

But then, without a word, Sycorax left.

After waiting in the silent devastation for several minutes, Alda carefully picked her way across the library until she knelt over Prospero's body. She stared at his lifeless form, thinking, doing her best to be logical and not emotional.

Where would Prospero keep her bubble? Had he hidden it somewhere? In a book, perhaps?

Was that what Sycorax wanted? The cauldron's bubble?

As Alda looked at Prospero's corpse, a memory flashed into her mind. She thought of the cemetery in Grand Ledge. The gravedigger singing tunelessly as he shoveled into the pit in the silence of the night. Alda's salty tears freezing on her cheeks, alone in her grief. Her grandmother, dead.

Of course, her grandmother. Prospero's robe was similar to Gramma's cloak. Alda tentatively moved the old man's lifeless arm and felt inside his robe's white folds. Yes, a hidden pocket, like the one where she first found the bubble. And secured inside were her cauldron's bubble, the percepstone, and a small, miniature book with a gilded pattern on its spine.

Despite her fear that Sycorax might return, Alda opened the book. It fit easily within her palm, and the interior looked like the others in the library, nonsense and emptiness, pools of ink and white space, crosshatched forms and faded letters.

She studied it for too long, turning the pages and tilting the volume as she scanned its contents. It was still meaningless, at least to her.

Was this what Sycorax wanted?

Alda reminded herself that Sycorax was not important, not to her, so she shook her head clear and started away, toward the door to escape.

But she hesitated. Something was not right. Something was missing.

Dreng. He had been tricked. Enchanted by the love spell. Alda could not let him marry the girl, especially now that Alda knew her true identity. Sycorax, she was certain, was evil, like the red spirits she commanded. Dreng was not safe.

Alda needed to save him, before he was forced — no, tricked into marriage. Before he married a woman who did not love him.

Before Dreng was killed.

Alda had her bubble now and knew that she should leave the palazzo to try to find a way off the island. If anything, she should try to find Ariel. But instead she turned toward the courtyard.

Chapter Nineteen: Sleep of Death

Dreng was awake. Alone and lost, it seemed. He sat near a crumbled wall in the courtyard, studying the destroyed fountain, the fountain he could not protect. He had failed at his one task, the one directive of his love.

At least the rain had stopped. He closed his eyes in the warming sun. When he opened them again, he noticed for the first time that windows along one side of the palace were destroyed, shards of glass still clinging in their frames.

He stood and cautiously walked toward the wall. What could have caused this destruction? Was it an earthquake?

As he neared the shattered panes, a single sheet of paper floated through the window. Dreng caught it gently and turned it over in his hand. One edge was torn, as if ripped from a book, and it was covered in what could only be words in a foreign tongue, each at irregular angles, with blank spaces and black spots.

Since the Danish prince had taught him to read seven years before, Dreng had seen relatively few books in his lifetime and read even fewer, but he knew this page was something more.

He stared at the parchment, focusing all of his attention on the words. He could not read them at first; the foreign symbols almost moved as his eyes followed them. He squinted, narrowing his gaze, and thought back to his time with the prince on the ship.

In a memory, so long ago it was almost forgotten entirely, Dreng grew angry during a reading lesson. "These two letters," the boy complained, pointing to a *d* and a *b*, "I cannot tell one from the other. How do I know what they are? And how can I even read if I don't comprehend the letters?"

Prince Hamlet was uncharacteristically patient, even kind, as he studied the boy's face, mindful of his young companion's frustration. "These are only letters in words, with no meaning in themselves. The symbols are full of sound, but alone they signifying nothing." The prince patted the boy's shoulder through the bars. "Look at the entire word, not its simple parts. Read the page, not the letters."

At the time, the boy was confused. How could he read the whole without the parts?

But now, in the courtyard, Dreng thought he understood the prince's meaning. The torn paper shook in Dreng's hand as he tried to focus on its entire face, not the foreign symbols. Suddenly, the ink rearranged itself, almost bleeding, and formed letters. Then words.

It was his own language, and he could read it all.

Still, their meaning was unclear. The words appeared to be a list of items. Ingredients for a recipe? Or something else?

And, perhaps more importantly, how could Dreng read it? Was it the prince's doing, some skill passed along in the hold seven years before? Or did Dreng himself somehow change the script?

"Ferdinand!" Miranda emerged from the crumbling doorway and walked toward him, concern heavy on her brow.

Instinctively, he slipped the paper into his torn sleeve. Dreng knew from the sea that some secrets must be kept, some treasure hidden. He could think on the paper later.

"What happened?" She asked about the fountain, not him.

"It was destroyed." He hesitated and added, "In the earthquake." Was it? Or had the beast or Alda destroyed it?

Dreng was reluctant to tell Miranda about Alda, but he could not explain why.

"No matter. You are safe, and the spring we exposed on the hill will suffice. For now." Miranda tenderly wiped the blood from his lip. "But you met resistance? Was it the monster, Ariel?"

Dreng nodded.

"Well, the beast is gone now. And so is Prospero."

Dreng shook his head and said, under his breath, "Such a man deserves worse than death."

Miranda took his hand comfortingly and smiled sweetly, too sweetly. She looked up through her fair lashes as she asked, "Are you ready, now?"

"For what?" Dreng's mind was clouded from his focus on the torn page.

"We can be bound. We are here, together, and finally alone. There is no need to wait."

He realized her meaning: a wedding. Dreng knew little of marriage and even less of weddings, but he somehow knew that this was not usual. He looked down, avoiding her gaze.

His thoughts turned to Alda. Where had she gone?

"I know a ritual. A rite." Miranda kissed his cheek, and he relaxed, his hesitations gone. She did not wait for a response as she continued, "Now, repeat after me."

Dreng was unaware of what he said. The words rhymed and rocked but meant very little to him. His mouth moved unconsciously as he followed her lead. He grew more than happy, elated perhaps, but he still felt incomplete.

Miranda was silent for a moment, and Dreng realized that she was gazing at him questioningly. She smiled. He smiled back, confused. Miranda raised her eyebrows and asked, "Do you have a ring?"

Of course, the prince's signet ring. But Dreng hesitated. Was it his to give? If he loved her, then it should be hers. And he loved her. Of course he did. He placed it on her finger. Surprisingly, it fit.

"Now, we kiss, and the deed is done." She leaned toward him, closed her blue eyes, and pulled his lips to hers.

As they kissed, the first real kiss of his life, Dreng felt drained, exhausted. And he thought he smelled rosemary. The rest was black.

* * *

Alda entered the courtyard too late. She watched, helplessly, as Dreng kissed the summoner, Sycorax. A flash of heat engulfed the couple, sending waves of white light radiating in all directions. Dreng collapsed, but Sycorax caught his body and lowered him to the ground, studying his unmoving face in the sunlight.

Alda could see that Dreng was dead. The kiss was enchanted, somehow, and she knew that Sycorax had killed him. He was gone.

As Alda stood in the unstable doorway, she felt she should flee. She had her bubble, so she should creep out of the palazzo and leave the island, somehow. Or try to find Ariel. Or simply hide. She should do anything to save herself. And find a way to use the cauldron's bubble to return to the moor. To see her grandmother. To get home. To escape.

But Alda did not do as she should. Instead, she felt an instinct from Netherfeld. This one was different, new. Before, the power had been intangible, hot. Invisible. Now, Alda heard whispers and whistling. Spirits-lights. Her spirits. That she could control. That she could summon.

Alda braced herself as the light shot from her fingertips, brightly colored shapes of animals and geometrics that swirled toward Sycorax, the summoner. The murderer.

But Alda's opponent was calm and brushed aside the lights with a wave of her wrist as she stood next to Dreng's body. Sycorax barely glanced at Alda as she sneered, "You have grown, but still not enough."

Alda loosed more lights. Sycorax again dissolved them with a slight movement of her hand. "I told you we would meet again, Alda. That I would return." The summoner stretched her fingers calmly and did not retaliate.

Alda could barely hear the words over the rush of blood in her ears. She shot again. Sycorax held up her hand, and Alda's lights froze, suspended. When the red spirit summoner lowered her hand, Alda's spirit-lights fell to the ground and dissipated into a kind of fog.

"Do you do not remember how this played out before? I will spark your memory." Sycorax finally opened her fingers and unleashed the red, flashing spirits. They whistled toward Alda, and she blocked them with crossed arms.

Sycorax laughed. It sounded icy, almost metallic. "Always the same with you. Building defenses." She lowered her voice, "Escaping." The summoner sent more spirits, and Alda ducked aside. "Only attacking those you think are weak, when you anticipate no resistance." Sycorax raised her hands aggressively. "If you had remembered Netherfeld, you would not have attacked now." The red lights streamed toward Alda in rapid succession.

Again, Alda blocked, but she felt drained. With pain in her arms and hands. Ringing in her ears. One red spirit broke past her defenses and tore into her shoulder. The burning of her flesh sizzled and popped, and Alda knew she could not hold the crimson lights at bay any longer.

She had to make a decision, quickly.

Alda could flee, perhaps, and save herself. Or she could fight, not with the immaterial lights but with physical force. For revenge. For Dreng.

So Alda gritted her teeth, clenched her fists, and ran toward the summoner, ready to throw her strength into a mortal battle, not one of magic and lights.

Sycorax's blue eyes widened, and she stumbled back. She had not expected this.

Alda was nearly upon her when a force grabbed her waist. Alda struggled, but two strong arms held her firmly from behind, a single hand grasping both of hers in place. Her opponent's hold grew tighter as Alda fought, uselessly, and Caliban's voice whispered in her ear, "She may use spells, but I need only strength. And mine is greater than yours."

Alda kicked wildly, trying to break free. The coarse voice continued, "Calm down, little girl. Shhh. If you like, I can take you to my cave instead of killing you. It has magic, too. You could be my wife, or my familiar."

Twisting her neck awkwardly, Alda bit Caliban's forearm, and he screamed in pain but did not release his hold. Sycorax laughed as she watched the struggling pair, but she did not intervene to help her son capture his prize.

After what seemed like hours, Alda felt her energy failing. She could not resist Caliban's strength much longer, so she looked to the sky and yelled, "Ariel!"

"That beast is dead," Caliban hissed in her ear.

Finally, desperately, Alda twisted and shifted her weight. Her foot firmly connected with her captor. Caliban moaned and eased his hold. She lunged forward, broke free, and ran, not looking behind as she fled the courtyard.

Sycorax did not attack again. Caliban did not give chase. It was almost too easy to get away.

Alda sprinted through the palazzo and out to the heathered hill.

Toward the cliffs that dropped into the ocean. She ran as she must have before, in Netherfeld.

Then she reached the end. Alda stopped at the cliff's edge and stared into the open sea before her. The gulls floated and dipped into the whitecaps. Waves crested and fell. The sand sparkled far, far below.

Alda's lungs clenched, and her breath came only in shallow gasps. Her limbs ached. The spirits' burn on her shoulder tingled. She could not remember being this completely and utterly exhausted.

As she composed her wits, the wind blew her hair and seemed to bring an unnatural calm. She turned around and surveyed her options. The forest, unseen past the field. The palazzo, now partially collapsed, in the distance upon the hill. Elsewhere, only emptiness. There was nothing here for her now. Ariel was gone. Dreng, too, was —

She was alone.

She pulled the cauldron's bubble from its hiding place in the top of her shoe. It was lighter, less heavy than she remembered, but still iridescent. And still useless, on the island. She was trapped. *On* the island.

Alda could almost hear her grandmother's advice, from so many years ago, when she was trapped in the oak tree, "Always hold onto something, and don't be afraid to fall."

So Alda inched to the edge of the cliff and watched pebbles scatter to the beach below. She took a deep breath, squeezed the cauldron's bubble in her fist, and jumped from the dreadful summit. Her white shift flapped in the wind, and she fell for what felt like an eternity. Then she vanished.

Chapter Twenty: What's Done is Done

Dreng awoke in the courtyard with a pillow under his head, disoriented. Miranda was at his side, and she tenderly told him that he had collapsed after their wedding vows. That he had slept through most of the afternoon, apparently exhausted after days with no peace or sustenance. She offered him food and drink, and after some recuperation in the palace, he decided to explore the wood, alone.

Not to explore, to search. For her. For Alda.

Now, the forest was cool and peaceful in the moonlight, and Dreng felt more at ease than he should. The trees seemed to whisper around him, cooing and swishing in the breeze. It was unnaturally calming, and he soon neglected his search as he enjoyed the tranquility of the otherworldly environment.

After some time, he came upon a shallow stream covered in floating flowers. Its surface sparkled and luminesced. The trees around it seemed to bend and bid him into its waters. The waves lapped invitingly toward his feet. It beckoned him. He obliged.

Dreng removed his shirt, exposing his scar from the St. Elmo's fire, and stepped in. The water was warm and refreshing. Perfect. He held his breath and dove under.

Suddenly, he was in a memory, back in the palace's courtyard, searching for the fountain. He knew it must be only a memory, but it felt real. Immediate. Wonderful. He saw her, Alda, and the action of the scene froze around him. The moving lights stopped. The rain suspended. The only sound was his heartbeat.

He had found her, again. At last. And it was everything and all.

But then his head broke above the stream's surface. And he breathed.

Another memory, terrible, from his distant past. He was on a ship, *The Tyger*. A young boy. The sea was calm, the sky clear and endless. The men laughed, slapped their knees, and sang a shanty on the deck. "Blow, blow, thou winter wind, thou art not so unkind..." The tallest man laughed the loudest and sang the sweetest: his father, the captain.

Then a sudden, loud crash. Red lights — like Miranda's but with less form and substance — danced across the deck of the ship and up the rigging. St. Elmo's fire.

A ball of smoke twisted above the mast and pierced his father's chest. The lights ricocheted across the deck, where they struck Dreng's shoulder. And burned.

A splintering snap, and the mast broke and fell. Dreng was on his back, pinned under the rigging. The deck shook beneath him, and the clouds churned with purple and green above. He thought that he heard a kind of ethereal music, distant and eerie:

"Double, double toil and trouble. Fire burn and..."

The song faded with the memory.

In the stream, Dreng fought for air, but something held him down. He kicked and splashed and willed his head to stay above the surface. He would not drown. He would not give up.

But he could not reach the shore. This time, it was too distant. Impossible. And the water was too inviting.

Dreng submerged again and returned to his memory of Alda in the courtyard. She smiled. He relaxed and succumbed to his past. To happiness.

Then a hand grabbed his arm. A small hand, dainty but strong. It pulled, and he kicked, and he was soon safe on the streambank, coughing and sobbing. His back convulsed as he breathed, and his savior soothed him and patted his shoulders reassuringly. He finally composed himself, his breath steadying as his eyes adjusted to the darkness.

In the moonlight, Dreng thought for a flash that his rescuer was Alda. But he heard Miranda's soft voice explain, "That is the Stream of Consciousness. It is enchanted. No one can escape it." She paused to let him realize that she had saved his life. "Now, tell me what it showed you."

Chapter Twenty-One: The Be-All and the End-All

Alda was in the nothing again. Netherfeld. Voices surrounded her. Noise without words. Forms without figures. All immaterial. Nothing solid. Nothing real.

"Who is here?"

Nothing.

She tried again, "*What* is here?"

Again, silence.

Alda angrily mumbled one of her grandmother's oft-quoted poems, one about a girl trapped in a tower, "I am half-sick of shadows." The words felt appropriate.

"So draw near and fear not." A disembodied voice replied in verse from the same poem. It was calm, soothing. Like her grandmother. *Her grandmother.* "Look around you."

"I am."

"Then, see."

In the distance, a green dome glowed. It grew brighter. Alda thought she could discern buildings. No, towers. Walls. A fortress?

"What is it?"

"Don't you know?"

"No."

"Yours," the voice explained.

"That is impossible." Alda stared for a moment, awestruck.

"Time will come." The voice continued, "For you to return. Here."

"But —"

"You must leave now."

"No."

"You must."

Alda felt a push. "But I don't want to —"

"— Leave." Alda was on the moor, beneath the purple fog of the stone circle. She was disoriented by her sudden change in scene and caught her breath, dizzy with fatigue and shaking with rage.

"But you only now arrived, girl."

The witches cackle-laughed as they approached her, their sharp tones a strange contrast to the calmness in Netherfeld.

All here was the same as when Alda left. The fire with an empty spit. The nearby cauldron. The stones themselves, regal and commanding, mysterious with their carvings of symbols and shapes, and the fog-dome, protecting them from the moor's rain and wind.

How much time had passed here? None?

"How?"

Alda was confused by the witch's question, but the weyward sisters did not wait for her to respond.

"She used the cauldron's bubble." They nodded to one another.

"It must be empty now."

"Yes, empty."

"Useless."

"Give it, then."

"No." Alda was stern, but the witches laughed.

"So where is Ariel?" For the first time, the witches were silent as they awaited Alda's response.

"Dead."

They gasped, "How?"

"Sycorax. Or Caliban." Alda realized, "I don't know exactly what happened."

"No."

"No."

"No."

"Prospero is dead, too." Alda thought this would please them, somehow, but the witches did not respond. "And his daughter, I think."

The bearded women huddled, whispering in hisses and snorts, glancing at Alda disapprovingly. Finally, the three turned to face her.

"Did you pass anyone else on the island?"

"Did anyone else go past?"

"On the island or elsewhere?"

"No," Alda lied about Netherfeld and her grandmother's voice. And about Dreng. She did not want to think about him.

"Then what did you bring for us?"

"Bring for *you*?" Alda felt her cheeks turn red, like fire.

"A bauble or a knick-knack?"

"A trophy or a spoil?"

"A tribute to try?"

"You sent me to an island that I could not escape." Alda clenched her fists angrily. "A prison, essentially. On a quest to free someone who was not entrapped. You had no regard for me or my safety. It was reckless."

"The girl does protest too much."

"I am not a *girl!* Not anymore. And what did you want, really? What was your game?"

"Another test."

"And we will tell it."

"But first, a tax."

"Ask her again."

"What did you bring for us?"

Alda frowned but finally relented. She was curious and frustrated. What had been the test, this time?

"I only have the percepstone." Alda lied again. Prospero's miniature book was safe in her shoe and her secret to keep, for now.

"Give it." Nona held out her wiry hand.

As Alda dropped the smooth percepstone into her wrinkled fingers, the witch — unchanged in appearance — grabbed her wrist and cut her open palm. Alda fought and writhed, but the sister was preternaturally strong. Despite her struggling, the two other witches held a coil of yarn below Alda's hand and caught her falling droplets.

They released their hold and moved away as they chanted nonsensical words over the bloody yarn. Alda was frozen, not with fear, but by something invisible.

When the witches suddenly stopped, Decima glared at Alda and began, "Your time-yarn is knotted now."

"We twist."

"We tie."

"We bind your time."

"Your time here is done."

"You are done, and time is past."

"No more to do here."

"Not to hear."

"Not to see."

"Nothing to remember."

"No more to remember."

"Back to the beginning for you."

"The knot is done."

"Untied.

"Undone."

"It is not done."

 "Time will remain elsewhere."

"Deeds will stay elsewhere."

"But no time for you."

"So go home for a spell."

"A spell to go home."

They ended together, "And forget."

Chapter Twenty-Two: Ending is Despair

The luminescent Stream of Consciousness rippled gently past the newlyweds, glittering in the moonlight as they both reclined against a tree, comfortable and thoughtful in their shared silence.

Dreng had told Miranda of his dream of the ship, his terrible vision. But not of Alda; it felt safer to keep that memory unspoken. After his tale, Miranda lapsed into contemplation, her blue eyes studying the surface of the stream but seeming to look beyond its waters.

As Dreng watched the calm waves and floating flowers, he realized that the water was shallow. He should have been able to stand, to easily escape, but some force had held him in place, pulling him into its murky depths. "What would have happened to me, in the stream, if — if you were not here?"

Miranda squeezed Dreng's hand, and the signet ring felt cold against his skin. "It would have swallowed you, of course. Your mind lost, elsewhere. Your body..." She did not finish. He understood.

His bride's brow furrowed in thought, which continued for some time as the water rippled in the moonlight.

Finally, Miranda asked, "Do you understand the song? 'Double, double' and the rest?"

Dreng shook his head, so she explained, "I recognized the words immediately. Witches' words, Ferdinand. A spell."

He considered for several heartbeats, not knowing how to respond. There was too much to comprehend, too many questions. The memory, the ghost, the witches.

He had enough of questions, so finally, he spoke simply, "Please, call me Dreng."

Miranda looked alarmed as her bright, questioning eyes studied his. He explained, "Dreng is what I was called before. On my ship, *The Tempest.*"

She smiled, and her worried expression eased. "Dreng?" He nodded, and she continued, "I thought for a moment you had some sinister secret."

She kissed his cheek and leaned into his shoulder, against the red lines of his scar. He wrapped his arm around her waist, took an unsteady breath, and confessed, "I do have a secret."

Before Miranda could react, Dreng revealed the torn paper with the unusual words, the page that fell through the shattered window in the courtyard. He handed it to Miranda, and she glanced at it briefly before laughing again.

"That? It looks like nonsense. Crooked marks and spots and spaces."

"No. It's a list of ingredients." He held it again and read, "Eye of newt, toe of frog, wool of bat, tongue of dog." He looked up and explained, "There are more items, but I do not understand them all. What is a witch's mummy?"

Miranda bit her lip as she studied his face. "How, how could you read that?"

Dreng told her about Prince Hamlet and his childhood reading lessons. Then, how the paper appeared to transform in the courtyard.

When he was done, Miranda sat in silence for several moments, deep in thought, before she whispered, "Do you know what it means?"

Dreng shook his head and admitted, "No."

"Instructions," Miranda explained. "For a potion. And there are more like it, maybe thousands more, in Prospero's library."

"A potion?" Dreng sensed its danger and whispered, "Do you mean a witch's potion?"

She nodded. Dreng wiped his forehead as he did his best to grasp this revelation. Miranda studied his expression, smiled slightly, and added in a soothing tone, "We can use a potion, now. To kill them."

Dreng met her eyes again, a question on his lips, but before he could ask, Miranda clarified, "The witches. In your memory. The ones who killed your father."

The young man sat up straighter, his shoulders tense. "Why would we do that?"

"Revenge." Miranda's blue eyes sparkled beneath her pale eyelashes.

Dreng thought of the ghost. His father's murder. All the wrongs that had happened to him since the night with the St. Elmo's fire.

He lowered his head into a nod and asked, "How will we find the witches?"

*   *   *

The empty cottage was too cold now, and Alda rubbed her hands together as her breath floated like smoke into the air. She wrapped her arms in her black dress and rocked gently, calming her shaking limbs.

Outside her window, new snow glistened, and the moon reflected off the Grand River and silhouetted the distant islands. The scent of freshly crushed herbs hung around her. She shivered in the heavy silence.

Alda was alone. In her grandmother's cottage on the seventh island. On the longest night of the year. Again.

But everything was different because she remembered. The witches' spell to end her memories had not worked, somehow. It must have been the fountain with the Netherfeld spring, she realized. Surely that. Or some unknown power?

And with the memories of all that had happened, Alda could not simply return to her life in the cottage. She had changed, too much, and did not belong here. But where should she go?

Thinking, Alda plucked the cauldron's bubble from its place in her shoe, but it was too light. She turned it over, wondering what part of it was missing, but it looked unchanged.

She closed her fingers around the sphere as she had the first time, when she found it in her grandmother's cloak, but nothing happened. After a moment of contemplation, she whispered, "Elsewhere." Nothing. She tried again, "Go to the bridge." Still nothing.

So she tried to envision a destination, but all she could see behind her closed eyelids were the blackness of the ship and the boy losing consciousness in her arms. Dark thoughts. When she opened her eyes, the cottage remained unchanged around her.

Desperately, she removed Prospero's miniature book from the top of her shoe. Yet its contents were meaningless, a tangle of symbols and letters amid spaces and spots. She threw it down in despair and, with more care, placed the cauldron's bubble in an empty vase as she slumped into a chair.

And she cried. No, she wailed, her voice like a wounded animal. She thought of the witches and their world, now closed to her. She thought of Dreng, gone. And Sycorax, with devious plans, no doubt. And her own, immediate helplessness.

What could she do, now, here? The bubble was useless. The book incomprehensible. She had no way to return to the other world, no magic. Or did she?

As she wondered, her tear-filled eyes searched the cottage, tracing shapes of familiar objects that now appeared mysterious in the moonlight. Looking for some lost clue, a message from Gramma, anything to help her get back all that had been taken.

Alda's eyes flitted across the cottage's contents and fell on her grandmother's porcelain teacup next to the sink.

A memory flashed into her mind. Days before her grandmother's death, during a windy snowstorm, Alda brought more firewood into the cottage and found her grandmother sitting at the kitchen table, staring into a cup of tea.

"What is wrong?" Alda asked as she added split logs to the fire. But she did not expect a response from one who had been silent or nonsensical for several weeks.

"I see them now. Rainbows on their curves."

"What rainbows?" Alda looked into the cup and saw that it was brimming with bubbles. "Did you put soap in your tea?"

The old woman looked up at her and frowned. "Do not worry if they flicker out. If the bubble bursts." As Alda emptied the teacup and barely listened, her grandmother added, "I have a recipe."

Alda had disregarded the conversation. It was one of dozens of senseless ramblings. But now it had a different context. And Alda knew it was important.

She darted into the kitchen and retrieved the recipe box from its place on the highest shelf. The cards inside were alphabetical: apple crumble, brown sugar syrup, citrus cookies... Alda dumped the box upside down and spread its contents over the table, searching. Nothing.

Perhaps her grandmother's words were simply another crazed rant after all.

But then Alda saw it. A perfectly folded paper, secured inside the bottom of the recipe box. Alda carefully opened it, her heart beating against her ribs.

Written in the smooth script of a younger woman were the words "Cauldron's Bubble" above a complex series of ingredients and instructions.

Now Alda realized, in the vast middle of the night, that all of her past was leading to this. Her grandmother's scoldings, instructions, even the snippets of poetry were in preparation for the coming obstacles Alda would face, for the spells and spirits. But how did her grandmother know about magic? And about the future?

Who was her grandmother, really?

And more importantly, Alda wondered, who was *she*?

Alda knew she was not a witch, but she was something different, surely. Perhaps something more, something magical. And now, with her grandmother's recipe, she had the guidance, the power to return to the world she had left.

But it would take time.

Volume Two: Double Double Toil

Doubt thou, the Starres are fire,
Doubt, that the Sunne doth moue:
Doubt Truth to be a Lier,
But never Doubt, I loue.

~William Shakespeare (1564-1616), *Hamlet*
Hamlet's letter to Ophelia, Act 2, Scene 2
First Folio, 1623

Chapter One: Midsummer Night's Dream

Alda hesitated on the rickety footbridge and looked toward the darkening east. The electric lights on the distant resort island twinkled in the dusk, like fairies through the summer leaves.

It was the start of the shortest night of the year. And though the day had been long, Alda still had more to do. Too much to do, always, and never enough time.

Six months had passed. Six months since the witches' quest, since Prospero and his island, since Sycorax and her spirits from Netherfeld.

Six months since Alda had watched Dreng die, his life taken by an enchanted kiss.

Six months since she had been returned to her home in Grand Ledge on the seventh island, trapped in this time and this place without a cauldron's bubble.

Alone.

Alda wiped her eyes and cleared her mind, as she had so many times before. Once inside her cottage, she felt some relief. Purpose. She dropped the basket onto the kitchen table and lit the oil lamp.

Shadows of green and pink fell across the single room.

Her grandmother's recipe for a new cauldron's bubble was still propped by the garden window, silhouetted in the rising moonlight.

Cans that once held the preserves that sustained her through the cold spring months now contained various ingredients: dried salamander, toadstools, herbs, wildflowers. This collection reassured Alda of all she had accomplished since she had returned to her own place and time.

Forced to return.

And, she kept reminding herself, there was hope, yet. If she could make the bubble, she could travel to the past.

When Dreng was alive.

She could save him.

Perhaps.

Alda pushed up her thin maroon sleeve as she reached into the basket. The cuff fell again to her wrist, so she rolled it up instead. Her body felt foreign, different, and her old clothes that she had worn before she had spent forgotten years in Netherfeld were too small. She instead wore her grandmother's dresses: outdated, threadbare calico fabric, but all she had.

Half a year ago, when the witches sent her away from their moor and back to her cottage, they had tried to erase her memory. To undo her mind's remnants of the talking birds, the nymphs in the stream, the bright spirits that shot from her fingertips on Prospero's island. But their spell did not fully work.

Her memories of the witches remained, and they haunted her. Yet the years she spent in Netherfeld, before she had tasted from Prospero's enchanted fountain, were still a void.

Alda shook her head, her ink-colored hair brushing against her cheeks. She had to be here, now, in the present. There would be time for the past, later. Now, she had to focus.

Gently, she removed a purple flower from her basket. It was conical, like a calla lily with its head folded over, almost bowing: a jack-in-the-pulpit. These flowers were scarce in the forest along the Ledge Path, and even the few she had found were either green or veined.

Gramma's recipe called for a purple one. And Alda found it today, finally, on the summer solstice.

For a moment, Alda let her mind wander. She remembered a walk with her grandmother, many years ago, through the oak forest on the far side of the river, above the sandstone ledges that stretched to the riverbank below. There, beneath the canopy of ancient trees, they had gathered pansies and daisies and Queen Anne's lace until Alda, who was still young and innocent, stooped toward a jack-in-the-pulpit.

"No, not that flower."

"Why not?" Little Alda started reaching for it again before Gramma could answer, so the older woman took her hand and led her away.

"That is a jack-in-the-pulpit, and it's not a flower. Not truly. It used to be a man, a preacher, who tried to drive out what he called heathen magic."

"What is heathen?"

After a moment of hesitation, Gramma explained, "Ancient and mysterious." She glanced at Alda, saw that the answer was sufficient, and continued, "The queen of fairies overheard his sermon, so she turned him into a flower to ensure he never spoke again."

Alda was instantly enchanted by the fairy queen, so different from the entrapped princesses of other childhood tales. She asked dozens of questions as they walked back to the cottage, but her grandmother refused to tell more. Instead, Gramma sang a song that began, "Loolla, loolla, lalla, never harm nor spell nor charm come near my little Alda."

And her grandmother never spoke of fairies again.

But later that month, Alda discovered a tattered book under her bed, a picture book with intricate illustrations of tiny people and their adventures, tales of lost realms and secret portals.

Alda did not ask her grandmother about the sudden appearance of the fairy book. And eventually, as years passed and she grew, Alda stopped asking about fairies.

But sometimes, under her breath, she hummed the song.

Now, so many years later, Alda knew the purple flower was just that, a flower. It was not a man who displeased fairies.

But it was more than that, too.

The jack-in-the-pulpit was the final ingredient for the cauldron's bubble, the key that had eluded her throughout the icy winter and pale spring.

So Alda retrieved her cast iron pot and held the recipe card to the glow of the oil lamp as she placed each ingredient into the bowl.

She hesitated. If this did not work, if something went wrong, she did not know how long it would take to find another purple flower. She tapped her fingers as she considered. Finally, she tore the jack-in-the-pulpit in half and dropped part of it into the mixture.

Nothing. No reaction. No puff of smoke or fiery spark.

So Alda waited and counted ten heartbeats.

Nothing changed.

More waiting, and her heartbeat quickened.

Something was wrong, but what?

Alda took a wooden spoon from a hook near the sink and stirred. She muddled the parts until they were broken down into a kind of powder.

Still nothing.

Perhaps they needed to be fused somehow, combined. So Alda dropped water into the bowl until it was a paste.

Again, nothing. What had she expected? Some magical metamorphosis? A sudden, furious reaction that created the sphere?

Alda bit her lip and thought.

Maybe she needed sunlight. Maybe the spell would only work during the day. Yes, Alda decided, she should wait until morning.

So she crossed to the chair next to the empty hearth. Even though she was exhausted now, she could not rest, not completely. Sleep had been elusive these six months.

She feared what dreams may come.

She retrieved Prospero's miniature book from the table at her side, the tiny volume that she had found tucked within the dead man's robes. Perhaps it could tell her a way to finish the spell, to make the cauldron's bubble.

If only she could read its incomprehensible language.

Now, as the moon shone directly through her kitchen window, she sat by the empty fireplace and lit a single wax candle to examine the book. Its leaves were strange: mismatched markings, spots and shapes of ink, blanks of white, scattered scribbles, and unknown letters. Crosshatching. Spaces. Nonsense. But she had them nearly memorized after so many months of study. She *had* to make sense of them. To understand.

She turned the pages again and tilted the book, her fingers running over the faces of words. Surely, she hoped, she had missed something. Surely, she could find something tonight. Surely, if she continued, hopeful and focused and uninterrupted, for hours...

And suddenly Alda was elsewhere. She had felt no movement, no warm sensation as she had when she travelled with the cauldron's bubble, yet she was back on the ship with the boy, with Dreng, in the hold with his blood dripping onto her hands. She wanted to save him, but she was frozen. She could not move. She forced her body into motion, her limbs heavy, but she could not stop his blood.

She could not save him, again.

Alda did not realize she was asleep, that Dreng was only a dream, until she awoke to a long, lingering scream that pierced the silence of the night.

*   *   *

Dreng's dream was like so many others before: his father's ghost rattling its words, "A witch." It flickered and added, forcefully, "Find her." Dreng wanted to flee from the eerie figure, its glowing features too much like his own, but his body felt bound. He could not move. He could not escape.

So for what felt like the thousandth time, the young man asked, "How do I find the witch?"

The ghost backed away, again disappearing into the forest.

Dreng followed him, desperately pushing aside branches as he was consumed by the black vegetation.

"Father, how do I find her?"

There was no answer.

With a gasp, Dreng awoke, alone. He was in the library of Miranda's palace, in an ornate wooden chair, leaning with his head atop a table. His arm was bent outward, and his fingers tingled. He rubbed his scar down his shoulder to his forearm, forcing the blood to reanimate his limb, as his eyes adjusted to the darkness around him.

It took several heartbeats for him to see clearly. Yet another symptom of remaining too long on land.

The palace was quiet in the vast middle of the night. Miranda, Dreng's wife, was either sleeping or patrolling the corridors with her red, enchanted spirits. Caliban was in his distant bedchamber.

Dreng was alone, again. As he had been so many nights in his half-year on the island.

So that evening, he had sought refuge among the books. At first, several months ago, Dreng had read to escape the monotony of being unnecessary. Miranda was often exploring the island, leaving him alone to search for meaning within the fragmentary manuscripts and broken bindings. But there was still not enough to keep his mind away from other distractions. Away from worries.

And, apart from books, there was the strange spiral etched onto the floor, the one that appeared after Prospero —

Dreng could not finish; he knew too little to end the sentence. Miranda knew, but he did not want to ask her what had happened during the fiery storm.

She had told him that Prospero was dead, but he could not imagine his wife capable of such a thing.

Some details were better unknown.

Yet he did have one burning question about that night, six months ago. What had happened to Alda? He had searched for her for days, then weeks. No trace. Now, he guessed that she was dead and gone.

Dreng did his best to accept this truth.

But he still thought about her. Too often.

Dreng wiped his eyes and stood, stretching until the tearing pain in his shoulders was enough to overpower his thoughts. He shook his head and, as he left the library, he avoided the spiral.

When he entered the palace's stony corridor, he realized that he missed the lapped planks of his former home. The sea, the camaraderie of his shipmates, the responsibility that felt, in a way, like freedom.

Even though he knew he had never been free, not entirely.

And now was no different: not free, not entirely. He had tried to leave the island, at first, but Miranda was unwilling.

After the night of the storm, after she spoke with him on the shore of the strange stream, after she told him of the witches, of her plan to defeat them, he had expected immediate action. But Miranda waited.

At first there were excuses, but as the weeks turned to months, the excuses became silence.

Dreng suspected his wife was afraid of something. What?

Miranda, who had led a crew of magical red lights against a sorcerer.

Miranda, who had died and come back to life. Miranda, who was afraid of nothing.

Or at least appeared to be.

What could frighten her so?

Or was she simply afraid to *tell* him something?

Dreng worried she was lying, that there was more she was not willing to reveal. That the island held secrets he could not penetrate.

And he was helpless here, in this world. No ship. No crew. No order. Not even a sword. But this was not a land of steel and blades. This was Miranda's world, a place of magic, a place where he was, quite literally, disarmed.

Now, as he wandered through the corridor and past the open doorway that led to the dilapidated courtyard, he glanced outside.

Beyond the courtyard, beyond the rubble of the collapsed roof and fallen walls, the shattered fountain and the fragments of frescoes, he saw a distant spot of light that flickered as it moved toward the cliffs above the beach.

He felt — no, knew — that he should follow the light.

For a moment, he hesitated at the threshold. Was it some type of magic? A spirit meant to lead him to destruction?

A wisp, like the Irish sailors feared?

Should he wake Miranda?

Or follow the light and keep a secret of his own?

He shook his head clear and left the suffocation of the palace.

After so many months of stagnation, he needed to seize this moment, this time.

*   *   *

An owl? A nighthawk? A lynx? Alda wondered, *what* could have screamed?

She feared it was a person.

Or was it Alda's imagination?

Yes, she decided. Her vivid dream, seemingly come to life. Her sleep had been short and shallow, so the scream must have appeared to materialize into reality.

The scream was her. Or rather her imagination.

She relaxed.

But then it happened again. Louder and sharper. A real scream. High.

A scream of fear.

And Alda was afraid. She clumsily stood, dropping Prospero's miniature book, her fingers shaking as she awkwardly bent and replaced it on the table by the fireplace. She straightened and stared at the door of her cottage. Waiting.

A third scream, louder. Was it closer? Alda ran to the door, holding it shut with all of her strength. She expected it to burst open at any moment, the weight of some unseen force bearing down upon her, a fearful, unknown something about to destroy her.

But then there was silence. Minutes of silence. The cottage grew darker as the moon passed overhead, its beams no longer breaking through the windows.

Alda counted her heartbeats. Once they slowed, she stepped away from the door.

Nothing happened.

She hesitated as she reached for the doorknob but set her jaw and forced her shaking hand forward. As soon as her fingers encircled the iron handle, she swung the door open, hoping to shock whatever was waiting.

Outside, all was calm. Silent. The smell of midnight dew on leaves. The moonbeams flickering through oaks, shining from almost directly above. The distant resort, dark, its electric lights extinguished in the midnight hour. The gentle flow of the Grand River, its waters unmoving and unmoved.

No breeze. No noise. No fireflies. Nothing.

It was not natural.

Alda knew she could not remain in the cottage, fearful and confined, so she summoned all her courage, screwing it into her heart until it stuck, and slowly walked across the bridge, her hands trembling.

She reached a fork in the trail and listened. To her left was the city and civilization. To her right, the railroad bridge and Sandstone Creek and, beyond that, the forest where the spiritualists had pitched their camp.

Earlier that week, Alda had seen them through trees as she stood on an outcropping above the creek. They sang and chanted and played with cards and divination. But Alda knew they were not magical, not like her grandmother. Still, the spiritualists had what seemed to be rituals, some of which could be dangerous. Perhaps one of them had screamed. Or caused someone to scream.

So Alda turned to the right.

After a few moments, the moon disappeared behind a cloud.

She stopped, waiting for its light to return. When it finally broke through, Alda could see the path as well as in daylight.

Despite this illumination, everything seemed different in the moonlight: shimmering shades and exaggerated shadows.

Above the Ledge Path, uphill from the river, were two boulders.

They looked familiar, but Alda knew she had never seen them before. Why did she recognize them?

Then she remembered the Stream of Consciousness, the nymphs' enchanted dwelling place on Prospero's island. This had all been in her vision: two enormous stones, low-growing ferns, and trees bent into the shape of a tunnel.

Why had she not noticed this path before?

Had it existed before now?

Did it even exist, now?

Without hesitation, before Alda succumbed to worry or fear, she clambered up the rise and between the boulders. The trees continued to bend above her head, leading her forward and preventing her from turning off the path. The ferns before her cleared. The way became covered in grasses and budded wildflowers until, finally, it terminated in a wall of close-growing trees.

At this dead end was a circle, a perfectly formed ring of blooming, light blue forget-me-nots. The dainty flowers glowed, almost fluoresced in the moonlight. A beam pierced the center of the ring like a spotlight and illuminated the exposed sandstone to a brilliant white.

Alda cautiously approached the flowered ring and knelt to the ground, tucking her faded maroon skirt beneath her knees as she examined the unnatural foliage. She reached out, her fingers quivering, and tentatively touched one of the tiny buds.

Something grabbed her wrist, something strong and cold and green that smelled of herbs and earth. It pulled, and she fell into the ring of flowers.

And then Alda was gone, vanished. The moon again disappeared behind the clouds, and crickets finally broke the silence.

Chapter Two: Stolen Away

Dreng left the still palace and followed the mysterious light past the heathered moor, down the cliff-path, and to the white sands of the beach below the palace. The water stretched out into darkness, and the rough waves crashed against unseen rocks.

As he carefully trod over the boulders along the shore, the light suddenly vanished. Had it been extinguished, or did it disappear?

Finally on the sand, Dreng remembered the day, six months before, when he came ashore. When his eyes had fallen on Miranda for the first time in all her perfection. Her golden hair and porcelain features.

Her apparent disappearance at the base of the cliff's wall.

Into the wall.

Although this stretch of beach was far from where Dreng's ship, *The Tempest,* met its fate, the same gray cliffs separated the sand from the rocky fields and palace above.

Did the cliffs harbor some secret?

With a prickling of hesitation, Dreng reached toward the cliff wall in the moonlight, expecting his unsteady fingers to touch cold, damp stones. Nothing. He stretched his hands as far as he could. No stone. No wall.

Cautiously, he took a step forward. Then another, and for a moment he was lost in darkness as boulders surrounded him. It was a tunnel, he realized, an optical illusion obscured from the outside by the surrounding rocks.

Or was it more than a trick of optics?

He kept walking, hunching forward and feeling his way for over a hundred paces until the air suddenly changed. The smell of stagnant water engulfed him, and he stood upright in an enormous cavern. This was not a cave, not low and dim like Caliban's lair. This place was beyond measure. Gems glistened from above, supported on finger-like protrusions of crystalline rocks. Pillar-shaped spears of sparkling stone erupted from the ground, surrounding him. And from each crystal, each gemstone, light glowed and reflected on shallow pools that shuddered with his steps.

He stumbled toward the center of the space, bewildered.

His first thought was of the wealth of this place. Men on his ship had died for less. And killed.

His second thought was fear. This space felt forbidden, dangerous. Unknown.

But curiosity overcame his urge to flee.

His third thought was of Miranda. Did she know of this?

If she did, then why had she not told him?

Dreng forced himself forward into the cavern's cool depths. On the far wall, primitive shapes and figures were etched into the smooth, shining surface: beasts and swirling lines, stick-like people with square torsos, birds and reptiles, and handprints of the makers of these images.

And as he studied them, the images seemed to pulse. Like a heartbeat. Alive.

The place was magical, like Caliban's cave where Miranda was resurrected, but grander. What powers were held here?

Before he could explore further, the light appeared again in a darkened corner of the chamber, in an area that seemed to be another tunnel leading to a darker passage without the glowing stones. Instinctively, Dreng thought to hide or to fight, but his reflexes seemed slower in this strange place; not only in the cave, but on the island itself.

Nonetheless, his heart beat against his chest and his fingers tingled, ready for defense. But then he saw the light's source: a candle.

Held by his wife.

Miranda, with the red lights of her enchanted spirits swirling about her form, stopped and stared at him, and for a moment the two were in a silence broken only by dripping water.

"What are you doing here?" Miranda's voice echoed.

Dreng did not answer. He wanted to ask her the same question, but he held his tongue. Instead, he asked, "What is this place?"

After a heartbeat of silence, Miranda finally smiled and extinguished the candle. "The island is laced with these caves." She crossed the cavernous chamber toward him, and he realized by her slow progression that it was much larger than he had originally thought. "They contain magic," she continued. "Prospero used their power for his spells. He read the symbols on the walls and understood ancient secrets. Then he wrote this knowledge in his books. I, however, am still discovering it." She smiled at him. "Still exploring. Learning more than the wicked old man knew."

Her tone was frightening, her lust for power evident. She studied Dreng's eyes and saw his concern. Her brow furrowed, and she added, "We should go home, now."

"No, let's explore. Together." Dreng intended to speak it as a command — no, a suggestion — but it sounded more like a plea.

Miranda swirled her hands, and the spirits disappeared as she approached him. "It's too dangerous. For you. There is too much here for you to understand." She was right, he knew.

Her spirits themselves were yet incomprehensible.

His mind searched for a response, but he muttered only, "Always." He wanted to say more but stopped himself and stood straighter.

"What do you mean?"

"There is always too much for me to understand." He moved closer to her and felt stirrings of courage. He spoke firmly, "So teach me."

Miranda started to speak and then bit her lip, so Dreng persisted, "I learned to write with water on a board. Then I learned to navigate and command and — before all of this, this island — I was —" He realized what was missing. Finally, he sighed, "I was *trusted*."

Miranda, who had reached his side, tried to touch his face. He turned away, disheartened, so she took his hand instead. "I trust you, but not myself." She squeezed his fingers, and he felt his shoulders ease. "Give me time to find myself, my place, and then I will guide you. I will be your compass. But I need more time."

She seemed to only ever speak in symbols. He had to guess her meaning. "Why wait?" Miranda looked away, toward the tunnel to the beach, so he persisted, "We're here together, now. We have time, now. We can explore now, until dawn. I can build a map in my mind and lead us back, safely." His eyes studied hers. "Please."

Her shoulders slumped, so he pleaded, "Please, my love. Let us go into the depths of this place together."

She avoided his gaze. He again reached for her hand as he asked, "Why do you *doubt* me?"

He did not expect Miranda to cry. He had never seen her cry. She was too strong, he thought. But now her grief, if that was what it was, seemed to consume her small frame.

He was helpless, so he only wrapped his arms around her and rested his cheek atop her head. As she relaxed into him, his arms again felt heavy, weak. She whispered, her voice shaking, "Never doubt my love."

After a moment of silence, Miranda recovered and wiped her face. She stepped back, but her eyes avoided his as she looked around the cavern. She focused on something over his shoulder, and her features softened as she relaxed. She even smiled slightly as she seemed to realize something.

What had changed in her, so suddenly?

Her eyes met his, and she whispered, "There are stories in the walls."

Confused, Dreng only stared.

After a moment, Miranda took his hand. "Come. I will show you."

*   *   *

Alda, in a dark and moonless forest, fought against the strong, damp hand that held her wrist. She could still see the blue ring of flowers a few feet distant and lunged toward it, but a force grabbed her waist and secured her hands together.

Then something covered her eyes. She was blinded and fell to the grassy ground, her captor wrapping a thin wire or rope tightly around her limbs.

And then movement.

She felt herself dragged along the ground, her fingers unable to catch hold of a root or a rock, and her feet scuffing uselessly behind.

After what felt like several minutes, her eye-covering came loose enough for her to see. She was in a wood, but not the forest along the Grand River.

The colors here were unnatural, vivid, almost glowing. Flowers hung from trees like garland. Blue light filtered through the foliage, and it smelled like a thousand bouquets.

The place was unreal. No, otherworldly. Like something from a dream.

Then she saw it, her captor. No, not it. Him. A green man with angular features and elongated limbs.

But *man* was not the right word, for he was not human.

He was clothed in exotic leaves and flowers, stitched and woven into something like fabric, with a sunflower pouch at his waist and a birch-bark hat.

Between his pointed ears and the brim of his hat, two small, silver horns protruded from his coarse hair.

On his belt was a dagger, its blade glistening silver and its tip the color of mint jelly.

Then she saw the ivy on her wrists, shifting as it grew around her arms. She tried to pry herself free, but it would not budge.

So she held out her palms as she had on Prospero's island, trying to unleash the spirits. Nothing happened. As she had expected. But still, she had hoped...

The spirits had not come to her since the return to her cottage. Since the witches forced her into banishment. Yet she had thought that now, in this place, the spirits might come to her aid.

And without them, she was powerless. Without the cauldron's bubble, she was trapped. Completely.

The green man was unaware of her struggles as he continued to drag her over the mossy ground — he barely acknowledged her — and turned toward a grove of trees.

Alda guessed that begging for freedom would prove fruitless, so she asked, "Where are you taking me?"

"Home." She felt a moment's relief before the thing added, "To the King of Shadows."

King of Shadows? Alda shivered. "No, no, that is not —"

As they entered the grove, Alda saw the trees turn and sway overhead. But there was no wind. She realized that when the green man approached, the trees bent outward. After they passed, the trees reformed their shape behind.

"This is not my home!"

The green man stopped and stooped, cutting the vine from her ankles and forcing her to her feet. She did not fight, not yet, as he pulled her into a clearing beyond the treeline.

Again, she protested, "I am not from —"

But Alda lost her words as she was awed by the surrounding wonders. Within the grove, the trees parted into a wide glade with branches stretching overhead and obscuring the sky. She was reminded of the European cathedrals in her stereopticon cards. Flowers glistened like stained glass, and songbirds twittered in an echoing chorus. Butterflies fluttered overhead, and bees the size of taffy buzzed among the flowers. Toadstools and mosses of every color littered the ground. And the sweet, almost tangible smell was overwhelming.

Alda asked, knowing it was a bizarre question, "Is this some kind of fairy land?"

"Have you forgotten where you are, my child? The forest is not so deep and wild."

No, Alda was certain she had never been here before. This was clearly not Netherfeld. It existed. Or seemed to exist.

So she asked, "Who are you?"

"You know my name. Is this some sort of game?"

Had Alda met him before, in Netherfeld? "I don't remember."

"Mortals do so easily forget, despite the introduction when we met. I am Robin Goodfellow, called Hobgoblin, called Puck. I am the one who brings some mortals luck, and others, who do not appreciate my charms..." He paused and narrowed his eyes. "To those, I often bring them harm."

Was this a threat? Alda held her tongue. Anything called Hobgoblin could not be kind.

And, *mortals*? What was this being?

"The king will return to us post haste, once he has completed with his chase." The green being made something like a smile and turned from her to study their surroundings.

So Alda did likewise. To one side was a throne on a raised pile of boulders, surrounded by toadstools large enough to be chairs. Opposite, on the far side of the moss-covered floor, was an ancient tree, a willow bending with burls and covered with tiny doors, each a different color.

It was a fairy tree, she guessed, like the one in her picture book, an illustration for a story about two children abducted by fairies, two children who escaped the fairy realm through such a tree and reappeared years later near their home, in a wolf-pit, with no memory of their missing time.

Alda suddenly realized that the stories could be true. That the book hidden under her bed was some sort of preparation for this coming trial.

Had her grandmother known this would happen?

Robin Goodfellow interrupted her thoughts as he announced, "The party has returned from being gone. Look, mortal, there is King Oberon."

As Alda stared, a brightly dressed line of green people appeared among the trees, carrying an array of flowers and food toward the throne. Their clothes were of the same flower-fabric as her captor, and, although they seemed to prepare for a feast or celebration, they were not cheerful. Instead, they seemed solemn, stoic. Without emotion.

Alda noticed, too, that they all had knives or swords in sheaths at their waists.

These were magical beings, yes, like the nymphs and the spirits. But they were more, too. Dangerous.

Behind this line of warriors, a taller, more human-like man appeared through the trees, smiling widely, his exaggerated grin out of place with those around him. His skin was lighter green, his limbs all proportional, with a beard and hair a nightly shade of black, his locks twisted with what looked like white ribbons. He was dressed as his comrades but with finer flowers and a short maroon cape that was nearly the same shade as Alda's dress.

Alda guessed that this being was the King of Shadows, Oberon.

The party did not see her at first as the king bellowed, "One more of the tyrant's darlings felled and forgotten! Let us wash our hands of his tainted blood and form our feast!"

Blood? As the group approached, Alda indeed saw traces of red smeared on the king's fingers. His eyes finally met hers, and his face flashed from a smile to a sneer to a frown.

"What is this, Puck?" He spoke as if Alda was not there. As if she was not worth acknowledging.

"I brought you Phillida, as you had commanded, and she deserves to be duly reprimanded," Robin Goodfellow responded.

Oberon laughed. The other green people stopped in their procession, glanced at each other, and also laughed. Even Robin chortled, but his sound was insincere.

"This is not my pleasant Phillida!" Oberon raised a fist, and the laughing abruptly stopped. Alda's heart pounded. "Look how she scowls! And her pigment is so pale. She is not my Phillida. I am positive."

Robin Goodfellow stared at Alda, as if seeing her for the first time. "Is it not she?" He blinked.

"No, this is a mysterious mortal. This is —" The king stopped and studied her more seriously. She felt exposed, measured. He finally nodded as if he already knew the answer, "Tell the others who you are."

Alda spoke up, "My name is Alda Reeding, and I —"

"Aldeering!"

"No, it's —"

The king continued without pause, "You are from a realm beyond our borders? Yes, you *are*. The land they call Gredge."

"Do you mean Grand Ledge?"

"I love that land, Aldeering. I know it, well." He stopped and studied her for too long, and Alda lost the courage to speak.

The king's focus shifted, and he seemed to look through her. "Puck, please fetch the proper human next time."

"I am deeply sorry, majesty. Their faces all appear so similar that none alone can seem familiar." Alda glared at Robin, but he did not meet her eyes.

"This is not a mere mortal, Puck." Oberon smiled at Alda, but he looked like a cat grinning at a mouse. "She is more."

Alda was not safe here, with this thing that thought her no more than an ant. And an apparent murderer who thought she was something else entirely.

Should she run? But where? The trees were like a fence, a cage. Alda could not escape, so she stood taller and did her best to look dangerous.

The king, who abruptly turned from her, merrily patted Robin Goodfellow on the shoulder as he comforted, "This is a momentary misunderstanding, Puck, but let it not happen again. Now, fetch Phillida, and bring her home."

Robin Goodfellow bowed deeply and dropped the vine securing Alda's wrist as he backed toward the trees. The loose end of the ivy snaked its way around Alda's forearms, tightening its bond.

"I'll put a circle round the earth in order to complete my search." Robin Goodfellow touched his hat respectfully.

Oberon nodded and added, as he made his way to the throne, "And ensure my love does not dare leave again, Puck."

Robin Goodfellow bowed deeply and sneered as he said under his breath, "I'll put a girdle on that girl, the one who made me seem to be a churl." He was seemingly swallowed into the trees behind him.

Alda watched him leave and found her voice, "Your highness, your majesty, please may I return to my home? If you show me the way to the flower ring, I can —"

"Nonsense! We are celebrating my foil's unhappiness. This is a funeral feast, after all. Come, eat, rejoice with us, Aldeering!" He motioned to one of the toadstools near the throne, at his feet, and Alda reluctantly sat and wondered whose death had sparked such celebration.

As she watched the armed courtiers place platters of food at her feet, she mumbled, "My name is Alda, not Aldeering."

No one heard.

She pulled helplessly at the bonds on her hands and forearms.

Chapter Three: Forms of Things Unknown

Dreng studied the drawings on the cavern wall as Miranda stood behind him, her arms crossed. "These are remembrances from the ancient people. The people here before." She paused, took his hand, and added, "They are dangerous."

He examined the wall further and raised his free hand, hesitantly reaching toward the stone. Miranda stopped him. "They have the power of memory, a kind of magic."

Dreng had learned not to ask about the magic. She never gave a clear answer. But he ventured anyway, "Whose memory?"

"Yours. Mine. Anyone who touches the cavern's wall-face. It captures their past, for those in the future to see."

He examined the images: herds of unfamiliar animals, people in groups, their arms outstretched, some people on the ground, prostrate. And between them all, ribbon-like lines of colors, like the spirits Miranda controlled. "Have you touched it?"

She hesitated. "No."

Suddenly, the ground shuddered. A tremor.

Another earthquake. They seemed to be growing more frequent.

The images on the wall glowed brighter and then dimmed.

Miranda's eyes widened, and she whispered, "We should leave." She pulled Dreng's hand, urging him to follow her.

But Dreng was tired. No, exhausted. Descending the cliff to the beach had taken a physical toll, and his continual patience was likewise waning.

He stood firmly. "What are you looking for here, tonight?"

She stopped and turned toward him. "I was simply exploring."

Nothing was simple with Miranda.

"Why?" Dreng had never pushed her like this, never questioned her authority, never refused a command or even a suggestion. Before tonight, he had simply obeyed.

Her eyes flashed in anger. "Because I can."

He understood from her tone that this was final. She would not answer, so Dreng hung his head, defeated, and followed after her.

But he stumbled on the slick rocks of the cavern floor as the vast space shuddered in another tremor. The surefootedness he knew on the sea was gone, and he fell toward the images on the rock. He felt his arms fling wildly into the air until cold, damp stone touched his fingers. A plume of sparks erupted, and pebbles rained down from the ceiling.

Light filled the dusty space, and a rainbow of beams connected Dreng's palm to the wall.

Miranda pulled him back, but something had started. "You have awoken the cave," her voice cracked. Was she frightened or furious?

The cascading sparks took form, becoming shapes like the images on the walls, small but in lifelike detail. Not like the spirits that swirled around Miranda. These seemed real, concrete. Like oil paintings come to life.

First there was a mother and infant.

Then a man, somewhat distant.

And a ship.

Dreng stepped back and watched the moving images unfold and realized he was watching his story. His life. The man, his father, boarded the ship and vanished. The infant grew into a child, and the father returned. The mother held his small hand firmly, the boy clung to her, but the man carried the child to the ship.

It was all rapid, changing and evolving before his eyes.

Dreng knew what happened next, so he looked away.

But Miranda stared at the colorful swirls, the lights of his life that danced around her.

And then she smiled. But it was not of love or pleasure. It was a sneer.

Her eyes met his, and she did not hide her expression. "Now, it makes sense." She seemed to forget the danger she had so recently feared.

"What does?"

"You." Miranda laughed and clasped her hands. "This frightened boy, this is still you. You are still scared, now."

She was right. He knew she was right, but he couldn't let her know that. He clenched his fists and looked to his feet.

"Don't be afraid." Her tone was softer, but he avoided her eyes.

Miranda stepped toward him, offering her hand, and he recoiled. He could not touch her, not now. He felt too exposed. Vulnerable.

The lighted images flashed. It was the lightning that struck the ship, the St. Elmo's fire that had killed his father, and Dreng unconsciously rubbed the scar on his arm.

More shards fell from the ceiling, and a pillar of stone nearby collapsed.

"We must leave. While we can. Come, now, my love."

Dreng scoffed at the final word and remembered something Caliban had said, "Love. That's a curse."

Miranda stepped back, and the red spirits returned and swirled above her shoulders. "Curse?"

In the dim light, emboldened by his fear, Dreng found courage. He had to prove he was no longer the boy hiding in the shadows. "This thing that we have, this arrangement —"

"Our marriage?" Her voice caught in her throat.

"— is made of one person. You. I am your footstool. You ask me questions, and I answer. You bid my service, and I comply. You give me nothing. No answers. No trust. No honesty."

"I do, I do, but there is so much —"

"I wanted a comrade, an equal, but I have a commander."

"No, that's not —"

He felt the anger flash in his eyes, and Miranda grew silent. She studied his face, ignoring the fantastical ship that still floated in the air.

As he stared into her blue eyes, he was reminded of the sea, the battles, all that he had overcome. He had been a leader, once. Respected.

At first, when he had met Miranda, that did not matter. He submitted to her fully. But now, after so many months, his esteem, his ambition suddenly returned. "Touch the wall."

Her face grew pale. "I can't."

"But you know me now, my love." He heard himself sound like Caliban, sarcastic and bitter, but he did not stop. "Show me your past."

"No!"

Before he could stop himself, he grabbed her wrist. The force of his anger felt foreign, even to him. Like his body was not his own.

Miranda fought back, and her spirits swirled about him, but he was committed now. Something had come over him, some strange passion that clouded his judgment.

Or, rather, something had been lifted. He could see clearly. See *her* clearly. And he did not like what he saw.

He pulled her toward the wall. "Dreng, stop this. Come with me, now. Leave. We can look for the portal together."

He paused. "What portal?"

Her eyes pleaded with his, "That is what I was trying to find. It leads to a place of nothing. A place of memories and spirits and power."

"Netherfeld?"

"Yes, but there is more, too."

"Tell me."

Another pillar crumbled. The dome above them shook, and the glowing crystals flickered in and out of darkness.

"I can't, Dreng. Not now. You — It's too dangerous." She paused and added, "I don't want to hurt you. I need you." She stopped fighting against his strength and seemed for a moment to trust him.

He hesitated for a heartbeat before he thrust her palm against the wall. Red sparks erupted, and the smell of fire pierced Dreng's nose. Flaming lights burst forth, and he shielded his eyes from the radiance.

When his vision adjusted, he saw an image of a girl, alone in a field of flowers. Her hair was the color of a vibrant sunset, hues of burnt orange and pale crimson.

As he watched, he realized the girl was not Miranda.

He looked at her, and she backed away from him, toward the tunnel, unaware of the shower of shards and light.

The image of the girl was joined by a boy, tall and fair with golden hair. For a moment, the boy looked familiar. But Dreng pushed the thought aside.

The images of the pair embraced. The boy left, and she fell to her knees in tears.

Again, Dreng looked to Miranda. Tears were likewise staining her cheeks.

"What is this?"

"I don't know." Her voice quivered as she lied.

The scene changed. It was a palace now, and the girl was older, in a gown. The boy was with her, also aged, and he kissed her hand respectfully.

Dreng glared at Miranda, her fair hair covered in the dust of the falling rocks. "Who are you?"

She wiped her eyes, set her jaw, and whispered, "Dreng, I — I'm sorry, but —"

Miranda was interrupted by a crash. The wall's images flashed a brilliant, dazzling white as rocks fell from above.

Dreng covered his head against the horrible shower of stones and shut his eyes against the cloud of dust. When he opened them, the glowing gems were extinguished.

All that was left was the red glow of Miranda's spirits.

*   *   *

Hours seemed to have passed in the fairy king's glade, but little had changed. The fairy courtiers still frolicked and feasted. The king consorted with them, occasionally returning to his throne to lead an elaborate, alliterative toast.

Alda still sat on a toadstool near the throne, watching and wondering. Her wrists and forearms still bound. Her mind wandering to memories and rhymes.

"Aldeering, drink with us!" Oberon called from across the clearing, brandishing a crystal goblet above his head.

She recalled lines from a nonsensical poem: "He had wholly forgotten his name. He would answer to 'Hi!' or any loud cry, such as 'Fry me!' or 'Fritter my wig!' But especially 'Thing-um-a-jig!'"

It was nonsense, all.

Alda did not stand or meet the king's gaze. After a moment, Oberon turned his dark-haired head and seemed to forget that she existed.

Alda struggled with the vines that still bound her. Was she a prisoner here? Or was she a maltreated guest?

And, for that matter, who was she? The witches had said she was more than human. Now Oberon, too, implied she was something above others. What did Alda really know of herself?

Ever since Alda was an infant, she had lived with her grandmother on the seventh island. Alda had never asked of her parents or other relations. It was not outright forbidden, but she simply had no desire to know. But now — no, since she had discovered the cauldron's bubble, she had questions.

So Alda thought back to the one time she remembered asking about her birth. It was her fifth birthday, her "whole hand" celebration, and Gramma had made sponge cookies that used an entire orange, sang old songs and recited verses as she cooked them atop the stove.

Alda, curious, had asked what her *real* birthday was like.

Her grandmother smiled and, without looking up from the rising disks of batter before her, said, "You were born below a dancing star."

Alda, of course, was confused, "How can stars dance?"

"It is an expression, my dear, that is meant to bring luck. It means you were born in happiness."

"Were *you* happy when I was born?"

Gramma glanced at her with a sly look, "I am happy now, and that is what matters."

"Yes, but on my real birthday, what did —"

"Fetch the breadboard, Alda! The cookies will burn if we leave them on a second longer."

So Alda did as she was told. Then she ate the cookies and forgot her questions. And she was content enough to not ask them again.

Oberon's loud laugh recalled Alda to the present as its sound echoed through the branches above.

She shuddered at the emptiness of its tone. It was not joyful or glad, and the other fairies did not follow his cue. The sound was empty and hollow, like the forced smile in so many sepia photographs.

Alda realized that she should not be scared of him, that she had seen worse. The witches, and Sycorax. And death. Dreng's death.

But Oberon was different.

If a man — or a fairy king — did not feel, then what was he capable of doing?

She thought back to the smudges of red blood on his fingers when he first entered the glade.

She needed to escape. But how could she get back to the ring of blue flowers? Could she find it again? And if she found it, could she use it to get home?

For a moment, Alda considered if this was a vivid dream. But no, she knew the stuff dreams were made on. This was more.

And she remembered the scream, the fierce cry that forced her from the cottage and led her to the circle of forget-me-nots. Who made that sound?

As more questions formed in her thoughts, questions she could not answer, Alda's gaze fell on the tree across the glade, its trunk covered with many doors, each small and brilliantly painted. Where did they lead?

Alda was too wrapped in her thoughts to notice the King of Shadows approach her from behind, so she jumped when he reached around her shoulder with an offering of food.

"Here, Aldeering. Dine with us. Enjoy this apple."

It was not an apple. The fruit's skin was red and leathery with a nub at the top and, although Alda had never seen one in person, she knew from a stereopticon card of Greece that it was a pomegranate.

"No, thank you."

Oberon's exaggerated smile faded as he cleared his throat. "Your highness."

Alda hesitated before she understood it to be a command to call him, "Your highness." She hoped that he would leave her alone to her thoughts, so she could discover some means of escape, but he instead lowered himself onto the throne behind her.

"Why are you not partaking of our revelries?"

"Prisoners do not revel." Alda raised her hands to show him the ivy that still tightly encircled her wrists.

"Oh, I noticed not." Oberon waved his hand, and the ivy withered and fell.

Without a word, Alda jumped to her feet and started for the fairy tree. If she could open a door and somehow climb through...

But the king likewise rose and grabbed her hands, lifting her off the ground as she struggled and kicked. He laughed and bellowed, "This fighter is little but fierce!"

He chuckled again as he steadied her by the shoulders. "I understand your apprehension, Aldeering. That you have fears and unasked questions. I will answer in a while. In time."

Alda relaxed, despite herself. She hoped that if there was indeed danger, it was not immediate. She could wait, for now.

"Music!" Oberon commanded. Somewhere above, notes like wind through reeds echoed through the leaves, and the unsmiling fairies mechanically moved and swayed haphazardly.

The King of Shadows grabbed her wrist and waist and forced her into an irregular waltz. There was no way to break free, but Alda had his ear. So she decided to learn what she could.

"Did you say this is a funeral feast?" She paused and added, "Your highness?"

"My late wife lost her beloved little Indian boy."

Alda was silent for a moment as she considered what to say. "What do you mean? What is an Indian boy?"

"A lad from that land, of course."

Alda was silent, wondering about the fairy queen, before she guessed, "I am sorry that your queen is dead, your highness."

Oberon laughed unexpectedly. "No, not of that fate, but she is former. First and former and current. So she is late. And she is still a queen, but not a queen of mine."

Alda stumbled, "I do not understand."

His smile widened, revealing teeth stained red with pomegranate juice. "We are at war, her and I. What a wonderful time for you to fall into our world!"

"But war is terrible."

"It is a folly, really, simply a folly."

Alda considered for a moment and ventured a question. "Are you not afraid of death?"

"I do not fear the impossible!"

"So you cannot die." Alda spoke this more to herself than to Oberon.

Alda glanced back at the tree as the king continued to twirl her to the strange music.

"Why did you kill the Indian boy?" Alda knew that her question may offend, so she quickly added, "Your highness?"

The King of Shadows stopped dancing, and the music suddenly fell into an eerie silence. Oberon held firm to Alda's waist and squeezed her

right hand in his as he whispered, "He was not *mine*, so I murdered him."
The king laughed heartily, and Alda shivered at his tone. "Ask no more
questions, Aldeering." He cleared his throat, and the music resumed.
Other fairies joined him, bending their arms and legs in awkward jerks to
the sounds. "Be joyful!"

Alda wondered why the king had revealed so much to her. Was it
because murder was so commonplace that it was not worthy of being a
secret? Or was it because Alda herself was so unimportant that her
knowing it posed no danger?

Or was it something else entirely?

She bit her lip, worrying, as her legs moved mechanically and her
ears did not fully hear the music. It suddenly became louder, and she
realized it was familiar.

Yes, she remembered. It was the same tune that her grandmother
sang, so many years before, as she picked wildflowers above the ledges.
*Loolla, loolla, lalla, never harm nor spell nor charm come near my little
Alda.*

As she sang the words in her head, she happened to glance at her
fingers, still grasped by the king.

Her nails seemed to glow slightly green.

But she assured herself it was simply a trick of the light filtering
through the leaves.

Chapter Four: Love's Wound

The sun had started to rise over the sea, and shadows from rocks offshore fell long and dark on the sand as Dreng emerged from the tunnel. Miranda was heavy and unconscious in his arms, and he soon realized in the sunlight that her injuries were worse than he first knew.

Moments earlier, after the cavern had collapsed, he had found himself trapped, his legs under a pile of debris. He worked desperately to free himself and reach Miranda's side and listened, fearfully, as he cleared the stones that had crushed his wife. A breath, shallow. Then another.

She lived.

But now, Dreng was helpless. He laid her on the sand and tore open her bodice. Purple blood pooled beneath her pale skin. Her breaths were irregular, her lips becoming the taupe-blue of seafoam. Blood trickled from her left ear, and her head drooped as he lifted her in his aching arms.

What should he do? He had no way to help her, here on the beach.

And he thought of Caliban, of his mysterious cave on the far side of the island, and how Miranda had been resurrected there from near death.

But Caliban was no longer in the cave. He was in the palace, Miranda's guest, brooding and lurking in the shadowy corridors and verbally jabbing Dreng whenever they crossed paths.

Dreng hated him. But he loved Miranda. Yes, Dreng assured himself. He did love Miranda, still. Despite her secrets and distrust. Despite his selfishness.

And even if there was no love, even if that had been lost in the words they slung at one another, he had caused this, the cavern's collapse and Miranda's injury. He should have left when she commanded.

He had to set this right.

Dreng looked warily up at the cliffs toward the palace and hoisted his wife in his arms. She was heavy. No, he realized, he was weak. So he took a deep breath and pushed on.

But his burden slowed his progress.

Finally, when he reached the base of the palace's hill, Dreng saw a deformed figure limp across a lighted window in the library.

Even in the dawning hour, Caliban was awake.

As Dreng started his final ascent up the rocky hill, carefully watching his feet pick their way through the thick grass, he heard the palace door open and a series of uneven footsteps quickly approach.

"Boy, where have you been?" The footsteps stopped suddenly as the crooked man saw the motionless figure in Dreng's arms. "What did *you* do to her?"

Dreng did not answer. Instead he lowered Miranda's form onto a mossy rise. He cradled her neck as Caliban loomed closer.

Caliban studied her for a moment, his eyes lingering for too long on the thin fabric beneath her bodice. "Is her body — is she dead?"

"Dead? No. But we must get her to the cave, where you saved her before." Dreng paused and added with uncertainty, "Somehow." The cave was many hours' journey, through the forest and across the island.

"No." The man hesitated. "There is another way." Caliban reached his angular arm down and tried to touch Miranda's cheek, but Dreng pushed him away. Caliban studied his face and sneered, "She should return to Netherfeld."

The place where she had disappeared, six months before. And when she returned, she had an army of spirits.

"No," Dreng said as firmly as he could. "Miranda told me not to go through the spring."

"Let *her* go. There is nothing for that woman on this island. Her body is brittle. Send her to the other realm, where she is a queen, and she may heal and live."

Dreng had questions, but he had not time to ask. "If she must go to Netherfeld, I will go with her."

Caliban scoffed, "If you insist on dying, sod-wit, at least give me the pleasure of killing you."

Dreng frowned and considered. Could he trust this man — no, this thing — who so openly loved his wife?

The crooked man persisted, "She is too weak, boy. She will not survive the journey to my cave." He continued to stare at Dreng. "The spring will take her to Netherfeld, safely." He paused and added, "It is the only way."

Without saying a word, Dreng awkwardly hoisted his wife's immobile form and led his companion to the waters that could save her.

Despite its powers, the spring itself did not look magical. It was a muddy hole in the ground with clear liquid bubbling and mixing with the soil into a puddle the size of a barrel.

Dreng struggled to ease Miranda onto the exposed dirt next to it, and he propped her awkwardly against his leg as he reached into the spring and cupped water into his hand. He held it to her lips, but she did not move. He poured it into her mouth; it trickled down her cheek.

"You may bring a horse to water, but you cannot make it drink against its will." Caliban laughed, and Dreng flinched at the unexpected sound, splattering the water onto the grass.

"What do you suggest, most gallant leader?" Dreng meant to speak with Caliban's sarcastic tone, but his voice cracked as he knelt beside his fallen wife.

Without a word, the malformed man pulled a stick from his shirt, the same branch from Ariel's tree that he had used to discover the spring.

Dreng thought it had been lost during the fiery storm.

"Why do you have that? It belonged to Miranda."

"No, it belonged to Sycorax, my mother. It came from *her* tree where *she* trapped that intolerable harpy, Ariel. So it is *my* rightful inheritance. Like this island," he mumbled the final phrase, but Dreng heard it clearly enough.

Caliban held the stick in his uneven fingers and twisted his arm awkwardly. Sparks sputtered into the air as mud cleared from the surface of the spring, and it grew to the size of a coffin, its smooth surface reflecting the brightening morning sky like a mirror. "Put her in."

Dreng shook his head.

"I said to put her in, you rag!" Caliban's eyes flashed in anger. "If you want Miranda to live, place her in the water!"

Dreng thought back to when Miranda had seemingly died, before. How Caliban led them to the cave. How he felt when she opened her perfect, blue eyes.

"I want Miranda to live. More than you know. Trust me, boy."

Dreng could not trust Caliban, but he also knew what it was like to not be trusted.

So grunting with effort, Dreng lowered Miranda's body into the water. The surface seemed to envelope her as he held her face above its surface.

"Release her."

Dreng hesitated and glared at Caliban.

He did not want to simply abandon her into the control of some magic he did not understand. He wanted to fight, to punch and grapple. To slash with a blade. He wanted to be able to do something to save his wife, to relieve the guilt he felt for her injuries. To undo the fury of his words in the cavern.

But he was helpless. He released her. Her body slipped below and flashed a brief, blue light.

Then the water froze, suddenly and completely.

Miranda was trapped.

Dreng tried to break through, but the ice was too solid and thick. His knuckles bled as he pounded the surface. "What have you done?"

Caliban had already started to limp away. He spoke without turning, "Your wife is in Netherfeld. Only her shell is here, preserved. And I finally see an end to this nightmare."

Dreng raced to his side and caught his shoulder, stopping him, and tried to form words, something about betrayal. But coherent thoughts evaded him, so when he could not speak, he swung.

Yet Dreng's fist only whisked through the air as Caliban ducked aside and returned the blow. Dreng felt the air pushed from his lungs as he fell back and struck a rock, scraping his back as he connected with the ground.

"Do not underestimate me, boy." Caliban stood over him, his foot on Dreng's aching chest and the stick pointed at his throat. "That is the last time you will fight me, if you want to see your wife again."

Dreng closed his eyes in defeat, and he heard Caliban's footsteps depart.

Dreng coughed, "Where are you going?"

"A storm is brewing. I must prepare for my journey." More footsteps, and then silence.

Dreng remained on the ground where he had fallen, his eyes pressed tight, wishing the earth would simply swallow him. That he could escape the place of his sorrows.

When he finally looked to the sky, he saw that even the clouds above darkened with his thoughts, his guilt for his wife's injuries. Her loss and potential death.

He pushed himself up uncomfortably and watched the coming storm and, finally, resolved to action: he knew he could find a way to save Miranda.

Among the books of Prospero's library, the books that he could read and others could not, there must be something to free her from the icy tomb. To heal her.

And as Dreng reached this resolution, the clouds parted as if attuned to his thoughts. A ray of light broke forth, and a beam illuminated an object hidden in the vegetation. Dreng stretched toward it and reached into the light.

Miranda's wedding ring. The signet of Prince Hamlet, given to Dreng so many years ago in the dark hold of *The Tempest*. It must have slipped from her hand, when...

Dreng steadied his breath and slid it onto his finger, fighting back tears as he felt wholly lost and abandoned. And under the weight of a thousand regrets, Dreng forced himself to stand.

He had not worn Prince Hamlet's signet ring for six months, since he had placed it on Miranda's dainty finger during their marriage rite. Now, it felt tight and foreign, its surface unnaturally cold.

And, for a moment, he thought that it glowed.

But the sky had darkened with the coming storm, so the metal's glint was merely an illusion.

He gazed at Miranda's frozen form for several heartbeats more, until thunder reminded him to return to the palace and its library.

Dreng knew of thunder, lightning, and of rain. He had survived them all, but some had left their mark. His scar ached whenever storms approached, and he realized it had not rained since the torrent with the red spirits. As he ascended the hill toward the palace, following Caliban's crooked footsteps, droplets began to fall.

Dreng wiped water from his eyes and stole one final glance over his shoulder, toward his wife's resting place. Movement caught his eye. A sudden flash of shimmering gray, a smell like lit gunpowder, and an ominous figure with ragged features and a grizzled beard.

The ghost of his father, standing — no, hovering — near the frozen spring. It stared at Dreng, as it had in his dreams, its mouth moving and voiceless. Dreng closed the space between them, and the figure met his eyes.

"Find her," it croaked. "Find the —"

"No!" The rain was heavy now, soaking Dreng's clothes through. He was cold and miserable, and his patience was gone.

The ghost continued, seemingly unhearing, "— witch. Seek revenge. Free me." Dreng wished that this, too, was only a dream. But there was too much misery here, now, to be simply imagination.

Dreng looked again at Miranda's frozen form and spat angrily, "My wife is in an icy grave —" the word stuck in his throat, but he pushed on. "Don't speak of witches or yourself. Tell me how to save *her*."

The spectre flickered, losing focus and then regaining substance. It did not speak, and Dreng could not wait. "Answer me! How do I save her?"

Nothing.

"Have I offended you, shadow? Or are you mute?"

The spirit seemed to blink in and out of existence before it answered, "The changeling, beyond the tree, can save her."

Dreng again wiped the rain from his eyes as he whispered, "What does that mean?" Did it speak of Ariel? But the harpy had been *in* the enchanted tree in the distant past, not beyond it. And no one had seen

Ariel since the fiery storm.

"Darkness comes, with ship-wracking storm and direful thunder." The ghost vanished.

Dreng was alone amid the rocks and grasses, pummeled by wind and rain. His wife was frozen, insensible and in a sleep of death, and the only other man — no, thing — that Dreng knew in this world was preparing for his own journey.

So Dreng scrambled up the hill to the palace as best he could, slipping on the grasses and stumbling over rocks. He had to find the answer, the meaning of the ghost's riddle. And he could only rely on himself.

As Dreng finally reached the palace, panting for breath, he felt his heart pounding beneath the signet ring and his clothes dripping with each step. He rounded the corner toward the library and saw Caliban stalking down the hall into the shadows, his form obscured by the blue cloak he so often wore.

Dreng ignored him and tried the library's heavy door. Within, he hoped, were answers, some kind of spell to save his wife.

But it was locked.

When he had left in the middle of the night, the door was open.

Caliban. Dreng rushed toward him and demanded, "What have you done?"

Caliban stopped, lowered his head, and said, "Nothing."

"Why did you bolt the library?" Dreng circled around him until they were face to face.

"Bolt? I walk slowly." As Caliban spoke, he shifted a canvas sack in his arms.

"What are you doing?" Dreng reached for the bag.

Caliban turned away and held it to his chest. "Saving my life."

"From what?"

"Death."

Dreng suppressed his frustration. "What *thing* will bring death?"

Caliban looked longingly toward the door at the end of the corridor, the door that was closest to the sea, and whispered, "What happened to her?"

Dreng realized that in his desperation, he had not told Caliban of the cavern's collapse.

So he recounted the events that led to Miranda's injury. But not the images that came to life when he touched the wall. Those, he felt, were too personal to share.

Caliban considered, shifting his parcel awkwardly in his uneven arms. His eyes focused on something far away. "Then it *is* dying."

"What is?"

Again, Caliban looked toward the door. He was quiet for several heartbeats but finally sighed and relented, "She told me weeks ago that the magic was waning. That spells that were once simple are now impossible. That the magic of this place is dying."

"Why did Miranda tell *you*?"

Caliban shook his head and stood up straighter, and Dreng realized for the first time that they were nearly the same height. "That is why she was in the cavern. To find a way to save what was left of the magic."

"How? With a portal to Netherfeld?"

Caliban looked away. "That woman is a mystery."

Dreng realized, "If she was trying to save the island, then that's why she would not leave."

"But I most certainly will."

Caliban turned away, and Dreng grabbed his arm. "Help me save her."

"How?" The crooked man's tone was clearly dismissive.

"You said —"

"I am leaving this cursed place, churl. Do not stand in my way." Caliban shook him off his sleeve and awkwardly spilled some apples from his sack.

Dreng took them and held firm as Caliban tried to snatch them from his fist. "Where are you going?"

"To sea."

"And then?"

"To land."

"To what end?"

"Death."

"You aim to die?" Dreng was confused.

"That is the end of us all."

Caliban again reached for the apples, but Dreng held them out of reach and laughed, despite himself. Caliban's equivocation seemed familiar, somehow. But Dreng would not give way. "Stay, and help me save Miranda. We can look in the library —"

Caliban snorted, "Books are only words. We need deeds to match."

"And magic," Dreng corrected

Caliban snatched the apples back. "You know little of magic."

Dreng crossed his arms and asked condescendingly, "If you know all, then what must we do?"

"Leave." Caliban raised his disproportionate eyebrows.

"Do you even have a ship?"

"Yes."

Dreng was skeptical. "Can you sail it?"

"Yes." Caliban lowered his head as he shifted the parcel in his arms. "But I need your help."

"And where will *we* go?" Dreng could not prevent the sarcastic tone from seeping into his words.

"The back door to Netherfeld."

"But you said it —"

"The path through the spring to Netherfeld is too dangerous, but there is another way to reach that realm. To help Miranda return to her body." Caliban studied his eyes and, for the first time, seemed sincere. "Help *me* save her."

Dreng uncrossed his arms and ran his fingers nervously through his hair. "This other entrance, how do you know it?"

"My mother told me. I can find it, I assure you." Caliban smiled slightly and added, "I am an honest man."

Dreng was still uncertain. "Where is it, this way into Netherfeld?"

"Through a tree."

Dreng's heart dropped. "A tree?"

"Yes, the Duke's Tree. It has a portal that leads, in a roundabout way, to Netherfeld."

Dreng's mind raced. The ghost. The changeling. Is this what the spectre had meant?

Caliban persisted, "It is a day's journey, at the most."

After a moment's hesitation, Dreng consented, "But we cannot leave in the storm."

"This storm will not pass. It is the magic of the island, what's left of it, unleashed. We must sail through it." Caliban paused and added, "Within a week, there may not be an island, without her. She must save it."

Caliban set his jaw and stared at Dreng. After a moment, he turned and made his way to the door.

Dreng stood in the darkening corridor and thought about the storm that brought down *The Tempest.*

And the storm on *The Tyger*, so many years before, that had killed his father.

Chapter Five: The Rude Sea

Alda felt her eyes open. Had she drifted off? Or had she been awake and lost in thought?

As her eyes adjusted, she scanned the scene around her. The king's festivities had lasted into the night, or at least until a time of longer shadows. She watched the fairies, their rejoicing: Oberon jovial and overstated, the lesser beings awkward, their faces joyless, but she still perceived them to be merry.

She felt her eyes close again. Did they close, or did only her mind sleep?

She was tired, exhausted. She had danced for hours, it seemed, and eaten nothing in — how long? Days?

How long had she been here?

Alda only wanted to get home. The cauldron's bubble, Dreng, everything that she had cared about before entering the fairy world and all that had happened six months ago — all that was immaterial now. She only wanted to return to her cottage, to relative safety, to what she knew.

Here, nothing was familiar. All was out of joint. Unknown.

But, Alda reminded herself, this was not the first time she had been lost in the woods.

Alda felt her mind wander again, to her past. As a young child, she often awoke with the sun, snuck away, and explored the muddy banks of Sandstone Creek, looking for crayfish and petosky stones. One particularly wet morning, she had discovered a morel mushroom near the woodline. Then she had found another. And another. And a whole path of them that led deeper and deeper into the dense forest between the creek and the rolling hills beyond the ledges.

But within minutes, she was lost. And the sky darkened with a coming storm, the kind that turned day into sudden night and threatened to cause mudslides on the Ledge Path and flood her grandmother's island.

So Alda ran. She had no direction, but she had speed.

And then she fell. It was not far, but when she opened her eyes, she was surrounded by blackness.

So she screamed. Yet no one came. After some time, she climbed, and the walls around her crumbled.

It was a coal mine, a chute dug by some town-dweller to gather fuel for winter.

When Alda finally emerged from the coal pit, the rain had stopped. She was covered in blackness and scrapes and bruises. But she was safe, and she realized as she calmed that she knew the way back to the river.

At the safety of her island's familiar bank, she washed herself in the icy waters. She later told her grandmother about the mushrooms, but she never mentioned the coal mine.

That was the first time Alda had overcome danger without her grandmother.

And now, sitting in the court of the King of Shadows, she knew she had to persevere alone. No one would help her.

She also knew she had to keep her wits. Fear would invite more danger.

So she sat on the toadstool and watched Oberon. The hollow music had stopped, and the king conversed with a male fairy with exceptionally green skin. The pair glanced at her occasionally: the green fairy only blinked profusely, and Oberon erupted in a wide, toothy grin that sent a shiver down Alda's spine.

In her unease, Alda turned her gaze to the fairy tree. Was it a means to escape? It was close, yes, but it was also dangerous in its uncertainty. Where would a door take her, if she could even pass through?

Perhaps it would be better to explore the woods until she found the blue ring of flowers. Surely that would take her back home.

She hoped.

But to escape, she needed to leave the glade unnoticed. She was watched too closely now. Guarded by all the fairies who stared and whispered since her dance with Oberon. And they were armed. She would need some distraction, some chance to sneak away unseen and unheard.

So as she waited for an opportunity, Alda studied the green pigment that had spread from her fingers to her elbows. It had no scent, no texture, no change in sensation. It was as if her skin was simply transforming into a new shade.

And it was expanding. As she watched, the color creeped nearly to her shoulders.

Would it continue to spread, covering her entire body?

What would happen, she wondered, if she changed colors completely?

But Alda's reverie was interrupted by a commotion at the edge of the glade.

Robin Goodfellow had disappeared some time before, so Alda had expected his return and was not surprised to see him.

Yet she was startled to see him with a young woman, who shrieked with a familiar scream. The sound that had summoned Alda from the safety of her cottage.

Who was this woman?

Although the newcomer was pale green, her features were less angular than the other fairies of Oberon's court. She appeared to be only some years older than Alda with hair that faded from silver to deep black. Her arms and legs were human-like in proportion and shape, her face contorted in fear.

Upon their approach, Oberon quickly took his place on the throne.

"I have discovered your lost Phillida, the girl who tried to make herself a ghost." Robin pulled on the ivy around her wrists as he spoke, bringing the young woman to her knees before the king.

"Lost?" Oberon repeated.

"I was not lost!" The young woman stood and twisted against her bonds. "It is the solstice, and I was trying to get home!"

Oberon placed his hand forcefully on her shoulder, and she seemed to calm. "You are home, now, and safe." He turned to another fairy and bellowed, "Fetch me the nectar!"

At the word, Phillida fought more. "No, let me go!" She kicked and lifted herself off the ground as two other fairies held her arms by the elbows. A third brought a purple flower, shaped like a chalice, and held it to her lips.

First Phillida spat the liquid, so Robin held her head. Then she bit her lips so tightly that red blood trickled out of the corner of her mouth. Robin used his free hand to pry her mouth open.

As the liquid was poured down her throat, Phillida's eyes scanned the glade for help, and they met Alda's.

Alda could not help her, but this was her chance to escape. A distraction. Alda swiftly fled behind Oberon's throne and was soon consumed by thick vegetation.

As Alda retreated into the forest's darkness, the last thing she could hear was Phillida's choking cough.

Soon, Alda could not see beyond her outstretched arms. The environment seemed a reflection of her fears. She was alone and confused, with known dangers behind and unknown dangers ahead.

How would she escape this world?

And her mind wandered to her memory of Netherfeld, the world of darkness. Of the swirling spirits and the green glow on the horizon. Of the time she had forgotten there and what might have happened during those lost years. Of Sycorax and how she seemed to recognize her on the island. Of her grandmother.

And then, in the gloom that enveloped the forest, Alda saw a tree with a fissure near its roots, a little hollow that glowed purple. She stooped toward the luminescent light and listened. A voice. Distant.

Was it her grandmother?

Was it even real?

Alda held her breath. The sound was not repeated, but she reached toward it anyway. Her hand was consumed by the purple light, and she blinked.

There was nothing. Alda still existed, but she was in a void. She felt and sensed and thought, but the world around her had ceased to be.

Rather, the world had changed.

The fairies and the forest and the tree with the purple glow were gone.

She was in Netherfeld, lost in the void.

She was here, now, and alone.

Trapped.

How could she get out without the cauldron's bubble?

And where were the spirits and the distant, glowing kingdom? Where was her grandmother?

So Alda called into the abyss, "Gramma, is that you?"

Nothing.

"Grandmother?" Alda asked more forcefully.

Noise rose, like voices from some distant audience, but it soon fell again to silence. Alda looked around. She focused on what she assumed to be the horizon, but the green dome that had tantalized her six months earlier was nowhere to be seen.

Alda tried again, "Are you here?"

"Yes." A voice, but sweet and young. Not Gramma.

"Who is this?" Alda could not see who spoke.

"Who is this?" Was it an echo? No, the accent was different.

"I am Alda."

There was a pause. Then, quietly, "Miranda."

"Miranda?" Was this the girl from Prospero's island, the girl whose form was taken by Sycorax?

"Yes. Who are you?" The sound was barely audible, and the final word drifted into nothing.

"I am Alda Reeding." She turned in a circle, squinting into the abyss, and asked, "Where are you?"

Silence.

Again, Alda tried, "Miranda, tell me where you are."

Nothing.

"Miranda, let me help you!"

"Alda, the witches are near." The voice was louder and shook with fear.

Alda's skin bristled as a chill enveloped her. She looked over her shoulder as she asked, "What witches?"

But there was nothing. The witches, if near, were invisible, or disembodied. Like the voice.

Miranda continued, "They have taken it."

"Taken what?"

"All of it. All of..." The formless voice trailed off.

Alda strained her eyes against the blackness around her. "Miranda?" She listened, then ran, searching, but saw no change in the lightless environment. She stopped and called again, "Miranda!"

Silence, still.

Alda counted her breaths and steadied her heart. After several moments, she whispered, "Miranda, what happened here? To the green city on the horizon?"

Alda expected no response, but the silence was broken by the sound of a crying child.

As Alda listened to its fearful screams, she wondered about the witches.

What had happened to Netherfeld in her absence?

*   *   *

On the beach, the waves were riotous as they beat against the shore, and the wind drove the rain horizontally against Dreng's face. He did not mind the rain, only the lightning.

It flashed into the distance. If there was sunlight in the sea beyond the storm, Dreng could not see it.

Caliban led the way along the sand, to a tiny inlet protected by the cliffs. There, beneath a thick canvas covering, was the raft that Dreng had started so many months before, the vessel he had hoped to use to take Miranda to sea. To escape the island.

Caliban, it appeared, had attempted to complete it. There were additional ropes and a mast secured with iron nails. The base seemed sturdy, as sturdy as an untested raft could be, and Dreng felt there was at least a chance they could survive the storm and escape the island.

A small chance. But more than none.

They had to try. To save her. To save the island and its magic.

A few moments were spent silently securing their supplies and readying the canvas that would serve as their meager sail. Dreng found two oars he had intended for Miranda and himself and handed one to Caliban.

This was not the journey he had wanted.

With a sigh, Dreng lashed a rope to the raft's floorboards and heaved as Caliban pushed. The surge had brought the sea close to the vessel, so despite tripping and cursing and fumbling, their work was soon rewarded as the unsteady vessel floated in the tidewater.

As Dreng steadied his feet, he again surveyed the sea. Waves. Whitecaps. Spray. Rain. Lightning. He looked to Caliban and saw the man clinging to the mast, unable to balance on the dancing boards beneath his feet.

Dreng found his voice, the tone he had used as boatswain. "Sit!"

Caliban collapsed on his knees, and Dreng handed him a rope. "Tie this to your waist. We must paddle together!" His words were nearly lost in the wind.

And in that moment, beneath his attempts at confidence, Dreng felt only fear and doubt. He was weak, weaker perhaps than he had ever been. Caliban would be little aid, if any. And so much was at stake. His wife, the woman he had promised to protect, had been struck down by his foolhardy actions. By his pride. If not for him, she would still be...

Dreng pushed against the current. Again, and again. The oar struggled with the tide forcing him back to the shore. Caliban did likewise, but the raft faltered. It was not made for this, for battling storms. And neither was its crew.

But Dreng paddled and fought until his arms burned and his fingers clenched in pain. His mind was focused on Miranda. On duty and obligation. On a debt he owed to save her.

Caliban swore oaths constantly beneath his breath but did not yield to the storm. Despite his abhorrence of his companion, Dreng was impressed by the crooked man's resolve.

Lightning flashed with a deafening roar. What had it struck? Dreng could not see amid the spray and fog, but he kept paddling. Stroke, stroke, stroke. Another crash. More light. The feeling of suffocating as the rain pelted his face and mixed with his tears.

For a moment, Dreng thought he should give in to the sound and the fury. That he should relinquish the oar and drift back to the island, where he could collapse at the side of his wife and await destruction. And as he was about to give in to despair, a streak of red lightning flashed.

Within a heartbeat, a boom reverberated.

And then all was still. The rain vanished.

Dreng's clothes were soaked through. His palms bloodied and blistered. His arms tingling from a thousand pinpricks. He sunk onto the boards of the raft and looked up to the clearing sky, more astonished than thankful.

And as Dreng watched the clouds shift to reveal a heavenly shade of blue, he heard Caliban whisper, "We are beyond the bounds of the storm. And alive for now. But there may be worse to come."

It was a miracle that they made it out to sea, past the storm that Dreng could yet see surrounding the island.

Dreng examined the raft's wood, lashed and fastened haphazardly but still secure enough to carry them into this vast expanse. For now, at least.

The vessel was, as the old sailors had said, held together with spit and prayers. Rusted nails and ill-fitting pegs. Only space for five or six men to stand. Only room for two to sleep. Insufficient.

Dreng mended what he could, the frayed ropes and straining boards, and adjusted the tattered canvas on the too short mast. He turned the rudder, hoping to catch a breeze.

He estimated they could stay afloat for a day. Perhaps two. Most certainly not three.

"We will be there soon enough," Caliban whispered as his eyes traced the horizon, seemingly reading Dreng's thoughts.

Dreng only nodded in response as he watched the island and its flashing storm grow smaller in the distance.

He stared at the crooked man for a moment and said, almost to himself, "I know you love her."

Caliban did not meet Dreng's eyes, his mind seemingly elsewhere. "Who?"

"Miranda. I heard you call to her in your sleep, one night in the palace." Caliban did not answer, so Dreng continued, "I heard movement in the corridor, and you were sleepwalking. Rubbing your hands. Sweating. Speaking of some 'damned spot.'"

Caliban still did not respond, so Dreng was blunt, "You do love her, don't you?"

Caliban's eyes narrowed as he finally looked up. Dreng saw his fists clench, the veins on top of his hands pulse.

Dreng persisted, "Do you deny it?"

"The labor of my love was lost." Caliban relaxed and added, in a quieter tone. "That woman is your wife. I am a fool, an empty purse, insignificant."

"Love is like a tree with many branches, many buds. It forever grows, until death." Dreng had heard that somewhere, long ago. He could not remember where, and he did not know why it came to mind now.

"Then I am the axe that fells it." Caliban considered for a moment and asked, "Do *you* love her?"

Dreng hesitated. "Yes."

"You seem uncertain." It was an assertion, not a question.

"I have known two things: the sea and Miranda. When I left one, I joined the other."

"Is that why you claimed that ridiculous moniker? Ferdinand? Because you had left the sea and thought yourself reborn on land?" Caliban laughed.

Dreng avoided his eyes as he explained, "Dreng is not my name. It means 'boy.'"

"How appropriate." Caliban chuckled condescendingly as Dreng scowled and continued, "So you feel like a house divided." Caliban met his eyes, and Dreng set his jaw.

"No, I am now a ghost of my former self, the person I was at sea. Some apparition without purpose. A spirit without a summoner." Dreng reflected on his words and asked, "Is Miranda dead?" He feared the answer and had avoided asking it directly until now.

Caliban looked away again, watching dolphins in the near distance as they skimmed the ocean's surface. "The waters will repair what is broken in her body. But she is splintered. We must reunite her parts."

Dreng was silent.

Caliban continued, his tone condescending. "That is her shell, frozen. Her mind — her soul, if you prefer — is in Netherfeld. The spring's waters took it there. We must go there, through the Duke's Tree, to lead her back." Caliban looked into Dreng's eyes, searching for comprehension.

Dreng thought of the past, half a year earlier, to when Miranda disappeared into the enchanted spring and returned with an army of red spirits. "How does the tree work?"

Caliban was silent for a moment, and he seemed to lose the sharpness that usually permeated his mood. They both sat in silence for several heartbeats before Caliban flatly stated, "It will take us to Fairy Land. Through that world is a passage to Netherfeld." He paused and added, "That is less likely to be fatal."

Dreng laughed. "Fairy Land?"

He had seen madness at sea. The Danish prince, for one, had the semblance of madness. But others had lost their minds, too, and spoken of mermaids and monsters that called them to the depths. These were men who had fallen prey to gambling and drink and worse, men who after years at sea had lost touch with the world around them.

Dreng feared that, if left unchecked on his galleon, *The Tempest,* he could have met a similar fate.

And now, if he remained much longer on this tiny, unworthy vessel, he expected that he would lose his grip on reality. Caliban, it seemed, already had.

What did Dreng really know of Caliban? The crooked man was raised on the island and formerly loved Miranda. Miranda, on the other hand, showed him no love in return. She was demanding and condescending, like a tyrant. But Caliban obliged. He let loose barbed words against her, but he always obeyed. He was her servant.

But Caliban must have been crazed before, to believe that Miranda had ever loved him. How could anyone love a thing so deformed?

This journey, too, was madness.

"You intend to take us to Fairy Land?"

Caliban did not share his humor. "Yes."

"There's no such place."

"There are more things in this world than *you* can possibly dream of." The words sounded vaguely familiar, like a whisper in a dream.

Dreng looked over his shoulder, back toward the island, a sliver on the horizon. The storm still surrounded it. They could not return, not safely.

"But this is a fool's errand," Dreng sighed. He looked directly at Caliban, "And you are the greatest fool."

Caliban stomped toward him, and the raft creaked under his weight. Dreng braced for a punch, but Caliban only shook his finger at him as he yelled, "Do not mock me, boy!"

Another creak as the wood strained, and then a snap. The vessel lurched, and Dreng reached for the mast. Caliban stumbled, lost his balance, and splashed over the side as the plank beneath him snapped.

"Man overboard!" The words were a reflex. Dreng knew no one could hear.

The surface of the water was too reflective to see into its depths, so Dreng reached his hand down over the side and felt. His fingers closed on an arm. He pulled, but Caliban's weight was too much to lift.

No, Dreng thought. He was too weak to pull his companion to safety.

In a split second, he made a decision: he let loose the flailing arm and jumped overboard.

Upon hitting the water, he felt strangely and suddenly awakened. A jolt, like when he had first landed on the island.

He reached out for Caliban's limp form and, treading water, grasped its waist and hoisted it onto the vessel. Dreng took a deep breath, kicked, and lifted himself to safety.

The former boatswain wiped his eyes and looked to the horizon, where he could no longer see the lightning and storm or the distant island.

They were finally, completely, beyond its bounds.

He expected to be exhausted from this excitement and exertion, but he was not. As before, on *The Tempest,* he felt invigorated. The lethargy was lifted. He had strength. And confidence. He was transformed to himself, again.

So he turned to Caliban, who was facing down in a jumble of awkward limbs and wet garments. Dreng knelt at his side, waiting for movement.

The ragged man breathed. Then coughed. And he finally turned and opened his eyes.

But he was not Caliban.

Dreng jumped back, unable to give words to his astonishment.

The other person smiled and stood with some difficulty, his knees buckling and arms reaching to the mast for support.

It was a young man, some few years younger than Dreng. Blonde hair, delicate features, and eyes as blue as Miranda's. As the young man raised himself to his full height, he did not look a monster. More like royalty, a beautiful youth.

Dreng tightened his jaw as he realized the young man was smiling at him with a sarcastic curl. The voice, undoubtedly, was still Caliban's, "Will you believe in Fairy Land now?"

Chapter Six: Tricks in the World

Alda was again enveloped in the silence of Netherfeld. Her pulse quickened. Moments became minutes as she listened for Miranda's voice or some sign of the witches. She began to panic, her breath coming short and swift, her fingers tingling. What had happened to the world she had known? And how would she escape?

Finally, another voice broke her panic: "I am trapped in a memory."

Alda did not know who spoke. It was not Miranda, and it was not her grandmother. The words were soft, feminine, confused but without fear. They seemed to float, as did everything else in Netherfeld, and Alda had no way to know if they were nearby or distant.

Even Alda herself was somehow less solid, like a figure in a fog. Everything else was like a curtain of black velvet.

Perhaps this was a different part of Netherfeld, a place far from the spirits and all she had seen before.

"I know that you're here." The voice again. Was it closer, or simply louder?

Alda was silent, waiting.

"Hamlet, is that you?"

Another pause, then, "No, he is dead and gone."

The voice was behind her, close. Alda turned and saw a walking shadow that became more solid and detailed as it approached. A young woman, nearly the same age as Alda, with sunken features and a furrowed brow. Her skin almost gray, her eyes bright blue, her gown a heavy brocade. Her hair the red of a flaming sunrise with shades of orange and crimson.

The shadow stopped. "Are you real?" The thoughts were Alda's, but the voice was the other's.

"Yes."

"Who are you?"

Again, she introduced herself, "Alda. Alda Reeding. I am from a place called Grand Ledge, and I —" Alda was surprised at her openness, at her trust in this stranger. She was silent for a heartbeat as she considered, before adding. "I am not a witch."

The young woman shifted a bundle in her arms and looked at her curiously. She opened her mouth several times before she replied, "I am Ophelia, daughter of Polonius. Of the Danes' royal court at Elsinore. I am also —" She paused awkwardly. "Not a witch."

Ophelia raised her chin as she spoke, and Alda felt as if she was being measured by her companion's gaze. Alda, likewise, stared back.

An infant's cry pierced the silence. In the nothing of Netherfeld, the sound floated into the echoless distance.

Ophelia patted the bundle, and the crying ceased. "Are you lost?" Alda nodded.

Ophelia lowered her voice, "Come with me."

Alda walked, or had the sensation of walking, yet the inky curtain of her surroundings did not change. She wanted to ask questions, but it felt somehow dangerous in this place of darkness. This was not the Netherfeld she had left so many months before. This place felt primitive, like the deep winters she remembered in her childhood, before electric lights.

She wondered, as her ears rang in the silence, if this was in fact an older Netherfeld. This place existed between place and time, so was there still chronology here? Or did multiple times exist simultaneously?

Perhaps, she thought, she returned to Netherfeld at an earlier time than her last visit.

Or, perhaps, something terrible had happened here and undone the green city that she had apparently built in the time before she remembered.

Alda counted her steps as she followed Ophelia and, as she reached two hundred, she saw yellow in the distance. Candlelight. The light grew and became a room, a kind of setting on a stage with three walls and an open fourth.

It was an elegant bedchamber, with golden candelabras and fine oil paintings of seascapes and a bed with curtains.

Alda entered the room and tried to touch a tapestry, but her fingers passed through it. Ophelia came to her side and also ran her fingers through the curtains, through the walls.

"It is like a candle's flame. Flickering and intangible." The young woman with the fire-red hair unwrapped the child and propped it against her collarbone. Its face was swollen and streaked with tears. It stirred, and Ophelia paced and hummed to ease its whimpers.

Alda's mind raced with questions. "Why is this room here?"

"It is from my memories."

"How?"

"I don't know, exactly." Ophelia paused and said, "I had hoped you understood and could tell me."

But Alda was equally confused and shook her head.

Again, she studied Ophelia. The baby calmed, and Alda felt herself staring at the infant, its lips forming tiny bubbles as its wide eyes traced the room's extravagant features.

Ophelia guessed Alda's question and said, "He is real, not a memory. I did not have him... before."

Alda waited for her to continue. When it was clear she would not, Alda ventured, "Before what?"

"Before I arrived." Ophelia paused and added, "He was born here."

Alda started to ask how that was possible but reconsidered. She tried to hide her shock with a question, "What is his name?"

"Hamnet."

Alda studied the baby's face. She had never before seen someone so young, so fragile. This child did not belong here, in this place of darkness.

She had to find a way to get him out. To get them all out. All three.

As Alda looked up, she saw Ophelia eyeing her with a worried look. "How did *you* get here?"

Alda noticed a slight accent. Where was Elsinore? But she did not want to pry about a stranger's past, so she answered simply, "Through a place that — I think was Fairy Land."

Ophelia suppressed a laugh. "Fairies? Fairies, no of course." Her tone became serious. She spoke to herself, her eyes unfocused over Alda's shoulder. "No, no, that is right. There are witches, so... Fairies, yes. Perhaps mermaids, too?" She chuckled, and little Hamnet sighed, yawned, and stretched his arm above his head before sinking into a calm sleep.

Despite herself, Alda smiled at the thought of mermaids. "How did you find this place?"

"I drowned." Ophelia lifted the baby and kissed his head again, as if reassuring herself. "I was gathering flowers near a stream and fell in. The water was beautiful and fragrant." As Ophelia spoke, various blooms appeared around them, brighter than the bedchamber and hovering in midair: pansies and thistles and columbine and others that Alda did not recognize.

Ophelia continued as if the flowers were not there, "When I was in the stream, I felt safe, and I remembered —" She smiled, and the flowers pulsated with light. "Then I realized I was sinking, and I swam. I was no longer in the stream but in a nightmare." The flowers turned to lights, like the spirits on Prospero's island, and darted around the flickering bedchamber. "So I stopped swimming. And I was happy, for a moment. And then I was here. With this nightmare." The floating lights sparked out.

"I know a stream like this. It is called the Stream of Consciousness, and it takes you to your fondest memory, but then —"

Alda could not continue. Two shadowy figures entered the bedchamber, like two actors coming onstage from the wings.

Ophelia glanced at the figures and then back at Alda. "I held them back as long as I could, but they keep reentering." Ophelia stepped away and turned her back.

Alda instinctively stood between the mother and the two figures, offering what little protection she could. One shadow was a young man, handsome but with darting and distressed eyes, dressed in fine black satin trimmed with furs. The other was a young woman, similarly dressed but in brighter colors. With long, red hair. They looked like something out of an Arthurian legend.

Yes, Alda decided, this second figure was Ophelia, but less sullen and younger. No, not younger, less strained. The two shadows interacted, their mouths moving, but they did not speak. They were mute, a mimed show of anger and anguish, finally both yelling, crying, tearing their hair and wringing their hands.

Alda turned to the real Ophelia. "What is this?"

"My worst memory. The beginning of the end."

Alda watched again as the two players finally embraced. Then they disappeared in a stream of smoke, like an extinguished candle. The bedchamber remained.

Alda struggled with her questions. She felt like a peeping Tom, staring into the private parts of a stranger's mind. "How does this —"

Her tongue caught on the word *exist.*

Could anything truly exist in Netherfeld?

"How does this work?"

Ophelia sighed and shifted her child in her thin arms. "At first, it was so solid. So immediate and present. I was there again, with my Hamlet, begging him not to venture down the path of revenge. To escape Elsinore with me. I could hear my pleas, 'No, leave them. Let me save you. Let me save you!' Then I forgot my exact words. And his. So there was sound with no form. After Hamnet was born, I forgot his father's voice, so Hamlet was silent. I was silent, too. There were no more words, only this poor play, this stage."

She looked around, into the darkness and back to the candlelight. "All this world's a stage, and we are the players. We can build here with our minds, but it is no more real than some pantomime."

To demonstrate, Ophelia lifted up her free hand. A butterfly flitted down from somewhere above and landed on her palm. She watched it for several breaths before she crushed it in a fist. When she opened her hand again, the butterfly was gone.

"Dust. And I am trapped in it." She wiped a tear from her cheek and sighed as she looked at her child, "No, *we* are trapped."

Alda thought of her last time here, six months before, when she met her grandmother and saw the green fortress in the distance. *You built it,* her grandmother had said. But Alda did not remember how. That had happened in the years she had lost, forgotten.

So Alda did her best to be sincere as she clasped Ophelia's free hand and squeezed it reassuringly. "There is a way out. I know there is. We will find it, together." She forced a smile and added, "Let me save you."

*   *   *

For at least thirty minutes, Caliban stared at his reflection in the smooth water. The raft continued away from the island, toward a flat and distant horizon that Caliban insisted was the proper direction.

Dreng felt more confident now, more at ease in his own skin. He was comfortable in the silence, too, as he watched dolphins leap in the near distance.

But Caliban, with his new appearance, was disarming, so Dreng did his best to ignore him.

Finally, Caliban turned and grinned at Dreng. His smile was unnerving. Beautiful, but full of malice and spite. "I love an honest surprise."

"I do not."

Caliban ignored him and continued, with clasped hands, "I had thought my former state, my transformation, was permanent. If I had known earlier, well, I never would have stayed on that accursed island."

Dreng glanced at Caliban and asked skeptically, "You think you could have escaped alone?"

"You underestimate the depths of my despair. I was more wretched internally than externally. For I was once, as I am again, beautiful. No, divine." Caliban added, to himself, "The curse is broken."

"What curse?"

"Did you not feel it, *friend*? Do you not feel stronger now? Lighter? Like an albatross was lifted from your neck? The island changes men. You had a curse, too." Caliban smiled, "Well, curs*es*." He laughed and continued, "It appears that once we were beyond the island, once it was out of our sight, we returned to ourselves. Me, this." He motioned to his body. "And you," he studied Dreng, "less incapable."

Dreng frowned and turned away. Caliban was seeking an argument, and he would not respond to his bait. So Dreng withstood his rage.

The beautiful youth leaned against the mast, an entitled easiness to his posture, and continued, "There is more to me than you know. I, like you, loved Miranda from the moment I saw her. But my love was real, not some deus ex machina. We were raised together. We played chess and laughed and learned." He glared at Dreng, who returned his look of disdain. "I knew that she loved me, too, so I tried to take her away from Prospero. The old man objected, as always, and made me look as I did with one of his deplorable spells. She, in turn, forgot that she had ever loved me. But she'll remember again, when I save her."

"You forget yourself. She's my wife." Dreng stepped toward him.

Caliban laughed. "There's the rub. It's a conundrum, you see. Your Miranda is not *my* Miranda. They are two but seen as one. *Your* Miranda, she —"

The boat lurched, and Dreng was glad of the interruption, the end of Caliban's nonsense.

But then the raft stopped altogether.

All was still. No wind. No waves. No movement. The two young men exchanged a glance. Caliban's eyes were full of fear, but Dreng felt only curiosity.

How could a vessel, even one so small, stop completely and suddenly?

Then a hand grabbed the side of the raft, a feminine hand with long, green fingernails and iridescent skin that shimmered like a flying fish.

Dreng started to reach toward the hand, but Caliban blocked his way. He whispered, his voice breaking, "Sea-maids."

Dreng pushed him aside and looked into the water. The fish-hand shot upward and grabbed the hem of his shirt. Ripped. He lost his footing and started to stumble over, but Caliban held his shoulder and pulled him back to safety.

"Mind yourself, boy." Dreng did not like being called a boy, especially by someone some years his younger.

"Boy," a feminine voice echoed.

"Boy!" Another, sweet and sultry.

"Come into the water with us, boy."

"We will show you our secrets."

"Our secret places."

"*All* our secrets."

The voices were sing-song, melodious. They echoed from the water's surface. Calming, peaceful. Dreng was enchanted and tried to return to the edge.

Caliban held him back and whispered, "Be like Odysseus and lash yourself to the mast if you cannot withstand their temptations. They are water witches. Do not trust them."

"Come, boy!"

Dreng wrapped his arms around the mast behind him and held tight to his own wrists, distrusting his instincts.

"Come with us!" More hands grabbed the edge of the boat.

"We will take you both."

Caliban called, loudly, "You are all too wet for me. I think better with a dry head."

As he spoke, the first mermaid hoisted her torso into full view. She looked like a woman in all but her skin, which was covered in small scales that glistened in the sunlight. She smiled kindly as she watched the two young men.

"We can always just pull you down. But would it not be easier for you to jump in?" She blinked flirtatiously, but her eyelids closed from the bottom.

Caliban's voice cracked, "No, we will not!"

"Then we will tear your raft from stem to stern." The voice was still pleasant, masking its threat.

"I demand an exchange. A trade!" Caliban sounded brave again, the fear leaving his words.

The fish-woman smiled. "A trade? Do you know who we are, boy?"

Caliban walked closer to her, boldly. "You are sea-maids, and you have no men of your own. You lure sailors to the depths, ensnare them, and then, when you are finished with them, bite off their —" He paused. "Heads."

Dreng understood his meaning. These creatures were dangerous, and they called him to the depths, somehow.

More scaly hands appeared on the boat, and its boards shook with their strength. Dreng knew it could not hold.

But, inexplicably, he hoped that it would break. That he would fall into the sea and spend eternity there. He wanted to follow them into the depths.

This was their call, the temptation of which Caliban spoke. He shook his head, trying to clear his mind.

The sea-maid blinked again. "Why are you not scared of us?"

"Because I am Caliban, rightful heir of the island formerly ruled by Prospero. Son of the powerful summoner Sycorax and betrothed to Miranda." He added, "The late Miranda."

Dreng started at the word *late*, but bit his lip and did not move from the mast.

Caliban continued, "I am owed a crown from my father and will be king, and all will know my name."

The mermaid laughed, and her mirth was shared by the unseen others surrounding the raft. The sound was eerily loud. "We can see lies, boy. Tell us the truth."

"Alright. I am the son of a madman and a nun. Born in a world without life and light and raised on a rock by a slave. I have lived much of my life cursed with a face that was not mine, possessing nothing of value and too little knowledge. I hate questions and impudence and, especially, sea-maids." Caliban drew in a deep breath. "Is that enough truth?"

Other sea-maidens peered over the side of the raft, their eyes burning like dozens of sunbeams. Dreng, feeling their lure and fearful of their powers, closed his eyes and focused on Miranda. He had to save her.

But as he thought, his mind shifted to Alda. For a moment, his heart seemed to stop as he yearned for her.

He closed his eyes tighter, cleared his mind, and listened.

A sea-maid's voice cooed, "You demand a trade but claim to have nothing of value." She was taunting.

"Nothing of value to *me*," Caliban laughed. The sound was awkward, forced.

"Then what have you?"

"This." Dreng, despite his curiosity, kept his eyes closed. He feared what he might do if he opened them, if the sea-maids took him.

"But we will have that regardless. When we destroy your raft."

"Yes, but you can have *it* without my wrath." Caliban lowered his voice. "You do not know my powers."

Silence. Dreng felt his heart pound against his chest, his eyes still closed. His breath came quickly as the sea-maids whispered around him.

Finally, the feminine voice whispered, "We agree to your terms. My sisters will allow *you* to go free and will only take your companion."

Dreng opened his eyes at the word *companion*.

He realized that he, himself, was the barter.

And suddenly he no longer wanted to join the maidens in the deep. He stepped away from the mast, searching for an escape, but there was none. The sea-maids had surrounded them.

Before he could return to the center of the planks, fish-scaled hands encircled his thighs and pulled him to the edge of the vessel. He could not break their grip. He was trapped. Helpless.

An idea flashed through his mind. If they would trade with Caliban, then —

"Wait, I want to trade!" He struggled to reach the mast again, but it was too far, so he braced his hands against the floorboards and leaned back with all of his strength. "I have a ring, a magical signet ring." The hands eased, so he continued, embellishing, "It can grant wishes —" They pulled again, not believing him. Caliban only watched, not lifting a finger in his defense. "No, no. That's a lie. I don't know if it's magical, but it may be. I've seen my father's ghost when I wear it. It was given to me by a prince. A Danish prince named Hamlet. Just let us both live, please, and the ring is yours."

The hands released him, and he fell onto the deck-boards.

"We will accept your trade."

"No!" Caliban leapt between Dreng and the sea-maid. Dreng struggled to get around him, to give the ring to the fish-woman. Caliban pushed him back. As Dreng stepped forward, he felt the force of a fist on his cheek.

The blow was weak; Caliban's new form had not known such violence. The beautiful youth bent over his hand and rubbed his bleeding knuckles.

Dreng again reached toward the sea-maid, the signet ring in his outstretched hand, but once more Caliban stepped between them.

"Take this instead!" Caliban threw something small and thin.

Dreng heard a splash, and the mermaid fell back into the sea, her tail lapping the water as she swam toward the item. The others released their hold on the raft and followed her, their voices sending incoherent shrieks into the wind.

The ship resumed movement, and both men sat in silence. In a moment, all appeared as it had been before.

Dreng, still shocked, asked, "Why did they retreat?"

Caliban rubbed his bleeding knuckles and muttered, "I threw them a stick."

"What?"

He stood and overly enunciated, "The stick, the stick, you cankerblossom. The magical thing from Ariel's tree that is our only protection against the coming dangers."

"Why did you give it to them?"

"To stop you from —"

"But you were going to give me to them?" Dreng was horrified by Caliban's betrayal. On The Tempest, this would have been mutiny. Punishable by death.

"I changed my mind. Man is a giddy thing." Caliban was silent for a heartbeat and added, "Surely you must understand. After all, you are a pirate."

"I am not a pirate."

"And I am not a prince." Caliban wiped sweat off his forehead and, in doing so, smeared blood from his knuckles across his brow. "But I only tried to trade you before."

"Before what?"

"Before I knew of the ring. I suspected, yes, yet —"

Dreng nervously replaced it on his finger.

Caliban leaned forward, his eyes a familiar kind of wild. "Tell me about Prince Hamlet."

Chapter Seven: Jaws of Darkness

Alda realized that she had never fully appreciated the phrase "in the dark." Now, after walking for what felt like days, she had no sense of time or place and was no closer to finding her way out of Netherfeld.

Before, she assumed that she had left with the aid of her cauldron's bubble but had no memory of how she escaped. Then, her grandmother had forced her out, back to the witches on the moor. Now, without such assistance, Alda was unsure of her next step.

And her mind kept returning to Miranda's warning of the witches.

"Are we closer to our escape?" Ophelia's optimistic voice broke her thoughts. Alda had been careful to suppress her own fears, for the sake of the infant Hamnet and his mother.

"I think so." Alda was not certain if this was a lie, but she hoped it was not.

"But you know this place?" Again, hope.

"I have been here before."

"What do you call this realm?"

"Netherfeld." Alda said it with a finality that she hoped would prevent further questions. She did not want Ophelia to lose faith.

The red-haired woman whispered, "Like a field of nothing."

Alda did not respond.

"How will we get out?" Ophelia's question echoed her thoughts, but Alda could not respond because she was uncertain of the answer. She imagined she was retracing her steps toward the tree with the purple fissure that could lead them back to the world of fairies, but all she could see was black. Without a landmark, she had to rely on her internal sense of direction.

But did this place even have direction?

Alda could sense Ophelia's increasing tension. Baby Hamnet slept in his mother's arms, and the silence between the two young women was only broken by his sighs.

"How do you know about witches?" Alda finally asked, trying to divert her companion's attention.

"Witches?" Ophelia looked over her shoulder, as if checking to see if they were being followed. "I know that people say witches do not exist." The young woman's voice rose at the end, almost questioningly.

"Then why did you say that you are not a witch?"

"Why did *you* say that?"

Alda did not respond. She continued walking, taking time to choose her words. Unable to think of a better explanation, she blurted, "I think my grandmother was a witch."

She expected Ophelia to laugh, but she asked seriously, "What was she like?"

"Kind. But overprotective. And secretive."

"At least she was kind." Ophelia adjusted Hamnet in her arms. "My father was only overprotective and secretive. But, he was not a witch." A pause. "Can men be witches?"

Alda thought of Prospero and his summoned spirits. Of Sycorax's son, Caliban. "I don't know."

Silence again.

Ophelia finally confessed, "I met witches."

Alda exhaled and admitted, "I did, too."

"How did you find them?"

"A cauldron's bubble."

"What is that?"

"A small orb that allows one to travel between times, between places."

"Can we use it now, to leave here?" Ophelia's voice betrayed her hope.

"No. It no longer works." Alda paused and added, "But I think I used it here, once before."

They walked in silence before Ophelia ventured, "Where else did you make this cauldron bubble take you?"

"Cauldron's bubble," Alda corrected her. "I could not control it. It took me —" She stopped, realizing she was out of breath. "Many places."

Ophelia stood at her side, waiting in the silence for her to continue. Alda instead sunk to the ground as her pulse raced, feeling her throat close with tears, but she only coughed as her eyes remained dry. It felt like a weight pressing on her chest, the force of her worries strangling her heart.

Alda was lost. She knew she was lost, and Ophelia knew they were lost, and they were going to be trapped in this place of nothing forever. Alda was helpless.

And in this helplessness, Alda's mind turned to despair. She always tried not to think about Dreng, about the boy she might have loved. No, might have known, at least. That would have been enough. The boy whose path she crossed so frequently but so infrequently, too.

The boy she could not save.

As she thought about him, or rather tried not to think about him, she heard something stir behind her. Ophelia looked at it first, and she did not move.

Alda followed Ophelia's eyes and turned and saw him. Dreng. Standing as she had seen him in the courtyard of Prospero's palace, bewildered.

"Dreng!" She started to stand, but Ophelia put her hand on her shoulder and squeezed gently, reassuringly.

"It is one of the walking shadows. Like my Hamlet. Your mind's creation."

Alda brushed away her hand and struggled to her feet. "Can I talk to him?"

"Yes." Ophelia frowned. "And no. It is not real, simply some kind of memory. An illusion."

Alda approached Dreng with caution and asked suspiciously, "Who are you?"

"Alda, is that you?" His voice sounded as she remembered.

"If you are Dreng, truly, you know that it is."

"I thought you were —" He moved closer to her, but she backed away.

"No." She hesitated and added, more to herself, "You're dead."

"I'm not." He smiled, "I thought you were dead."

"If you're not dead," Alda hoped, "then where are you?"

"Alda, stop." Ophelia again put her hand on her shoulder, more forcefully. "Don't do this to yourself."

He continued, as if not hearing her, "I searched for you on the island for days, but..." His voice started to fade, as did his form.

"Dreng, where are you?"

A look of realization crossed his face. "Is this a dream?"

"Where are you!?!"

He grew silent, and his figure turned darker as his eyes flashed with confusion. He was a blur now, an image in a faded photograph. Alda realized that Ophelia was right; he was one of the walking shadows. Alda gasped, "What do I do?"

"Forget him. Do not think of him, and he will not reappear." Alda closed her eyes and inhaled deeply. When she opened them again, Dreng's shadow was gone.

She finally wiped the tears from her cheeks, the tears that she had tried so hard not to shed. Once she was certain that her voice was steady, she asked, "Why do you not forget about Hamlet, make him vanish?"

"That scene is my penance. To relive it is my punishment."

"For what?"

Ophelia pressed the baby to her collarbone, took Alda's arm, and whispered, "Lead me, and I will tell you what I know about the witches."

Alda took some minutes to decide which way to go, finally setting on a direction that had — she was not sure how to describe it — some kind of magnetism. Then Alda led the way slowly, and Ophelia walked beside her through the void, silent for some time.

Or, at least it felt like some time. Alda was aware that time was not measurable here, not like seconds on a pocket-watch, but the silence seemed to last for too long.

Finally, Ophelia drew a deep breath and spoke in a trembling tone.

"I knew my Hamlet loved me, despite everything." Ophelia's voice was quiet in the darkness, barely audible over their slow footsteps. "He told me of the supposed ghost and suspected murder. Of his plan to feign madness. To seek revenge. He asked, so I played my part for him: the pure and innocent lover. I let him insult me in front of them — my father and his uncle — for show. To trick the court and convince them all his madness was real. I was part performer and part audience, at once."

She stopped walking and added, "But none of that is important now. Not since he was taken and I —" Amorphous lights formed around her head, like a halo, and Ophelia stopped abruptly.

Alda watched the glowing lights intently. They grew, stretching upward like the aurora borealis that she saw one winter, rising above the Grand River.

Although Alda had questions, she knew this story was not for her.

This was Ophelia making sense of her past. Her private, secret past. So Alda let her continue.

"I have to be vague about this time with Hamlet, you see, or else the memories will come alive. And this, this scene, no, this act is not for you to see. For anyone to see."

Ophelia's voice raised in pitch but not volume as she continued, "I knew, at the end, that my Hamlet needed help. His feigned madness became too real, and my father — I feared Hamlet would not be able to overcome whatever transpired. He no longer wanted my assistance, but I resolved to help him, in spite of his reluctance." The lights intensified, so Ophelia stopped again, steadied her breath, and continued, "I had heard, earlier, from some traveling players — actors — that there were witches in the wood, three old women who offered spells and potions. For a price."

Ophelia shut her eyes. Lights appeared around them. Trees grew. As she remembered, the story came to life before them in shadows and silhouettes. Still dark and nebulous, but full of inarticulate sound and fury.

"I found the witches that night, and they gave me a potion to end Hamlet's madness." Her eyes finally met Alda's. "I would have done anything to save him. I would now, as well. But it was toil, useless toil. And then, ultimately, the toil was for nothing, when Hamlet — So it felt doubled again."

Ophelia steadied her breath, opened her eyes, and whispered, "It is double, double toil, to fight to save someone who cannot be saved." She lowered her head and added, "Someone who does not know you are trying to save him."

Her words were muddled, but Alda understood their meaning: the frustration of seeking to save one so beyond redemption. Beyond hope.

Ophelia shifted her child and squeezed her eyes closed, fighting back tears. The silhouettes from her memories took form, and then became clear beings with features and faces.

Three old, bearded women appeared.

Alda recognized them immediately: the weird sisters from the moor, the ones who had sent her to Prospero's island and had tried to erase her memory. As Alda watched, they interacted with a shadow of Ophelia.

"The witches offered me something to help my love, to save Hamlet. In exchange for this potion, they asked for the fruit of a secret, hidden seed. I did not know what they meant, but still I agreed." The scene dissipated as Ophelia sighed and wiped her face with her free hand. "I did not know that they spoke in metaphors and that I was with child. I would never have agreed —" She patted the sleeping babe's back and continued as another scene appeared.

"But when I returned, my father had been killed, and Hamlet sent away to England. I heard whispers that he was to be executed there. I was alone. So I returned to the witches." Again, the scene transformed before them as Ophelia described her memories. "They saw my grief and offered me a place in their circle. I could join them, their coven." Ophelia choked on a sob and continued, "And, then, at that moment in time, in that instant, it was a fine temptation. I could have power like theirs. Be free from the court, from the gaze of others. Finally make my own way in the world."

Her voice cracked. She cleared her throat and continued, "I agreed, and I think I went mad for a time because I only remember —" The scene burst in a cloud of smoke. "Flowers." These appeared around her, floating above her head like a wreath. "The witches sent me to fetch herbs and flowers. So I did. And the last flower that I needed grew above a stream."

A new scene appeared: a shallow stream like the Stream of Consciousness, luminescent and inviting. Ophelia's shadow figure hung precariously on an outstretched willow branch, stretching higher to reach a blue flower. The figure fell, and the image abruptly disappeared. "As I told you, I drowned and am now here."

Alda considered the story as they stood in silence for several heartbeats.

"Have you met anyone —" Alda corrected herself "— any *thing* here?"

"Not until you." Again, her voice raised at the end, questioningly.

"Have you tried to escape?" It came out like an accusation. Alda felt bold here in Netherfeld, somehow. Like she belonged. Like she could command. Or break free.

Ophelia spoke slowly, obviously embarrassed, "I thought this was the afterlife. Heaven or hell or something not yet dreamt of. But then Hamnet was born, and I wondered if..." Ophelia let her voice trail off as she kissed her infant's head.

"How was Hamnet born here?" Alda immediately regretted her probing question and its implied disbelief, so she avoided the other woman's eyes.

After a moment of awkward silence, Alda continued walking, and Ophelia followed. Was she certain this was the way back to the tree that led to the fairy realm? It did not seem so far before.

"How do you know about this place, Alda?"

Alda continued walking as she spoke, "The witches, mostly, and a raven."

"A raven?"

"It could speak. And, and I spent several years here, some time ago."

"What did you do here?"

"I don't know."

"Why not?"

"I don't remember, not entirely. You lose memories of this place when you leave. At least sometimes, you forget."

"If I leave here, will I, too, forget?" Ophelia's voice shook on the final word.

Alda lowered her head but continued on. "I don't know."

"If you have forgotten, then how do you know that you were ever here?"

"I aged, and I met someone who had — had known me." Alda barely spoke this above a whisper, like some secret she was scared to tell.

"Whom did you meet?"

After seeing Dreng, Alda was careful not to let the past overtake her mind. Elsewhere, her memories were safe. Here, they were a threat. Alda was hesitant to speak of Sycorax, so she pretended not to hear.

But Ophelia persisted, louder, "Who?" Baby Hamnet awoke with a squeal, and Alda stopped walking.

"Should you feed him?"

"No, he does not eat. He fusses because he is scared."

"How does he live without food?"

Ophelia hesitated for a moment before she answered, "I don't know." She bit her lip and added, "I don't know if he truly lives."

Alda tried to hide her uncertainty, her fear, so she nodded and walked confidently in the direction that pulled her.

Ophelia trotted up to reach her side. "Who had known you?" The young woman was persistent to a fault.

Alda did her best to answer vaguely, to keep the walking shadows at bay. "A woman named Sycorax. She was a powerful summoner, a kind of sorceress, who tried to kill me on an enchanted island, outside of

Netherfeld. She had so many powers," Alda could hear something like respect in her tone. No, not respect, fear. She lowered her voice and continued, "But she killed — she murdered the boy whom you saw, who appeared earlier."

Ophelia waited for a moment, apparently giving Alda a chance to elaborate, before she asked, "What was this summoner, Sycorax, like?"

"Terrifying."

The infant nuzzled against Ophelia's collarbone and sighed. She stroked his fine hair and whispered, "Sometimes, I wish I had been more terrifying. Then I might have saved Hamlet."

Alda confessed, "Sometimes, I wish the same."

Ophelia continued, almost to herself, "She may be like the devil, but the devil holds power."

They walked farther as Alda let her thoughts turn to Sycorax.

When the two had met in the island's palazzo, it was clear that Sycorax knew her. And then Sycorax attempted to kill her — But was that true? Sycorax had murdered Prospero — Alda had seen his body — and he was apparently a more powerful sorcerer. Yet somehow Alda had escaped from her.

It was too easy. Perhaps it was a trick.

Alda felt her jaw ache and unclenched her teeth as she continued to walk at Ophelia's side into the endless nothing.

Chapter Eight: Whips and Scorns of Time

Dreng did not know he had nodded off. But he awoke with a start, his eyes searching toward the darkening horizon. The words *where are you?* were ringing in his ears, and he did not know why.

The sea was still and smooth. No land was in sight, and darkness would soon be complete and comfortless.

Caliban was still sulking in a corner of the raft, as he had since Dreng told him all he knew of Prince Hamlet, the prisoner who had taught him to read and abandoned him bleeding in the hold of *The Tempest*.

But Caliban refused to reveal the reason for his curiosity about the Danish prince.

Or his sudden interest in the signet ring.

Despite his shipmate's persistent ill temper, Dreng felt revived from his nap. Uplifted. He broke the silence with a simple, "Thank you."

Caliban did not turn as he spat, "For what?"

Dreng considered what he had meant, "For making the sea-maids leave."

"I will always regret it. That tiny branch from Ariel's tree was worth more than a thousand of you." Caliban again lapsed into silence.

Dreng still had a question, "Which story was true?"

"Story?"

"You said you were both a prince and the son of a madman. Which was true?"

"Doubt truth to be a liar."

"What?"

"It's part of a rhyme. No, not simply a rhyme, a kind of riddle that my mother used to recite: 'Doubt thou, the stars are fire, doubt that the sun doth move, doubt truth to be a liar, but never doubt I love.'"

Dreng was silent for a moment as he considered. "It's beautiful."

"It's nonsense."

"Why?" Dreng frowned and, before Caliban could respond, he added, "Whoever wrote it loved someone."

"No. It's archaic, old. The meanings have changed." Caliban was silent for a moment before he continued, "'Doubt' was not always simply 'disbelieve.' When this was composed, 'doubt' could also mean 'suspect' or 'tentatively believe.'" Caliban sighed, "Nothing is ever as simple as it seems."

Dreng narrowed his eyes suspiciously, so Caliban explained, with a condescending tone, "The riddle is in the rhyme's wordplay. Alternately, the final line could be, 'Never *suspect* I love.'"

Dreng thought, for a split second, that the rhyme seemed strangely familiar. Where had he heard it?

Caliban continued, "So does the poet confess his love, or express that it is uncertain?"

"Or he does not believe in truth." Dreng paused and asked, "What do you think it means?"

"I am, by nature, uncertain," Caliban said, turning toward him with a sneer.

"Are you never serious?"

"Mostly sometimes." The beautiful youth furrowed his eyebrows and did his best to look solemn.

Dreng laughed, despite his frustration and despite their situation. There was more to Caliban than he could understand, but one question above all others needed to be asked.

Dreng knew that Caliban loved his wife. So his laugh faded as he worried aloud, "Will you steal Miranda?"

The phrasing felt strange because Dreng knew that "stealing" implied ownership, and no one owned Miranda. Yet he did not know how to better express his fears.

Caliban grew melancholy and stared at the horizon. Dreng studied his face and clarified, "I mean, will you take her from me?"

Dreng was still not entirely certain if he loved his wife, not completely. Not after their words in the cavern. But he was loyal. If she survived her time in the frozen spring, if he could save her, he would never leave her, not willingly. And in the past, he had trusted that she would not choose anyone, especially Caliban, over him.

But now, after Caliban's transformation...

"Six months ago, when I saw her on the beach — with you — Miranda and I had not spoken in years. Not since I was..." Caliban took a deep breath, "Changed. And in those years, I thought I wanted a bride. Not her, just someone. Anyone. A companion. A stranger, even." He stared at Dreng and lowered his voice, "I did not want to be alone." He sighed, "But in these recent months — seeing her with you —" He paused, his voice slightly higher. "Have you ever felt that there is one person in the world made for you, some soul that was written to intertwine with yours, that calls to you?"

Dreng nodded, his thoughts involuntarily turning to Alda.

Caliban continued, without looking at Dreng, "If Miranda is that — for me — then I will find her, and she will return to me. Willingly." He gazed directly at Dreng, his blue eyes pleading. "Will you let her?"

Dreng knew he had no power over Miranda. He was helpless in her will, a ship on her tide. "Miranda will always do as she pleases." Dreng's tone dropped. "If we can save her." He looked down at his hands, considered, and asked, "Did you see a girl on the island, when Miranda and I —" He did not want to refer to their marriage rite. So instead, he finished, "After the red storm?

"I saw many things." Caliban was silent for a moment and looked away, studying the horizon. Several moments passed in silence before Caliban shouted, "Land!"

Dreng followed his gaze. On the horizon, silhouetted by the setting sun, was a mountainous sliver.

They both forgot their conversation as they watched the brave new world grow against the sky.

Within minutes, Dreng could discern the coast: smooth and grassy, like waves of green. Beyond the dunes and meadows, Dreng could see trees.

But he had little time to admire the scene. The waves were much smaller than those near Prospero's island, but their raft was a shambles now. The pressure of the storm and burden of the sea-maids had worn the vessel to splinters held with broken twine.

Dreng knew that they had to reach the shore. Soon. And, he knew, they would not be able to return to sea. At least not on this raft.

They would be the land's prisoners.

Caliban's face revealed a similar concern as he studied the coastline.

"What is this country?"

"We are near Athens." Caliban smiled as he spoke, as if the word inspired some happy memory.

Dreng ventured, "How did you find this place?"

"Luck."

"Luck is not my friend."

"Nor you mine."

Dreng glared at his companion. "How will we find the tree, the Duke's Tree?"

"We simply will."

"How?"

"I have a will, so there's a way."

"Determination is not a guide."

"Would you feel better if I said I had been here before?" Caliban sneered at Dreng, who frowned.

"Do not lie."

"I would never!" Caliban lowered his tone and added, "I want Miranda more than you. We will find her. Even without the blasted stick that you made me sacrifice to the sea."

"You are a fool," Dreng mumbled as he continued to avoid Caliban's stare and instead watched the waves, measuring the distance to the shore.

"I am an absolute knave."

Dreng ignored him. After a moment's reflection, he narrowed his eyes at Caliban. "Can you swim?"

Caliban studied his limbs, as if seeing them for the first time, "If I must, but I am out of practice."

Dreng pushed him overboard. When Caliban's head breached the surface, Dreng dove in and swam toward the low, seagrass-covered dunes that lined the beach.

The current was stronger than Dreng had expected. Its power was deceptive, and he pulled himself toward shore with all that he had.

When Dreng reached the sand some minutes later, exhausted and dripping, he scanned the whitecaps until he saw Caliban bobbing beyond the bar, more moved by the waves than by his own merit. But not in real danger.

As Dreng watched him, his mind returned to the last time he had washed ashore, when *The Tempest* sank and he was alone.

When he had first beheld Miranda.

Dreng shook his head, clearing his thoughts. He felt star-crossed, like fate was working its machinations against him, forever taking those he could not protect.

Like his father, his crew.

Like Alda.

Caliban's coughs broke his reverie. The blonde youth had finally reached shore, hunched over and vomiting sea water.

"Are you tired, friend?" Dreng was aware his words had taken on the sarcastic air of his companion.

"I feel like Caligula, fighting Neptune."

Dreng did not understand this reference, but he gleaned its meaning. "Were you victorious?"

"Always." Caliban coughed again, gagging.

It occurred to Dreng that the youth may have never tasted sea waves. "How do you feel?"

"My stomach is not constant, but all will be well in a moment."

"Then let's find our way to your magical tree."

Caliban straightened up, lost his balance, stumbled over his feet, and fell onto the sand. He did not try to stand. "I suspect *you* are too tired. We should wait until morning."

"I?" Dreng laughed. "It's barely dusk. You're all talk and no action."

"I suit my words to the action." Caliban's banter seemed familiar, but again Dreng could not place it.

"But words are not deeds," Dreng retorted, proud of his wit.

"You speak nonsense." With that, Caliban reclined, propped his head on his arms, and closed his eyes.

"No more than you."

Caliban did not respond. Soon, he snored.

Night was quickly upon them, but Dreng could not sleep, not in the open, exposed in an unfamiliar territory.

So he explored. He walked easily across the sand and counted fifty paces in all directions. No sign of danger. Or habitation. Or life of any kind. The birds were all a-roost, but the night animals had not yet awoken.

It was the time between sunset and moonlight when life was suspended.

As Dreng stood overlooking the beach with the trees at his back, he returned to his thoughts.

He had barely spoken to Caliban in the six months he had spent on the island. The crooked man, although seemingly always underfoot in the palace, had been perpetually sulky and silent. Distant. Dreng had attributed it to jealousy; it was no secret that Caliban had once been betrothed to Miranda.

But was it actually melancholy instead? Did Caliban harbor real, human feelings? Regret, even? Remorse?

Is that why he hid his true meanings behind sarcasm and equivocation?

Equivocation. Suddenly, Dreng realized why Caliban's conversation seemed familiar.

It was Hamlet.

Of course. Caliban's tone. His sudden interest in the ring. Even the young man's transformed appearance.

The Danish prince and the fair youth shared some connection, somehow.

Dreng half considered waking him immediately, to ask some penetrating question and perhaps surprise him into being honest.

But Dreng's questions could wait. Miranda could not. He needed

Caliban now, to reach the tree and save his wife. Confrontation could happen later. This pettiness, after all, was insignificant.

He twirled the signet ring on his finger as he resolved to focus on finding Miranda.

As he finally reclined on the cold sand, he wondered briefly if Miranda was worth it. She had been, after all, less than kind. But, no. He pushed the thoughts aside. He had done this to her. And she was his wife. That was sacred, unbreakable. He could worry about Caliban and Hamlet later. And his father's ghost. And the witches and the changeling and all of that. Now, he needed to rest, to sleep.

*   *   *

"What should we do?" Ophelia spoke with a whisper as she stared into the vast expanse of nothing before them. She nervously shifted sleeping Hamnet in her arms.

They had walked for hours, days. Or only minutes? Alda had no sense of time. She was disoriented. And confused. And, she admitted, frightened, as well as completely and utterly and hopelessly lost. Without a way out.

"I wish my grandmother was here."

"The witch?"

Alda nodded. Then an idea struck suddenly, an idea so perfectly possible that Alda was surprised it had not come to her sooner.

"The scenes you build here are memories, correct?"

Ophelia nodded.

"But I could interact with Dreng?"

"If the memories are strong enough, you can alter them. Speak with the shadows. I did, at first, with Hamlet, before he faded."

"And you can ask them questions?"

Again, Ophelia nodded. "Yes. But the shadows' answers are your memories. You can learn nothing new, nothing you did not already know."

"Yet if I cannot remember some part of my past, but the memory is still there, trapped in my mind, then..." Alda smiled. She envisioned her cottage, a fire blazing in the hearth, a glow from the oil lamps illuminating the kitchen, the bundles of herbs and the worn books lining crooked shelves and the fading, yellow wallpaper peeling around the windows.

She saw it in her mind, and then she saw it before her.

Ophelia turned away, leaving Alda with her memories.

At first her grandmother was a silhouette, black against the tapestry armchair, poking the fire into an eruption of sparks. Then she took form. A younger version of the woman who was buried last winter. The Gramma of Alda's childhood.

Alda clenched her fists and stepped into the scene. Her grandmother rose and faced her, smiling and clasping her hands on her laughing belly.

"Alda, you have grown! I remember when you were no higher than my knee."

Alda smiled, but it faded quickly. "I remember that, too." She paused, considering what to ask. A way to safety, a route out of Netherfeld, was pressing, but first Alda needed to know: "Gramma, who am I?"

"You are my granddaughter."

"Yes, of course, but *what* am I?"

"You already know."

"Am I a witch?"

The walking shadow smiled, her eyes blank.

"Am I more?"

The figure tilted her head questioningly and, again, smiled.

"Gramma, what am I?" Alda's voice rose and echoed into the distance.

Ophelia turned toward her and whispered, "If you do not know, then she cannot know."

Of course. So Alda continued, "What did I do, before, in Netherfeld?"

"You fought a queen."

"Sycorax?"

Her grandmother's shadow nodded. "And built a kingdom."

"A kingdom?" The city with the turrets, the green glow on the horizon.

"Where is it now?"

The shadow lowered her voice, "It is yet to come."

So Alda was in Netherfeld's past. "And where is Sycorax, now?"

"She is here."

"Here?" Alda glanced around, her nerves suddenly on edge. "How can we escape? How can we leave Netherfeld?"

"Remember the tree —"

"Remember?"

The shadow smiled knowingly.

Alda realized, "Then it will be created. But will it work if it is only the stuff of memories? Will it take us back to the world of the fairies?"

Her grandmother's shadow was silent.

Alda considered for a moment if that was truly where she wanted to return, so she persisted, "Is there a way to reach Grand Ledge, to get home from here?"

Again, silence.

And as Alda's thoughts returned to the distant seventh island, she knew she needed another answer. "Who were my parents?"

Ophelia whispered, "If you do not know, then —"

But the scene before her changed. Spring sunlight poured through the cottage's windows. The fire disappeared. Flames glowed within the black iron stove, and Gramma stood over it minding orange sponge cookies.

A shadow of Alda, not yet as tall as the older woman's waist, appeared at her side.

"On my real birthday, what did —" Alda's voice was high, innocent.

This was the memory of Alda's fifth birthday. Why did it appear?

"Fetch the breadboard, Alda! The cookies will burn if we leave them on a second longer."

The shadow of Alda did as she was told. And Alda, the real Alda, remembered what happened next: she ate the cookies and forgot her questions. And then she was content enough to not ask about her past again.

But this time was different. Her grandmother's shadow turned toward the child, and smiled, "You were born in a world far away. A forest with magic and magical beings and..." Her voice trailed off.

"Is this only a story, Gramma?" Little Alda asked.

Her grandmother laughed, "It is a fairytale, but it is real. There was a war there, where you were born, so your mother brought you here."

"Where is my mother now?"

"She is in the other world."

"When will she come back?"

"I don't know."

"What is she like?"

A pause.

"The cookies are cool enough to eat now, Alda." The small shadow of Alda took a bite, and smiled, and then laughed. The child wiped her eyes as if she had just woken from a nap and asked, "Can we get a puppy?"

The two shadows in the cottage suddenly vanished, and Alda turned, wide eyed, to Ophelia. "I do not remember that. Was it real?"

Ophelia shrugged and kissed Hamnet's head. "It was true."

"What is the difference?"

"Truth is not always real. Doubt truth to be a liar." Ophelia smiled to herself, as if remembering some half-told joke.

"What?"

Ophelia met her eyes and explained, "It is one of life's riddles. We may say something that seems true without knowing it is a lie." She paused and added, "Or we may say something true that is perceived to be false."

Alda considered this, "If we can't even trust ourselves, or our memories, then what can we believe?"

Ophelia was silent. Alda realized that her companion was carefully considering her answer, so she was silent as well.

After a moment, Ophelia said, "To thine own self be true." She laughed slightly and added, "My father and brother used to tell me that. Frequently. We must believe in ourselves, be honest with ourselves." Her smile faded as she added, "They did not live by their advice."

Alda nodded. "My grandmother used to say, 'Know thyself.' But she never told me who I was. About my mother. Anything." Alda added, "I think she made me forget."

"Perhaps she wanted you to learn for yourself." Ophelia moved closer to her and said, "Or she was trying to protect you."

"From what?"

"The past."

Silence.

And then Alda heard it. A rumbling, like thunder, distant and foreboding.

Ophelia looked at her, her eyes wide.

Alda stammered, "Is — is that a storm?"

"It does not rain in Netherfeld."

Before Alda could respond, a bony hand grabbed her wrist. Its nails dug into her skin and held firmly as she struggled to break free.

"No!" Ophelia shrieked, and Alda saw two cloaked figures reach toward the young mother and child. Ophelia fell to the ground, shielding her baby from their menacing holds.

These were the strange women from the moor, the weyward sisters.

"Time is come," Decima cackled.

"For you to come," Morta added.

"To make time," Nona finished.

Alda fought against her oppressor, but the grip only tightened as the being reached to ensnare her other wrist. As the thing took hold of Alda's free hand, a burst of light and a wave of heat flashed over her.

Alda squinted against the powerful beams. Through her lashes, she could see red lights — like those Sycorax loosed on the island — stream from Ophelia's outstretched hand.

For a split second, Alda thought she saw Sycorax, surrounded by her army of lights. But she blinked, and it was still Ophelia, her face sweet and serene, yet powerful.

The young woman stood, her babe cradled in one hand and the spirits shooting from her other palm, as the three attackers fell to the ground under their force.

Ophelia calmly held the witches in place with her spirits as she commanded, "Alda, think of the tree! Create it!"

Alda rubbed the scratches on her wrist and closed her eyes, envisioning the tree and its purple fissure. When she opened them, it stood before her, shining in the red lights.

"Ophelia, go into the fissure! I will follow."

Ophelia shook her head. "I must stay here until you are safely through."

Alda looked at the witches, covering their heads with the folds of their robes, crumbling beneath the strength of Ophelia's red lights. Would Ophelia be able to escape once she released them?

Alda wondered if Ophelia truly wanted to escape.

"Follow me," Alda pleaded.

"I will."

"Promise me!"

"Trust me."

Alda took one last, desperate look at the mother and her child, the witches on the ground before them, and the vast darkness of Netherfeld before she placed her hand within the tree's fissure and vanished.

Within a heartbeat, Alda was back in the realm of fairies. All was vibrant green and blue and oppressingly fragrant.

Desperately, Alda turned back to the tree.

But it was gone.

Rather, it did not exist.

It was real in Netherfeld because it was of her memory. But her memory could not manifest itself here.

And when she left and took her memories, did the tree also vanish in Netherfeld?

Alda's breath came quickly, gasping in the perfume of the thousand flowers. Sweat pooled on her forehead, and she wiped it from her brow.

She had no way to return, to save Ophelia and Hamnet.

And Ophelia, trapped on the other side, had no way to escape.

Chapter Nine: Lack of Wit

When Dreng awoke on the beach the next morning, he felt like he was missing something.

After a few moments of reflection, he realized that the something was most likely Miranda.

He had never been on land without her. And now, on this new and foreign shore, he had no ally. He had no confidant. No one to trust.

Caliban, his only companion, was more likely an enemy.

And this unknown land seemed itself a threat.

In the morning light, the nearby forest felt alive, its trees staring menacingly. Dreng quickly jostled Caliban awake, ready to begin the quest for the Duke's Tree, but it took several moments for the beautiful youth to finally acknowledge Dreng's anxious concern.

"You quiver at nothing, boy."

"I know danger." Dreng frowned. "More than you."

"Then you do not know me." With that, he turned away.

Dreng paced impatiently as Caliban further delayed entering the woods. The youth stretched and spit and wandered along the waves, kicking the foam and muttering under his breath.

After what felt like hours, Caliban reached into the surf and retrieved his blue cloak, washed toward shore during the night. He wrung it, waved its heavy folds in the wind, and fastened it around his neck. Finally, he turned to the trees and, without speaking, strode confidently between their trunks.

Dreng followed warily, glancing over his shoulder at every snapping branch or rustling leaf. The thick, ancient canopy above obscured the sun, and they walked in a twilight of shimmering blue and shadows.

Dreng's senses were on edge from their encounter with the sea-maids. Again, he wished he had a sword.

After some time and no apparent progress toward their goal, Dreng considered asking Caliban how he knew the way to the Duke's Tree. But he decided he would rather have silence than an intricate, nonsensical explanation of Caliban's navigational strategy.

Finally, after Dreng had decided that they were completely lost, the pair arrived at a road that showed signs of recent travel: wheel tracks, footprints, and the hooves of some foreign animal.

Caliban silently motioned that they should follow the road to the south. Dreng was hungry, and short-tempered, and impatient, but he kept thinking that each step brought him one step closer to finding Miranda. So he trudged on.

And then he heard voices. Deep voices, and merry. For a brief moment, Dreng imagined he was back on *The Tempest* with his crew, celebrating after some fortunate adventure.

Caliban stopped abruptly, and Dreng nearly walked into him. The beautiful youth held his finger to his lips as he led Dreng to a thick-growing bush spotted with white flowers. Dreng followed his companion's motions and peered through the branches into an open glade where four men held papers and spoke in awkward, forced rhymes.

Beyond them was a tree, an ancient oak with a trunk several cannon-lengths across and limbs so heavy that they were held aloft with haphazard planks. In the center of the tree was a crack, a triangular hole that led into purple-hued darkness.

This, Dreng surmised, was the Duke's Tree. The oak that would lead to Fairy Land.

But the four men stood in their way. Dreng studied them: they wore clothes no finer than that of common sailors, and their hands and faces were stained and dirty. They were laborers or mechanics. Or worse.

Each had a sword at his waist.

"They might be bandits," Dreng whispered. "We should circle back and reach the tree from behind."

Caliban shook his head, "These are not criminals. But stay a moment. It may be a trap."

"A trap?" Dreng looked anxiously over his shoulder.

"Fairies are mischievous. We'll watch for a moment and then —"

A terrible cry shattered the peace of the forest. Dreng leaped aside and looked for an enemy. Caliban turned pale.

Foliage shivered across the road behind them, and a strange animal sauntered into the open, its mouth full of sunflowers.

"What kind of horse —" Dreng backed away.

"It is an ass, you fool! A donkey," Caliban hissed and returned his attention to the men in the glade as Dreng continued to stare at the beast.

It met his gaze, swallowed, and brayed again. Dreng had never seen such strange a creature. "Why does it make that noise? Is it ill?"

"Quiet, or we will be discovered," Caliban hissed.

But it was too late. The four men had stopped talking, and Dreng turned in time to see them part the bush.

Dreng clenched his fists, ready to fight, but Caliban stepped between him and the gang and flashed a winning smile. "Gentlemen, we have found you!" The beautiful youth glanced back at Dreng and mouthed, *smile.*

Dreng did not smile. He shook his head and planted his feet, his mind focused on combat, heightening his senses.

Caliban continued, "I am the great Prince Hamnet of Denmark, and this is —" He cast a sly look at Dreng "—my lowly servant from the wilds of India." Dreng scowled at him, but Caliban continued, "I have heard of your miraculous feats of exhibitionism and wish you to perform at my court in Elsinore."

The four men smiled at one another, and the shortest, who appeared to be their leader, stepped forward. "I am honored but in no way surprised that word has spread of our greatness, your majesty. We are great, as you can see. Skilled and great, your highness."

"And eloquent," Caliban suggested.

"Yes, great and elegant. Thank you, sir." The short man bowed deeply and stood upright with some difficulty. He swirled his hands extravagantly, and all four bowed in unison.

Dreng stood speechless. Who were these men, and what was Caliban's aim?

Caliban waved his hands in a flourish, and the quartet stood upright and looked at one another awkwardly. Then Caliban turned to the short man and demanded, with an air of regality, "What is your name, *great sir?*"

"I am Nick Bottom, your highness."

"Will you show us a scene?"

"We are not yet rehearsed, your highness."

"Well, what is your part?"

"We are still assigning roles, your highness. It is a new work, sir, your highness, a most lamentable comedy about a playwright who is stabbed to death in a bar fight. We lack a man to play a wall. We always need a wall, you see, because we do not have a wall on the stage. The last man to play the part did not perform to task and made fools of us, so we are short a player, your highness."

Dreng understood. These were actors, rehearsing a play. He had never seen a play before, but Prince Hamlet had told him of a fine one called *The Mousetrap*.

This did not appear to be a trap, as Caliban had warned, but Dreng did hear an unexpected noise from behind the Duke's Tree. He bit his lip, watching intently, and allowed Caliban to continue with the rouse.

"If you need one more player, then use my boy —" Dreng glared as Caliban corrected, "I mean servant."

"They could build a wall instead," Dreng suggested to Caliban.

The youth threatened Dreng with the back of his hand and commanded, "Indian boy, do as this *great* gentleman says."

Dreng rolled his eyes but obliged and stepped forward.

"We can make a scene now, then, your highness." Nick Bottom eyeballed Dreng up and down, critically, and asked Caliban, "Can he speak from memory?"

"His mind is rather poorly, so he cannot speak the speech. He trips on his tongue." Caliban was joyful in his tyranny. Dreng felt his cheeks burn with indignation, but he was too aware of the men's swords to attempt any reckless feat.

The players exchanged papers and read in whispers for a moment. The foliage rustled again, closer, but the others seemed not to notice.

Nick Bottom explained condescendingly, "Then stand here, boy. Hold your arm out, thus, with a crack between your fingers, like so. This will serve as the opening where the playwright, the character playwright, watches the play that he wrote through the wall that is this Indian boy."

"Why is there a wall between the writer and his play?" Dreng had lost all patience. This was ridiculous. A waste of time. A distraction.

Nick Bottom did not respond as he flipped through pages and whispered directions to the others.

Caliban glared at Dreng and mouthed, *play along.* Dreng, not knowing what else to do, obliged. He held his arm out straight while Nick Bottom peered through his fingers and the other players positioned themselves on the opposite side of Dreng's hand.

"If it pleases you, your highness," Nick Bottom said to Caliban. "We will begin our scene thus, post haste." He paused and added, "Your majesty."

As Caliban nodded and waved them to begin, the players looked nervously at one another and stood in silence. A sharp cackle broke the peace. The actors exchanged confused looks while the tallest one shuffled pages.

The tall man whispered, "You are not to laugh, Bottom."

"I did not laugh."

"Nor did I."

"Nor did any of us, for certain of it."

"Are you sure?"

The tall man had no time to answer because the pages flew out of his hand and scattered in the wind. "It is the haunting, Bottom. It has come for us *again!*" The man backed out of the clearing nervously, and Dreng heard his footsteps thud as he ran up the dirt road.

Dreng looked at Caliban, who raised his eyebrows questioningly. A sly smile spread across his lips as he nodded toward Dreng and mouthed *trap.*

Dreng did not have time to respond as Nick Bottom threw himself before Caliban and pleaded, "This is not our regular level of greatness, your highness. The inn was too busy for our rehearsal again this evening, so we came here to the Duke's Tree to seek privacy. It is not haunted, your majesty. We *know* it is not haunted because we are of sound mind, your highness. But there are superstitions about this place, your highness. We ourselves have seen strange happenings here, but we have not the minds for superstitions."

Dreng imagined they had minds for very little as he positioned himself to take possession of one of their swords.

But then the donkey, who had been munching grass nearby, brayed and charged one of the remaining players, chasing him out of the clearing. Dreng felt a chill and looked at Caliban, whose eyes were wide. Did the beautiful youth fear this unseen enemy?

Were these fairies' games?

Caliban, his voice cracking, suggested, "Perhaps we should all exit, I mean exeunt, as you would say."

More movement, closer. Dreng saw a flash of green and reached for Nick Bottom's sword. As Dreng unsheathed it, the player turned to run but tripped over a root.

The branches above the short man shook, and a limb fell onto his shoulders. The fourth player backed against another tree, petrified, as the ground began to quake. More branches broke and fell around them, and the air filled with leaves swirling and flapping.

Dreng ducked through the whirlwind, toward the Duke's Tree, with the sword held at the ready. Caliban joined his side and yelled above the rumbling and cracking, "If you want to save Miranda, run into the fissure. I will be on your heels."

So Dreng turned toward the tree and ran. For a moment, he was dizzy and felt suspended in air, as he had when he was washed from *The Tempest*. His eyes struggled to focus, disoriented, as he smelled a sickly sweet odor.

Where was he?

Suddenly something grabbed him from behind and secured his arms to his sides. He dropped the sword, and all was black.

Chapter Ten: Larded with Sweet Flowers

Alda was still reeling from her sudden return to the fairy world with the image of Ophelia holding back the witches burned into her mind.

She steadied her breaths and looked around. All was the same: trees and flowers and the too-sweet fragrance. No trail. No path.

No ring of forget-me-nots.

No way home.

Before Alda could determine what to do, a feminine voice rang out, "Aldeering!"

It was one of the fairies. So Alda crouched behind a tree trunk and listened. Footsteps. Closer. Closer, still.

Then a hand touched her gently on the shoulder. Alda whirled around and saw Phillida, the apparent prisoner dragged into Oberon's court, whose capture was the distraction that Alda had needed to flee.

Had Phillida escaped, too? Alda noticed a bruise growing brown on her pale green cheek and fresh scratches of red on her forearms.

"Phillida, what happened?"

"I left them to find you, when I heard there was another mortal, I knew I had to find her, and I have found you, so we can go home now, together."

Her words were soft and swift, not separated by breaths. When she finally stopped speaking, she gasped like someone breaking the surface of water.

Alda hesitated and studied the other woman's face. "Home?"

"Yes, Aldeering, I can take you there, if you follow me and stay close, then we will not be separated again."

"My name is Alda."

"Of course, Alda is a lovely name, the fairies have difficulty remembering mortals' names, my name is not Phillida, it is —" she inhaled deeply. "Well, I have been here for so long that I do not remember my human name."

"You are a human?"

"Yes."

"Then why are you green?"

"You are as well."

Alda glanced nervously at her hands. Phillida was correct. The green had spread beyond her shoulders and onto her collarbone. She imagined that her face must be green as well. "Why is this happening?"

"It is one of the effects of this world, you see, the pigment of skin reacts with the vegetation, to change those of us who are chosen to be green."

"What do you mean, chosen?"

"Those that are with the evil queen are of a different caste, they are like metal and cold, and their skin is the color of their swords, not natural and beautiful like us." Phillida paused and smiled at Alda, her eyes wide and seeming to focus on something distant. "Take my hand, Alda, and I will lead you home, and we can go together."

But Alda was suspicious. "How did you escape from Oberon?"

"I simply told him that I had to leave to find you and that I could not stay with him a moment longer, and he understood and allowed me to leave, to find you."

"Why would he do that?"

"Because he loves me."

Alda thought back to when she had last seen Oberon, forcing the liquid down Phillida's throat. She frowned, and Phillida's eyes dropped to the ground.

"I have tried to escape before, I had searched for the blue flowered ring every year on the solstice, and I never found it again until this past night."

Alda felt the suspicion in her voice as she asked, "You know of the forget-me-nots?"

"Yes, of course, and tonight I discovered the circle's secret, rather the secret of this place, and that secret allowed me to reach you as well."

"What secret?"

"If you want to find something, if you focus on it and wish for it and think only of it, then the forest will show you the way to reach it."

Still, Alda was skeptical. "How do you know?"

"Because I wished and I thought and I hoped to find you, and here you are, but before this night I was distracted and selfish and did not wish hard enough, so that is why I could not find you for all of these years."

"All of these years?"

"Yes, Alda, how many years has it been, since you have lived on the island with your grandmother in the little cottage with the garden and the wooden bridge?"

Alda thought, amazed, and breathed, "Fourteen years, but I am older, since I spent time —" she stopped herself before saying *in Netherfeld.* "I am at least sixteen years old."

"Well, then I am sorry to have missed you for so long, and I look forward to finally getting to know you now."

"How do you know about Gramma and my cottage?"

"Why Alda, I am your mother of course..."

Alda's mind raced, but Phillida did not notice her distress as she continued, "... and I am sorry to have missed you for so many, many years, my dear, you must understand that I have been busy during this time, so please forgive me."

Alda realized that her jaw was slack, so she closed her mouth. "My mother?"

"Of course, sweetie, but I suppose I look different from that old daguerreotype because I am grown now and have spent so much time in Fairy Land."

"But this is impossible. You are no more than twenty!"

"We do not age here, which is why I wanted to find you and bring you here, to be happy and young and with me always." Phillida drew in a deep breath, squeezed Alda's hand, and continued, "Now tell me everything that has happened to you and everything that Mother, that your grandmother, has told you about me." She smiled, waiting.

Alda's head still swirled, so she stammered, "Take, take me home. And I will tell you everything."

Phillida smiled again, patted the back of her hand, and led the way between the trees.

The pair walked in silence as Alda searched her memory for any mention of her mother. But there was nothing. No photographs. No drawings. Not even a name scribbled inside the cover of a book. It was like Phillida had been erased from Alda's life.

As if she had never been a part of it.

Was it her grandmother's doing?

Or was this all a trick?

As Alda wondered, she realized that she had a question. "What is that tree, the one with the many doors in Oberon's glade?"

"The willow is a fairy tree, of course, one that has many enchanted portals that lead to many exciting places, I imagine, but I have never known anyone who has passed through and returned to tell of their adventures."

So it was, as Alda had suspected, a pathway to other realms. Could it lead home? Or back to Netherfeld? Or was it simply random, a game of chance?

The forest grew suddenly darker, and Phillida lowered her voice as she continued, "Before we return, I must warn you that Puck has been exiled, which has happened before, and this time it is because he frightened you and then allowed you to escape."

"Exiled? Where did he go?" Alda did not trust the hobgoblin. She pushed some hanging flowers from her face. The trees were thicker here, darkening the way.

"Since he has been banished from Oberon's court, he may return to the world of mortals, I hope that he does not return to the evil queen once again for she is not to be trusted and may bring harm to him or to the others, and I do not like it when the evil queen hurts my friends."

Alda did not conceal her surprise, "The fairies are your friends?"

Phillida smiled, her eyes distant. "Why yes, they raised me, you see, and I would be nothing without them, after I left the island and came here, and without them I would be old and ugly and die."

Alda thought of her grandmother, so different from her mother. Should she tell Phillida about her death, or wait until they were safe on the seventh island, away from the perils of this world?

Alda held her tongue as Phillida inhaled and continued, "And Oberon especially was kind to me and so patient because I am not like them, I am not beautiful or clever, but he saw something in me that the others did not, and he saved me."

"From what?"

"Life."

As Alda opened her mouth to express her surprise, Phillida parted a curtain of flowered garland and stepped forward into the vast space of

Oberon's court. "We are home!"

It was a trap.

Alda turned to flee, but Phillida's grasp on her wrist was too tight. As she was pulled into the center of the court, a circle of fairies formed around them. Alda could not escape.

Oberon approached, his smile stretching unnaturally across his face and a chalice in his outstretched hand. Phillida took it and drank as Oberon bellowed, "Phillida, you have found her!"

Phillida offered the chalice to Alda, and she carefully sniffed the liquid. It smelled like boiling rhubarb: bitter and earthy. Without drinking, she tried to return it to Phillida, but Oberon caught her hand and squeezed too tightly.

"I was doubtful initially, Aldeering, but Phillida has lessened my qualms!" Alda tried to pull her hand away as Oberon turned to the fairies surrounding him, "This is my lost daughter!"

Alda dropped the chalice, and the liquid splattered onto her ankles. Phillida energetically hugged her, and Oberon continued to beam. The others showed little emotion but clapped, their beating hands matching the rhythm of Alda's heart until the sound grew into a fury of drums.

This, Alda knew, was what she had wanted. To discover her parents.

But not like this.

When Alda was a child, she often found herself daydreaming about them. Her father, she imagined, was a circus performer. No, a ringmaster. A great man who could juggle flaming torches and tame wild tigers. Her mother was a princess disguised as a fortuneteller who ran away with him because her family only wanted her to marry a prince.

So Alda had convinced herself that she had to live with her grandmother because her parents were traveling the countryside with elephants and lions and a grand, striped tent, like the one on her stereopticon card. When she was old enough, Alda had hoped to join them. Maybe she could learn trapeze.

But this, this was not what Alda had expected. To find her mother to be a mindless, frivolous girl enslaved by an overpowering, unfeeling creature who hid behind a smile as he ruled over emotionless beings in another world.

If Alda had been like the girls in her childhood books, she would have fainted. But Alda was of a different mettle. Instead, she asked, "Then I am a princess?"

Phillida whispered near her ear, "Their world does not work like ours, the king cannot die, so he has no heirs, they are all immortal here, as are you since you will stay with me, we will be young forever."

Life like this was not worth living. Loveless, thoughtless, petty, warring. Alda shook her head and whispered, "I want to go home. My real home. To Grand Ledge." She looked at Phillida, pleadingly, "Come with me." But she felt Oberon's eyes studying her.

"Nonsense!" Oberon laughed, "Your mother and father are here. As is your husband!"

"Husband?"

Phillida smiled as the king continued, "Cob Web was reluctant because you are lesser and human, after all, but his family influenced him to accept." Oberon stepped into the circle of observers and patted the back of the bright green fairy that Alda had seen earlier, the one with whom the king had whispered before she escaped.

Cob and Alda exchanged uncomfortable looks. It was clear that he was equally unwilling. "I cannot marry him."

"You must."

"But I am already married," Alda lied. "To a pirate. A powerful, fearsome pirate who will kill anyone who tries to take my hand."

"A pirate?"

"Yes. A captain."

Oberon narrowed his eyes suspiciously. "What is his name?"

"Dreng." Alda spoke the name without thinking, and her cheeks burned at her instantaneous remorse.

"But Daring is not here."

"Dreng," she corrected, and her heart sank again at the word. "And he is coming for me." Again, a lie. Her grandmother always told her to tell the truth. But Gramma had never fully told her about fairies.

Oberon pulled her toward the young fairy and laughed, "Nonsense! Mortals do not know of Fairy Land, so your human husband cannot help you here. Now, take Master Web's hand." The king forced Alda's fist into Cob's and clasped his large palm around them. "In my presence, we have come together to witness the marriage of —"

Alda saw a look of terror in the young fairy's eye and whispered to him, "I am not ready."

Phillida, standing uncomfortably close behind Alda, must have heard, "My Oberon, this is not what the daughter of a king deserves, let us bring the ambrosia and light the wisps and set a stage worthy of human royalty!"

Oberon laughed and looked at the mossy floor, "Of course, my dear! How foolish of me!" He turned toward the others and commanded, "Let us fix a feast!"

Alda stepped quickly away from Cob Web and hurried to the edge of the court. Phillida followed at her heels and placed her hand on her shoulder, preventing Alda from slipping away between the trees.

Alda turned to her. "If you are my mother, how can you let me marry someone who does not love me? Someone whom I do not love?" She felt her cheeks glow in fury.

"He will love you, and you him!"

"What, will I *learn* to love him?" Alda could not contain the anger in her voice.

"No, you will love him now..." Phillida reached into her bodice and removed a scrap of white fabric. She continued, "I found this handkerchief in my mother's trunk with a note about its magic, it is from an Egyptian sorceress who cast a love spell on it." She paused and looked at Alda, "If you give it to a man, he will fall in love with you, and if he gives it to you, you will love him." She tore off a strip, ripped that in half, and cupped the two pieces in Alda's palm, "Exchange these with Cob Web during your ceremony, and you two will love one another."

Again Phillida smiled, waiting for a response. Alda only frowned as she asked, "Does Oberon have part of this handkerchief?"

Phillida tucked the remaining fabric into her bodice, patting it against her heart. "Yes, he wears it next to his heart, as do I, but if it ever falls from his touch, then the spell will break." She grinned slyly, "So I have sewn little scraps into all of his clothing and tied some into his hair and beard, thus he is never without it."

This was not love, Alda knew. It was not fair to trick Cob Web as Dreng had been deceived into marrying Miranda — no, Sycorax. Yet Alda relented, "I will marry Cob if I may speak to him first. Privately."

Phillida nodded slightly, "That is not custom, so I must speak to the king, to plead your case..." Phillida's voice trailed off as she trotted toward Oberon.

As Alda waited for her mother's return, she examined the two scraps of handkerchief. They were cotton, white, not extraordinary in any way. Would they work?

Did she want them to work?

At Phillida's approach, Alda tucked the two pieces of fabric into her sleeve. "The king has allowed you to speak to Cob Web, but you must do so before the last of the wisps is lighted."

Alda looked above and gasped. The tree canopy was aglow with floating flowers and black orbs. As she watched, the orbs burst into rainbow lights, flickering brightly below the dark leaves that were silhouetted against the sky. The fairies who had previously encircled her now stood in the center of the glade, looking upward and swirling their wrists as they arranged the flowers in the air above.

"The wisps will all soon be lit, so hurry, Alda." Phillida stepped aside to reveal Cob, and then returned to Oberon's side.

Cob Web's angular features were calm and stoic as he approached Alda, and he avoided her gaze as he whispered, "May I shake your hand?"

Alda obliged. His fingers were cold and smooth, like stems of an iris in the early spring. Despite herself, Alda shuddered. "Do you want to marry me?" Her tone was more direct than she had intended, and he pulled his hand from hers.

"No." She saw relief flash briefly across his face before returning to his solemn expression.

"Then let me leave." Alda glanced at the other fairies. Oberon had an arm around Phillida, while also laughing and holding his belly. The others were busy with their decorations and preparations. Alda could easily slip out of the glade unnoticed. If Cob Web helped, she could put some distance between herself and the others before they discovered her absence.

"I cannot."

"Why?"

"I am honor bound to —"

Alda punched him. It was a reflex, no, it was an instinct. He stumbled backwards and touched his lip but did not try to stop her as she ran.

And as Alda fled between the dense trees, she realized that she could almost be happy there, with her mother and father and something like love for a husband. She could have a family, finally, and a home.

But it would all be a lie. And Gramma had told her not to lie.

Chapter Eleven: As This World Goes

As Dreng regained consciousness, he felt weak, like he had back on the island, before he escaped with Caliban.

After a moment, though, he realized that he was not weak. The thing that had captured him was simply more powerful.

Then he remembered what had happened with the players, that he was now beyond the Duke's Tree, and the world slowly came into focus. First, a scent, sweet and strong like rotting fruit. Then bright, blue sky burst through openings of heavy foliage. Trees hung with fantastical flowers passed overhead, moving quickly into blurs of purple and blue.

Constant movement, scuffing, pain in his back and shoulders.

Dreng realized he was being dragged. His arms were still pinned to his sides, held in place by something thin and strong. A cord. Before him a green figure, with disproportionate limbs and a hat of white bark and two horns rising beneath its hair, pulled him across the grassy forest floor.

A dagger hung on the creature's belt, its silver hilt scrawled with symbols. Its blade tipped with sparkling green. Was it poisoned? Dreng did not want to test it.

What had happened to Dreng's sword, the one he lifted from Nick Bottom? Dreng realized that he had dropped it when he was captured. Was it here, or on the other side of the tree? Regardless, it was gone.

And where was Caliban?

More importantly, how could Dreng find Netherfeld, find Miranda?

At the thought of his trapped wife, Dreng struggled more fiercely against his bonds. The creature dragging him across the forest floor jerked the cord until Dreng's arms bled from his efforts. Still, he persisted.

Dreng wanted to barter for his freedom, so he looked to his hand.

But Prince Hamlet's signet ring was gone. When had he lost it?

Thirty seconds passed as he was helpless, his shoulders aching as they scraped over moss and roots. A full minute. Dreng felt his shirt slide from his shoulder, exposing the St. Elmo's fire scar to the rough soil. Then something wet ran down his side: blood from his skin rubbed raw against the ground. He tried to regain his feet, but there was no break in the movement, no opportunity to find footing.

Finally, breathless, he tried, "Where are you taking me?"

No response.

Two minutes passed, and Dreng stopped counting his heartbeats. The ground felt softer, and the flowers smelled sweeter, the trees were gone, and the light was more filtered and blue-green.

Suddenly they stopped. Dreng forced himself into an awkward sitting position and looked around. They were inside what looked like a ship-sized nest. Thorny vines and woven saplings formed a great circle that peaked into a dome above. Candlelight flickered, but there were no candles. Voices echoed, but there were no speakers. There were no windows, no natural light, and only one opening that was now some distance behind Dreng and his captor.

"Reveal yourselves, fairies," the green man demanded.

Fairies? The voices grew louder.

"I hear you near me now, Queen Mab, so do not be afraid to show your men." He paused and added, "Or would you rather be called Titania, then?"

The voices ceased. A flicker of candlelight pulsated and intensified. It multiplied into scores of sparks and took the form of a woman. A shadow woman, but made of light and not darkness.

As Dreng watched, amazed, the sparks strengthened and became solid. The lady was radiant, quite literally, and glowed like the moon above the sea. Her hair was thin and fine like a spiderweb, her gown the blue of waves before dawn, and her face serene and kind.

If not for Miranda, Dreng might have loved her, at least for her beauty.

The majestic woman — if she was indeed a woman — eyed Dreng and his captor suspiciously. "Robin Goodfellow, did your master send you here?"

"No, your majesty's suspicions are not right. King Oberon sent me out into the night, in exile to the mortal world, so now I seek to find a better fold."

Dreng's eyes met the woman's, and she circled him closely, too closely, but spoke not to him.

"And you want my patronage now, little Robin? My protection from the King of Shadows and his unruly band? To be *my* servant?"

The captor lowered his head. "If your majesty so pleases to allow."

As Dreng wondered at this celestial being, she touched his bloody shoulder. The pain stopped. He turned his head and saw that the wound remained, but it was numb.

"What is this ragged offering, little Robin?"

Dreng held his chin up higher and set his jaw.

"This is a second Indian boy, Queen Mab. Owned by a lofty prince. I found him in the mortals' woods and knew you had —"

"Knew that your *former* master, the great King of Shadows had so recently —" She paused and stared at Dreng, studying him "— well, that is past." She turned and placed herself before Dreng's abductor, who deeply bowed before her.

"I accept your offering, Robin Goodfellow."

Offering?

The green man bowed into the shadows as he whispered, "I will remember this."

The queen returned her attention to Dreng, looming over him, her eyes oppressive with radiating power, and snapped her fingers. The vines securing Dreng's arms withered away and fell to the stony ground, and she clasped her sharp fingernails into his cheeks and pulled him to his feet.

The queen studied him like this for some time, her eyes flitting across his features in silence, her breath icy. Dreng did his best to meet her gaze, to suppress his terror. Finally, she bit her lip, and a drop of silver liquid trickled down her chin.

She did not wipe it away as she whispered, "Tell me, Indian boy, what is your name?"

Dreng finally flinched and avoided her gaze as he answered, "Dreng." She released her hold on his face, and he stumbled back. He felt wet on his cheeks and wiped away blood, but he did not feel the injury.

"Fairies, welcome Dreng to our bower!"

The room erupted in a cascade of sparks, and dozens of shining figures appeared, beautiful men and women with silken hair and glowing skin dressed in thin garments of various shades of blue and silver. They looked like stars come to life, vibrant as they shouted in a chorus of welcome.

And, Dreng observed, they all had swords. These were warriors, the queen's men. And the fairy king, Dreng suspected, had his own band of fighters.

The two monarchs appeared to be at odds. At war, perhaps.

Dreng knew, war was havoc. And lines from an old ballad rung in his mind, "All was lost, but that the heavens fought."

The queen, again too close, whispered into his ear, "You are a part of our clan, now, our tribe of immortals. The lesser fairies call me Queen

Mab, but you *must* call me Titania, my sweet boy." Her breath on his cheek was like a northern wind as she added, "And you must honor and obey me, always."

Somehow, Dreng felt even more imprisoned now than when he had been bound.

She laughed, a hollow sound that echoed into the dome above. "Of course you will be loyal, dear Dreng. And swear your fidelity to me and to your new radiant comrades. So this honor must be celebrated."

The other luminous creatures scurried about, bringing trays of exotic fruits and goblets of gem-colored liquids. Dreng watched in amazement, feeling as if he was in a dream come to life.

For a moment, he forgot danger. He forgot Caliban and Netherfeld and Miranda and his obligations and worries as Titania offered him a new suit of the finest blue silk and shoes that were light but sturdy. He was presented with food and drink unlike any he had tasted before. He was pampered and regaled in ways he could not imagine. The light-formed beings treated him as their superior and Titania as their god.

No, he realized as the queen forced cherries into his mouth, he was not treated as their superior. He was a pet.

And Dreng remembered his lost wife, his reason for living. He glanced at Robin Goodfellow, who sulked across the room and stared at the others, brooding. Dreng knew he was not safe here. There was more to her, more to this world. This was all a distraction, an obstacle preventing him from finding Netherfeld.

His hands suddenly felt cold, and he noticed their tips glowed light blue.

What was happening?

He returned his attention to Queen Mab — Titania — who led him to a throne of crystal and lowered her regal form onto its cold surface as she sipped fruit-smelling liquid from a sapphire chalice. The queen motioned for him to sit at her feet and placed her hand on his head, as one would caress a beloved dog, as another radiant person offered him seeds from a red fruit.

These creatures, he realized, were like the ancient gods. Immortal and unfeeling, toying with mortals and subjecting them to their whims. He needed to escape.

And he needed a sword to do so.

Time passed slowly as Dreng watched the creatures eat and laugh and dance to twinkling music that floated from above. Their movements were sudden, not graceful or soft, for they clearly did not fear injury to themselves or others.

Suddenly, the queen stood. The ethereal music stopped, as did the revelers, as light shone directly from the opening at the top of the dome and illuminated a circular patch in the center of the bower.

Titania raised her hand, and all bowed. She reached behind the throne and withdrew a bejeweled sword. Its blade glistened as she stepped into the spotlight, its steel cutting into her fingers and blood like molten silver dripping down her wrists. She was insensible to her wound as she summoned Dreng before her.

He understood: an oath of fidelity. He had heard tales of such ceremonies in the principalities on land. But on sea, oaths were of a different kind.

He lowered himself on one knee as the queen placed the hilt on his shoulder. "Those among us who wear a sword are under the command of the queen."

She paused for emphasis as she looked at the other fairies in the bower, her eyes glowing. "If you accept this gift, you promise to give your life for me and for mine, to follow me to the last gasp, with truth and loyalty. And," she paused again and stared through her glittering lashes. "You must promise to use this blade against the first foreign creature that you encounter."

Dreng considered. He had no love for any in this land. Miranda was in Netherfeld. If he met Caliban again, he would not hesitate to deliver a blow to the boy who tried to sacrifice him to sea-maids. And Dreng knew no one else. No one living.

Above all else, he needed a weapon. To escape. To save his wife. To save himself.

He saw no reason to refuse the sword. "I will."

She presented the hilt to him, and he closed his hand around it and held the sword. It felt odd. Was it cold? No, he decided. It actually did not feel.

He realized that *he* did not feel. At least not fully. His blue fingers tingled, and his wrists ached, but his hands lacked external sensation.

Spurred by curiosity, he ran his fingertip over the blade. Red blood trickled down his knuckle, but there was no pain.

He realized his hands were shaking and tightened his hold on the hilt. As he examined the blade in the shimmering light of the creatures around him, Dreng lost himself to memory.

For a moment, he felt as though he was on *The Tempest*, steadying a different sword in his untested hand.

Dreng, as a boy, had been raised with weapons. After his father's death, the men of the ship made sport of sending him with a small stiletto after rats and birds that ventured aboard. They wagered on his success, and he found some small profit in his skill. As he grew, he used wood scraps to practice against his shipmate's rapiers and improved his defenses. But then Prince Hamlet escaped. And Dreng, with his injury and Ernesto's death, was thought to be an accomplice. It was treason.

After several months in the hold, months in waste beneath the crew, months alone and hopeless, months that Dreng remembered only as flashes of fear and desperation, he welcomed death.

But he had no will, no power to bring death upon himself.

So when the captain, an old man called Billy with a thick beard and an earring, offered a trial by sword, Dreng knew he could finally rid himself of his mortal prison.

The stakes were clear, as were the rules: if Dreng could defeat any and every man who challenged him, then he could live; one opponent at a time, and first blood won the bout.

Dreng expected the opening blow would be more than blood and hoped his opponent would end it, that he could finally escape to the regions beyond this earth.

At the start of the trial, Dreng, still weak from the infected wound between his ribs, held a proper rapier for the first time. It was heavier than he had expected, and he needed two hands to support it. The blade shook as he planted his feet, the men forming a circle around him.

Young Dreng took in two breaths before the first man stepped forward. It was a burly Spaniard whom the crew sarcastically called Duke. A man with a good and strong arm. Dreng knew this man had some degree of honor and would not kill an unarmed boy, so he held the rapier loosely but defensively, its tip barely above his waist.

Duke studied him for a heartbeat, spat, and snarled, "I knew your father, boy, before the St. Elmo's fire. He was a better man than you will be, but you deserve to be a man." Duke raised his sword and sliced his own fingertip. He held it above his head to show the others, and the crew nodded and murmured.

In all, five men stepped forward to challenge Dreng, and all five drew their own blood. Dreng had more friends than he knew, and Ernesto, it seemed, had made many enemies before his death. And Prince Hamlet's escape, he learned, was not enough to warrant a boy's execution. Some, perhaps, even felt something like regard for the boy who appeared not to fear death.

Little did they know how he had welcomed his own end.

So Dreng was saved not by combat but by respect and honor. This made him want to live, to succeed, to serve the ship and its men.

And for years thereafter, the crew trained him as an equal until he proved their superior. And then, after more years, they elected him boatswain, a position he held with equal parts fear and compassion.

But it all ended in a storm and a shipwreck.

For many months thereafter, Dreng had no need for a blade. On the island, such a weapon was useless against magic, and Miranda had enough power to protect them all. But now, without her, he had to depend on his own strength and skill.

But was he still capable?

In the beam of light inside Titania's bower, he swung the sword to test its balance. It was adequate. He could defend himself. And, if required, he could attack.

But he hoped to escape before then, despite his commitment to Titania.

As Dreng lowered the blade, he heard a rustling outside the bower's walls. He looked to Queen Mab, who curled her thin lips, raised her shimmering eyebrows, and commanded, "Danger comes. Defend me. It is your duty, Indian boy."

He reluctantly held the sword en garde and faced the only door, readying himself for an attack.

Chapter Twelve: Fortune's Fool

Alda ran over roots and under limbs and through the thick floral odor of the forest. She ran until her lungs ached and her legs tingled and her heart flittered like a hummingbird. When she finally stopped, she still felt watched and in danger, even with her distance from Oberon's court.

She steadied her breathing and her shaking hands and looked around as she rubbed her aching knuckles. Nothing was familiar, but all was the same. Trees and flowers and vines. The overpowering floral scent. Green, fading into more distant black. No landmarks.

But she remembered Phillida's strange advice: if you think of something, it will appear. So she stopped running and pictured the circle of blue flowers, glowing beneath the heavy oak leaves.

But her mind wandered. Back to her mother and father and Cob Web. She closed her eyes, pushing her thoughts from her recent strife.

And instead, she thought of Dreng. She had lied about him being her husband. But was it a lie, or a wish?

Did it matter, since he was dead?

As she wondered, she heard footsteps. No, it was merely an echo. She listened harder.

It was indeed an actual sound. Quick footsteps. Running. Getting closer.

She wanted to hide, but it was too late.

A cloaked figure appeared before her. She stepped back but stumbled over her skirt and fell. As the figure approached, she eased. It was a human, not a fairy. And he seemed familiar, somehow.

He lowered his hood to reveal a handsome boy, nearly her own age. Blonde with bright, inquisitive blue eyes. Pale and scowling, but beautiful nonetheless. She realized that her mouth was open, so she closed it as she stood.

He likewise stared at her. His eyes flashed with realization as he spat, "You're that little girl. That witch who summoned the colored spirits." He paused and added, "But you've turned green."

Alda stood and stretched her neck, trying to look taller. "I'm neither a little girl nor a witch."

The boy laughed. "Say what you will."

"How do you know me?"

"I know many great and mysterious things, Alda."

Alda was quiet for what may have been too long or perhaps not long enough. Finally, she asked, "Who are you?"

The boy did not answer. Instead, he asked, "Why are you here?"

"I am lost and searching for a way home."

"Aren't we all?" He smiled slyly.

"Do you know of the flowered circle? The circle of flowers? With the blue flowers that help you remember?" She had meant to ask one question, but her mouth did not stop.

"I may have seen them, but I forget," he raised his eyebrows. "Do you know how to reach Netherfeld?"

Alda narrowed her eyes. "What do you know of Netherfeld?"

"Everything and nothing. I was born there."

Could this be — No, he was too old to be Hamnet. But time was not linear, not always.

So again, Alda asked, "Who are you?" The boy shifted his weight and did not answer, so Alda tried, "Do you know Ophelia?" As she said the name, the guilt of leaving her behind and her inability to save her pressed on her heart.

"I know *of* her."

"What do you know?"

"Many great and mysterious things."

"Of Ophelia?"

"Yes, I know of her."

Alda shook her head. Speaking in circles reminded her of the witches, so she took a deep breath to steady her nerves and asked, "What do you want in Netherfeld?"

"To find a girl."

"Who?"

The boy paused, drew in a breath, and exhaled as if considering how to answer. Or avoiding an answer. "Miranda."

"Miranda?"

"Are you a parrot?"

Alda scowled at him as she asked, "How do you know Miranda?"

"I loved her, once." For the first time, the boy appeared to be serious.

"Well, I did not see her in Netherfeld—"

The boy frowned.

Alda continued, "But I heard her speak."

His eyes widened, "What did she say?"

Alda answered provokingly, "Words."

He gritted his teeth, "What words did she say?"

"Who are you?"

"And what did you say?"

"No, tell me who you are, or I will say no more." And to prove her point, Alda crossed her arms and planted her feet.

The boy paced and ran his hands through his hair. Finally, he turned and spat, "Fine, I am Caliban. Or I was. Now I am back to myself."

"Caliban? You do not look —" Alda shook her head and stepped toward him, but he backed away. Of course, he had the blue cloak that Miranda had given her on the island. The cloak he stole when she had fallen into the pit. "You tried to — to what?" She laughed at this coincidence, the sound harsher than she expected. "You wanted to make me your wife, you said."

"You bit me."

"And you tried to have your mother, Sycorax, kill me."

"Mother would not have killed you."

"How do you know?"

"Because she loved you, once."

Alda stepped back, as if slapped in the face. "No, she sent spirits at me and —"

"To make you leave the island."

"— she killed Dreng."

Caliban shook his head. "Dreng is still alive."

"No." Yet Alda had hope. She wanted to believe him.

"He is, he is." Caliban removed a golden ring from his finger and thrust it into Alda's hand. "This is Dreng's ring. My father's ring, too. It has the powers to awaken the dead, so do *not* wear it. But when you find Dreng, give it to him."

Alda took the ring and placed it carefully in her sleeve, next to the scraps of Phillida's enchanted handkerchief. "Where is Dreng?"

"In this world, with the fairy queen."

Alda was suspicious. This boy, after all, spoke in riddles. "How do you know?"

"I saw him taken. To the queen's bower."

"And you let him be captured?"

"I am not a warrior. And my Miranda, she needs —" His eyes revealed his desperation as he ran his fingers nervously through his hair. "What did Miranda say?"

Alda sighed and relented, "She warned of witches and said they are trying to take something from Netherfeld."

"Witches?" Caliban said it to himself, as if lost in a daydream.

Alda nodded. "I saw them, too, before I escaped."

"What did they want?"

Alda only shrugged provokingly.

"Did you see anyone else? Anyone?" His voice rose as he asked.

Alda shook her head and looked down, avoiding his gaze.

She could hear his teeth clench as he asked, "How do I reach Netherfeld?"

"I don't know." Alda considered telling him of Ophelia, asking him to find her, but she did not trust him. So she added, "The way I got to Netherfeld, the fissure in a tree — I think it no longer exists."

Caliban scowled. "You *think*?"

Alda felt the hair on her neck bristle. "Maybe if *you* think about Netherfeld hard enough, you will get there." Alda spoke sarcastically, despite her belief in her words.

"There must be another way."

Alda offered, "Well, there is a tree in Oberon's court, a willow with many doors that lead to other realms." She paused and added, almost questioningly, "One must certainly lead to Netherfeld." And if the tree took Caliban elsewhere, what was it to Alda? After all, he had attacked her on Prospero's island, and Alda was not quick to trust someone so devious.

"How do I reach Oberon's court?"

"How do I reach Dreng?"

Chapter Thirteen: Sick at Heart

Dreng held his breath as shadowy movement flitted across the opening to Queen Titania's bower. Then a figure, a slim silhouette. It was a woman, or a girl.

"Dreng?"

Alda stepped into the room and looked around, her eyes moving past the other figures and focusing on him. Her hair was longer and more unkempt than when he had last seen her, her skin an unnatural shade of mossy green, but it was Alda. Alive.

Why was she here?

She gasped, "You *are* alive!"

Dreng did not share her joy. Instead, he held up his hand to stop her as he looked to Titania and pleaded, "I know her."

Alda moved closer, and the fairies parted around her. "I thought, I thought I saw you die —" Her voice was lost in a sob as she quickly closed the space between them.

And Dreng realized that she could not see the others, could not see the danger, just as he did not see them when he arrived with Robin Goodfellow.

Alda was almost to him, but Dreng turned his back to her, facing Titania. The queen sneered at him and whispered, "Remember your oath."

"No, I cannot. She is not a threat." He turned back to face Alda, his eyes wide with fear. His heart pounding. And the sword, the bejeweled sword, held before him.

He had thought Alda to be dead, gone, vanished. He had wished to find her, spent days searching and weeks hoping. But she was not on the island.

Yet, somehow, Alda was here, now.

Titania hissed, "She is one of them, allegiant to wicked Oberon. Only his tribe are stained so unnaturally." The queen stepped behind Dreng, forcing him forward.

"Dreng, you can't what? Who are you talking to?" Alda was at his side and reached for him, but he backed away. She continued, "Come with me, I can —"

Alda could not finish. The sword shifted in Dreng's hand, willing its movement with a momentum of its own. He felt it pull toward her heart, and he used all of his strength to keep it higher, to hopefully strike her in the shoulder or dash it through the air above.

But he felt it connect with the muscle in the top of her arm, the force of her flesh pressing against the blade, and he pulled it back as quickly as he could.

Blood dripped down Alda's elbow beneath her red sleeve, and liquid seeped through the front of her dress. She stumbled away from him, seeming more in shock than pain, and whispered only, "Why?"

His heart ached, and it was all he could do to keep his throat from closing. Creating harm without cause was not — and to a woman. Especially her.

"I, they —" He stood straighter, glanced over his shoulder at Titania and the others, at their sneers and angry gazes, aware that Alda could not see him. With a shaking voice, he commanded, "Run."

Alda did.

He wanted to follow.

As she escaped, the fairies did not give chase. They instead closed around him, encircling him with frowns and stares.

Titania's glare was the worst. "You did not kill her."

"I never swore to kill for you. Only to use the sword. And protect you. And she was not a threat." Dreng immediately regretted this insubordination.

The queen struck his face with her flat palm, and he fell back but quickly regained his footing.

"She was one of them! One of the filthy tribe that killed my last boy!"

"She is a mortal, like me!" Titania struck again with her other hand, and Dreng felt blood drip from the side of his mouth. But there was no pain.

Queen Mab raised her hand a third time, but he did not flinch. Even if he had felt pain, it would not be enough to make him bend to her will.

His resolve was too hardened, now that he knew that Alda lived.

Instead, he gripped the sword in his hand. "That girl is, is my friend. Not a fae. I will not kill her."

"She is a foreigner, boy, a changeling, and better dead than alive." Dreng started at the word as he remembered the ghost's prophecy, *the changeling beyond the tree can save Miranda.*

The queen's mouth curved into a strange smile, and she gently wiped the blood from his lip. She cupped his chin in her hand as she stared into his eyes. "If you do not kill that beast, then *we* must."

Queen Mab pushed him aside, and Dreng felt the hair on his neck rise in a shiver. He could not allow more harm to befall Alda, so he straightened as the queen crossed toward the exit and stated flatly, "No."

Titania turned, looked to the circle of fairies around her, and laughed. It was not a sound of hatred but an actual, gleeful, melodious laugh. She placed her hand over her heart as she paced, circling behind Dreng as he self-consciously altered his grip on the hilt.

"I have never been commanded so, Indian boy! What an entertaining jest." Her tone dropped. "Now I will tell you this: I see your hope. I see that you want to use the sword against me, to chase that creature down and somehow align with her, to leave this world with her and take *my heart* with you." She laughed again, clasping her hands. "You forget that you are mine, my dear boy."

The ring of fairies had parted somewhat, leaving a clearing between Dreng and the bower's opening, as Titania haughtily added, "And you cannot wield the sword against me."

Wield? Dreng wondered if she was literal. He weighed the weapon's balance in his grip, inching his hand down the blade until he felt it slip in his painlessly bleeding fingers.

Swords were forged to be held, to thrust and to slash, not for this. But, if there was a chance, even a chance to save Alda...

"I am not a boy, madam. I am a boatswain. And you, majesty, are not my captain."

He threw the sword like a javelin and silently prayed to any superstitious power that might hear his wishes.

Somehow, it soared straight and pierced the queen in the chest.

But the force did not even knock her down.

The others erupted in a scream and rushed to her aid as Dreng escaped into the forest. Above the pounding in his ears, he could hear her laugh, and he knew she would soon follow, so he ran like there were feathers on his heels.

The forest was dense and claustrophobic. It was how Dreng had imagined the jungles of tropical isles, the ones foreign sailors spoke of, with rainbow birds as large as dragons and wild cats as black as ink that could swallow a man whole.

What dangers lurked here, yet unseen?

And how would he find Alda? He needed her now, more than anything. To save her. Finally.

Alda.

Alda, the girl who could have saved him. Alda, who was not dead. Who was somehow here, in this fantastical place, who had found him once again in a time of need. Was *she* here to save *him*, this time?

Time. Where had Alda been all these months?

How did she escape from the island?

More importantly, how would they escape now?

As he worried, he could see her in his mind. First, her joy at discovering him, then her fear at his apparent betrayal. The ache in her eyes as his sword met her flesh.

Dreng felt a worsening ache in his heart.

Suddenly, he heard a whimper and a rustling of leaves. Even before he beheld the source of the sound, he knew it was Alda. And he knew she was gravely hurt.

He took a deep breath and revealed himself. She was on the ground, holding her bleeding arm, her face a paler shade of green than her surrounding skin. He stared for a moment, his mouth agape and thoughts swirling, unsure what to say.

She stood, stumbled backward, and caught herself against a tree.

"Alda, let me —"

She glared at him before he could say *help*, so he stopped. She hissed, "You have done enough damage to me."

"I didn't mean to. I would never —" He thought back to when he encountered her on the island, when he had inadvertently injured her in a scuffle, "I would never deliberately cause you harm." He reached toward her. "There were others with us, in that place, invisible fairies who forced me to, to do that. To you."

She backed away, but her eyes softened somewhat as she breathed, "You're hurt, too."

"Not enough to notice." He wiped his hand across his face and looked at the blood on his fingers, but he could feel no pain.

Alda nodded. Her tone eased as she asked, "Who were the fairies?"

"Silver beings, led by Queen Mab — Titania — and her band of warriors."

"Oberon's wife," she whispered to herself. Her eyes met his, and she snapped accusingly, "But why did you —?" Alda lifted her bloody hand from her arm, and fresh droplets fell to the ground.

Dreng stammered, "I — it was against my will." He could feel Alda glare at him as he added, "I can bind it." He stepped toward her, but she again recoiled. "It was an oath, the sword — I could not stop it."

Alda eyed him suspiciously, "Why are you here?"

"To help you."

"No, I mean, why are you *here*? In Fairy Land." Alda looked up, indicating the trees and the forest.

Dreng finally understood. "To save —" He blushed, involuntarily, at the thought of his wife. "I came here to find a way to Netherfeld —"

"Yes, with Caliban." Alda seemed to relax as Dreng looked at her questioningly. "I met him, earlier, in the wood."

"He is here?"

She nodded. "But why are you his ally?"

"The island — we had to leave, together. Where is he?"

"I sent him to find a way..." Her voice trailed off. She shook her head and continued, "He will soon find a way to Netherfeld."

Dreng felt himself scowl. He did not trust that boy to rescue Miranda. But still, she should be safe enough if Caliban could find her. Safe for a time. And Dreng had more pressing problems now.

Before he could warn Alda of the approaching fairies, she continued, "He gave me something of yours. A ring."

Dreng's heart lifted. So Caliban had taken the signet ring.

But why did he take it? Did he need it, for —

Before Dreng could wonder further, Alda shifted awkwardly, her hand still held tight to her wound. "It's in my sleeve —"

She raised her eyebrows at him and nodded toward her right arm.

He approached cautiously, hesitant to further cause her distress.

Without moving her hand from her injury, she said, "Just unfasten the button, and —"

Her cuff was wet with blood, so he fumbled to open her sleeve. As he did, his thoughts involuntarily escaped his lips, "I thought you were dead."

Alda smiled slightly.

"I thought the same of you."

His fingers closed on something small and soft near her arm. "I'm glad you're not."

As he removed a bundle from her sleeve, his skin brushed against hers. Their eyes finally met, truly met, for the first time.

Within her orbs, he saw fear and confusion. Dread, perhaps, but a shadow of hope, too, an impression that she wanted to find peace and happiness. And he wanted to share in her future joy.

He wanted to share her future.

Before he knew what was happening, his lips touched hers. He forgot the forest and the uncertainty, the questions and danger. The queen and her threatening approach. His lost wife.

He forgot everything in that moment except Alda and himself, and their lips together at last.

*   *   *

This was not the time for a kiss.

Something had happened. Alda knew, despite her inexperience with love, that something was wrong. So even though she wanted his lips to linger on hers, she pushed him away.

Then she saw what was in his hand.

He was startled, his eyes pleading. "Alda, I —"

"Drop it."

"What?"

"I said to *drop it*, Dreng."

He hesitated, his eyes still locked on hers. "As you command, so I will."

He released the scrap of the enchanted handkerchief from his bloody fist and looked at her again, confused. As he wiped his forehead, his eyes lost their distant look and returned to their normal gaze. "I — I'm sorry. I don't know what —"

Alda ignored him as she reached for the fallen handkerchief. Then she hesitated, fearful to take the thing that had dropped from his hand, afraid that the magic would transfer to her. Instead, she pushed dirt over it with her foot.

"What was that?"

"A piece of handkerchief, with magic," she stammered. "Enchanted, given to me by —" She stopped herself from saying *my mother* and finished, "a fairy." She glanced at him, and she felt herself blush. "It makes a person fall in love with the one who gives it to him."

He turned away from her, his face also red. He whispered, "I didn't — I mean, I never would have — It was not an honest thing, to — to do that."

Alda met his eyes and added, "The spell only works if one is touching the handkerchief, so it, the spell, is now undone." She looked away, avoiding the anger that might be in his eyes.

In her heart of hearts, Alda wished the kiss had been sincere. Maybe someday, she hoped, but not here or now.

She glanced up and saw him looking down, biting his lip. She studied his face and saw it was more worn than when she had left him on Prospero's island. Sun had darkened his brow, and lines creased the corners of his eyes and mouth. He did not look like one who had spent these months in happiness.

And there were fresher wounds. Bruises forming on his jaw, scratches on his arms. Blood trickling unnoticed from his mouth and fingers.

His fingers. They were a silvery, metallic hue. He was changing, like her.

Dreng felt her gaze and shifted uncomfortably. He lost all appearance of confidence, and cleared his throat awkwardly before he spoke. "Titania — Queen Mab is coming, with her men. We must escape. But let me —"

Before she could stop him, he tore the bottom of his silver-blue shirt and wrapped it several times around her upper arm. Its pressure, and his touch, eased the pain.

As he worked, Alda considered. "How did you get here?"

"I was taken through a tree."

"Can you find it again?"

He hesitated. "I do not think so."

"Do you remember it? What it looked like?"

"I did not see it clearly, not from this side." He looked at her questioningly. "And you?"

"I entered through a circle of blue flowers." As she said it, she saw it in her mind and closed her eyes, focusing on its details: the small petals of the forget-me-nots, their star-like centers, their narrow stems and oval leaves.

She felt Dreng step away, the bandage secured, and opened her eyes. Nothing had changed. The ring did not appear before her, magically. Perhaps Phillida had been wrong.

But a flash of blue caught the corner of her eye as an unexpected breeze pushed aside a garland of pink flowers.

There, in a narrow opening behind a wide tree, was the flowered ring, with filtered sunlight dappling its surface.

She approached it, and Dreng followed, amazed. "It was so close?"

"In this place, you find what you wish to discover." But Alda wondered, *did she create the circle of flowers*? Had some of her Netherfeld abilities spilled over into this world?

There was no time to consider further. Dreng had said the queen was coming for them, so they had to act quickly. Alda looked at him firmly and whispered, "Come with me."

"Where?"

"To my home. We will be safe there, through the ring."

Dreng bit his lip. Alda saw his mind work behind his eyes. And she remembered that there was a ring of a different kind, his signet ring, still tucked within her sleeve. She retrieved it and placed it in his hand. "This is yours."

He wiped her blood from its golden surface, sighed, and shook his head. "I cannot go with you."

"Please." Alda stepped toward him and reached for his hand. He backed away. "When we reach my cottage, I can finish the cauldron's bubble, and we can go anywhere. Anytime." His eyes flashed with confusion, and she realized that he did not know of the magical sphere.

"I have — an obligation. No, a duty. An honor. I cannot, I can't —"
He wiped his hair from his eyes and again shook his head. "You must go
without me. I must find Netherfeld."

"But the queen —" Before Alda could finish, leaves rustled behind
Dreng. Branches bent and broke, and he turned and backed toward Alda.

Alda could not see his face, but she heard the fear in his voice as he
stood tall and demanded, "Let her go. As I said, she is a mortal —"

Laughter erupted around them, and Alda realized they were
surrounded by the invisible beings. But she could still reach the forget-
me-nots. And so could Dreng. She reached for his hand, but he was
pulled forcefully away from her grasp.

A beautiful woman materialized before her, with Dreng's shirt
clasped in one hand and a sword dripping in silver liquid in the other.

This, Alda knew, was Titania. Queen Mab. Oberon's wife.

She easily lifted Dreng off the ground and hissed, "Treason is a sin!
And this slumber, your penance." The queen blew a deep breath onto his
face, and he went limp. As she threw him to the ground, his form
crumbled, and he lay unmoving.

Alda started to step forward, but her fear of the fairy queen
prevented her from crouching at Dreng's side. Instead, she yelled, "Do not
harm him!"

Titania seemed to notice her for the first time. She laughed and
clasped her hands, the sword in her hand scraping her cheek. But the
beautiful woman did not recoil from its blade as shining blood trickled
down her chin. "Who are you to tell *me* what to do, human?"

Alda gritted her teeth and stated with as much force as she could
muster, "I am Aldeering, daughter of Oberon, and I will not allow you to
cause injury to this young man."

The queen's laughter grew louder. "Oberon's daughter?" Her voice dropped. "Guards, destroy this pretender."

Within a heartbeat, Alda had to choose between the flowered circle and — and what other possibility existed? If she passed through the ring and reached her home, she may not be able to return. No, she could not leave Dreng, unconscious — or worse — on the mossy ground. She had to escape from here, to get help for him.

But how?

Where could she go?

Up. The flowered garlands, the vines that led to the treetops. Alda had not climbed in half a year, but still —

She jumped and swung her arms, bending her elbows and twisting her feet around their coils. Invisible hands pulled at her calico dress, so she reached higher, stepping lightly on branches and grasping for vines until she felt she was well past her unseen enemies.

Finally, Alda released her grip and rolled onto the ground, hitting her injured arm and losing her breath. She recovered as quickly as she could as footsteps pounded closer. Then she ran and hoped and thought only of her mother.

The footsteps grew quieter, more distant. The terrain changed. More blue light streamed through the trees, vivid green, a chorus of birds.

Then she saw Oberon's glade ahead, the dense trees that lined its exterior. And she ran harder, knowing that whatever dangers awaited her return to court were less than those that approached from behind.

*   *   *

Dreng was trapped in darkness. In a dream. In death?

No, his mind worked. But he could not move. So, instead, he

thought.

More than anything, more than all the dangers and the unknown, the kiss was on his mind. The kiss, that was so long in anticipation. The kiss, that felt like the sweetest honey. The kiss that, he knew, was a trick.

Did Dreng love *her*?

He should.

Yes, he decided, he *should* love Miranda.

Miranda, after all, was his wife, and a man should love his wife. Or, at least, be loyal to her.

But Dreng knew from his years at sea that loyalty was not always aligned with love.

A memory flashed into his mind's eye.

It happened months ago, several nights after his marriage rite. The island air was cool as Dreng watched the moonlit ocean through an open window in their bedchamber.

He thought Miranda was asleep, her golden hair spread across her pillow, but then he heard her whisper, "Where do your thoughts bend?"

"I'm thinking only of the waves."

He turned from the window to his wife in their bed and saw her spinning the signet ring on her finger, watching him intently. After a few breaths, Miranda sat and shifted, reaching to smooth the coverings where he had slept. "Then come to bed. The sea will still be there in the morning."

"As will I." He turned fully to her and smiled, attempting to conceal the sorrow that accompanied his reply.

But it was clear that his words stung her. "You would rather leave?"

"You know I can't."

"Because you have no ship." It was not a question.

"Because I have you." He crossed the room quickly and embraced her, but he could feel she was not soothed by his touch.

Miranda rested her chin on his shoulder and said, her voice distant, "Do you think love should be like this? Wanting something else?"

"I don't want —"

His wife pushed him back and met his eyes. "You want the sea. To leave. But you must wait until I am prepared to go with you."

He was silent for a moment as he feared her implication. "Do *you* want something more?"

"No." He knew Miranda was lying as he stood and returned to the window.

She sighed and continued, "Dreng, you are not my first love. You know —" He focused on the distant horizon, bracing himself for her words as she sighed and continued, "The man whom I loved, before, was my everything, and he haunts me, still. But he made oaths he could not keep. Madness took him, and he changed." Her breath shook as she inhaled deeply. "I did as well."

Caliban, Dreng guessed. Their intimacy had been clear: the crooked man's longing looks and frequent sighs.

Miranda stood and crossed the room, wrapping her arms around his waist. "Just know that this love is different. It is built of the stuff of stars, the magic of the universe. I know that you will love me until I die."

On that night, as Dreng stood in the darkness, he understood her to mean that they would love each other.

But now, with the distance of memory, he saw her words for their true, simple meaning.

Their love was his to give and hers to receive.

She seemed incapable of loving anyone, even her husband.

Except, perhaps, her mysterious first love.

And Dreng, within his cloud of thought, realized that whoever or whatever Miranda had before him, whatever emotions she shared with Caliban, would return the moment she saw the beautiful youth. Miranda should, *would* get what she wanted, and he could not stand in her way.

Yet he must still save her. He owed it to her, as her husband, as the one responsible for — It was his honor at stake.

But first, Alda.

And in his memory, Dreng knew what he had to do.

So as he stood in the memory of the palace's bedchamber, he closed his eyes, thinking of the forest. He opened them, expecting to see the green tapestry and smell the overpowering flora.

Instead, he was underwater. In a different memory. Tossed amid the waves as colored lightning flashed overhead, the shadow of *The Tempest* looming above. He kicked and pulled and willed himself up, but the surface was still so distant...

His hand broke through. Then the other. Finally, his head was above the whitecaps. And he breathed.

In the forest, Dreng sat upright. His silver-blue garb soaked with sweat, his dark hair dripping into his eyes. He stood, shaking, and steadied his gasping breaths, reassuring himself that he was again in the present.

Queen Mab and her guard were gone. As was Alda. But there was no blood, no sign of injury to her. Had Alda passed through the flowered ring?

Dreng parted the curtain of pink flowers, looking for the circle of forget-me-nots. But it had vanished.

He ran his fingers nervously through his hair and, in doing so, looked up. The vines above were torn. Broken flowers littered the forest floor, trampled by footsteps.

Dreng smiled. Alda, it seemed, had escaped. And those who had given chase left a trail that he could follow.

But what would he do when he discovered her, when he again confronted Queen Mab and her tribe? What *could* he do?

He needed a weapon. Not the queen's bewitched sword. Something honest and simple and dependable. A branch? No, he needed steel.

Like the blade he had snatched from the clumsy player, Nick Bottom. The sword that had dropped from Dreng's grip when he had been captured by Robin Goodfellow.

As Dreng followed the trail of the fairies' footsteps, he remembered Alda's words and wished for the fallen sword. If Alda was correct, if this place could deliver to a man that which he most desired, then…

Dreng shook his head as thoughts of Alda and Miranda and Netherfeld and all that he had lost came crowding in. He stopped and breathed deeply, calming his pounding heart until all he could see and want was the weapon. He let the longing overtake him.

Once he was calm, he took a step. And another. And more. And within ten paces, Dreng saw a glint of metal in the soft, blue light.

Chapter Fourteen: Love Never Did Run

Alda knew that the queen's band was quickly approaching, so she burst through the curtain of trees into Oberon's court. Her lungs ached as she gasped for air and finally wheezed, "Queen Titania is —"

"TRAITOR!" Oberon's voice bellowed through the glade, echoing from the canopy above. Even the leaves seemed to quake in terror. "You disobeyed, me, your father, the *king*."

Alda's eyes searched for a friendly face among the emotionless, green beings that quickly encircled her. Oberon stood at the far end of the glade near his throne, with Phillida on a toadstool at his feet.

Even from this distance, Alda could see the tracks of tears on her pale green cheeks.

Two guards moved in and took hold of Alda's arm, the one on her left pressing painfully on her injury. She let out a shallow cry as Oberon crossed the space and the others parted before him.

"You abandoned your bridegroom. And your mother. And *me*." His voice lost its sing-song tone as he shook with rage, and his gaze flew over her form as she struggled to break free.

Finally, his eyes landed on her wound. On the red blood. And the bandage.

The shimmering fabric torn from Dreng's shirt.

Oberon's eyes somehow grew even wider, his lips curling and teeth gnashing as he spat, "And you have aligned with *her*! Why, why did you betray me so?"

Alda stopped struggling against her captors long enough to stammer, "She — she is coming for me!"

"So you do not deny it?" Oberon's tone revealed something like remorse.

"No, no, Titania wants to kill me —"

"Then the queen will have to wait her turn, you disobedient wretch." The king lowered his eyes and returned toward his throne as Phillida audibly wept. He avoided Alda's fiery glare as he placed one hand on Phillida's shoulder and wiped his eyes with the other as he commanded, "Send Aldeering through the willow tree."

A murmur spread across the glade, and the two guards holding Alda dragged her toward the fairy tree with its many portals. As Alda grew closer, she could see each door, each unique, all covering the willow's trunk and lower limbs.

Where did they lead? "No!" The fairies in the mob around her did not react to her objection, but the tone of their whispers was foreboding.

Alda turned her attention toward her mother. Phillida finally stood, her voice high and quick, "Do not send her there, my lord, to a place unknown, allow her to stay with us, please, I beg you!" She covered her face as a sob wracked her slim frame.

Oberon looked to Alda's mother. "This child has refused my command and denied her bridegroom. The injustice is not mine alone to bear." Alda was now at the base of the willow, the length of the glade stretching between her and the king. She could not read Oberon's expressions, but the anger in his voice was apparent.

The king stepped toward the center of the clearing and rubbed his chin. "But where is Cob Web? He deserves justice as well."

Cob emerged timidly from the treeline and bowed before the King of Shadows. Oberon waved his hand angrily as he asked, "What say you?"

Alda felt the grip on her arms loosen as the others waited in silence for Cob's response. She twisted free and ran to Cob's side, reaching into her sleeve as she fell at his feet.

"I am sorry for running away, before, master Web. I was scared. But now, I need your help." She looked up, pleading, "The queen is coming, and you must protect me and rescue my, my friend."

Alda clasped his hands, waiting for his response. His grip was cold, inhuman. But in a moment, his fingers enthusiastically encircled hers.

He helped her to her feet, looked placidly into her eyes, and turned to Oberon. "I must do as my fiancée commands, my lord."

Phillida choked as her sob transformed into something like a cheer. Oberon turned away, hiding his expression and pacing before his throne.

Shocked whispers echoed below the trees and their flowered garlands.

"I am not one to stand in the way of love, my boy, but this enthusiasm is a sudden turn."

Alda looked at her feet and smiled.

She still held Cob's hand.

And still pressed the scrap of enchanted handkerchief against his palm.

Cob met her eyes, "What is your command? Simply say the word, my love, and I will destroy an army for you."

Carefully, Alda tucked the piece of handkerchief into Cob's cuff. His eyes never left hers, and she was unnerved by their lack of emotion, despite his professed fidelity.

"I must beg you —" Alda paused. "My love, to lead some soldiers into the forest with me. To find my injured friend." She saw confusion in his eyes. "He is a human, a mortal, like me."

Cob nodded and summoned five others from the crowd gathered in the treeline. As he did so, Alda felt a momentary pang of regret at her deceit. But she shook her head and reminded herself that Cob and all the others could not die.

There was nothing at stake, for them.

But Alda, and Dreng, could lose all.

The small band paused at the edge of the glade, as Alda bid them to wait. If she could find Dreng and the ring of forget-me-nots, then she might not return. At least, not directly.

So Alda turned to the king, who flashed a sneer of indignation. Alda's words — words that she might say to a father — were lost, so she stated simply, "Titania is coming. Prepare for her."

She then took Phillida's hand and affectionately squeezed her fingers. "I will return, Mother." She paused and muttered, "If I can."

Phillida patted her hand and smiled weakly. "You will, as there is a way."

Finally, Alda turned to Cob and the others. She knew that the mob of Titania's guards approached, and she wondered why they had not yet appeared. Perhaps they were not giving chase, after all?

So Alda grew bold as she looked to Cob Web and commanded, "I will lead you through the woods, to my friend. Stay close." She took two steps toward the trees that lined the glade before staggering back, a silver sword held to her throat.

The trees parted of their own accord, revealing Titania, regal and commanding as she brandished her weapon with the strength of a seasoned soldier.

The sword's tip punctured Alda's skin, and she felt blood trickle down her collarbone.

Alda stumbled back, into Cob's arms. In one swift movement, he steadied her and stepped between Alda and the queen's blade.

Titania's glistening footmen trotted into the clearing, now fully visible in their array of silver and blue, and the green fairies receded into the shadows, their piercing cries sounding like crows escaping some common enemy.

Oberon rushed forward and furiously spat, "You are not to be here, you haughty hag! There is a truce —"

The queen turned toward the king but kept her weapon trained on Alda. "Is this thing *your* child, my husband?"

Oberon's face burned brighter green.

"Ah," Titania continued, circling her prey. Cob maintained his stance between Alda and the aggressor, but his sword remained tied at his waist, useless against the mightier, bejeweled weapon.

Then Titania laughed. The sound was gleeful and unexpected, and Alda shivered as the queen continued, "I think you mistook the truce for an annulment. It is not so."

With her eyes still trained on the King of Shadows, Titania slashed Cob's chest. He stumbled and fell into Alda's arms. She tripped back, his weight pushing her to the ground. As Alda struggled to sit with his head on her lap, she thought of Dreng, a boy in the darkness of the ship's hold, breathing shallowly as he had bled in her arms.

Alda pushed the thought away as she measured Cob's pulse. Dark green liquid spilled from his chest, yet he was conscious and seemingly unaware of his pain. He reached for her face and whispered, "It is a small price for your love, my dearest."

But Alda could not respond. Her voice closed within her throat, the guilt of her trickery weighing on her heart.

She wiped the blood from Cob's face and undid the cuff of his sleeve. The scrap of enchanted handkerchief fell to the ground at her side, and he was released from its powers.

Cob Web blinked twice as something like confusion crossed his face. He turned from her and sat upright, holding his arms across his chest to stem the bleeding.

Titania laughed again, her glee apparent in her tone, "No one stands between us now, changeling."

She raised the sword to strike.

As Alda looked up, she saw a green blur. A flash of metal. An airy cry, and a thud before her.

"No!" Alda barely felt the word escape from her lips as she crouched at her fallen mother's side, pressing her hands against the red blood that fell from her injured breast.

Titania wiped the crimson liquid from the blade and studied its color on her hand for a moment before she readied for a second blow.

"Treachery! The blast of war has sounded!" Oberon's voice boomed, its volume igniting a fiery cry from the surrounding trees as the greens loosed their weapons and lunged against the sparkling silver beings.

The king himself, brandishing a golden sword, charged toward Titania, who met his attack with fierce parries.

Alda barely noticed. She looked helplessly into her mother's eyes as the blood pooled around her green fingers.

In spite of everything, Phillida smiled. "I found you, Alda, I found you, and after all these years, I had so hoped we could be together, and be young forever." The injured woman's eyes widened. "But we can't, Alda, we can't because I'm dying."

"No, no, I can help you." Alda knew the words were a lie. The wound was too deep, the hole too near her heart.

"I cannot stay here, now, so take me, Alda, take me, take me to the willow, and let me pass through a door."

"But the tree is dangerous."

"What danger should I fear now, child?"

"Where will you go?"

"I don't know, that is the beauty of it, the willow tree is a mystery, a chance that you take to...." She coughed, and blood trickled down her cheek.

"But you will die."

"I will die here or anywhere so let me have an adventure at the last, I have looked at the willow for years and always wondered where its doors may lead, and now I want to wonder no more."

She reached for Alda's face and added, her voice shaking and her tone more urgent, "And I do not want my daughter to see me die, that is too much for one still so young."

Alda felt the tears on her cheeks, blinding her to the frenzy of blades and blood that enveloped them. "Mother, we can't reach the tree. I can't carry you."

"I can."

Dreng stood above them. How long had he been there?

He crouched and took Alda's hands off her mother's wound. "Take my sword." He hoisted Phillida into his arms, examined the fray, and commanded, "Stay close."

Alda remained in Dreng's shadow, nearly touching him, holding the sword as best she could. The fairy warriors were too preoccupied with their own conflicts to notice the humans skirting their game, so they crossed the glade unobstructed.

When the trio finally reached the willow, Dreng lowered Phillida against its trunk as Alda stared worriedly at the turmoil around them. Phillida followed her gaze, coughed, and with a steadier voice whispered, "They are like gods, we are their ants, they will battle to the end of time, and we will follow each other to our graves."

Alda nodded, pretending to fully understand, as she studied the doors on the fairy tree. All were miniature, intricate, like something from a dollhouse. Finally, Alda asked, "Which door?"

"You can choose, darling."

Alda selected one of bright purple, adorned with hinges made of gold. The most regal. It emitted a white glow when opened. "Mother, I —"

Phillida interrupted, "I will come back to you, somehow, and we will know each other again." She wiped blood from her lips, coughed into her palm, and kissed Alda on the cheek. "This is not the end, so you must save yourself." She looked up at Dreng and smiled. "And him."

As Phillida reached for the tree, a realization flashed across her face. "I remember my name now, it is Hecate!" But her face fell as she added, "No, that was your grandmother, I think I have always been myself. Only Phillida." Alda watched as her mother thrust her hand into the portal.

And vanished.

Dreng's eyes were filled with confusion as Alda stood and placed the sword in his fist. She held his free hand and whispered, "Follow me."

"Where are we going?"

"To safety."

But before they could move, Dreng lurched forward, a look of shock on his face.

A silvery-green dagger was embedded in his back, near his shoulder. The tip cut through the front of his shirt.

"No!"

Dreng's sword fell to the ground, and blood stained the silver-blue fabric as his eyes searched Alda's, brimming with confusion and fear.

But Alda had no time to tend his injury.

Standing over them both was Robin Goodfellow. With a sword aimed at her heart.

Alda planted her feet and held Dreng's sword in both hands, its blade threatening the green man.

"Alda, don't." Dreng coughed. "He's too strong."

But Alda stood firm.

Robin ignored Dreng as he hissed at Alda, "Your grave is gaping wide." He was within striking distance of Alda. Two steps, and he would have her. "There is now nowhere to hide."

Alda knew she would be killed. She had no experience, no skill, in matters of combat. But she withstood her trembling hands, forcing the blade to be steady as she braced for a blow.

Then, suddenly, Puck was felled with a blow from behind.

As Robin Goodfellow hit the ground, unconscious, Caliban stood over his crumpled form and rubbed his knuckles, sneering, "I've always wanted to hit a hobgoblin."

For the first time, Alda was glad to see the strange youth. Caliban stretched his fingers and said, "Give me the sword, witch."

Alda smiled with relief and handed him the weapon. "You're late."

"You gave terrible directions." As Caliban spoke, he studied the doors on the tree.

Alda helped Dreng to his feet, steadying him with her shoulder. Nervously watching the forces around her, she asked the beautiful boy, "Which door will you choose?"

Caliban glanced at her and scoffed, "The one to Netherfeld." He pointed to a green door, its hinges made of intricate wrought iron.

"How do you know that's the one?"

"I can always find my way home."

Caliban reached for the door, but Alda grabbed his arm. "There is a woman there, in Netherfeld, named Ophelia, and she needs —" Before she could finish, Dreng swooned. Alda caught his weight and looked questioningly at Caliban.

The beautiful youth nodded gravely at Alda. "I already told you, I *know* her." He hesitated and asked, "Can you save him?"

Alda looked at Dreng and nodded. "I think so. No, I *know*."

"If you have that knowledge, then I'll be along." Caliban glanced one last time at the battle around them and murmured, "Once more into the void." He thrust his hand through the green door, and vanished.

For a moment, Alda stood amid the chaos but felt completely alone. It was like being in a moving painting, swirls and colors and, amid the clang of metal, a perceived silence. Then pounding in her ears.

She watched her father, the King of Shadows, as he swung and leapt and thrust opposite Titania, his face ecstatic in what should have been a scene of despair. Queen Mab was likewise joyful, gracefully dodging and attacking in time to his movements. It was like a dance, a bloody waltz.

Her mother was correct: these beings would battle to the end of time.

Alda was suddenly aware of Dreng's weight fully on her shoulder, his eyes fluttering beneath his lids, as she was overcome by her burden.

She had to get him to safety. This time — she *had* to save him. "Can you walk?"

Dreng did not respond.

*   *   *

Dreng only felt dizzy. Like a sickness after a turbulent storm. Not injured, but he felt something lodged in his shoulder and could not move his left arm. He also saw darkness approaching, clouding the outside of his vision and threatening to cover his eyes completely.

As Alda guided him through the forest, he became aware that his feet were barely moving. His weight was on her, and he felt strangely light.

Then came flashes. Green, like a tunnel. A clearing. Blue flowers in a circle. The sensation of falling and falling and then somehow falling up. On his feet again. Darkness. Natural darkness, and moonlight. Yellow stones and more falling. Alda under his arm, limping. Walking, moving. A trail with a river and gray stones. The creak of wood. Yes, a bridge. A door slamming and a smell of herbs. Rosemary, the smell that he knew so long ago. More falling, but not as far, and a soft cushion. A blanket and a candle. No, not a candle, something brighter. The scent of other herbs, and cold liquid on his shoulder.

And, finally, pain. Excruciating pain. Numbness. Water on his lips. And nothing.

Chapter Fifteen: Poison of Deep Grief

The first hours in Alda's cottage, in her home on the seventh island, were chaos. After she removed Puck's dagger, Dreng moaned and fought in his delirium, unaware of her aid and fearing some unseen danger. She did her best to ease his suffering until he finally collapsed on her little couch, his eyeballs active beneath his lids.

As the sun climbed above her windowpane, Alda examined Dreng's wound. It was green, a mossy shade that spread across his chest and down his arm, mingling with the iridescent silver that radiated from his skin.

Alda delicately smoothed her green fingers across the wound's surface. At her touch, an emerald-tinted liquid trickled from the puncture in his shoulder. She pressed harder, and more seeped out.

It was poison.

Alda worked patiently for what felt like several hours, squeezing his injury until the liquid turned to blood. Her mind drifted to a song from her childhood, an old ballad about a young man who was bitten by a rattlesnake: when his true love tried to suck out the poison, she too died.

Molly had a rotten tooth in which it stuck, and killed them both, she sang in her mind.

So Alda shook her head and changed her thoughts. But her memories were all darkness and death.

Her father, an emotionless tyrant.

Her mother, incapable and lost.

Her grandmother, deceptive and gone.

Finally, she decided to end her worries with words. Dreng was still unconscious, his head turning and sweating amid his moans. She brought a wet rag from the kitchen and wiped his forehead as she whispered, "I really don't know you at all, Dreng."

It seemed like a good place to start, an introduction. So she wiped more poison from his shoulder and continued, "My name is Alda Reeding. I know a little magic, but I am not a witch. I grew up on an island, alone except for my grandmother."

Her voice caught, so she shifted the rag and continued, "I met you, when you were a boy. On a ship. First above the waves and then again, later, in the hold below the deck. I wanted so much to take you with me, to save you. But I didn't know how. And here, now, I still don't know how. So I need *you* to help me save you."

He moaned, and she wiped his damp hair from his forehead. "You are something to me. Important. I feel like we know one another. That we have some shared connection." Alda smiled as she remembered a passage from one of her grandmother's old books, "As if I had a string somewhere under my left ribs, tightly knotted to a similar string in you."

She shook her head. That was a romance. The words weren't right for this. This felt more tragic. The wound he inflicted in her arm reminded her of the grim reality of their fates.

She leaned to his ear and whispered, "Dreng, I need you to live so I can know you." She hesitated and added, "Fight, for me."

Alda wiped a tear from her cheek as she sat straighter and studied his face. It had eased, somewhat. The sweat was less abundant, his eyes still. At peace, finally.

She lowered the rag into a bucket near the fireplace and saw something flash on his hand. Dreng's ring that Caliban had given to her, glistening beneath dried blood on his finger.

The ring was important, she knew, and it needed her care. To be cleaned, to be made new. Resurrected, in a way. So she slipped it over Dreng's knuckles and held it on her forefinger, examining it in the light of the fire as she wiped his blood from its surface.

The ring was old but not extraordinary. Gold, with one side flat and an engraving of some sort of seal. Not a wedding band or any sort that appeared sentimental. Or magical.

But Caliban had said — How could a simple ring awaken the dead? She doubted him.

Alda glanced at Dreng, now peaceful in slumber. The green near his puncture had nearly vanished, replaced by the shimmering iridescence that radiated from his skin.

Alda smiled, somewhat at ease. And with her thoughts on a happier future, she absentmindedly slid the ring until it was fully on her finger.

For a moment, all was as it should be. Nothing changed. But Alda had a strange sensation, a ticking in her ears and the feeling that she was being watched.

She turned toward the kitchen and there, between the oak table and the sink, was her grandmother.

The form was immaterial, transparent. Ghostly. Alda shivered as she gasped and asked, "Is it really you, Gramma?"

The apparition nodded. But Alda knew better than to trust some magical being. So she stood between Dreng and the thing and asked, "If you are truly my grandmother, then who is my mother?"

The ghost flickered and whispered, in a rough voice, "You know, now."

"Tell me."

It blinked several times before answering, "Phillida."

Alda relaxed for an instant before her grandmother added, "A foolish girl who trusted too easily."

"You were her mother, and it was your duty to protect her from — from whatever dangers might come!" She drew her breath and continued, with heartbreak cracking her voice, "Why did you never tell me about her?"

"You needed to learn for yourself."

"But you deceived me!"

The ghost was silent.

"You withheld information. Secrets. Knowledge." Any joy that Alda felt upon seeing her grandmother vanished as she asked, "What else have you not told me?"

A pause, interrupted only by Dreng's peaceful breathing.

The ghost flickered. "You are — as I was — a witch."

Alda shook her head and looked to the floor, focusing on the knots in the boards as she avoided her grandmother's gaze. "I know you are called Hecate."

As Alda spoke the final word, she remembered the witches on the moor: *Hecate? But how can that be?*

"Yes, the witches' leader. Or I was, once, long before." Silence for a moment, and then the rattling voice demanded, "Look at me, child!"

Alda raised her head and glanced at Dreng before she faced the apparition. "How can I trust you?"

"You don't have to trust me. Just *believe*." The image flickered again, disappearing for a heartbeat and then reforming. "The weyward sisters are draining Netherfeld — consuming its magic. You must stop them."

"How?"

The ghost seemed not to hear her as it continued, "Soon the magic will be theirs alone, none left for others." Its eyes pierced into Alda's as it added, "They have already stolen many of your powers. When they transplanted you here. You must hurry. While you can still reach Netherfeld."

Alda thought of her inability to form the lights, both here and in Fairy

Land. Her magic, it appeared, was in fact waning. "What must I do?"

Again, the apparition did not respond.

"How can I stop them?"

Nothing.

"How!?"

The being shivered as it finally disappeared. Alda, her fingers shaking, removed the ring and wiped the beading sweat from her forehead.

*   *   *

When Dreng's eyes finally regained focus, he was covered in sweat on a narrow bed, or rather an oblong chair, alone in a small room. It was night, and long shadows flickered from a round, lighted globe that cast strange shapes across the ceiling. Detailed paintings in shades of black and brown hung on the walls, which were themselves covered in an intricate pattern of yellow loops and flowers. Old coals smoked in the hearth, and bundles of herbs hung above a long table opposite some sort of empty cistern.

Where was he?

This place was foreign. Nothing was familiar, yet he felt safe.

Why?

The smell. The scent he knew from his boyhood on the ship, the scent that had preceded his meeting with Alda.

Rosemary.

This place, he guessed, must be Alda's home.

But where was she?

Dreng tried to stand, but felt too weak. So he sat again and examined his body, his injuries.

A small puncture near his chest was healing and covered in a thick scab. He ran his hand over a wound on his back and found his fingers covered in a tacky, amber substance that smelled of unfamiliar herbs.

Had Alda done this? To return him to health?

He was not fully mended, but he was also not in danger of death.

He would recover, he knew.

In time.

And, Dreng realized, he could feel again. Pain. In his shoulder and back. Not sharp, but the dull throbbing of healing. How long had he been here, helpless and unconscious?

As he wondered, he studied his hands. The luminous glow was gone. His skin had returned to its natural tone. He was becoming himself again, sensation and all.

He felt his face, and its growth was of a week. No more than two.

And in that time, what else had passed?

His thoughts quickly turned to fears. Caliban, searching for Netherfeld. Miranda, entombed in an icy grave. Both needed his help. But he was trapped, here, now. How could he reach them?

How could he save them?

He would need help. Where was Alda?

Gone.

How could he find her?

His mind seemed overflowing with questions, without answers. So he scanned the room for clues.

A flash of gold on a small table near the hearth caught his eye. A welcome distraction. He struggled to his feet and painfully inched toward his goal until he collapsed in a chair next to the table.

Prince Hamlet's signet ring. It, at least, was safe.

Dreng held it in the filtered moonlight, turning it over several times before placing it on his finger.

Then he saw a tiny book, smaller than his palm, beneath where the ring had rested. He examined it, skimming its pages. The writing was miniscule, at first blots and shapes and nothing discernible. But this was the language he could read, so he waited until the words formed.

Within a heartbeat, the shapes bled and shifted into letters and then words and phrases: rhymes, in all likelihood spells, written by a shaking hand. With names like "pricking thumb" and "trouble fire" and "something wicked."

He could not suppress his smile; this was useful, somehow. But he did not yet understand its potential.

As he studied the book's pages, a cold breeze blew through the room, and Dreng looked up as a door creaked open and a familiar figure entered from the darkness beyond.

Chapter Sixteen: Such Sweet Thunder

Outside the cottage in the moonlight, with stolen medicine in her hand, Alda hesitated amid the flowers lining her garden's flagstones. Distant thunder roared, and she watched lightning flash red on the horizon upstream.

Elsewhere, she would fear magical spirits. Yet here, in Grand Ledge, she knew that it was only a summer storm. She was safe.

But in the days since they escaped from the fairies, Alda had been in a state of constant anxiety. Dreng was slow to recover from his poisoned wound, despite her attempts to make him well, and she was still reeling from all that had happened.

Even though her skin had returned to its natural hue, the events of Fairy Land were still etched in her mind. The loss of her mother. The last glimpse of her father, smiling in a battle that could not be won, a battle that he enjoyed.

Now, as she hesitated on the threshold of her cottage on the seventh island, returned to the year eighteen ninety-seven, Alda had one nagging question:

What next?

There were witches and fairies and magic out there, far away, but she could leave them all and be safe here. And she would not have to be alone.

She could make Dreng well and start a new chapter. They could ride the resort island's rollercoaster or attend an operetta or skate hand in hand like the couples she envied from a distance.

They could be happy — finally — and together.

And maybe, after some time, they could forget the witches and fairies and magic.

When Dreng awoke, she decided she would ask him to stay. Yes, she would propose this plan.

She took a deep breath as she felt raindrops on her bare arms, opened the door, and almost dropped the medicine bottle.

Dreng was gone.

No, he was awake, moved. No longer on the couch but instead slumped in a chair near the empty fireplace, his hand resting on the little end-table. He saw her, but his eyes were distant, lost in thought. Yet he smiled as she sat on a little stool opposite the hearth.

As Dreng rubbed his eyes, Alda said, "You look like you've seen a ghost." She immediately regretted her attempt at humor and continued, "I'm glad you're awake. Does it hurt?"

He only smiled meekly, so she was silent for several seconds before she offered the medicine bottle. "Here. It will help."

"Thank you." He read the paper label, furrowed his brow, and turned it over several times. Still avoiding her gaze, he opened it and started to pour it into his hand.

"No, no." Alda took the bottle from him, its contents dripping down the side. "You drink it."

"Why?" He looked at her, and she saw his eyes were full of ache.

He did not understand this time, this medicine. "It will make you feel better." She wiped the bottle and offered it again.

He hesitantly took it, eyed the liquid suspiciously, and finally drank. He coughed and cursed under his breath.

Alda suppressed a smile as she crossed the room into the kitchen and poured water from a floral pitcher into a chipped mug. As she returned to his side, she found the courage to express her relief. "I had thought, all these months — since I saw you on the island — that you were dead."

He thanked her for the water and drank. Finally, he murmured, "You were mistaken."

Again, she smiled. "I know, and I'm glad."

"How did you escape?" He raised his eyebrows questioningly, and she saw the lines on his brow ease as he relaxed.

Alda had wanted to ask the same question, but she answered, "I ran. After I saw —after I thought you were dead — I ran until I reached the cliffs. And I used a cauldron's bubble to, to reach safety." She paused and added, "It is a magical object, a kind of spell, that takes one to other times and places. I mentioned it before, in the forest, but—" She stopped herself and watched him until he nodded. Then she asked, "How did *you* escape? From Sycorax?"

Dreng appeared not to hear her as he twisted the signet ring on his finger, his thoughts seemingly elsewhere. Finally, he asked, "Why did you think I was dead?"

Alda sighed. "I came into the courtyard. After, after Prospero — was killed — I came into the courtyard, and —"

Dreng's voice trembled. "Did you see him die?"

"No, but he was killed by Sycorax." Alda spat the word with disgust.

"Caliban's mother?"

"Yes."

Dreng's expression darkened. "You saw her?"

"Yes, in the library, with Prospero's body."

Dreng's eyes overflowed with confusion. "You saw Sycorax? On the island?"

Alda frowned, "Of course. As did you."

"I did not." His tone was firm.

Was he delirious? Did the poison still linger? Had the medicine somehow harmed him?

Alda spoke slowly, "You did. Of course, you did."

He shook his head, clenching his hands into fists. Why did Dreng insist on this falsehood?

Alda steadied her voice and sighed, "Yes. She kissed you, and you collapsed — that is why I thought you died."

Alda knew that her frustration was apparent in her tone, but Dreng laughed. "That was Miranda, not Sycorax. And I must have fainted. I awoke some time later, in the courtyard. And you were gone."

Alda's heart beat heavily in her ears.

She understood now.

He did not know about Sycorax, that she inhabited Miranda's body.

What had happened in these months since?

Before Alda could explain, Dreng continued, "There was no danger, you see. It was all a misunderstanding. If you had stayed, then —"

The heartbeat in her ears turned to ringing as Alda blurted, "Sycorax tried to kill me."

She had. Had she? But Caliban — Had Caliban, in the fairies' forest, been honest?

Alda shook her head. "I was *not* mistaken. After I *thought* Sycorax had killed you, and after she attacked *me*, I had no choice but to run."

"But —"

Alda took hold of his hands, her palms sweating and fingers shaking. "Dreng, listen to me. The woman you know to be Miranda is Sycorax."

He studied her eyes, and his lips curled into a sneer as he asked suspiciously, "What do you mean?"

"Sycorax, through some spell or magic, took control of Miranda's body."

Silence.

"The woman is dangerous, Dreng."

"You speak of my wife, Alda."

"Wife?" Alda's heart sank. Sycorax had entrapped him. "That makes her no less dangerous."

He shook his head and struggled to his feet. "*You* are mistaken."

Suppressing her anger, Alda held his elbow until he was steady. Once he found his feet, he straightened and said with certainty, "My wife is in danger. She may even be dead by now. She was consumed by a spring on the island, frozen while I have wasted time here." A look of pain flashed his on his face. "She is in peril, and she is not evil. And whatever I had thought in the world of fae, however I had felt there, about y— about anything else — those feelings were forgeries. They were not true, not real."

Alda returned his proud tone. "You doubt truth to be a liar."

His eyes burnt into hers as he whispered, "What?"

She repeated the words as he ran his fingers through his hair.

"Where did you hear that?"

"From a — a friend." Alda tripped over the final word, her heart aching at the thought of Ophelia trapped with the witches in Netherfeld. "It means —"

"I know what it means. It's part of a riddle. Caliban told me."

"Caliban?"

"Yes. It's nonsense."

"How did he come to know it?"

"From his mother." Dreng paused and added, with sarcasm seeping into his voice, "From my *wife*, apparently." He lost his balance and caught himself on the back of the chair. "I need air."

"Let me help you." She reached for him.

He evaded her touch. "No."

Before she could intervene, Dreng crossed the short distance to the doorway and let himself out.

Alone, Alda realized that her ears had stopped ringing. All she could hear was pounding rain.

*   *   *

Outside, in the torrent, Dreng finally felt at ease. He understood storms, their chaos. And even though lightning had killed his father and disfigured him, he was not afraid, not now.

But he was angry.

He leaned against the door for support as puddles formed at his feet. His mind searched for something to grasp.

Sycorax, he knew, was a sorceress. No, that was not what others called her. She was a summoner. She was evil, a villain, a killer.

But why?

What had she done, exactly?

Dreng only knew of her through Caliban, and it was clear he had no love for his mother. If Sycorax was indeed Miranda, then Caliban would have known.

But did he know?

Caliban had spoken of Miranda loving him, of Miranda being somehow trapped in Netherfeld when Dreng knew her body was encased in an icy tomb.

Had Caliban spoken of Dreng's wife, or his own love?

As Dreng wiped the water from his eyes, pain shot from his elbow through his scar, the remnant of the St. Elmo's fire. The scar's racking pain was greater than his recent wound, and he clenched his fist until it subsided.

Suddenly, his mind felt clearer. Like the rain's water had washed away his delusions. His anger, his doubt vanished. And he remembered Caliban's words on the raft:

Your Miranda is not my Miranda. They are two but seen as one.

Dreng should have suspected sooner that something was amiss. He should have questioned Caliban's words immediately, but the sea-maids and fairies and everything in between and since had kept him from the truth.

Caliban knew.

He knew that Sycorax had taken Miranda's form. He may have even aided her. What appeared to be Miranda's resurrection in the cave, when Dreng first arrived on the island, might have been something else entirely.

And Dreng remembered her eyes. The sudden change from jet black to vibrant blue.

More recently, her midnight wanderings, her unspoken secrets, the images in the enchanted cavern.

Did Dreng know her?

Did it even matter?

She was his wife, whoever *she* was.

Miranda or Sycorax, it made no difference.

He was bound to the woman trapped in the frozen pool. He owed her loyalty.

And he had to save her.

Again, he let the rain run down his forehead and felt the weight of uncertainty lift from his shoulders. He had a goal, a mission, something concrete. A rescue.

And after she was safe, he would have time to determine if she was a hero or villain.

As Dreng's focus returned to the present, to his surroundings, he realized the rain was harder now, the pool near his feet risen above his ankles.

He reached toward the door but smelled the scent of the sea, brackish air that was out of place in a heavy storm.

He turned. Standing silhouetted in the moonlight was the ghost. His father's figure, its eyes glowing red.

Dreng held himself against the closed door, his legs suddenly unsteady and his breath coming in gasps as he squinted through the torrent.

Like each time before, the apparition's mouth moved like a landed fish before it creaked out, "The tide is turning, you must find three witches, quickly, and—"

"Who are you?" Dreng had the courage to directly ask the question he should have asked when the ghost first appeared.

"You know me, son."

"Do I?" Dreng laughed, the sound bitter. "You may be the devil, for all I know. I don't even know my own wife. Or myself."

"But you do." The image flickered and reappeared, stronger.

"Then what is my name?"

"What's in a name?"

Dreng stepped away from the door, emboldened by having so little to lose. "I am in a place out of joint with my time and home, married to a woman who is out of form, embroiled with magic and witches and fairies and a strange land that is nothing. And yet, I am called by a word that means 'boy' in a foreign tongue. *If* you are my father, tell me, what is my name?"

"Trust me, son."

"No, you trust me. If you do not, then you are some vile *thing* that is not my father."

The spectre was silent.

"Tell me who I am!" Dreng felt his fists clench. Rain ran over his injured shoulder and down his scar.

But, amid the turmoil of the storm and his pain, Dreng's attention was only on the ghost. He listened with every nerve of his body as the figure opened its mouth and whispered two words into the night.

*   *   *

Alda closed her mouth. She had wanted to speak to Dreng, to calm him, but he left too quickly. For a moment, she considered following him into the rain but reconsidered.

After all, she had loosed a secret that may have been better kept. So instead of walking to the door, she crossed the room to the kitchen.

All was as she had left it. The herbs. The list of ingredients. The remnants of the jack-in-the-pulpit. She scanned the items quickly. Yes, she had enough for one more attempt.

One more chance to make a cauldron's bubble. One more chance to escape from here. One final chance to stop the witches and save Ophelia.

As Alda assembled the ingredients, she thought about Ophelia, the young, lost mother.

Ophelia, who had said *doubt truth to be a liar*.

Ophelia, who had birthed a son in a realm of nothing, who could spin spirits out of air.

Ophelia, who seemed strangely familiar, like words to a lullaby that had not been sung in years.

As Alda muddled and mixed the herbs, an unexpected thought creeped into her head.

What if — before Sycorax was Sycorax — she was Ophelia?

Alda stopped mixing as she stared at the yellow wallpaper, her eyes tracing its pattern as her mind reached into her memory.

The magic. The spirits. The son. It all aligned. The only differences were the names and appearance.

No, not the appearance. Alda realized that she had never seen Sycorax, not in her true form.

And Alda had even told the young mother about Sycorax; Ophelia could have taken the name in some strange paradox.

In the Fairy Land forest, Caliban had told Alda that his mother knew her. Alda had assumed this acquaintance was during her forgotten years, the time she lost in Netherfeld, before she could retain her memories. But what if he had meant earlier than that, earlier in his mother's timeline?

And Caliban had said that he had been born in Netherfeld, that he knew his way home. Was Caliban, in fact, Hamnet? The son of a prince?

Six months before, when Alda had met Sycorax on Prospero's island, the summoner could have killed her. It was clear that she had superior powers; she could have shot spirits and spells and easily ended Alda's life. But she did not. Instead, she let Alda escape.

Maybe Dreng was right. Maybe Sycorax was good. Maybe it was all some misunderstanding, the result of Prospero and others building stories in their minds full of prejudice and fear and little fact or compassion.

And if Sycorax was indeed Ophelia, the kind, young mother pining after the man she had loved and lost... then Alda could believe that Sycorax was not evil.

But she would need proof, somehow. And the only way to get that was to help Dreng save his wife from the frozen spring. Then she could ask for herself.

For a split second, Alda's heart sank. Rescuing Dreng's wife would most likely mean losing him. But that did not matter. In the end, even after his recovery here, she barely knew him. Her feelings were an illusion, like an actress putting on a show.

So saving his wife was the only way to help Dreng.

As Alda reached this resolution, her cottage returned to focus around her. Suddenly, she was aware of the spoon in her hand, the herbs in the cast iron. Muddled and mixed.

All that remained was the jack-in-the-pulpit, its unused half still on the table.

The spell's final ingredient.

Alda held her breath as she added it. But nothing happened.

Again.

It was as it had been before, on the night she was taken to Fairy Land.

And, as she had six months earlier — alone in her cottage after her grandmother's burial — Alda allowed herself to cry. Her head on the table, cradled by her arms. Tears dripping from her wrists.

But this time was different.

When she finally lifted her head, there was no magical omen that appeared to lead her way, no word written in the crumblings and herbs. She was trapped and helpless, still.

And the rain beat harder on the windows.

Chapter Seventeen: The Rest is Silence

Dreng opened the cottage door with a burst of energy. The ghost had told him of the witches, of a way to find them and save his wife, but there was more, too.

Finally, he had a name.

And it meant nothing to everyone else, but to him it was everything. "Alda, I —"

She interrupted, despondently, "I can't help you."

"What?"

His eyes adjusted to the golden light of the interior, and he saw Alda leaning over a black pot at the long, wooden table.

"I can't help you save your wife. The spell doesn't work."

His hands were still shaking from the excitement that came with finally learning his identity. But his attention was turned as he closed the door behind him.

"Spell?"

Alda nodded. As if he fully understood, she said, "For a cauldron's bubble."

He steadied himself against the wall and wiped the rain from his face as a wave of exhaustion passed over his limbs. Alda seemed unaware of his weakness as she stared into the pot, her eyes red from recent tears.

"How does it work?"

Alda sighed as she repeated, "It takes a person between time and place, and —"

Dreng shook his head impatiently. "No, the spell."

Alda hesitated. "Like a kind of recipe. There are ingredients. Which I combined, as instructed. And then, nothing happened."

He thought back to the island, to what he knew of magic, what he had seen and heard with Mir— with his wife. "Some spells need words."

"I don't know them."

He smiled. "I do."

He limped to the table near the fireplace, to the miniature book with the unusual writing.

But as he stepped away from the door, it burst open with a wave of water. Alda rushed to it and forced it closed.

Dreng turned to help her, but she dismissed him. "It is only a summer flood. They are common." Her voice cracked on the final word, and Dreng knew she was lying.

She knelt and barricaded the door with a rolled carpet and a metal statue of a ship.

Dreng sank into his chair and flipped through the miniature book's pages.

"That book is nonsense. I've tried —"

"Alda, I can read this tongue." Finally, he pointed to a page, "Cauldron's bubble." He did not conceal the pride in his voice. "It's here."

She straightened and twisted water from her skirt as she crossed the room to his side. "Read it."

Dreng took a breath and began, "Flames of mortal lights here show, as within the cauldron grows, a charm of power and of trouble. Like a hell-broth, cauldron's bubble."

Dreng waited with bated breath. Nothing happened. He glanced at Alda, and something between fear and excitement was etched on her face.

No, it was anticipation.

Suddenly, a boom like a cannon reverberated as the black pot splintered into shards. The force of it cracked the table and shook the door open. More water rushed inside, but Alda seemed not to notice as Dreng watched her anxiously.

She moved the fragments of the broken pot, clasped something in her hand, and smiled.

In his excitement, Dreng forgot to tell her his true name.

*   *   *

Alda's heart leapt as she closed her fingers around the sphere. "Dreng, it worked."

Her heart again pounded as she crossed the room and crouched beside his chair. She held it out to him, beaming, "The cauldron's bubble. We did it."

He looked at her questioningly, his focus shifting from the orb to her eyes.

"How does it work?"

Alda thought back to Leana, the raven in the Canyon. "It will take us where we *want* to go. But we need time to ready ourselves, to assemble supplies and create a plan to —"

Alda stopped as she realized the door had been forced open. The water was nearly to her knees.

This was not simply a summer storm.

This was more.

This was dangerous.

Dreng stood, a look of panic flashing across his face.

As Alda turned toward the door, hoping to hold it closed against the rising river, she heard a harrowing crash as waves fell through the kitchen window and hurled toward them.

She turned to Dreng, looked forlornly into his eyes, and put her back between him and the current. As the water pushed them together, she reached for his hand.

His fingers closed on hers, and they clasped the cauldron's bubble, palm to palm.

Then they vanished.

The oil lamp above the fireplace flickered in the empty cottage. Soon, it was extinguished by the floodwater rising swiftly up the yellow walls.

The smell of rosemary lingered.

Volume Three: Trouble Fires Burn

Double, double, toile and trouble;
Fire burne, and Cauldron bubble.

~William Shakespeare (1564-1616), *Macbeth*
Witches' Chant, Act 4, Scene 1
First Folio, 1623

Chapter One: Perchance to Dream

Dreng saw nothing. Rather, he could not see. All was black, an inky curtain thrown over reality. He knew Alda, so close to him moments ago as floodwater rushed into the cottage, should be nearby. So he reached for her.

Yet his fingers grasped only air.

He felt a brief wash of panic, like being swept under waves, but he pushed the fear into the pit of his stomach and struggled to his feet. Surely there was an explanation. Something real in this impossible situation.

Had he been transported somehow?

Knocked out by the flood and dreaming?

Or dead?

For a terrifying moment, Dreng wondered if he had been taken down into the vast depths of the beyond, to some ancient place of demons and ghosts and unimaginable tortures.

But he felt no immortal anguish. And he could *feel*: the hard stone at his feet, the chill prickling his arms, the damp shiver on his neck. The rough-woven fabric of his clothes, the river's water in his hair and leather boots. Prince Hamlet's signet ring, tight on his finger. The damp pages of the miniature spell book within his leather belt, pressed against his waist. The ground was solid, too. Wet and cold. There was a smell, like stale water. Fresh water. Mold and mildew. Rust. And dripping.

Finally, he drew a breath. "Alda?" The word echoed. "Alda, where are you?"

No answer.

He waited for footsteps, breathing, something worse, anything to indicate that he was not alone.

All was still.

He must have been transported somewhere, here, to this so solid place.

With a jolt he remembered the bubble, the glimmering sphere that he had held in the cottage, the object that Alda said could move one through time and place.

That thing had surely vanished both Alda and him.

But where was the mysterious bubble now?

Gone.

Most likely, it was with Alda. Elsewhere. But how?

He focused his mind, remembering what he could.

Days before — days, or weeks — he had been in the fairies' realm. Subjected to the whims of the tyrant queen. Threatened by the king. Given a sword and wounded by a dagger. The poison. The recovery. The pain in his shoulder remained sharp, but less intense.

If he had time, he could fully heal. But now, well, perhaps time was all he had. Too much time, alone. Or too little.

He thought back to Alda's cottage and the brief calm, like an eye of a storm. Then turmoil, an emotional tempest. His father's ghost. A flood. The cauldron's bubble, made and used and... lost.

Before that, before all that, he had placed his wife's body in a frozen pool.

Wife. What else could he call her? Not *Miranda*, not any more. Not after what he learned from Alda. But *Sycorax* felt wrong. It was an evil name. The moniker of one bent on destruction.

But were Alda's words in the cottage true? Were Miranda and Sycorax one in the same, the kind maiden and the fiery summoner?

What could he believe? *Whom* could he believe? Alda, a stranger he met only in flashes, darting in and out of his life, complicating and risking it? Or the woman he knew as his wife, the young islander once loved and once loving, but who also brought a cavern crumbling down around them as her past came to light?

Then he remembered. The stench. The dripping. The darkness. The cave.

He was in a cave. But it was not the same vast cavern on the enchanted island, not with the lights and illuminated walls that collapsed as his trust was shattered.

Now, there were no gemstones, no way to find focus. No vision.

But Dreng could not be still. He had to move, to escape, to save himself, at least.

He took a tentative step, pain shooting from his leg to his shoulder. Then another, holding his unseen hands before him. Then a third, and he heard a clink like glass upon the ground.

He had kicked something, something small, so he knelt and reached and felt with his fingertips until his hand connected on an object other than damp stones.

He examined the thing in his palm, feeling its surface. Smooth. Small, yet heavy. A perfect sphere. No. Half of a sphere.

It was the cauldron's bubble. Cleaved in twain. One of two halves.

The other part, he suspected, was with Alda. But where was she?

He fumbled to place the broken orb in his pocket, its fabric threadbare and damp. It was safe, he hoped.

Hope.

Again, he took a tentative step. Then he paused and listened.

Laughter, sudden and short. Dreng cocked his head, listening. Again. No, not laughter. A cackle. Malicious.

It grew in a crescendo. No, not louder. Closer.

Dreng knew in his heart of hearts that it was not safe. Whoever was

laughing in this place of absolute darkness could be nothing but
malevolent. Yet he followed the noise, groping in the dark, his arms
outstretched before him.

Then he felt warm. No, not warm. Less chilled. The smell dissipated.
The moisture dried. The rocks below his feet gave way to — to nothing.

And there was light, a green glow in the distance.

But there was nothing else. Only Dreng, his heartbeat, and the
distant light. The rest was black, empty.

This was somewhere else. Somewhere new. Not the lightless cave
where he so suddenly appeared after the flood. This was a place of pure
blackness. A void.

In a breath, Dreng knew where he was. This was the place of which
he had been told, the place he could not believe. A place of spirits and of
nothing. Netherfeld.

The laughter returned, sudden and overpowering. Not a single voice,
but a chorus. A cacophony.

And three figures appeared, three women robed in black, draping
silk, silhouetted against the glowing horizon. Laughing and tossing the
tangles of dark hair on their heads, their faces obscured by shadows and
beards.

Dreng backed away, but it was too late. He was seen.

The figures moved closer, their faces clearer. Dreng knew them
somehow, distantly, in some memory that had been pressed below the
surface of his thoughts. They were familiar.

And he knew they were dangerous.

"The waters worked, sister."

"And washed what we wished."

"Whisked what we wished for."

He stilled his instincts and stopped backing away. His feet held firm, even if his heart was not.

He stuttered, "Who, who are you?"

"A poor introduction."

"A name for a name."

"Give us yours first, boy."

They spoke quickly, one voice bleeding into the next.

He gulped and whispered, "Dreng."

"A lie."

"But he believes it."

"No, he knows."

"He did not."

"Now knows."

"Now, and then."

"So speak the truth."

They paused, waiting.

And he tried to hold his tongue, but the words felt forced from his throat. For the first time, Dreng parted his lips to speak his name, his true name, the name that his father's ghost had told him outside Alda's cottage, a name that felt simultaneously foreign and familiar yet, somehow, ill fitting. Like an assigned part within a play.

"Thomas." He gulped. "Thomas Chatterton."

The women spoke together, ignoring Dreng. He stood awkwardly, trying to unravel their thread of words.

"Do we know?"

"Some."

"More."

"It is all and nothing."

"Nothing to us."

"All to him."

"That is all?"

"Enough."

"'Tis not."

"And him?"

"Nothing."

"To us?"

"No, some."

"Yes, more."

"His name?"

"His?"

"What's in a name?"

"A boy by any other."

"Is still a boy."

"This, the boy."

"Still, the boy."

"I am not a boy," Dreng interjected. He thought of Caliban, of his insults. These women — no, creatures — were cut from the same cloth. "Tell me your names." He strained to sound more confident than he felt, but his voice cracked on the final consonant.

"Ask a question."

Dreng narrowed his eyes, "Who are you?"

"Us."

"We are us."

"We are three."

"No, what are your names?" Dreng's eyes flitted from one face to the next. The strange women were nearly indistinguishable, different only in height.

"Morta."

"Decima."

"Nona."

"But that is not *the* question."

Before Dreng could stop himself, he blurted, "*What* are you?"

"Weyward."

"Weird."

"Sisters."

"Witches."

And Dreng remembered. That night, so many years ago, amid the colored lightning that surrounded his father's ship, *The Tyger,* amid the chaos and the rain and the screams of pain, he had heard voices. A chant. A spell. And laughter.

Their laughter.

These were the witches who had killed his father. He had found them, at last.

A brief smile flashed across Dreng's face, despite his attempt to conceal the sudden joy he felt at this discovery of the witches. No, not joy. Relief. "I know you."

The tallest laughed at his words, the sound high and shrill. "You know so little."

"His false heart knows."

"Heartless."

"Broken."

Dreng clenched his fists. Should he fear these creatures? Their powers? "What do you want?"

"A word."

"Some."

"Words."

"Words."

Dreng felt his nails dig into his palms as he asked, "What words?"

"Yours."

"You speak by the book."

"But they are yours *only now*."

"Ours soon."

Dreng decided that he had seen and survived worse and suppressed his fear. He drew a breath and blurted, "Then let us trade words for words. I know you murdered my father. With some spell or charm. But why?"

They turned toward one another and spoke in loud whispers, seeming to ignore him as they conspired.

"He is still so little."

"But fierce."

"Should we tell him, sisters?"

"Or let him grope in the dark?"

They turned their eerily beautiful faces to him, and the shortest smirked. "Knowledge for knowledge, boy."

"Tell me of my father."

"He is dead." More laughter.

Dreng felt the hair on his neck stand on end. "By your hand."

"By our words."

"Our words and a blow."

"You tried to kill me." Dreng felt sweat bead on his brow.

"Kill?"

"Never."

"You were in the way."

"Collateral, some would say."

"But you stole from us."

"That night."

"On *The Tyger*."

Dreng reflexively reached for a weapon, but he was unarmed. "I am not a thief."

"A man of character."

"A pirate of principle."

"I am not a pirate," he hissed.

"And a liar."

"Yet I am no fool." Dreng crossed his arms and tried to stand taller. "I will give you more of my words. The words that you want. If you tell me why you attacked our ship."

The witches stopped circling and stared, unblinking. He guessed the meaning of their sudden silence. He had hit upon the vein.

"Tell me of my father's death, and I will give you what you want. Freely."

"We could take it now, boy." The witch sneered.

"Why not tell him, sister?"

"It matters not to us."

"But will it pain him?"

"With certainty."

"Then do."

The shortest witch reached within her black robes and withdrew a sphere of water. It hovered above her palm as she whispered into it, spat on its surface, and threw it to the black void at Dreng's feet.

The liquid expanded into a pool that shone like a looking glass. Upon its surface, the reflection of a figure appeared: a young woman with rosy cheeks, carrying a basket. Her arms tanned and muscular as she walked a dirt path at the base of a barren hill. She looked to the ground with a tear in her eye. Her face was serene yet forlorn. No, sad. And familiar.

Her aspect was like a painting from a memory, distant and almost magical. Dreng grappled with his mind, weaving images until his past became more clear. A tapestry formed from his thoughts.

And he realized it was the face of his mother.

As he watched the image in the water, he wanted to reach for her. To save her. But shadows descended. Three cloaked figures surrounded her, performing a kind of animalistic dance. They were witches — these same witches — pulling at his mother's dark hair and ragged dress, ripping the basket from her hands and scattering its contents across the muddy earth.

Colored lights flashed, and the young woman fell to the ground. The witches in the watery image took the basket and ascended into the foggy sky.

Dreng looked up, tears obscuring his vision. "Did you kill her?"

Silence.

He looked again to the water. The woman did not move. Finally, he dashed its surface, and the pool evaporated in a burst of steam.

Dreng faced the three sisters, his voice shaking in anger. "You did, you killed her. And why? For what?" He drew a breath, waiting. "What was in the basket?"

The mid-height sister snickered. "Chestnuts."

"Chestnuts? You took her life for, for chestnuts?"

"She would not share."

"Said they were for her husband."

"On *The Tyger*."

"Near Aleppo."

"Coming home, soon."

"But she had stolen the nuts."

"From our tree."

"Thief."

"Death to thieves."

Dreng's mind whirled, fitting together pieces of his past. "So you three sent a spell to my father as well? To our ship."

"A curse."

"To sleep."

"To waste."

"To die."

"But not yet."

A strange calm washed over the witches, and their eyes focused on something beyond Dreng, something far away. He thought for a moment that they spoke to one another, not to him, as their whispered voices lost their rough edges and smoothly blended together. As one witch spoke, another started:

"You, Thomas Chatterton, will live a life. Yet a lie. A full life. Until you perish. Atop a crimson, singing mountain. As it burns."

Dreng had heard tales of prophecy, of supernatural beings whispering omens to men at sea. Was this such? If so, he would not die today, now. He took a breath to screw his courage as he rolled up his sleeve, revealing the red scar that coursed from his chest to his arm. "You did this."

The sisters' focus snapped back to him. They did not look at his scar but instead gazed into his eyes.

"We have told."

"Given you our words."

"So now you give."

"Give, give!"

Goosepimples formed upon Dreng's neck. "Give what? What words do you want?"

"Nothing."

"Nothing."

"Nothing that you can live without."

And before Dreng could flee, their wiry hands were upon him.

Chapter Two: Such Stuff as Dreams

Alda stared into her palm, her fingers shaking. The cauldron's bubble was broken. In half. Useless.

Dreng was gone, again.

And she was alone. Again.

But where?

Inside a palace, glittering and golden. Emerald-tinged light filtered down from some unseen source high above. All was grand. Gilded. Every candlestick, chair, even a long, sturdy table were encrusted with shining jewels and precious metals. Tapestries adorned the walls, images of ancient gods in love and battle, and a fireplace surrounded by glittering tiles that sparkled around gold-green flames.

Alda had never seen such glorious wealth, such excess. Whoever inhabited this place was powerful. Alda also hoped they were benevolent.

She carefully tucked the broken bubble into her sock as she explored her surroundings. There appeared to be no windows and no door. Only the tapestry-clad walls and great hearth.

She was trapped.

So she turned to the grand table that stretched through the center of the circular room, its surface scattered with books. Alda tried to read their covers, but all were in Latin or Greek or other ancient tongues.

As she studied them, several marbled volumes materialized before her eyes. *Life of Lord Byron*, one of her grandmother's beloved poets. She opened the top book and read, "So we'll go no more a-roving, so late into the night, though the heart be still as loving, and the moon be still as bright. For the sword outwears its sheath, and the soul wears out the breast, and the heart must pause to breathe, and love itself have rest." She did not read the final stanza as her words echoed disconcertingly. It sounded strangely like eavesdroppers calling back from above.

As Alda closed the book, the volumes vanished. So she turned her attention instead to the tapestries. She recognized Athena from her illustrated mythologies, with her owl and helmet. Zeus with his lightning bolt. Hera with her crown and staff, so much like the one held by Prospero.

At the recollection, Alda's mind filled with questions. What could have created this place, with its materializing books and extravagant furnishings? Or rather, *who* could have created it?

As if on cue, a tapestry fluttered. Alda stepped back, clutching a chair that might serve as a weapon if violence came. But the tapestry parted to reveal a second chamber, small with stone walls and narrow windows that showed only black night beyond. And in the threshold of this lonely room was a familiar figure.

"Ophelia!" Alda stepped toward her, relief flooding her face. "I thought the worst, that you were taken by the witches or, or —"

"Ophelia?" The young, red-haired woman did not share Alda's joy at their reunion. Her eyes revealed some inner turmoil, her mouth twitching between a forced smile and a sneer. "That is what I was once called. Once, before you abandoned me in this place of nothing. But why dwell in the past? Here, sit." It was clearly a command, not a request.

Alda felt her knees buckle and slipped into a curved-leg chair as Ophelia continued, her voice rising into a shrill crescendo, "I, too, had questions at the start, Alda. Foremost: why? Why did you escape into the land beyond and leave me to endure the witches' fury?"

"It was an accident. I thought, I thought that you would —" The red-haired woman raised her hand, and Alda felt her throat close.

"Old excuses! Old, and tired." She sighed. "And when you returned, after so much time had passed, why did you imprison me in this gilded cage?"

"Cage?" Alda paused and wondered, "Are we in Netherfeld?"

Ophelia slapped her hand on the table, sending pages swirling into the air with supernatural force. "Do not play the innocent! It does not suit you."

Alda tried to stand, to confront her, but she was trapped. Her hands could not lift from the chair's ornate arms, and her torso could not rise from its seat. But she summoned the courage to object, "No, I would not do that! I did not imprison you!" She took several breaths and steadied her tone, "Why would you think that I did?" Her voice broke on the final word as she thought of several, including the witches, whom she might throw in a dungeon.

Alda swallowed and continued, "Ophelia, I —"

"No! That is not my name. Not *now*."

And Alda realized that this was not Ophelia, not the girl she knew before. This was someone else. This was a later version of the young mother, alone and trapped and born anew. Dangerous. This was Sycorax, the woman Ophelia would become. The woman who wanted to kill Alda.

"Sycorax? What happened when I was gone?"

The sorceress laughed. "Ah, you have forgotten." A wry smile flashed across her face. "Now, now, now, in this petty place I record my time." She motioned to a book that flew open, revealing a journal with calligraphic handwriting. "Light, candle!" She snapped her fingers, and a candelabra burst into sparkling flames. "No more shadows, now. Only a tale of sound and fury."

The young woman paced around the table and stopped as she faced Alda, her eyes aflame and hair lifting in some unseen breeze as she ran her finger over the journal's pages.

As Alda watched, a scene formed before her, lighted figures in miniature moving across the book's faded surface. Dollhouse toys come to life, like costumed players on a diminutive stage.

Like those Prospero had shown to her on the island.

Ophelia — no, Sycorax — curved her finger in the air, and Alda recognized the scene: a young woman with red hair, with an infant clasped to her chest, lights shooting from one hand, holding back three cloaked figures, the witches.

Alda had seen this before she had passed through the tree into Fairy Land and, in doing so, abandoned the young mother she called Ophelia in Netherfeld with her infant son, Hamnet.

"This is the story of my creation." Alda's companion narrated the scene. "Of course it began much earlier, with my Hamlet's madness and my early devotion to the weird sisters, but I confided that secret already." The young woman paced, wringing her hands. "After you left, I was trapped here, with my son, surrounded by the witches who had, had —"

Alda's companion paused, searching for the right word, "Who had led to my Hamlet's downfall. And mine. And they were here, but they did not seem to know me, as if I was a stranger. As if they had not met me. Not yet." She stopped and stared directly at Alda, her eyes sparkling. "I met them before they had met me. In their past. So I told them I was Sycorax, a powerful summoner. And that my son was named Caliban and was rightful heir to a realm of magic." She lowered her voice menacingly, "And that I bowed to no one."

The witches' figures cowered as she spoke, their images flickering like a sputtering candle. "I told them to let me be free. They agreed, if I would let them live. So they transported us onto an enchanted island."

The scene evaporated, and a new setting appeared. Alda recognized the banks of the Stream of Consciousness amid the bowing trees and greenery of Prospero's island. "My son was whole, complete for the first time in the real world, out of this wretched plane where he was born. But I — I was not."

A shadow appeared against the calm surface of the water. The figure of a woman, a black silhouette, holding a too-solid infant. The images evaporated as the young woman said, "He grew, yet I was fading. My body had died, you see, drowned, and I was merely a walking shadow. A shade."

She sighed, "Years passed. I taught my son some magic, what I could, but I was only a figment. Not of the earth. Not tied to it. Weak. And then one day, a sorcerer arrived, a man called Prospero." The storyteller's eyes met Alda's as she warned, "If you ever meet him, do not trust him."

Alda thought back to Prospero's story of his past. Sycorax, dark-haired and power-hungry. Caliban, a grotesque monster. Miranda, a helpless victim. And the old sorcerer himself, the hero of magic and savior of the island.

Who lied, Sycorax or Prospero? A knot formed in Alda's throat as she realized the answer was, most likely, both.

Sycorax waved her fingers, and more figures appeared. The robed man that Alda recognized as Prospero, and a girl with fair, blonde hair. It was Miranda, Alda knew, but she remained silent.

"The old man wanted only power. Magic. Knowledge. To control what was not his. First, he commanded my help, my spells. I yielded what I could, but he wanted more." The figures interacted: the boy and girl played and danced while the robed man bent threateningly over the female shadow.

Sycorax took a deep breath and continued, "The sorcerer was so trapped in his mind that he could not understand the world around him. Not nature or beauty or, especially, love." The boy and girl embraced. "So when my son and his daughter —" She choked back a sob. "The old man cursed my boy. And banished me here. To this empty realm."

Alda wanted to ask more questions, to know more fully about Prospero and Miranda and also Ariel, but she held her tongue, silently waiting for her companion to finish the tale, not wanting to reveal what she already knew.

With a snap, the figures vanished. Sycorax wiped either sweat or tears from her face as she murmured, "Then you came. And found me here, in Netherfeld. But you, too, did not know me."

Alda watched as a version of herself, dressed in the black clothes of her grandmother's mourning, appeared suddenly above the page. Sycorax waved her hand, and it vanished.

Alda gasped, "What happened? What did I do?"

Sycorax stood taller and choked on a laugh. "You *know*."

Alda shook her head as her eyes filled with frustrated tears. "But I don't remember!"

Laughter erupted from Sycorax's lips, shrill and long and echoing in the space above.

"You are always the *ingénue*, Alda. Never in control. Pushed and pulled like foam atop the ocean during a storm." Sycorax filled her words with deep and hateful wrath.

Alda shuddered, "Whatever happened, I am certain I can help you fix it."

"Here is your chance." She raised her arms, motioning to the palace around her, and let them fall helplessly at her sides.

"I don't understand."

"Undo what you have done, Alda. Release me."

"From what?"

Again, Sycorax slapped the table. Pages flew in a whirl of parchment, hitting the tapestries and floating like feathers to the marble floor. She spoke slowly, enunciating each word. "From this prison you built for me."

Alda tried once more to rise from her chair, but she was still held tightly to its surface. "This is surely not a prison! And you were not trapped here for so long. I saw you on the island several months ago, with Caliban and Dreng."

A shadow seemed to fall across Sycorax's face. "Who is Dreng?"

Alda stammered, "The boy from the ship. Shipwrecked. You, you —" She could not finish. The confusion in Sycorax's eyes was unsettling. "How do you not know your own husband?"

"Husband?" She laughed, a sound of joy this time. "Surely not."

"Yes, you married him the night you defeated Prospero. The night you drove me from the island. Surely you must remember."

"Remember?" Sycorax again paced and rubbed her hands anxiously. "Yes, I will remember. But that has not yet happened." A smile held strong on her lips. "But I will defeat him, you say? Defeat Prospero?"

Alda nodded, uncertain how much more to reveal. The bubble had apparently taken her to Sycorax's past, into the time between when she was Ophelia and when she took control of Miranda's body on the island.

This was not the Ophelia that Alda knew nor the Sycorax she would later meet. This was someone else. A new form.

And despite being trapped in the extraordinary palace with red-haired Sycorax, despite being trapped in a realm with no time and no form, Alda remembered a conversation with her grandmother, many years before, as the older woman taught her how to transform skeins of yarn into scarves and blankets.

Alda remembered that the cottage was especially cold that winter, and she shivered as she watched her grandmother.

"No, twist it this way, dear, and hold this needle thus." Her grandmother was patient, but Alda was not.

"I'll never learn, Gramma!" Alda's voice was high with youth and frustration. "This will take forever."

"No, not forever. But it will take time." Her grandmother set aside the knitting needles and the ball of coarse, brown wool as she embraced young Alda. Over her shoulder, Alda stared at the wooden needles in the candlelight and tried to calm herself as her grandmother soothed, "You know, time is a funny thing. For you, it is like the needles: straight with a knob and a point, a beginning and an end. But the time of others, the way you see them, is like the yarn. It is full of loops and twists and turns that only sometimes cross the needle."

Alda was calmer now, able to think. "Is this a riddle?"

"In a way." Her grandmother examined her eyes. "You know the novel I am reading, about the artist who ran away to live in the abandoned mansion, the book with the split binding?"

Alda knew the volume and nodded, so Gramma continued, "It was written over fifty years ago, and the woman who wrote it has since died. But to me, that book is now. I am reading something from the past but in my present." She held the yarn deftly in her fingers and twisted it over the tip of a needle, showing how the wood and wool seemed to intersect. "And I read that novel before, when I was younger, so that was another time it crossed my straight line." Again, she looped the yarn. "And someday, after I am gone, you will read that book." She picked up the second needle. "And it will be the author's past, and my past, and your present, all intersecting." She twisted the wool and crossed the needles, and soon an entire row was complete.

"We all have our own time-needles, Alda. Our perception is straight. But the world around us loops and twists and doubles back. Sometimes, it is even cut and retied with a new yarn."

Watching her, Alda commented, "That is a silly riddle." But she likewise picked up her knitting and mimicked her grandmother until, sooner than she expected, she had the beginning of a scarf.

Now, in Alda's present in Netherfeld, and Sycorax's past in Netherfeld, Alda understood the analogy:

People likewise crossed paths and crossed time, as did the yarn and needles.

Alda thought of Dreng, how he had grown up during her time with the witches on the moor when she had barely aged. Of how she had met Ophelia, a young mother who later became Sycorax. Of the babe Hamnet, whom she had known as the monster Caliban, who later transformed into a beautiful young man. Of the woman she knew as Sycorax, this woman, who did not yet know of the wicked deeds she would perform.

These lives of others were the yarn, crossing and intertwining, at times overlapping. And Alda's life was the needle, straight and linear.

Sycorax snapped her fingers, and Alda's mind returned to the present as the chair on which she sat collapsed into splinters beneath her. Alda stood awkwardly as the fiery woman caught her wrist. "You will help me escape, Alda. You will undo this prison you have erected and free me into the world beyond, your world, where I can fulfill my duty and reclaim my island."

Alda recoiled as the fingernails dug into her wrist like talons. She did not know what to do, how to save herself and help Sycorax. If she *should* help Sycorax. But now, she had no choice, or rather only small and rotten choices. So she nodded weakly.

What else could she do?

Chapter Three: Night's Black Agents

Dreng felt weak as the weird sisters loomed above him. Exhausted. Drained. His heartbeat was a whisper as a stream of light connected his scar to the witches' fingers.

Could he run? If so, where? But he could not stand.

Could he fight? With what? But he could not raise his arms.

Could he live?

Not for long.

Whatever they were taking from him, whatever they were tapping from his body, was something that he could not live without.

So he pleaded with the strange sisters, his voice coming in whispers and gasps. "Let me help you! Whatever you need, whatever task, I offer my aid." He searched their blank, unfeeling eyes and forced out, "I can read, read magical tongues. I can be of service —"

"You can do as we."

"This skill is ours."

"Not yours."

"And ours again."

The yellow rope of light intensified, pulsating in its increasing energy.

Dreng's heart felt cold, as if seawater pressed against his organs. One blink, perhaps two, was all that remained.

With a breath — his last — he let loose a scream like a baited bear, deep and animalistic. Instinctual.

A pause. A moment suspended in time that seemed at once an eternity and a heartbeat.

A flash like sunlight. Heat. And then a suffocating blow. Dreng's face and arms wrapped, pinned, held beneath a fabric net from which he could not break free.

Then all was quiet. Apart from the ringing in his ears.

Dreng sat upright and pushed a blanket from his head. As his ears pounded and limbs tingled, he squinted into the gloom.

A slim form was silhouetted against the horizon's dim, green light. The figure replaced a sword on its belt as it approached Dreng.

"Who are you?"

"*Deus ex machina*, it would appear." Dreng recognized the familiar sneer as his companion crouched at his side.

"Caliban?"

"I, in this analogy, am the god. You are the machine. And a broken one at that."

Broken, indeed. Throbbing ache from his too-recent injury in Fairy Land. And now, the damage caused by the witches... But Dreng suppressed the pain, as he had so many times at sea.

His jaw clenched against his will as he asked, "How did you find me?"

The beautiful youth tore off a corner of his shirt and gently touched the blood that trickled from Dreng's scar. "Find *you*? No. I found the witches. You simply had the good luck, or the misfortune, to be with them when I did."

Dreng struggled to stand, but his knees buckled. Caliban caught him and continued, "You must wear the cloak, friend. It will protect you."

A cloak, not a net or a blanket, had covered his head. The sapphire blue cloak that Caliban had fished from the sea before they set forth into Fairy Land. "Those witches are up to something, something wicked. I've been on their trail, and when I saw them ensnare you —"

"You were here? Watching, while they were —" Dreng pushed him away and steadied his feet. "While they were killing me?"

"I intervened before they succeeded, of course."

"Barely."

"Surely that is worth something."

"Little more than nothing." Dreng examined the wound on his chest, the dark circle around it that smelled of cooked meat.

Caliban followed his gaze, his eyes filled with concern. "You should not deal with those devils."

Dreng self-consciously covered the wound with his shirt. To his surprise, it did not hurt. Rather, it did not feel. "What do they want?"

"Apart from killing you?"

"Apart from taking the supposed something," Dreng corrected.

"Of course. The *something*." Caliban's words were heavy with sarcasm.

"What is it?"

"*It* is of great importance."

Dreng tried to conceal his smile. "You do not know either."

"I know more than you."

"Such as?"

"I know where we are."

"As do I. Netherfeld."

Caliban scoffed, "But what is Netherfeld?"

Dreng shook his head, so Caliban continued, "When I was a child, my mother told me of a realm of pure magic. Where one could imagine a lion, and a lion would appear. Where the impossible could happen, simply from one's thoughts. That it was once lush and populated with thousands of magical creatures. Then witches came. And the creatures scattered. The fairies, to their world. We to ours. And others, so many others, to different, faraway realms. The world of pure magic became black. Void. And, if the witches have their way, they will do to our world what they did to Netherfeld." His voice broke, and he continued, "I have startled them away, for now, but they will return soon enough. We must move apace."

Caliban turned, and Dreng followed his footsteps, his limbs aching with exhaustion. "How can we stop them?" Dreng's voice trembled.

"We cannot."

"Then what will we do?"

"Die, perhaps."

Caliban led the way briskly, and Dreng trotted painfully after him. After too many minutes of silence, Dreng grew weary of walking through the nothing with his moody companion. He had questions — too many questions — but doubted that Caliban would answer any. Still, he tried, "How did you get here?"

"Through a tree. And several detours and distractions. And a loss, but — Let us speak of the present, not the past."

"Fine. Then what of me? What did the witches want?"

The two walked in silence for a dozen or more paces, through the nothing of Netherfeld. Dreng, wrapped in the blue cloak. Caliban, nervously fidgeting with the hilt of his sword.

After what felt like too long, Caliban relented, "Your wife told me there was something in you that was different."

Dreng's heart sank to his feet. He could not speak of Miranda — no, Sycorax — not now, not after so much with Alda in the cottage, so he remained silent.

Caliban seemed to grope for words, speaking slowly, "You have a gift. No, a curse. No. That is not right either." He looked at his feet and slowed his pace. "You have an ability."

"Ability? Like swordplay?"

"No, something innate. Like an intuition. Or a power. Yes, a power."

"What power?"

"They said they wanted words, yes? You have the power of speech." Caliban laughed. Dreng did not.

But he thought about the cauldron's bubble. How his words helped to create it.

"As the witches said, you stole this power. It somehow bonded with you that night on the ship."

"How?"

To Dreng's surprise, Caliban stopped and studied him for several heartbeats before parting the cloak and lifting Dreng's shirt to reveal the scar. "They left their mark on you. A symbol of magic. Like a rune or sigil."

"Was it intentional?"

"We mortals cannot guess." He walked again, purposefully toward some unknown destination. "We merely see the present and the shadows of the past. Those dark and midnight hags see more."

"More? Then how can we stop them?"

"More, but not all."

Dreng considered. "Are they gods?"

"Ancient, of a sort. Primordial. Of the chaos, before worlds."

"How do you know?"

Caliban grinned. "Do you not trust me?"

Dreng started to respond but bit his tongue. He was alone here, confused, torn from Alda and all that he knew. Alone and in the dark, most literally. He did not need to cause offense and risk what little safety he had in the company of his companion.

"The witches, they want to kill me?"

Caliban laughed, "Don't we all?"

Dreng scowled, "Then why have they not done so before now?"

Caliban stopped walking and considered. "As a boy, you were nothing to them. Perhaps they forgot about you, or perhaps they were preoccupied elsewhere. Regardless, once you were on my island, you were safe."

"Why?"

"The spells. My mother's. Prospero's. The island was protected. Later, in the realm of the fairies, you were likewise safe. But when we were at sea —"

"Mermaids."

Caliban nodded. "Sea witches, rather, some cousins of those you met moments past."

"But we escaped."

"They are lesser than these."

"How do you know of these things?" Dreng's brow furrowed with suspicion.

Caliban only laughed. "I am the son of a prince. And a witch."

It was an echo of the words spoken on the raft. Familiar but altered. "If that's so, then I'm descended from Neptune himself." Dreng's tone dripped with sarcasm.

But Caliban was serious. "I jest not. I expected you to know by now, but you are not the brightest star in the heavens." He cleared his throat and pulled himself up to his full height. "I, Caliban, was by birth called Hamnet. Son of Hamlet, Prince of Denmark."

Dreng laughed. "He had no son. He never spoke of one." Dreng had suspected a resemblance between Caliban and the Danish prince before, after their raft had been destroyed, but now, to hear such a connection spoken aloud — it was surely the stuff of fantasy.

"He did not know. I was a posthumous child. Born after my mother died."

Nonsense. Dreng scoffed, "Do not continue this, this poor joke. I knew him."

"Skepticism does not become you."

"Then speak truth."

"Truth? None of this matters." Caliban waved his hand as if swatting a fly from his face. "There are more pressing worries at present."

The two walked in silence for some minutes. Dreng began to feel something like suspicion, then regret, and his face burned. What if Caliban was indeed Hamlet's son?

Dreng finally spoke first, his tone soft. "How did you defeat the witches here, today?"

"With all of my strength. I cannot do so again." The beautiful youth paused and added, "How many days did you spend with your witch?"

"My witch?" Dreng paused. "Alda?"

Caliban nodded soberly.

Dreng cleared his throat and continued, "Days. A week. I am not certain."

"Then she is more powerful than I anticipated, if the witches did not find you with her. We will need her help." Caliban again stopped. "Where is she?"

Dreng bit his lip. "I do not know."

Chapter Four: Fabric of Vision

Alda's wrist bled as Sycorax pulled her to a gilded wall and thrust her face against its bejeweled surface. Alda tried to back away, but the summoner's other hand held her head tight as her knee jabbed into Alda's spine. She could not move.

"This, this prison is from you! You did this, Alda! You are my jailor!" Sycorax released her, and Alda crumbled to the ground. "Get up!"

Alda struggled to find her feet but lost her balance. Sycorax impatiently grabbed her raven hair and hoisted her to full height. She kept a tight hold on her locks as she commanded, "Make it vanish!"

Alda felt tears on her face but resolution in her heart. She would not budge. "No!" If she had constructed this place for Sycorax, to hold her here against her will, then she must not destroy it now.

Even if Alda could no longer remember building it, or why it was created.

Sycorax released Alda's hair as she paced toward the far end of the room. Alda steadied herself and stood tall, her chin high and defiant like an armored warrior in one of her stereopticon cards.

When Sycorax turned again toward her, her face was calm and smiling. Alda stepped back as the summoner cooed, "We were friends once, Alda. We built a city, a vast city beyond these walls. It glowed a beautiful green, the same color as these lights." She looked to the ceiling above. "And we were happy, you and I. Queens. Friends."

Her tone darkened. "But then you changed, Alda. You heard whispers of Prospero's lies and took his side against me. Then you imprisoned me here. And vanished. And all these years — years? who knows time in this place? — I have waited for you. For your help." Again, she smiled. But there was no kindness in her eyes.

Alda subconsciously backed away as her companion spoke and was suddenly aware that her shoulders touched the golden threads of an intricate tapestry. She turned only to see Medusa's head smiling down at her, held in the hand of victorious Perseus. She stepped away, and Sycorax joined her side.

"You and I wove these, Alda, together. As I said, we were like sisters. Our looms here in Netherfeld were our minds, and we could spin gold into anything with simply our thoughts." She took Alda's hand reassuringly but then held tight as Alda tried to pull away. "We can be friends again. Tear down these walls, Alda. Burn the whole tower down. Let me be free again."

Alda reclaimed her hand and stepped back toward the tapestry. Again, "No!"

Sycorax calmly eyed her as she stepped past Alda and parted the tapestry, revealing a solid wall adorned with a simple spiral.

Alda recognized it immediately. A witch-trap. The magical symbol that could entrap and torture witches.

Sycorax spoke again, her voice like an angry mistress scolding an unruly child, as she repeated, "You did this, Alda. You placed these here, encircling my tower. To keep me in place. To trap me. But they can trap you, too. Trap you, and worse." She paused. "So help me destroy them, or I will deal much worse."

As Alda looked from the summoner to the spiral, her thoughts sped through possibilities. She could release Sycorax, yes, and face the consequences of unleashing evil. Or perhaps Sycorax was sincere. A friend. And all would be well. Or Alda could resign herself to the trap. She had been ensnared by one before, in the Canyon. And although she might die in the real world from the elements or starvation, she faced no such danger in Netherfeld. Only weariness and, perhaps, torture. She expected she could withstand both.

And, perhaps, Sycorax was bluffing. She was trapped here, after all. Seemingly helpless.

Alda bit her lip, thinking. Then, while she weighed her options, Alda heard a whisper. Faint at first. Distant. And then the spiral erupted in a green light, its beams ricocheting from the room's countless jewels.

Alda was momentarily blinded, and Sycorax held her hand before her eyes to block the rays. The voices grew louder. More distinct. Closer.

"Against the wall." Faint, commanding.

"What now?" Worried and confused.

And Alda recognized their tones, so she turned to Sycorax, her eyes wide. "You must touch the spiral."

"No! That is surely death." The summoner's voice cracked with fear. "This is a trick."

More sounds. The first voice continued, a string of words muttered incoherently. And Alda knew the sound.

"Sycorax, that boy calling you from the other side is your son. He is performing some kind of spell for you to enter the island. If you follow his call, you will survive."

"How do you know?"

Alda took a deep breath and appeared as confident as she could. "Because it has already happened."

This was Alda's chance. An opportunity to escape. To overpower her captor. And, if her supposition was correct, to align her past with her present.

Alda held her breath as Sycorax bent toward the symbol, listening as she kept one hand on the tapestry. After a moment, she held a finger tentatively toward the spiral, like a child daring herself to touch a boiling kettle, but then recoiled. "I cannot. Alda, I don't —"

But Alda did not hear the final words. As Sycorax turned away from the symbol, Alda lunged and pushed her toward its glowing surface.

A sputter of sparks, like electric lights snapping suddenly out. A cloud of dark smoke. When it cleared, nothing. The spiral was gone. Sycorax was gone. And the room had lost its green glow.

The walls themselves were less radiant, almost dull. Like a faded photograph. And as Alda watched, the gilded room disappeared.

At first it was gradual, like fog lifting after sunrise. Then more violent: golden stones crumbling, jewels bursting, metal twisting and bending as colored lights streaked through the air above. Alda dove beneath the table and pulled a fallen tapestry over her shoulders as the tower collapsed around her.

Rather, it did not collapse. It simply vanished. Alda first felt the tapestry grow cold and quickly realized she was grasping only her own palms. Then the table shifted to one side and fell like a coin into an invisible well, vanishing into the enveloping dark.

Soon Alda was alone again in the black, silent void of Netherfeld.

She stood and pressed her shaking palms together. Sycorax was gone, thrust onto the island with Dreng and Caliban. Into Alda's past. The tower was likewise vanished, somehow.

Alda surveyed the space beneath her feet. There was no indication of a foundation, no trace of the walls that had so recently enclosed the summoner. It was as if it had never existed.

Yet there was life, still. Or rather movement.

Spirits stirred above, lifting like wafting smoke from a dying flame. Slow and thin at first, then faster. Their numbers swelled, and Alda was surrounded by dancing swirls of light and color, their luminescent hues of green and blue dazzling her eyes.

And, like on Prospero's island, the spirits spoke to her. A form like a Luna moth flitted toward her, its voice high and sweet as it whispered, "You are returned to free us as you did so long ago."

She recognized this spirit from Ariel's magical feast and remembered what those spirits had said, as she realized, "You were trapped?" The moth flitted up and down as if nodding.

"Yes, and then we vanished you." This voice was lower, belonging to a robin-like spirit.

"We saved you from this place as you saved us from her." It was the moth again. Her voice was familiar, somehow.

A starling added, "And we sent you to seek Leana the raven in the Canyon. To ask for her aid."

"To escape from *her*."

"To escape the summoner."

Until this moment, Alda had assumed that either the witches or the bubble had taken her to the Canyon. She broke the spirits' brisk chatter. "What did Sycorax do?"

"She stole us."

"Used us."

"Took our sisters and mothers and cousins."

"She built us into her walls and palaces."

"Used us as material."

"I don't understand." Alda knew enough of Netherfeld's magic to glean that one could create with her mind. That she could imagine something and then make it real, somehow, simply by being in this realm. So why did Sycorax need to use the spirits?

"Her own magic dwindled." Again, the moth's words ran smoothly together. "The magic within her was like a dry well so she needed to use another source and she chose us."

The robin interjected, "She chose to use us like so many bricks."

"And I allowed her to do this?" Alda felt a knot in her stomach rise to her throat. These spirits were creatures, sentient, not to be forced into some act against their will.

"You did not know until we told you."

"And then you helped us stop her."

Alda understood. "You helped me build the prison? Rather, you were the prison. To protect the other spirits. And you helped protect me as well."

Again, the green Luna moth flitted an affirmation. "She tried to attack and destroy you but we would not let her."

"Why would you save me?"

The moth hovered near Alda's face, its luminous wings obscuring the other spirits who continued to swirl and bend in the air around them as it whispered, "Because I am your mother of course."

Alda gasped, and her voice cracked in disbelief, "Phillida? Is it truly you?"

The moth flitted above, as if startled by a sudden blast of wind. The other spirits followed her, swirling up into the sky like some ominous cloud. Green light flashed in the distance. Again, brighter. Or closer.

"Quiet! It is coming. We must go to the floating waters." The robin's words were high. Urgent.

Despite herself, Alda felt her jaw clench with fear. "What is coming?"

"Danger."

The spirits swirled away like leaves on a brisk breeze, but Alda hesitated in the darkness. The spirits, in the past, were her allies. Should she trust them, now? Could she believe them?

But there was no alternative. Nothing else, no one else, to help her find her way in the endless, empty realm.

So Alda followed as best she could, trotting beneath and behind the spirits. She asked with unsteady words, "What are the floating waters?"

The hovering spirits remained silent as they led her through the vast expanse of Netherfeld's darkness.

*　　　　*　　　　*

As they walked through the darkness of Netherfeld, Dreng told his tale in quick whispers, relaying the events at the cottage to Caliban as they approached a crumbling, dilapidated tower. "And the flood, it, it separated us..."

His voice was lost as he saw that the lonely tower was not crumbling. Its form was gray in parts, invisible. Like a painting with a chipped surface. Or chalk letters washed away by water.

Caliban entered through a stone archway at the base of the tower, and Dreng reluctantly followed. The doorway led to a small corridor with a spiral stairway that ascended into blackness above.

Dreng stopped and stared. "What is this place?"

"My chateau." Caliban smiled, and Dreng could not tell if it was pride or sarcasm that penetrated his tone. "I created it."

"Why?"

"I needed a place to hide bodies." He motioned to the stairs, as if they held some sinister secret.

But Dreng understood his sarcasm. "You live here now?"

Caliban scoffed, "This is something less than living." As Caliban spoke, the archway filled with mossy stones as pieces of stairway vanished before them.

Dreng stared, amazed.

"But this place is sturdy enough. And safe." Caliban held out a hand expectantly, and Dreng returned the cloak to him.

As Caliban tied it over his shoulders, he stepped on the first stair and touched a faded stone. It became solid at his fingertips. He turned back to Dreng and studied his eyes. "You look like you've seen a ghost."

"I have." As soon as Dreng spoke, he regretted revealing this secret.

Caliban laughed. Dreng did not.

Caliban's eyes brimmed with curiosity as he descended the step. "A ghost? What kind?"

Dreng remembered it on the island, outside Alda's cottage. In the curtain of rain. The bearded spectre, its skin glowing yet transparent. It was a spectacle of horror. Not real, not human. But Dreng could not describe it thus, so he shrugged and avoided Caliban's gaze. "My father."

"When?"

"On several occasions."

"What did it say?"

"When?" Dreng skirted the question and wished he could take back his words, but he remembered its warning. Its command to kill the witch that had taken his life.

"On those several occasions."

Dreng sighed, "I don't remember."

"Speak the truth."

"It's insignificant. Worthless."

"It is not." Caliban stepped forward boldly, gripping tightly to his sword. "Tell me what the ghost said, when you most recently conversed with it."

"My name."

"Is that all?"

"No."

Caliban crossed his arms and feigned anger. "What else?"

Dreng clenched his fists and looked for some escape, some way to turn their discussion. But he was trapped. "He said that in order to stop the witches, I had to give them what they wanted."

"Which is?"

"I don't know."

"You don't?"

"No." But Dreng now suspected that they wanted *him*.

"How do you know that ghost, as you call it, was truly your father?"

Dreng shook his head. He had no answer.

"Did you test it? Ask a question only he would know?"

"Yes, I asked the spectre for my name."

"But how would you know if what it spoke was true?"

Dreng met Caliban with silence, so the beautiful youth continued, "Did you ever doubt its words?"

Doubt. The word brought him back to Miranda — no, Sycorax — before the cavern crumbled, and the anger he felt then rose back into his voice as he hissed through gritted teeth, "I may not have known my father. But I know who *I* am. And I can still recognize truth."

Even as he said it, he knew it to be a lie. His wife, her false identity, proved it so.

Caliban laughed again and held his haughty chin aloft as he met Dreng's stare. "What is truth, boy?"

"Don't call me that."

"It is what he called you, isn't it? Your Danish prince?"

Dreng avoided his eyes. Caliban was right — the word *dreng* meant boy — so he quickly changed the subject. "What are you doing in

Netherfeld?"

"Searching."

"For what?"

"Truth."

"And what is truth, oh great seer?" Dreng's sarcasm weighed on the final word.

"Truth is the backside of falsehood." Caliban made a movement to indicate another meaning of "backside."

Dreng did his best to suppress a snicker. "You cannot define a concept by what it is not."

"Then you define it."

Dreng considered. "Truth is the end of reckoning."

"That's a start."

Dreng scowled, "How could you determine truth, if you do not know what is false?"

"There's the rub."

"The what?"

"Dilemma." Caliban wiped his fingers over his chin and sneered, "Tell me, where is your wife?"

"Trapped in a frozen spring." Dreng answered without hesitation. But he suspected there was more to it than that.

Caliban raised his eyebrows. "Do you want to save her?"

Dreng drew a deep breath and exhaled slowly. "Yes." He immediately regretted his response. Finding Alda was more important.

"Then help me discover what is true."

"What do you mean?"

Caliban turned abruptly and walked away from the stairs to an empty area of the small room. "Come with me."

"Where?"

"To meet someone."

"Who?"

Dreng could hear the smile behind Caliban's words. "No one."

As Dreng watched, mouth agape, Caliban waved his hand, and the stones at their feet disappeared. A new set of stairs appeared, straight and narrow, that became obscured by darkness some distance below the ground.

"Once more into the breach!" Caliban stepped lightly down the stairs, and Dreng hesitantly followed. The walls became more ruinous as they descended, parts entirely obscured in blackness and others transparent. Soon, Dreng had the sensation that they were deep below ground. If such a realm had a ground.

Finally, the beautiful youth reached the final step and entered a windowless corridor, his pace quickening. Dreng forced his weakened limbs to match his companion's steps as he panted, "Where are we going?"

He half expected some sarcastic response, a reference to death or such, but Caliban was serious. "To interrogate my prisoner."

"Prisoner? Who?"

"Time will tell."

Chapter Five: False of Heart

As Alda continued to follow the spirits in the unbroken nothing of Netherfeld, she could no longer hold her tongue. So she trotted closer to the moth and whispered, "Are you truly Phillida?"

It cooed only, "Yes."

"But, how did you get here?" Alda needed a way to test it, so she lied, "In Fairy Land, I saw you pass through a circle of flowers. What happened after that?"

The moth stopped its wings and glided for a moment before it replied. "I did not enter the flowered circle child, you helped me into the door in the tree."

Alda was satisfied. "Of course. Where did the door lead?"

"To a land of flowers."

"Flowers?"

"Yes fennel and columbine... daisies... violets... all so lovely."

"And then what happened?" Alda realized her pace had slowed, so she ran faster to not fall behind the other spirits.

"The witches found me there and wanted me to join them because I am descended from Hecate... but I did not." It fluttered anxiously. "The witches destroyed my body and sent me here with no form" The moth paused. "But over time I repaired myself and became a Luna."

"But I met you before, as a moth, on Prospero's island. Why did you not speak to me then, tell me who you were?" She paused and corrected, "Are."

"It was not time my child."

Alda studied the other forms, swirling above. Some were only lights like ribbon, flitting through the darkness, some geometric shapes like cubes or pyramids. Others were animals a-flight, their glowing wings cutting through the dark. "Were these all people, once?"

"Some were and others have only existed in spirit form."

"Who were they?"

"We do not speak to one another of the past, my child, because that is not where we are." The moth moved to Alda's other side and flew higher than the others. "We see what is before us and with us now and hold blinders over what has been because that is not where we want to be."

"And what is the danger you fear now? Is it the witches?"

Again, the moth stopped beating its wings and coasted gracefully through the air. When it reached Alda's knees, it flapped urgently and lifted to the height of her face. "They are close."

Alda felt a lump form in her throat as she asked again, "What is the floating water?"

She was met with silence. So she followed obediently, her thoughts bending to Fairy Land and her discovery of her lost mother in that enchanted forest. Broken and confined. Lacking will and empathy. And love. She was cold and, worse, deceptive.

Alda knew that Phillida was not a mother, not truly, which is why she did not mourn her injury in Oberon's court or her passing through the many-doored tree into an unknown realm. She was like a stranger, a character in a book of fantastical tales. Still, Alda knew that she should love her mother. But she could not.

Yet she was grateful for some connection, no matter how distant, in this place of nothing.

Although she would have preferred to find Dreng. Or her grandmother.

"Where is Gramma?" Alda had not intended to speak the words aloud, but they escaped from her lips along with her thought.

The moth sped farther ahead, so Alda quickened her pace to remain below it as she persisted, "I have seen her here before. Where is she now?"

Several moments passed in silence before the moth whispered, "She is weak."

"Why? What happened?" Fear raised the pitch of Alda's voice.

"She tried to hold them at bay."

"Tried? Did she fail?"

Again, silence.

"Phillida, tell me what happened!" The sudden exclamation felt like a knot in Alda's throat. She pressed her hand against a cramp in her side and gasped for breath, suddenly winded. For a moment, she thought she could not take another step.

"We are here." The robin's timely words quelled Alda's worries. Or rather, redirected them. Above the spirits, some distance above Alda's head, was a swirling torrent. It looked like the Grand River after the spring frost: foamy waves lapping and dancing, splashes sending droplets into the air. Blue light shown through, reflecting on its glistening surface.

But the water was above them all, perfectly suspended, its edges fading into the surrounding darkness. Like a distant galaxy on a moonless night. Alda reached above her head, trying to touch its glistening surface, but it was too far.

"You cannot reach it." The voice echoed through the nothing, sending some spirits scattering up and out.

It was human. Soft and light. A girl.

"Sycorax?" Alda held her breath, fearing the summoner might have returned too soon.

"No." The unseen girl laughed, high and jovial. "She is dead, of course. My father killed her. And even if she somehow survived, she would be old and crooked by now."

Why did the girl not reveal herself? What was she hiding? *Why* was she hiding? "Who are you?"

"Yes! I *do* know you. You are the strange person from the beach, the girl to whom I gave my cloak." Her tone darkened. "I should have kept my cloak, I suppose. I might not be here if I had kept it."

"Miranda?"

The voice laughed, high and innocent. "Who else? You and I are the only girls ever to be on Father's island."

The spirits stopped their frantic whirling and hovered once more in the air, their light illuminating the darkness below the floating water.

Yet Miranda was still hidden. "Where are you?"

"Here!"

"Where?"

"I am standing next to you, friend."

Alda turned and looked to all sides. "I cannot see you."

"Nor can I see myself. Here, let me show you my hand. Look up!" Above her head, Alda saw a silhouette of long fingers and a narrow palm, its form like a shadow against the blue waters above.

Unlike the walking shadows Alda had encountered earlier in Netherfeld — the forms of those born from Ophelia's imagination — this figure was black, like all around it.

"Why are you invisible?"

"Invisible? Yes, I suppose I am. I thought it was more like a trick of concealment, as seahorses hide in ocean greens. This is how I have always been, since I have been in this place."

"How did you get here?"

"Oh, that is such a story! I was bored for so long that I finally summoned the courage to find my Cali, and I took my cloak for protection."

"Cali?" The spirits swirled excitedly at the name, streaking past Alda's head.

"Caliban! You must certainly know him! He is the only boy on Father's island."

Alda nodded, suppressing questions.

"And then I saw you on the beach, and I was so close to Cali's home in the cave, and I thought I could surely get there before Father's spirits came for the horrible men from the ship. So I gave you my cloak. But I was too slow. And the spirits were too fast. So they took me here."

"You are dead." Alda intended to speak questioningly, but her tone dropped too much on the final word.

"Oh, no! Father would never kill anyone. He is far too kind."

Alda felt her brow furrow. Moments before, this girl had said her father had killed Sycorax.

But Miranda continued, unaware of her mistake. "No, his spell simply separates a person's being from his body."

Alda bit her lip and did her best to look squarely at the voice's source. "Is that not death?" The spirits around them once again swirled, their forms flitting beneath the water above.

"Of course not! For the being only comes here to wait for a reunion with its flesh."

"You are in limbo, then." Alda shivered. The girl's light mood was unnerving.

"I am awaiting my return to my body, yes."

Alda knew that Miranda's body was already in use. Sycorax had taken it. "And what if you cannot return to your body?"

"Oh, I will not return by myself. My father will find me and restore me."

"How?"

"He is ever so clever, my father, Prospero. He will send his harpy to find me and make me whole again."

"But what if he —" Alda paused, worry pressing her brow. "Cannot?"

"Then I will have to wait longer, I suppose." An awkward silence. "But I am patient."

And Alda realized she had another question: "Why were you going to Caliban's cave?"

"To see him and to play games." Her words were innocent, as if the answer was universally understood. She frowned. "I told you, I was bored."

"Did you plan to run away together, or —"

"Oh, no. Cali did not know I was coming. Years have passed since I last visited him. It was a surprise. He loves surprises."

Alda suppressed a snicker.

Miranda did not seem to notice and continued, "And Father had kept me away for so very long. But I am older now, old enough to make my own decisions. And I told Father such earlier, but he would not listen to me. So I snuck out when he was busy with the invading ship and went to see my Cali and tell him that I love him still, despite —" She paused, her breath audible as she searched for the proper word. "Despite his unfortunate appearance."

Again, Miranda paused, her breathing fast and heavy in the void. "And now that you are here with me, my friend, you can help me return to him."

"How?"

"The waters above are part of an enchanted stream that leads to Father's island. My father told me stories of it, warned me not to go near it. It is like a tunnel between this world and mine. So I can use it to return. Just hoist me up to touch it, and then I can go home."

"But what of me?" Alda's tone shook with worry.

"Yes, I suppose you should come along as well. Can your lights lift you up once I have passed through? Can you command them to do your bidding as Father commands his to do his unwanted labor?"

Alda looked to the spirits, her eyes filled with unspoken questions.

"We will help." The melodious voice of the robin whispered in Alda's ear. Its words grew softer so only Alda could hear. "But this girl is dangerous."

Chapter Six: All the Devils

Dreng descended into the depths beneath Caliban's tower, following the beautiful youth into the darkness below. He expected some odor, some smell of tepid water and rot. But this place, the realm of Netherfeld, had no such scent. Rather, it had no scent whatsoever, no discerning features apart from the grim tower, its underground labyrinth, and its vanishing form.

Twenty paces. Fifty. The ceiling lowered, and Dreng had to bow his head as he stayed on Caliban's heels, the position reminding him of being in the hold of *The Tempest*. Ten more steps, and they reached a small, solid, metal door in the floor. Etched into its surface was a spiral, matching the one on the floor of the library in Prospero's palace.

And near the door was a simple, wooden lever.

"What is this place?"

Caliban stooped and moved his cloak aside as he placed his hand against the lever. "An *oubliette*. A place to forget. But we must remember. And find truth." He smiled and added, "And wisdom." The beautiful youth pulled, and the door fell open with a rusty squeal.

Dreng leaned over the small opening, his eyes unable to adjusted to the darkness within. "What's ins—" Before Dreng could utter the final syllable, he felt himself hit a stone floor, his shoulder crumbling beneath the weight of his body.

For a moment, Dreng lay as he had fallen, confused and stunned. The darkness enveloped him, like in the cavern, except for the opening some ten feet above his head. It closed with a screech, and he heard a latch as the remnants of light danced behind his eyelids.

His vision adjusted, and the phantom lights ceased as he considered what to do.

He could call out. For help. For Caliban. But this was his doing, some game, some trick. And Dreng doubted there was danger, not real and immediate danger, yet his heart pounded against his ears.

And his shoulder throbbed. It was out of joint, bent strangely forward above his tingling arm and useless fingers. This was not the first time it had been injured thus, so he held his breath and clenched his jaw as he twisted and popped it back into position.

Only a slight hiccup of pain escaped his lips.

He wiped the fresh sweat from his forehead and tried to reason through Caliban's words: "A place to forget, but we must remember, and find truth and wisdom."

But he had mentioned a prisoner. *Prisoner.*

The word stuck in his mind as Dreng realized that he might be Caliban's prey. Perhaps this was indeed a trap, not a trick.

Perhaps Dreng was the prisoner.

But, if the witches had spoken truth, it was not Dreng's time to die. There was no singing mountain, no fire. If Dreng had more confidence, more optimism, he might even think himself invincible because surely stones could not sing or burn. But he had seen so much since he had arrived on Prospero's island.

And before that, Dreng had survived worse.

Years earlier, after Prince Hamlet had escaped, when the young ship-boy had been bandaged and his wound from Ernesto began to show its first signs of improvement, he was suddenly thrown into the dank hold and bound to a munitions barrel, his shoulders twisted behind him and his wrists searing against rough rope. He struggled to stand but could not brace his feet against the slick planks. So he sat in the damp and listened to the scurry of rats, waiting for what punishment would come.

After what felt like days, a hooded figure appeared. Dreng expected execution, but he instead got a bloodied nose and aching jaw. The boy pleaded and begged and cried and offered to tell the man anything, to do anything, to make the beating stop. Only silence met him and then, again, Dreng was alone. The next day was the same. And the next and the next until his every breath rattled with pain and hunger and thirst and his pleas that sounded so empty as they echoed against the wooden beams.

Finally, Dreng stopped speaking. He took the punches and kicks and worse.

And then, suddenly, they stopped.

One night, after passing out from exhaustion and agony, he awoke to find the ropes gone. Stale bread and flat ale had been placed on the barrel. He ate and drank and, after settling his nerves, snuck to the deck above and slumbered in relative peace on his old coiled rope.

The next morning, as the sun rose, he reunited with the crew.

He counted their number. It measured the same as his beatings. Each had his revenge firsthand.

And no one ever spoke of what transpired in the hold, not even on the day of his trial by sword.

But Dreng had learned the importance of revenge and silence. And he was also taught to be hard, to outlast the men who caused pain and fear, to guard himself against what danger might come.

To survive.

As Dreng's mind returned to his immediate predicament, he shuddered and rose unsteadily to his feet, outstretched his arms, and took tentative steps into the darkness.

Four paces ahead, and his fingers touched a wall. Two to the left, and another wall. He turned around, toward the direction that had been his right, and his third step landed on something soft.

He knelt and felt a jumble of rags. Skin, warm. Long hair, coarse. A beard. Breath. He gently shook the figure, but it did not stir.

Should he speak?

Should he cry out for aid, for Caliban?

No, this was Caliban's aim. This, the prisoner. So Dreng leaned closer to the inanimate man and whispered, "I can help you."

Silence. So Dreng continued, "Tell me who you are."

A deep breath, held, and released with a sigh and a cough.

Dreng felt his companion move and steadied his shaking form as he tried to sit. Finally, after the man could sit unaided, he responded hoarsely, "I am Prospero."

The name was unexpected here, in the prison of forgetfulness. The man who had destroyed *The Tempest* and killed Dreng's crewmates. A murderer and a tyrant.

Prospero was dead. Miranda — no, Sycorax — had told Dreng so. He had died in the library, somehow, and the only trace of his struggle was a spiral on the floor.

The same spiral that adorned the trapdoor above.

So Sycorax had lied. The old man, the one who commanded spirits and controlled the enchanted island, lived but had been transported to another realm.

For a brief flash, Dreng wondered if she had spoken truth. Perhaps this was death, the world beyond. Perhaps, as he had feared, the flood had indeed washed him and Alda not to another realm but to a watery grave.

But no. Sycorax had lied, and this was real. Dreng could feel his existence, even now. He was yet alive.

And so was Prospero.

After the shock had subsided, Dreng asked quietly, "How did you get here?"

"Who are you?"

The question caught Dreng off guard. He had two names now and had to choose. "My name is Thomas Chatterton." The words immediately felt foreign. The title of a stranger.

And he was met with silence again.

So Dreng continued, "I can help you, if you tell me how you got here."

Again, the old man did not respond. So Dreng persisted, "What does Caliban want with you?"

"How would I know the wants of a monster?"

Dreng felt his fingers curl into a fist, and it took all his resolve to hold his temper at bay. "*You* are the monster."

The sorcerer laughed, the sound quickly becoming a cough.

"You are three steps behind him, boy. Caliban will destroy you, as he has ruined me."

A sly smile spread across Dreng's lips, unseen in the darkness as he lied, "Yes, I know. Certainly. How can we defeat him?"

"With wisdom."

"What kind of wisdom?"

The old man shifted away, and a chill rose up Dreng's neck as silence once more permeated the black chamber.

And, finally, the old man spoke...

After some minutes of repeated questioning, Dreng shouted for Caliban's help and begged for their release from the *oubliette*. But Dreng could hear the reluctance in his captor's reply as he refused to lift him to safety.

Finally, Dreng lied and told the beautiful youth that Prospero had revealed the secret wisdom.

Caliban was still suspicious, his tone clear even as his words were lost in echoes, and it was not until Dreng swore an oath not to retaliate that a rope hit the stony floor in the darkness, and Dreng pushed the old man up to safety and then awkwardly heaved his own weight into the tower's underground corridor, wincing in pain from his too-recent injuries.

In the relative light above the cell, Dreng could examine his fellow prisoner for the first time. He had not seen Prospero previously but had heard enough from Miranda — Sycorax — to paint a picture in his mind.

This man before him was not what he had anticipated. His emaciated form was shrouded in a thick robe. His face obscured by a beard. His hair gray and thinning. The man's eyes were cast downward, ignoring those near him. He was weak. Frightened.

Dreng looked from him to Caliban, his eyes full of questions.

With a snort, Caliban spat, "You two have not had the pleasure of a formal introduction. This specimen was until recently Dreng, the once and future Thomas Chatterton, former pirate and current — I don't know what."

"Yes, I already —"

Caliban paid Dreng no regard. "And this abomination, miscreant, stock-fish, this, this spongy mushrump is Prospero, father of Miranda, former sorcerer, usurper, and then destroyer of my hopes and dreams." The young man spat.

Prospero cast a wicked look at Dreng, who stood and looked down at the man's ragged form. One who had once controlled unknown powers now looked only sad. An old man to be pitied, not feared.

"Did he give it to you?" Caliban glanced at Dreng, and his eyes appeared more mournful than his tone revealed. "He refuses to even speak a word to me. And if he speaks, I expect only lies."

"Why should I tell you what he said?" For once, Dreng was a step ahead of Caliban, and he did not attempt to hide the victorious sneer on his face.

"I saved your life. I protected you from the witches." Caliban leaned toward him, slowing to enunciate each word with the full weight of his threat. "And if you do not help me now, I will make certain that they find you again. And then there will be no *deus ex machina* to save you."

Dreng laughed, despite the shiver that tickled his neck. This was not the boy on the raft, not the same sarcastic witticisms or insolent sneers. This was something dark; some madness had overtaken the beautiful youth. And where would that madness lead? To Dreng's death, or his own?

Or both?

But Dreng suppressed his worries and focused with the steadiness of character that he commanded as boatswain, his voice unwavering as he spoke to Caliban. "How long have you held him here?"

"This place has no days or months or years. There is no moon or sun. No seasons, so —"

"How long?"

"More than long enough for him to give me what I want."

Dreng crouched by the old man's side and reached for his bearded face, which turned away not in fear but in some kind of haughty pride. After a moment, Dreng stood and sighed, "He told me that he has the wisdom you seek but would not share it with you or anyone." Dreng set his jaw and added, "So we must kill him."

Even Caliban gasped, but Dreng did not flinch. He had seen this resolution before. In himself.

And now, above the *oubliette*, Dreng saw a familiar, steely look in Prospero's eyes as he stood above the captive. So Dreng repeated to Caliban, "Kill him."

Chapter Seven: Deepest Consequences

Below the glistening, floating waters, Alda felt an unsettling sense of urgency as the spirits swirled around her, their forms brushing against her arms and skirt, their lights unnaturally bright in the surrounding nothing of Netherfeld.

And Alda did not attempt to suppress her smile as Miranda's empty silhouette again broke the silence. "If we are to leave this place, then I must bid it farewell properly."

The girl was so innocent, so sweet and kind. Sincere and pure. Strangely, she was the opposite of Caliban. Perhaps the cliché about loving opposites was true after all.

Or perhaps what they had together was not love. Only some trick. Like Dreng's enchantment.

But Alda shook her head. Surely there was good in the world, and this girl was of it.

"Goodbye, my dear spirits." The forms of light spun wildly like bees kicked from a hive as Miranda spoke.

Alda stepped back, growing worry weighing on her brow.

The innocent girl continued, "Goodbye, sweet, black nothing."

Some spirits flashed, their lights sparking into the blackness.

The moth form of Phillida glided closer to Alda, the only calm spirit in the pandemonium. "Alda my dear," she whispered. "You must prepare yourself."

Before Alda could respond, Miranda continued, "Farewell, my newfound friends!"

Lightning. Again. A third flash connected a few yards from Alda, the light dazzling her eyes to near blindness. And when she opened them, she saw three familiar figures.

Witches.

"All hail, Alda!" The voice was hoarse, its words sarcastic.

"Hail, heir of Hecate!"

"Hail, the living girl."

"Who will die."

Alda backed away from the weird sisters, positioning herself beneath the Stream of Consciousness. She could feel the spirits swirling above and behind her but dared not turn her head toward them as she retorted, "We will all die someday."

"She sees the truth, sister."

"Too little, though."

"And too late."

"The rest she'll know in the grave."

"Let's not speak of such morbid things!" Miranda's enthusiastic voice broke though the whirring spirits. "Friends, do you already know one another?"

The witches laughed as Alda pleaded, "Miranda, come with me!" She could not leave Miranda with them as she had abandoned Ophelia.

But what might happen to the girl without a body on the other side of the stream?

Surely she would be a shade, as Sycorax had been. But Alda could protect her there, on the island. Then she could find Dreng, somehow. And together, with the cauldron's bubble, they could find Caliban. And —

Alda's hopes were interrupted as she realized she was suddenly suspended, lifted toward the Stream of Consciousness by the spirits.

Again, she tried, "Miranda, these beings are dangerous! Do not remain here!"

But Miranda laughed, and the sound revealed that the formless voice had moved closer to the three witches.

"But these are *my* friends. They found me here. And helped guide me to this stream. And then they told me to wait — here — and that an enemy would soon come."

"Enemy?"

"You." Four voices spoke in unison.

Miranda laughed, and Alda realized that her innocence was a ploy. This girl was clever. And the spirits were correct: she was dangerous.

So Alda reached for the stream, her fingertips only inches from its enchanted waters. But then she fell. Not completely to the ground, but near enough. She wiped her hair from her eyes and saw plumes of smoke dissipate above her head. Yet she was suspended by the spirits, despite their dwindled numbers.

She realized that the spirits were the smoke. The witches had destroyed them.

And a cold grip encircled Alda's ankle as some unseen force pulled her down, toward the witches.

Before Alda could react, the robin and starling and several formless swirls dove at the witches, who with a wave turned them to pillars of smoke that quickly dissolved. As if they had never existed.

But whatever encircled her ankle loosed its grip as the five spirits that still hoisted Alda aloft lifted her closer to the stream. The Luna moth flew at her side, its voice shaking as it gasped, "Only a little farther my dear and you will be safe... but you must not forget me when you are gone."

"No! Let me stay and fight!" Alda struggled and dropped again, but the spirits held firm and moved faster toward the stream. Three spirits let loose and again charged the witches, only to be instantaneously dissolved as well.

Each time the witches waved their hands, they cackled. Miranda joined in their mirth, her laugh more shrill than the others. "Yes, yes, let her stay!"

Alda could not determine if the girl found joy in the spirits' destruction or was unaware of the witches' wickedness. She shivered.

Now, Alda ascended slower as only a sparrow and the Luna moth remained at her side, hoisting her arms toward the underside of the water. She reached, and her fingers felt its droplets.

As she was thrust into the stream's depths, Alda's last thought was of her mother, trapped in Netherfeld with the witches. But Phillida had escaped worse, surely. She was strong enough to survive the witches' wrath.

And suddenly, Alda was elsewhere. Her worries distant and overpowered.

She knew it was a dream — no, a memory — but that did not make it easier to overcome. Although she was within the depths of the Stream of Consciousness, she had no sensation of its waters.

Instead, she was a little girl again on the seventh island in the cottage, looking at stereopticon cards as her grandmother kneaded bread on the large wooden table.

"Tell me a story, Gramma."

"No, I want to hear *your* story."

Little Alda lowered her stereoscope and gave her grandmother a serious look, one that felt too mature for her age. "I don't have any. I'm not old enough."

"Nonsense! You have your stories there, in your hand. Tell me about them."

"These are only pictures."

"Then give them words."

Alda hesitated and sorted through her cards. Her favorites were of the flora and fauna of distant lands, watercolored images of Australian marsupials and South American jungles. She selected one of a reef and placed it carefully on the wire rack. As she looked at its image, the corals seemingly so close that she might touch them, she whispered, "There was a mermaid who lived in an enchanted reef, a young mermaid. A girl, like me. And she found a fish trapped under a pirate ship's anchor, so she freed it."

"Go on."

"But it wasn't an ordinary fish. It was the color of amethyst, and it could talk. So when the mermaid freed it, it gave her three wishes."

"And what did she wish for?"

Alda lowered the stereoscope and bit her lip. "She wished to see the world." She sorted through other cards, grasping for inspiration. "She wished for knowledge, more knowledge than she could get beneath the sea. And..." Her voice trailed off as she watched her grandmother turn and pound the dough. "And she wished to find her family."

"Well, the mermaid should know that she can see the world without help from a magical fish." She smiled slyly. "And that she can find her own knowledge."

"But family —"

"Family, too." Gramma stopped kneading long enough to smile at Alda and wiped a floury hand across her forehead. "You can choose those you are with, those whom you love. Or you can choose to be alone." Her eyes narrowed as her gaze became more intense. "Remember this, Alda. But now, be like your mermaid. Swim!"

And Alda became aware of her legs and her arms, flailing in the stream. She imagined its smooth surface, the flowering dryads above, and she kicked and pulled and finally gulped the island's air.

But then she fell into another memory, one more recent. In her cottage with Dreng, delirious from his poisoned wound. Sweat dripping from his forehead, his shoulders shaking and breath heaving from his chest. She wiped his hair from his face with a cold cloth, and his eyes opened for a flash before turning upward, their spheres only white.

His lips moved, urgently, but no sound escaped.

Suddenly, his mouth opened in a silent scream, and then he was still. Too still. And for a moment Alda was on edge. No movement. So she felt his chest. Nothing. No heartbeat, no breath.

Alda gasped and choked on a sob, and for a flash her eyes focused on the present, on the stream's shoreline. She pulled again, knowing that Dreng was only a horrible dream. That the shore was real. That she had to reach it. That she had to save herself.

But she fell into her memory again, and her cheeks were wet with tears. She held her wrist over Dreng's lips, feeling for air. Nothing. She held her shaking finger to his neck, as her grandmother had taught her to do, and waited in the deafening silence.

Finally, Alda felt her hand close on a root, and she dragged her body from the enchanted waters.

She was on the island, again.

But as she coughed and choked and finally smiled at her successful escape, her mind was still with Dreng.

She thought he had died then. For a terrible moment, she feared he had left her alone in the cottage. But she had felt a distant echo of his heartbeat. And then his breaths returned, steady. His fever broke, the poison somehow sweated from his quivering form. And as he slept on her tapestried sofa, she cried over him. Tears of relief and sadness and fear and uncertainty.

And now, on the bank of the Stream of Consciousness, she felt tears again flood her eyes. But she quickly brushed them away.

He was alive, somewhere, she reminded herself. She had saved him in her cottage.

As the fear from her memory faded, Alda had only one desire: to save him again.

But first she had to find him.

Chapter Eight: Mischiefs Manifold

As they stood in the vanishing tower's depths, the corridor's ceiling weighing down on them, Dreng tried to make himself look larger than he felt. Intimidating.

Prospero remained defiantly silent, scowling, so Dreng continued, "In the *oubliette*, he told me that he has a pearl of wisdom, some secret of knowledge, but that he could not share it."

"Why not?"

"He said that we are too simple to use it."

Caliban laughed. "We? Us? Too simple? I? I am the heir to a great kingdom. And you, the — well, you are still alive, so surely that is significant."

"Caliban, it is a trick." Dreng enunciated each word slowly as he wiped his hand across his brow. "That is why we must kill him."

"But then we will never find the pearl of wisdom!" Dreng disregarded Caliban's protest and took hold of the sword at his companion's waist as Caliban objected, "No, no, not yet. What if, what if..." His words faded into the depths of the corridor.

"Why do you hesitate?"

Caliban mumbled, "Conscience makes me a coward."

"I have no such reservation!" Dreng held the sword aloft, its blade pointed at Prospero's throat. But Caliban pushed the weapon aside and stood between them as the old man cowered on the stony floor of the disintegrating tower.

"Do I want him dead? Surely. But not enough to kill him. Let him suffer instead. Let him wither. Let him be forgotten. But do not kill him, Dreng. Death is too kind."

A wail echoed through the dim light. Not a scream of pain. A sob. Dreng smiled and lowered the blade as Caliban crouched beside the old man.

"You would let me live, boy?"

"Only as you let me live. A miserable outcast, torn from —" Caliban
stood as he added, "I loved your daughter once. And still, despite myself.
That makes you somewhat more like kin. Though less than kind."

The old man broke down into a wretched pile of tears and wails, so
Dreng dropped the sword to his side as he turned to Caliban. "If you
won't let me kill him, then what shall we do?"

"You and I can return to the island. *My* island. There is enough
knowledge in the library to help us stop the witches." He took a deep
breath as he replaced the sword on his waist. "I hope."

"Take me with you!" Prospero's voice cracked as he pleaded. "I will
be at your service. You will command my obedience. I swear to you, I
swear to you on —"

"On my mother's grave?" Caliban's voice shook with fury. He again
bent to the old man and studied his face. "Usurper, if you want to be free,
tell me where to find the damned pearl."

Confusion flashed over Dreng's face. Did Caliban want a pearl? A
literal pearl of wisdom?

Prospero shook his head, so Caliban grabbed him roughly by the
front of his shirt. "My mother and I tore apart your staff when we sent
you to this wretched place! It was in splinters, but its magic was gone.
Disappeared. The seed that let its power grow was nowhere to be found."
He spoke through clenched teeth. "Where did you hide the blasted pearl
of wisdom?"

The old sorcerer coughed and turned his head away silently. The
young man relented, a look not of anger but of profound disappointment
crossing his face. "My friend was going to kill you, Prospero. He is mad.
But I stopped him. I let you live. And still, you will not surrender the one

token that I need to free your daughter from an icy grave."

Dreng turned, concealing the look of surprise on his face. Caliban knew that the grave held Sycorax, not Miranda, so this was a purposeful lie. Dreng could not let his unchecked expression betray whatever his companion was planning.

"Let me save her, Prospero!" His voice cracked. "The pearl. Now."

"You are like the devil, Caliban. Spinning a web of deceit and ensnaring those around you."

"You confuse me with a spider. Harmless if left to my own devices."

The old man scowled and coughed again, the sound deep and worrisome. He raised himself up on one elbow and reached his free hand into his mouth. His face twisted in pain and effort until he produced in his palm a single, white tooth.

But Dreng could see it was no tooth. Its shape too round, its surface too smooth. It was a pearl.

Prospero thrust it into Caliban's hand as he proclaimed, "Here is the pearl of wisdom. Now let me go free!"

Caliban smiled at the tiny jewel and placed it within the fabric at his waist. His expression changed suddenly as he looked back at the old man. "Free you? I said that I would let you be forgotten." He lunged forward and pushed Prospero back through the open door of the *oubliette*. A deep thud echoed from below before Caliban dropped the metal door with a reverberating clank.

"You will leave him here to die?" Dreng's words shook.

"One cannot die from hunger or thirst in Netherfeld. He will survive." He paused and added, "But what is it to you? You were going to kill him."

"I told you it was a trick."

Caliban smiled slyly. "And I played my part as well. Are we offstage now?"

Dreng nodded reluctantly. All was deception with Caliban. Well, most. So he doubted that he would receive a clear answer, yet he asked, "What is the pearl of wisdom?"

Caliban, to his surprise, was earnest. "It is like a prism that magnifies the sun. But this jewel intensifies magic. Any spell, any power, is amplified by its touch."

"Then it can find Alda."

Caliban cleared his throat, the sound unnaturally loud in the empty corridor. "In time, friend. First, we must awaken my mother. Your *wife*." The word felt cruel, like a dagger.

The beautiful youth turned and started down the corridor, and Dreng shivered as the cries of the prisoner echoed hollowly beneath him.

*   *   *

The island was not as Alda had remembered. The sun's orb was still as bright and the sky was the same shade of azure blue, but the sounds and the colors were all muted. No, not muted. Absent.

Flowers. Leaves. Life. All gone.

No naiads emerged, sparkling and misty, from the enchanted waters of the Stream of Consciousness. The dryads — oaken nymphs — no longer dipped and swayed above the streambank. They stood white and barren, like an elephant graveyard in one of Alda's stereopticon cards. White. Sun-scorched. Dead.

Alda shivered. How much time had passed on Prospero's island? Had she arrived at some distant point in the future, after years or decades or centuries had done their work?

Or had something horrible happened?

Another shiver. Alda wrung the dripping water from her black hair and gray skirt and hesitated longer than she should before she approached the naked trunk of a deceased dryad.

For a moment, Alda recalled a moment from her childhood. When she was younger and happier, she was tasked with trapping a wild squirrel that ravaged her grandmother's herb garden. So she rigged a trap from broken planks and frayed rope and waited patiently for her target to creep beneath its wooden prison. The squirrel finally came, and she captured it with ease.

But then she discovered that the squirrel was injured, its foot bleeding from the weight of the crate. So Alda nursed it back to health. And in the end, it was hers and lived in a box near the dry well on her grandmother's island, spending the summer frolicking within the treetops.

The next autumn, the squirrel was gone. At first Alda had thought it found some warmer place to ride out the coldest months, but she had been mistaken.

One frosty morning, she discovered the dried remains of her animal friend near a rock pile at the far end of the island. Its sparse fur was matted with brown blood, its neck contorted at an unnatural angle. Parts were missing. It had been killed.

And as Alda stared at the squirrel's remains, she only wanted to kill the thing that had taken its life. But, helplessly, she knew she could not. Even if she could find the predator, she could not bring herself to harm it.

All these years later, Alda rarely thought of the squirrel because the image of its corpse overpowered any pleasant memories she had of the friendly creature. She only remembered it in death.

Now, looking at the dryads' remains, she felt the same stirrings of anger and vengeance combined with the knowledge that this, this would be her predominant memory of the magical beings. This is how she would forever see the dryads in her mind's eye.

Alda took a deep breath and summoned the courage to touch a branch. She remembered what the dryads had told her so long ago: their dead sister, the tree that had once held Ariel, still contained powers. So she bit her lip and, with pangs of regret, snapped a branch.

It turned to dust in her hand, blowing away in a sudden breeze.

So she instead examined the tree's trunk. It was cold, of course, and dry. Her fingertips ran over its surface, loosening pieces of bark that fell to the ground as powder.

On the smooth, white interior of the tree, crisscrossing over its surface, were marks burnt by some unknown flame. Strange lines seared in a complex pattern that reached up and down the tree. As Alda peeled more bark from its limbs, she saw an ever more intricate pattern of branching, irregular lines.

She had seen a pattern like this before. On Dreng. The red scar on his shoulder, the scar she had been too self-conscious to acknowledge out loud. To question. But she should have asked about its cause.

Because whatever had left its mark on Dreng had done the same to the dryads.

And she could guess what had caused this damage.

When Dreng was fighting the poison from Puck's blade, he fell in and out of consciousness, in and out of bewilderment. At times, he had spoken to his mother, mistaking Alda for the woman who had birthed him. Often, he swore and cursed at unseen sailors, thinking himself at sea.

But once or twice, he had whispered a chant and clutched his shoulder in agony.

Alda suspected the chant was more. Something wicked. Words of death and destruction. A spell.

And though Alda still knew relatively little of witchcraft, of the scope or scale of its powers or the numbers of those who practiced it, she guessed which three of its followers were likely culprits.

The weird sisters. They could have done this, destroyed the dryads and wrought havoc on the island. They could have done it, but did they?

And if they did, were they finished with their deed?

Or was worse yet to come?

Alda felt despondence overpower her, so she stood suddenly and wiped dripping water from her forehead. She was dizzy, tired. Somewhat disoriented. But she needed to persevere. To find a way home.

To find Dreng.

And she knew this place. So she pushed herself through the leafless forest. Over the stony fields. Up the grassless moors. And finally, after too many hours, the palazzo. Prospero's palazzo. Dilapidated. Abandoned. Still and quiet and void of colors. Like everything else in this cursed place.

Alda's feet dragged over the smooth stones of the palazzo's floor. The corridor smelled of wet decay. Holes in the roof let sun shine through, onto pockets of gray moss and brown leaves. She started down a corridor, changed direction, and turned again until she found herself in the library.

She remembered it from before, when she had learned that Miranda was Sycorax in disguise. When Alda hid from her, quaking with fear. And when Alda let loose her powers, shattering its massive windows and saving herself. When she searched Prospero's body and retrieved the miniature book, now missing in her flooded cottage.

But so much in the library had changed. The great Corinthian columns were crumbling, their stones pitted with time. The timbers above were warped and bent. The bookshelves were empty, their wooden planks battered and fallen into heaps. Not a book or manuscript or shred of parchment remained.

And in the center of the room was a great spiral. A witch-trap.

What had happened here, in her absence?

A snap. A jolt. And Alda felt her feet leave the floor and her back hit a toppled bookshelf.

She stood, stunned. Her ears ringing and shoulders aching. But she had to move, quickly, to avoid whatever invisible force had attacked her.

So she ran and ducked, sliding behind another bookshelf. It offered little protection as she peered through its shelves, searching for her adversary.

Another movement, like a wind, rattled a toppled bookcase across the room. And another. Like something was searching for prey, stalking to find her.

She ducked lower, her pulse racing. After several heartbeats of silence, she held her breath and again peered out, scanning the apparently empty library.

Except it was not empty. Movement caught her eye, in the far, shadowy corner. She squinted into the darkness and finally saw a faint flash of something. Hair? No. Skin? No.

Feathers.

And Alda felt a smile spread across her lips. She stood tentatively as she called out, "Ariel? Ariel, I mean you no harm!"

Silence.

She walked forward, slowly, avoiding the remains of the bookshelves and the spiral etched in stone.

"Ariel, I'm Alda. Show yourself. It is safe."

"This safety is a lie, but —"

A thud.

She saw him now, collapsed on the floor with his head propped against a wall, his great wings spread loosely at his sides. The harpy looked like a fallen angel from her grandmother's illustrated *Paradise Lost*, a celestial figure struck down by some mighty force.

"Where are the books? What killed the dryads? What happened here?" Her questions were soft and hurried as she rushed to his side.

But Ariel did not speak. Instead, he shifted until he was more upright. As she knelt at his side, she saw blood smeared across his cheek.

"What happened to you?"

"I thought you one of them." He sighed and added, "I'm nearly spent."

"Who did this?"

"They're gone. For now." His metric words were short, chopped, and he paused for breath at the end of each phrase.

"Who?" Alda lowered her voice as she guessed, "The witches?"

The harpy nodded, his breath rattling as he inhaled.

"What do they want?"

"A book. A book of spells." His eyes widened as he whispered, "The book of Prospero."

The miniature book, the tiny volume that contained the words to make the cauldron's bubble. Alda had last seen it in her cottage. Before she was whisked away by the rising waters of the Grand River.

Antediluvian. The word slipped into her head, inspired by the angel-like figure before her. *Before the flood.*

"Why do they want the book?"

Ariel coughed. "For knowledge. Power. All."

He coughed again, and more blood dripped from his mouth.

"Your injuries — Shall I help." Alda had intended it to be a question, but it came out with the force of a statement.

Another cough, deeper. "The island, its magic —" He gasped like a diver too long below water.

Alda reached for his hand. His claw-like fingers were cold, unmoving. "What can I do?"

Silence. Then, in a soft voice, "You tried to save me once before, and 'twas too early. Now, it's too late."

"No, no. What can I do, Ariel? Let me help you." A tear on her cheek. She cried too easily now for someone who was once so strong. She barely knew this creature, and their brief meetings had been born of mystery and violence.

"This is my island, child. Not Sycorax, nor Prospero, nor anyone could command it. Only I. And along with it, I must die."

"No, no, I can save it. Dreng, my friend — my friend and I will save it. And you. Please wait, Ariel. Wait before you, you sleep."

But it was too late. A shadow covered the sun, and the room turned to twilight shadows.

And instead of sadness, instead of grief, Alda only felt guilt. The harpy's energy was spent to attack her. If she had not come here... If she had announced herself... If she had never found the cauldron's bubble in the first place...

No. That would mean never meeting Dreng. She needed him in her life. She needed to find him.

And as she stood and turned from Ariel's motionless form, her thoughts leaped quickly from the harpy's death to what the future might hold.

How would she escape this place? Stop the witches? Return home?

More importantly, how would she find Dreng in the vast labyrinth of time and place without a cauldron's bubble?

Chapter Nine: Restless Ecstasy

The wet smell of the cave stung Dreng's nostrils as he followed closely behind Caliban when they passed from Netherfeld into the too-solid world.

"Do you need my hand, friend?" The words were heavy with sarcasm.

"Why did we not enter Netherfeld here before? Why did we take the raft to the Duke's Tree?"

"I did not know then what I know now."

"What is that?"

"My way."

Dreng only sighed. He continued walking in the dark, trusting the sound of his companion's footsteps more than his own instincts.

Caliban, Dreng knew, must understand these caves that connected Netherfeld to the world from which he came, the lightless tunnels that transected Prospero's island and bridged the land above with the realm of nothing.

Dreng, as well, had passed through one such cave after the flood, when he came into Netherfeld. So surely they must lead out as well.

Or was it another of Caliban's tricks?

Yet soon enough, Dreng saw a glimmer of light. A beam. Then an opening. The entrance to a cave. Not the grand cavern that had collapsed, but a lesser cave. Smaller, narrower, lit with glowing jewels that sparkled like stars beneath their feet. They climbed up a steep slope, passing dripping water and eerie formations of slippery stone, until the weary travelers withdrew from a shallow hole near the island's clifftops.

The sun was a golden shimmer in the distance, like a piece of gold glittering above the sea. Dreng barely noticed. Caliban looked only to the ground as the pair persuaded their tired forms to silently take one step, and then another, until after too long they were nearly at the frozen spring that had so recently engulfed Sycorax's body.

But was it indeed recent? The trees in the forest's edge drooped, their limbs barren and bark stripped. The grasses of the open moors were brown and brittle. No foliage. No life. No birds or bees or sounds. The island was desolate. Dead. Silent.

Dreng remembered the too-familiar songs that he heard nightly when he lived in the palace. They were so common that they became like a breath, nearly unheard.

But now, the sounds' absence was deafening.

As silent as the grave.

A fitting turn of phrase for what appeared before them: Sycorax — or rather Miranda's body — entombed in a shallow pool of clear ice. Her form still, in a magical sleep. Or death. Like a living statue that had lost its animation. Not aged or broken or decayed. The same as when Dreng had last beheld her. Unmoving and unmoved.

As Dreng knelt next to the frozen spring, he ran his fingers over the surface. He could break the ice or melt it with a flame, but then what? Her body had been injured, perhaps destroyed, in the collapse of the cavern. Could they resuscitate her? Or had so many weeks, or months, or years, made this an eternal tomb?

"We need a spell." Caliban's quiet, uncertain words broke Dreng's reverie. Since they had returned to the island, Caliban had barely uttered a sentence. Now his tone was distant, soft. Lacking the charisma and sarcasm that usually weighed his words.

"What spell?"

Caliban sighed, the wrinkles near his eyes somehow becoming deeper. "I do not know. *She* would know. But she is not here..."

Dreng was unsure if he spoke of Sycorax or Miranda, but it mattered naught. He looked up the hill to the palace above, its form vastly more ruinous than when they had left on the raft.

How much time had passed when they were away, in Fairy Land and Netherfeld?

"Should we go to the palace's library?"

"Perhaps." Caliban wiped his eyes and, for what was likely the first time, admitted, "I don't know what to do. Without a spell, the pearl —"

"Perhaps this will help." Dreng set his jaw as he retrieved the miniature book from the folds at his waist and passed it to Caliban.

"Where, where did you get this?"

"Alda."

Caliban smiled, "She is a witch and a thief. No wonder you love her."

"I — I don't. I mean, I —"

Caliban silenced his protest with a wave of his hand. "It matters not." He thumbed through the tiny pages, searching.

Finally, he landed on his mark. Pointing, he handed the book back to Dreng. "Read this, *paramour*."

Dreng scowled but did as he was told and read a spell entitled "trouble fire:" "Come deadly flames to charm the air and cast about the mortals' games, to take from each his deathly share and cloud the sun, until the hurley-burley's done."

As Dreng spoke, Caliban held his hand, the pearl clasped between their palms. When Dreng finished, he waited, his breath shallow. Nothing.

Caliban shifted away and rubbed his fingers nervously. Moments passed. Caliban stood and peered at the ice. Then he paced, the blue cloak flapping rhythmically against his legs.

And Dreng remembered the words of his father's ghost: "The

changeling, beyond the tree, can save her." He had assumed the changeling was Alda, somehow, so perhaps they needed her to revive Sycorax.

Or he was the changeling. Or Caliban.

Or the ghost was wrong. Or deceitful.

After several excruciating minutes, Caliban turned to Dreng with a cruel sneer, "You must have tripped on your tongue. Read again, and speak apace."

But before Dreng could repeat the spell, they both leapt back in surprise. Above the frozen spring was an orb, its surface burning in green-red flames. A wisp, like the Irish sailors had described in their tales of fairies and little people. It quickly spread and fell onto the ice, its flames growing taller and transforming into deep, blood-red. It suddenly burst into a white light, and then vanished.

Dreng blinked as his eyes adjusted to the scene before him: the spring was a low, liquid pool, barely ankle-deep. Steam rose from its surface. Within the shroud of mist, Miranda's form convulsed as white foam trickled from her lips.

Before Dreng could react, Caliban was at her side, cradling her head as her limbs thrashed uncontrollably. He looked to Dreng helplessly, "Help me hold her!"

Dreng took her shoulders and eased them up until her torso was well above the water. As Caliban stroked her hair, Dreng could see that her eyeballs were streaked in red, unseeing and flicking unnaturally.

Despite her uncontrollable ferocity, Caliban calmly soothed, "This is home, Mother, you are safe, open your eyes —"

Dreng was helpless, as was Caliban, who continued to speak softly, his words either prayers or curses.

And Dreng expected the worst. When he had placed his wife's body in the spring, when its waters enveloped her form, she was injured. Gravely. And even though Caliban expected some miraculous cure, some resurrection, Dreng had his doubts. Surely mere waters could not sustain a person so long. Surely she could not be healed.

But suddenly, the body of the blonde girl took a deep breath and relaxed as heat radiated from her form. In the still quiet of the evening, Dreng could hear her voice fill with happiness as she whispered, "Cali?"

The beautiful youth first recoiled and then bent forward, touching her neck tenderly as tears welled in his eyes, and Dreng turned his face to hide the conflicting emotions in his eyes.

This was not Sycorax. This was someone much kinder, younger. Someone whom Caliban knew.

A trick, indeed.

"Miranda..." Caliban's voice shook with emotion. "I can't — I can't — Now, I —"

Dreng knew he should be happy for his friend. And besides, perhaps Miranda could help them stop the witches. She could have yet unknown magic, after all.

But Caliban's voice shook with emotion. Not hope. Not love. Desperation. "Not now, my once-love. It is not your time." Caliban's voice grew louder as he spoke a string of words. A spell. The same he had muttered when he resurrected Miranda in his cave.

And as Dreng watched the pair, the girl sat bolt upright as red light swirled around her form. It quickly faded, and she looked to the sky and blinked, then stepped from the shallow pool and stretched her arms above her head as one awaking from a long slumber.

As Caliban hung his head and quietly wiped tears from his eyes,

Dreng was again struck by how his companion's face had changed. More somber, yes, but also aged. Worn. No, forlorn.

The yellow-haired girl looked first to him and then to Dreng. "We have work, my boys." Her tone was icy, condescending. "The witches are coming. They're close. And we must strike first." Her eyes flashed. Blue eyes. Sycorax's eyes.

And in that moment, Dreng regretted waking the woman he once loved. But, still, he needed her. To find Alda. But what would be the price of her help?

*   *   *

Alda, alone in the vacant library of the crumbling palazzo, felt her body become limp, numb. She was tired. No, exhausted. No, beyond even that. Bone-dead tired, her grandmother would have said.

Bone. Dead. Tired.

Ariel was dead. She had come here, so many months ago, to find him. To free him or capture him or somehow bring him to the witches on the moor. She had a goal then. A purpose. And now, she was helpless. Without a path forward.

She could not bring herself to look at the harpy's body across the room, breathless and motionless. Still, she felt safer with him nearby. As if the form of the great harpy might drive away any threat. A rouse. A trick.

Her mind wandered again to the witches. To the fear she felt before them in Netherfeld. To her mother's spirit-form, trapped in the void. To Miranda. To Dreng.

Her thoughts became swift and disconnected, the flashes of her memories and wishes as she lingered between awareness and sleep.

Images from her stereopticon cards. The Sphinx. Parthenon. Colosseum. Then they became more real, recollections of her life in Grand Ledge. The Folly Hotel. The Opera House. The Ledge Path. Alda's hand passing over the tourists' graffiti, etched into the sandstone cliffs. Names. Dates. Initials. Hearts. A cowboy with a pipe. A chief with a feathered headdress. A mermaid holding an anchor.

Then the carving on her grandmother's gravestone: Able Reeding. Alda's fingers running over that, too. And the name changed before her mind's eye, its letters reworking themselves: Hecate. And Alda was alone in the cemetery. An open grave before her with a new stone above its void. Blank. No name. No date. Alda peered inside and saw a mirror. No reflection on its surface.

She was suddenly back in her cottage. Orange and red and yellow leaves outside. The colors of autumn. And flames. And heat. Sudden heat. Not from the fireplace, but from Alda's hands. Burning. Engulfing her. Surrounded by fire.

And Alda choked amid the black smoke as it burned her eyes and scorched her skin. She was burning alive. Combusting. Searing. And she could not move. Frozen.

But then she gasped. Clean air. Again. And again. And. Again. Until her breath became even. Calm. Until she awoke in the reality of the palazzo's empty library.

Long beams of light pierced the broken windows, streaming down from holes above.

Alda was safe. For now. And alone. Again. She shivered in the darkness, goosebumps forming on her sweat-drenched skin.

And then she cried. Not the silent tears she felt on her cheeks so many times before. Not the tears of sorrow she wept over Dreng. But the wailing howls of a caged animal. A bereft mother. A lost soul.

She cried until the tears turned hot on her skin. Until her hands shook and her throat ached.

Until she no longer felt like a girl trapped in the hands of fate but like a woman who could control her own destiny.

And then she stopped, wiped her face, and stood. She had to move. To do something. To find Dreng. To stop the witches. To get home, safely, to her cottage.

She shut her eyes, focusing only on her goals and wishes, and she felt a rush of wind, as she had so long ago when the windows shattered at her command. Her hands felt warm, powerful.

And when Alda again opened her eyes, her fingertips glowed with a fierce, white light.

Chapter Ten: Strange Bedfellows

Dreng strained to follow Sycorax in the waning light as she raced up the hill to the palace. He could not match her speed.

He remembered so many months before, after she had returned from Netherfeld with her fiery spirits. How he had loved her then. No, worshipped her. And the memory brought shame. Dreng blushed, despite himself.

He regretted being so easily susceptible to her apparent spell. To falling so quickly. And for a flash, he wished that he had never known her. That he had immediately lashed together the broken planks of *The Tempest* and set out that same day onto the sea.

He might have died, yes, but he might have lived. Reached a port. Found a place in a new crew. Returned to sea again. The same. Unchanged.

But then he would never have known the wonders he had seen since. Fairy Land. Netherfeld. Or Alda.

A life without Alda was not worth living. So, in the end, his past lapse was worth his current regret.

Now, as Dreng watched Sycorax approach the palace, he realized her pace was something more than mortal. Caliban soon fell behind and finally settled into step alongside Dreng, adjusting his sapphire cloak as they walked.

"You are angry?" It might have been a simple observation, but Caliban's voice rose questioningly, seeking an answer.

Dreng clenched his jaw as he thought of wide-eyed Miranda awaking from the frozen waters. "I do not understand you."

"I am beyond comprehension."

"No, what you did at the spring."

Caliban sighed. "We need my mother *now*, Dreng. She knows —"

"And what of Miranda?"

Caliban lowered his voice. "She could not help."

"But she came back, to you, and you, you did what with her?"

Caliban avoided his accusatory stare and looked up to the figure outpacing them.

"And for *her*?" Dreng shook his head in frustration. "You traded the woman you loved for your mother."

"You loved her once."

"That spell is gone." Dreng had felt it lift on the raft. And now, it had no hold on him.

Caliban glanced at him. "She is more powerful than any of us."

Dreng scowled.

"And she is your wife."

"She is not."

"Denial does not make it less true."

Dreng shook his head and studied the ground as he walked. "And what of Miranda?"

"I returned her to Netherfeld."

"You mean you exiled her soul and stole her body."

Caliban stopped and caught Dreng's shoulder. "She is safe there. And I will rescue her, soon, as Orpheus led Eurydice from the jaws of Hades."

Dreng felt confusion flash across his face, so Caliban sighed and explained, "I will lead Miranda from Netherfeld into our world, as I led you through the caves. When it is safe here. But until then... Without Sycorax, our world may cease to exist."

Dreng shook his head, "You trust Sycorax, but —"

"I do not trust her. Nor should you. But use logic. My mother has awoken from the place of nothing after how long? Years? She has seen the witches there, and has heard whispers of their plan. She *knows* them, knows them from before I came to be. And, like us, she wants them destroyed. More than we. So we *need* her if we want to save this world. Regardless of trust."

Dreng's shoulders slumped as he relented. He felt weak, beaten down, ready to surrender. "I understand, but I cannot obey her."

"Then trust me."

Despite himself, Dreng laughed. "You ask the impossible."

Caliban likewise grinned. "Then simply do not die."

"As always."

They shared a smile. But Dreng's grin quickly faded to concern as they reached the doorway of the crumbled palace.

As they passed over the threshold, Dreng caught a flash of the palace from the time it had been his residence: warm and candlelit, the scent of Mediterranean herbs overpowering the salt of seawater, the soft tread of Miranda's footstep echoing down the corridor.

But that was a mirage, both then and now. He had never known Miranda. It had always been Sycorax, disguised in a stolen form. And now, the truth was before him: crumbling stones and the smell of cold, wet decay. Nothing warm. Nothing loving. Nothing safe. All ruins.

Yet soft footsteps echoed down the corridor.

The trio stopped, their silence shared as they listened.

The steps were hurried but light. Caliban started forward, but Dreng held out his arm.

"I know more stealth than you. Give me your sword, and I will find whatever danger waits ahead."

Caliban shook his head and whispered, "Sword? No. This will do."
He retrieved a dagger from a concealed lashing around his calf and thrust
its hilt into Dreng's palm. "Something of this size is more fitting for you."

Dreng scowled as he positioned the dagger in his right hand, his
boots nearly silent against the cold stones as he turned a corner and lost
sight of Caliban and Sycorax.

He traced the sound to the library. Hurried footsteps, seemingly
back and forth. Pacing. Sighs. Heavy breaths. As he grew closer, he
heard muttering. Angry. Guttural. Like a caged animal. Yet familiar.

He stood against the wall outside the library's doorway and listened.
When the footsteps were at the farthest end of the room, he ducked
inside, expecting to conceal himself behind a bookshelf.

But the shelves were likewise in ruins. The seemingly endless rows
of volumes were gone.

Dreng moved quickly to the far wall and hid within shadows. Beside
him, half-reclined in a corner, was the lifeless form of the harpy Ariel.

Ariel. Here. Dead.

Dreng knew not to gasp. He knew not to show surprise. Or
hesitation. Or fear.

But whatever had killed the harpy was more powerful than any
being Dreng before had encountered.

Holding his breath, Dreng bit his tongue as he watched the
murderous figure across the room, its back turned toward him. It glowed
in an unnatural, brilliant, white radiance. Sparks trickled from its fingers.
Ethereal. A spirit? A ghost?

It turned, and its black hair swirled. Inky black. Like midnight. And
Dreng knew, "Alda!"

He leapt from the corner and ran to her. She hesitated at first and
stepped back, the white glow disappearing as she returned to her normal,

familiar self.

They spoke at once, their words overlapping.

"How did you get here?"

"What happened?"

"Where were you?"

"Were you in Netherfeld?"

"Did you see the witches?"

"Are you hurt?"

"You killed Ariel?"

"No, I, I —"

"Why were you glowing?" Dreng realized that his left hand was upon her waist, the dagger still clenched in his other fist, and he stepped back self-consciously.

Alda likewise blushed and looked away before her voice took on a skeptical tone. "Glowing?" She laughed. "I was warm, yes, flushed perhaps. But glowing?" Her cheeks burned crimson as she shyly met his eyes.

"It was —" He searched for a word and, unable to think of one better, whispered, "Magical."

Alda's brow furrowed, and the corners of her mouth bent down slightly. "I, I don't know. I wasn't aware I — I was only thinking about you and how to find you and how I am trapped on this blasted island, and then my fingers, well, they — well, here *you* are." She smiled, and his heart eased somewhat. "Do you have half of the cauldron's bubble?"

He nodded. "And you?"

Her smile broadened. "In my sock. We can combine the parts somehow, I suspect, and use it again to escape and —"

Alda stopped suddenly as Dreng summoned the courage to take her hand and, squeezing her fingers, said, "I am glad to be here, with you, but,

but —" He glanced over his shoulder and quickly dropped her hand as he concealed Caliban's dagger within his boot. "We are not alone."

"What do you mean? Who else is —" Alda could not finish.

Sycorax burst into the room, her golden hair whipping as she rushed Alda and felled her with a powerful blow.

Dreng was torn between helping the victim and stopping the aggressor but quickly held Sycorax back as she readied for a second swing.

Alda lifted herself from the ground and rubbed her bleeding cheek. Caliban tried to wipe her blood with a corner of his sleeve, but she pushed him away and looked to Dreng as a condemned man might glare at his accuser.

He held firm to Sycorax's arms, knowing full well that she could level him with a magical word. Still, he did not let go.

Finally, Sycorax ceased her struggle. "Here you are, *dear* friend! Always interfering. Always standing in my way. Always under foot." She stomped, and the palace quaked as more stones crumbled from its walls.

Sycorax twisted free from Dreng's grasp and again rushed at Alda, but Caliban stood between the two women. Alda looked to both sides, searching for an escape, as Sycorax pointed threateningly at her face.

Sparks erupted from the summoner's fingertip. "You have done nothing but deceive and betray me, girl, and it is time now to —"

Dreng started toward them, but Caliban pushed his mother's hand aside and hissed, "Not now. We need this one's help." He glanced nervously at the corner where Ariel's body was slumped and added, "The books are gone. We are alone. She is all that we have here, now. Do not kill our only ally."

Sycorax spat and turned her back to the others, her arms crossed and her foot tapping angrily. Finally, she faced them and smiled threateningly as one might at a naughty child, an expression Dreng had seen so many times before when they were together on the island.

He looked away as his wife explained, "The witches are growing stronger by the minute. And these three are not simply magical women. They are of the ancient times, of fate and destiny and elemental knowledge. And in those ancient times, some force — some god or act of nature — bound our world together with magic. So all that is invisible — love and honor and sacrifice, hope, knowledge, joy — are made up of this primordial magic. And all physical things contain some traces of it as well. So when it vanishes, when the witches have destroyed all magic, we are left with nothing."

Caliban nodded, "Like my decaying tower in Netherfeld. All the worlds will be gone, flung into chaos."

Dreng clenched his jaw.

Sycorax smiled at her son, sincerely, "Yes, the state of confusion that existed before order. These weird women are of that. Or perhaps they made it. And now they want it to return."

Dreng glanced at Alda, saw her backing away from the others into the shadow of a toppled bookshelf. She wanted to be unseen, so he asked skeptically, drawing attention to himself, "What happens if they succeed, if magic disappears?"

"Chaos is a state of nothing, you puppet." Caliban smirked. "You would be a part of it as well."

Dreng turned his back to Caliban and faced Sycorax instead. "How do you know that is the witches' goal?"

The woman he once loved glanced at him and quickly averted her gaze, shaking her head as she seemed to study her feet. After several deep breaths, she straightened and faced Dreng again, her chin held unnaturally high. "Do you know who I am?"

"Sycorax." The name still sounded forced, and she lowered her head slightly at the sound.

"No, that is what I am called now. But that is not who I *am*." She avoided his eyes and paced, her feet scattering dust from the toppled shelves. "I was young once, in love."

She glanced at him, and Dreng bit his tongue. The word stung, but he remained silent, so she continued, "I was called Ophelia then, and the man I loved — Caliban's father — was mad. To save him, I aligned myself with the weird sisters. And then, even then, they wanted chaos. They destroyed me. And him. They meddle in the lives of mortals, until there is nothing but disorder. That, somehow, brings them peace. Or..." She paused. "But they do not think as we do. They are elemental. And dangerous. And when I was trapped in the frozen pool, they grasped their chance and started to seize power."

She stopped pacing and whispered, with too bitter tears in her eyes, "The witches bring only death and despair. Without them, I would still have my Hamlet."

Dreng stumbled back at the name, "Who?" But she did not meet his gaze. "You were — what you said —" Caliban had spoken truth about his parentage. This woman — his mother — and the Danish prince. And Dreng felt a pang of regret for not believing the beautiful youth sooner as he realized, "On the ship, Hamlet spoke of a lost love."

She smiled weakly and stepped closer to him as her demeanor changed to something calm and soothing. "When I first saw you, Dreng, I recognized *his* ring. He would never lose it, never barter with it, never let it be taken by violence. Since you had it, I knew that he gave it to you freely. That you were a good man. That I could trust you. So help me now. Believe me. About the witches. Despite what has passed between us."

She reached for his hand, and he did not immediately pull it away. Her fingers were icy, foreign on his. A memory, once joyful and now forlorn.

He retrieved his hand and held his fists behind his back. "We need Alda."

Sycorax sneered, "You may, but *I* do not." She glanced at Alda, who hid in the shadows some distance behind Caliban, rubbing her cheek and glaring at the others.

"The Indian boy is right."

Dreng glared at Caliban, who continued, "And she is powerful enough to kill a harpy."

Alda's voice cracked, "I did not! Ariel, he —"

Sycorax held her palm upright to stop Alda as she spoke to Dreng. "Why do you need her?"

"She glows."

Chapter Eleven: Insubstantial Pageant

Alda hoped that Dreng was mistaken. That she was not a necessary tool to fight the witches. After all, she felt no different when she had apparently glowed, apart from a brief sensation of heat. She had seen no light emanate from her body, only white illuminating her fingertips. She seemed as she had always been — not entirely normal, but not overtly magical.

And she still hoped that she could escape with Dreng and forsake Sycorax and Caliban to battle the witches themselves.

So when Dreng revealed her apparent ability to the others, his betrayal stung.

"She glows?" Sycorax eyed Alda like a wildcat about to pounce.

Alda stood behind Caliban as she admitted, "I might have some magic in me, but I cannot use it. Not well. Not well enough, at least."

Caliban turned to her, and she was startled by the sincerity in his eyes. "Some is better than naught." He rifled through his clothing and retrieved a small, white bead.

Sycorax grinned, "You found it."

"How do you think you were awoken, Mother?"

"Let me have it!"

"I know what *you* would do with it, but I want to see how it reacts with the witch."

He held it before her in his palm, but Alda refused the offer and instead asked, "What is it?"

"The pearl of wisdom. It intensifies magic."

"Where did you get it?"

Dreng looked away, his face revealing some inner turmoil.

Caliban explained, "From Prospero's staff."

Alda spat, "When you killed him."

"I? Never! And I have a witness." Caliban's face was a mockery of innocence as he turned to Dreng, who meekly nodded. "See? Now, take it. Then we'll all know what powers you hold."

Alda still hesitated. This was too much. Dreng's sudden appearance had been welcomed. Wanted. And she had so much to tell him. So much to say. But now, now, with the others... She could not speak her mind. And she was not in control. Once again, she could only act on the whims of those around her.

Alda was aware of Sycorax's defiant stare, her arms crossed angrily below Miranda's tumble of yellow hair. Dreng watched her anxiously, his fingers fidgeting at his sides. Caliban again thrust his open palm toward her, so Alda held her breath as she touched the pearl with a shaking finger.

A rumble, low and deep. And then higher, closer, its pitch rising and its intensity increasing. An earthquake. No, more. As the ground shook, the air grew hot and thick. Lightning. Simultaneous thunder. And in a fraction of an instant, a shot of cold reverberated from Alda's hand as white light enveloped the ruined library. The ground heaved, and then all was dust and blackness.

Alda felt pain on her back first, weight from the roof's timbers that pressed her down. Her head was protected, her hands wrapped instinctually above it. One ankle trapped, but the other free. She kicked the wall-stone that held her in place and reached up through the debris of the collapsed palazzo until her fingers pierced sunlight above. And she pulled. And pushed. And heaved herself free from the rubble.

As she brushed the dust and blinked in the dimming light, she saw that Dreng was already standing above the ruins, his feet on a great

column as he reached into the depths to pull Sycorax free, her fingers
clasping his wrist. As he helped the summoner to safety, he looked up
and saw Alda. His expression changed.

"You're injured."

She felt a drip between her eyes and smeared blood across her
forehead. "A scratch." Yet she felt dizzy and closed her eyes as she
repeated, "A scratch. It's not so deep."

But she slumped onto the rubble for a moment, the world spinning
before her, and surveyed the ruins. She felt like a lone survivor after
some devastating war, or like the first woman thrust out from paradise
and into desolation.

However, she was not alone. Dreng was quickly at her side, Sycorax
sitting some distance behind him, similarly shocked and stone-faced.

"Where is Caliban?"

"He was here, before me, when I touched the pearl."

Both Alda and Dreng leapt to the place and reached into the rubble.

Alda's fingers found him first, his blood-wet clothes cold against her
fingers. As she dug, with prayers unspoken on her lips, she saw the
rubble likewise stained red.

Dreng removed debris relentlessly, silently, until Alda could see
Caliban's swollen and bloodied face emerge from the ruins. They
extracted him together and carefully carried him across the ruins to the
open space of the courtyard. Dreng gently placed him on a long-stone
that had once encircled the fountain's pool — the fountain that Alda had
destroyed during the fiery storm so many months ago — and Alda
wrapped Caliban in his torn and dusty cloak.

And then they waited.

Alda stood beside the injured youth, her hand on his bleeding
forehead. She looked at Dreng and remembered the care she gave him in

her cottage. The worry and panic. The same feelings fell upon her now, but less intense. Less powerful.

Still, she feared. For some moments, Caliban's breaths were irregular. The three watched in silence as they became more shallow, barely audible. His chest barely moving.

Then, they ceased.

Silence.

Sycorax stood in shock, her hands on her stomach and tears streaming down her cheeks. "He cannot leave me, he cannot leave me…" she repeated again and again.

Dreng turned away and covered his face.

Alda, however, remained at Caliban's side, his hand clasped in hers. She was surprisingly calm, not frightened or panicked. Yet there was hope. There was always hope. So instead of weeping or cursing, she whispered into his ear, "She is alive, still. Miranda. I saw her, and she needs you." Alda waited and thought she felt something like a flutter in his palm. "Caliban, Miranda needs you. She needs you. We need you. Come back. For us."

A tear fell down Alda's cheek, trickled down her chin and onto her neck. She released Caliban's hand to wipe it away, but more tears quickly followed. She hid her face in the folds of her skirt until a cough broke her sorrow. Then a deep, rattling breath.

Finally, "If I return from the dead, it will be for my own sake. Not for you lot of foot-lickers."

Alda did not expect such a flood of relief, not for someone who was at best a stranger and at worst an enemy. But she wiped his face with her sleeve until he pushed her away and sat wobbling atop the long-stone.

Dreng turned pale at the sudden resurrection, and Sycorax's shoulders relaxed beneath her faded dress.

Caliban stared at them as if they were lunatics until he finally spat, "Why is the witch more moved by my rising than are my kin?"

Alda wiped the remainder of her tears and laughed, "I am not a witch."

Sycorax knelt at her side and, glancing at Caliban, took Alda's hand. "But you *are*. And we need your help."

Alda looked at the others, all staring expectantly at her. Dreng with his quiet hope. Sycorax with her intensity. Caliban, bloodied and destitute. She could not disappoint them or abandon them. She could not take Dreng and flee with the cauldron's bubble. She had to stay and fight.

So, as resolutely as she could, Alda nodded. "What should we do?"

Caliban inspected the wounds on his chest and arms and then sadly examined his bent sword as Sycorax spoke: "The witches have drained this island. And nearly Netherfeld. And, most likely, the worlds beyond as well."

Alda felt her eyes widen. How many worlds were there? But she was silent as the summoner continued, "We must find them. And soon. But it will take ages to discover them in the web of realms."

Dreng cleared his throat. "We need a trap."

"A trap?" Caliban scoffed, "No cage will hold them, you lily-liver." He pressed his foot on his blade, trying unsuccessfully to bend it back into shape.

Dreng retorted, "You should not turn the tip like that, you... egg."

"You speak of country matters," Caliban spat.

Dreng scowled, turned from him, and continued, "But surely our combined magic can hold the witches at bay. And with Alda's help —" He looked at her with a mixture of hope and something else. "We only have to lure them here."

Caliban angrily sheathed his sword, its blade still bent. "And how should we call them? Ask politely? Say *please*? Whisper our wishes into the wind and hope they hear?"

Dreng frowned. "They want *me*, remember. In Netherfeld, you saw them —"

Alda gasped. "You confronted the witches?"

But Dreng continued, "They wanted something from me. Let me be your bait. I will call them, somehow."

Caliban's tone lost its notes of sarcasm. "Somehow is the dilemma."

Alda thought back to the last time she encountered Sycorax on the island, of the spirits the summoner used to storm the palazzo. For a moment, Alda thought that might work again, and then she blushed. Now that she knew the truth, now that she understood that those spirits were enslaved from Netherfeld, she could not suggest such a feat. And she regretted having summoned them herself. She bit her lip, trying to think of some alternative.

"We need a spell." Sycorax's face was stern, distant. "But the library, it —" She looked at the rubble behind them. "I do not know such magic. Not by heart."

She looked at Alda questioningly. "I, I don't —" Alda studied her feet, avoiding the enquiring gazes of the others.

Dreng placed his hand reassuringly on Alda's shoulder. "I have your book."

He reached within the folds at his waist and retrieved the miniature book, the volume Alda had taken from Prospero's body in the library. The book that Alda had thought was lost in the flood. It was safe. And her shock shifted quickly to relief.

Sycorax smiled, and Caliban looked up from his unhappy sword.

As Alda's mind raced, her three companions said at once, "I have a plan."

*   *   *

They laid out ideas, their words weaving over and through their thoughts until three separate plans slowly became one.

"But we need the pearl of wisdom for this to work." Dreng's heart sank as he realized it was likely in the rubble, lost amid the broken stones and cracked timber.

But Caliban laughed, the sound quickly becoming a cough as he bent over and clutched his stomach. He spat, wiped blood from his mouth, and shuddered as he straightened himself. In his open palm was the pearl of wisdom. "I may be rather grave, but I still have a grip."

Dreng smiled despite himself and looked to Alda, "When they arrive, you must take the pearl and —"

"No." Alda's tone was resolute. "I touched it once, and nearly killed us all. I will not do so again." Her voice became softer, pleading, "I will face the witches to protect you." She looked to Caliban and Sycorax. "But I know that whatever magic I perform will be instinctual. I cannot control it. That jewel, that pearl is dangerous in my hand. Dangerous to us all."

"Then I will use it." Sycorax was too eager, and Dreng wanted to object, but he held his tongue as she took the pearl from Caliban. "The witches once taught me a spell that I can use against them, if it comes to that. And Dreng, what of you? Do you know what to do?"

He nodded. Two spells in the book seemed the most likely to lead to their success, or their survival: "pricking thumb" to summon the witches, and "trouble fire" to stun them.

Then Alda and Sycorax and Caliban would finish them, each in their own way.

"Well, what are we waiting for? Let's call the blasted devils and save the world!" Caliban stood, with his bent sword in hand, and struck a pose that Dreng could only assume was meant to be heroic. But he swooned like a man sick at sea, doubled over, and fell to his knees.

Before Dreng or Sycorax could react, Alda was at his side with her arm around his shoulders. She eased him back onto the rock, wiped the wounds on his head with a corner of her skirt, and spoke softly, too softly for Dreng to hear.

But he could see the kindness in her eyes, the care that she gave even to someone who had wronged her in the past. She looked like one of the haloed figures whose paintings were prized by Spanish sailors: all peace and forgiveness and compassion. And he knew that his friend was safe with her.

Finally, Alda looked to Dreng. "He needs water."

"I will fetch some." Again, Sycorax was too eager. She started to pick her way over the ruins as Dreng turned to Alda, nodded, and followed the summoner away from the ruined palace.

Dreng still did not trust Sycorax. Especially when she would so soon command something as powerful as the pearl of wisdom.

Besides, Dreng had no purpose at the moment. He felt breathless as he watched Alda with Caliban, like someone swept overboard in rough seas. His emotions were in his throat, dangerously near to suffocating him. So he pushed them down. For now, at least.

"There is rainwater trapped upon the rocks at the cliff's edge."

Sycorax's words startled him, and his mind seemed to snap to attention as she led the way toward some great stones.

"Should we go to the spring instead?"

"No." Sycorax averted her gaze. "Those waters are… too powerful."

Dreng doubted her words but did not protest. He instead looked out to sea as she bent over the hollows and filled a dented pewter mug with clear water.

"Where did you get that?"

"From the ruins." She smiled at him, the way she always did when his foolishness amused her. "Your mind is elsewhere, Dreng."

"It is not. I, I only —"

"You love her."

The words were not a question. Sycorax stood at his side, her eyes studying his as she took a draught from the mug.

"I — I do not know what love is."

"I am, I am sorry." Sincere remorse permeated her words as she filled the mug.

Dreng shifted his gaze from the sea and looked instead at his boots, their leather scuffed and coated in dust from the crumbled palace.

He could feel Sycorax's eyes on him as she continued, "Dreng, I did not wish for this. Any of it."

"Nor did I." He did not attempt to conceal the loathing in his voice.

"I — I am sorry. For the spell —"

"Curse."

"Dishonesty —"

"Deception."

"I did love you, once."

Dreng scowled. "Lies."

Sycorax lowered her tone and leaned toward his ear. "Those months with you, here, as my husband —"

"Do not call me that."

"With you, that was the happiest time since — since I came to this island."

His anger lifted somewhat as he realized she was right. He had been happy as well. But he could not speak the words, he could not vocalize agreement, so he only nodded.

She continued, "Yet that time is past. And we are here. Now."

They stood in silence. Dreng felt his pulse quicken as he realized that he was trapped. "Release me."

"What?"

Dreng took her hand as one begging an executioner for mercy. "We had a rite, a ceremony. We are married, still, in some way. Even though the curse is passed. Even though I — I —"

"I know you did not love me. Not truly. It was all a deception. So those words you shared with me, the words that bound us one to another, were not honest. They had no truth. They were like lines in a play, spoken by someone performing a part."

She held both of his hands in hers, as she had so many months ago in the courtyard of Prospero's palace, when he wanted nothing more than to be her husband and to be bound to her for eternity.

"Forget them, Dreng. Forget the words, the rite. Forget our lives together. Forget me." She squeezed his palms, and he likewise pressed his fingers into hers. "I suspect you would be luckier now, if not for me." Sycorax glanced at the nearby palace, at the figures of Alda and Caliban, their forms huddled close. "You can find happiness yet."

Dreng released her hands and wiped his brow. "Happiness is not my lot." He felt regret cross his face for a moment but quickly set his jaw, hoping resolve would conceal his true feelings, his sense of foreboding.

"What do you intend to do?" Her tone echoed that of the ship's captain, commanding and earnest.

"I cannot let her come to harm." He licked his lips, suddenly dry. "I must protect her, Sycorax. If all else — Alda must be safe."

The summoner's voice lowered to a quiver. "No, Dreng. That is not your lot. We will all survive."

But Dreng could see the lie behind her eyes, the sadness and acceptance, and he understood.

Dreng clenched his jaw. "What should we do?"

Sycorax smiled.

Chapter Twelve: Mercy Itself

Caliban was silent as Alda tended to the blood seeping from the wound on his head. She could sense that he did not wish to speak. But she could not remain silent, so she began, "This will be over soon, one way or another. And we will all be safe, or dead."

"The dead are safe," he muttered.

"Then we cannot lose." She smiled at him, and his glare eased somewhat. So she continued, "Were you in Netherfeld, all this time?"

"Yes, and no."

Alda waited for him to elaborate, but he did not. Instead, he merely twisted the hem of the blue cloak nervously in his fingers.

"And were you alone there?"

"Yes, and no."

Again, several heartbeats of silence.

"I was in Netherfeld as well." Alda paused, waiting, and continued, "And I was not alone."

"I suppose you were not, witch. I expect you had spirits you could control, to do your bidding. Like my mother. Were they your slaves as well?" He slung the words like weapons, but Alda did not recoil as she sat at his side.

"I saw her, Caliban. I saw your Miranda."

He stopped fidgeting. But he still did not meet her gaze.

"She told me — She told me that she cared for you. Always. Despite how you — how you once appeared."

"No, she could not care for me. That was a lie, taught to her by her father, to be cruel to me."

Alda disregarded his objections and continued, "And she told me that on that day, the day I arrived on this island, she was going to you."

"To torture me further."

"To tell you that she loved you."

Caliban broke. His hands shook as he reached for his face, concealing the tears on his cheeks. Alda was stunned for a moment, surprised by his sudden and unexpected change. She had thought him incapable of powerful emotions, numb with sarcasm and wit.

So she wrapped her arms around his shoulders, bent close to his ear, and whispered, "She is waiting for you in Netherfeld. And she believes you will find her, now that you know she still loves you. And that she has always loved you. She will be there for you, waiting until you arrive."

There was more, but Alda could not bring herself to speak of Miranda's dealings with the witches. She was likely an innocent, lured in by them as Ophelia had once been duped. And that would be for naught soon enough, when the witches were gone.

Caliban finally looked up, and his eyes met hers, their orbs filled with heartbreak and regret. "Alda, I, I had her, here, for a moment, and I —" He hung his head. "I didn't know why she was on the beach that day. I never, never would have…" His voice faded, his final words lost in a deep breath.

"It's not too late, Caliban. You can go to her."

"Now? But you need me. For the witches."

"You are too injured."

"I am not!" He attempted to rise again, but his legs gave way beneath him.

"See? And what can you do that we cannot?"

"I can do many great and mysterious things."

Alda laughed as she wiped a tear from her friend's eye.

His tone grew more serious. "Alda, let me stand with you. There is too much at stake — We could all die."

Alda shook her head. "And if you try to fight now, *you will* die."

Caliban looked toward the sea, toward Sycorax and Dreng bent over a great rock above the cliffs. "I can fetch her, Alda. Bring Miranda here so she can help us." His voice rose with excitement. "I can reach her through the caves and bring her back, leading her like Orpheus out of the underworld."

Alda frowned. "I know that myth. It does not end well."

"But this is different. If I go to her now, quickly, I can return to fight. We can return together." He shifted his gaze again and looked imploringly at Alda. "Will you wait until I return?"

Alda lied, "Of course."

He seemed to know and hesitated. "Or I can wait until after the battle..."

"Caliban, you may be able to talk. You may even be able to will yourself to walk. But you cannot fight. Not now. Not soon. So you can stay here, an invalid, and force us to protect you. Or you can take my advice and return to Netherfeld."

He was silent. Alda heard the waves in the distance, beating against the shore so far below.

Caliban again looked toward the cliffs, and his face softened. "He is a good man."

Alda followed his eyes. "I know."

"No, you do not. Not fully. He would die for you, Alda. He would die for any one of us." He took her hand pleadingly. "Ensure that he survives."

"I will."

"And, and will you tell them why I left? If I wait to take my leave — they won't let me have it. Tell them, please."

"Of course."

"Also tell them I will return. Soon."

Alda nodded. "As you did in Fairy Land."

Caliban smiled as he raised himself and balanced on shaking legs. "Yes, to strike a hobgoblin."

They shared a silent, knowing gaze.

"Stay but a moment —" Alda stood and quickly pulled a broken timber from the rubble and tested it with her weight before she handed it to the beautiful youth. "Now, go." She paused and added, "May your journey end with a lover's meeting."

"'Til we meet again."

Caliban turned abruptly and limped through the dilapidated courtyard and over the low wall, toward the moors and distant beach. As Alda watched him leave, her heart seemed ready to burst. She doubted she would ever see him again.

His wounds were worse than he knew, internal and unseen, and there was no magic powerful enough to heal a broken body.

If there was, her grandmother would have surely taught her to use it when she first became ill.

At least in Netherfeld, Caliban had a chance of survival. If not survival, then perhaps some kind of existence.

So with a sigh, Alda turned back toward Dreng and Sycorax, slowly approaching over the palazzo's rubble. She took several deep breaths as they grew near until her voice was calm when they reached her side.

"Caliban is left to find Miranda."

"Should I go after him?" Dreng's voice broke with concern.

Sycorax shook her head and looked sadly at Alda. "Why?"

Alda lied, "He knew she was in danger and could not wait another moment."

"Is that all? Are his injuries more severe than we thought?" Sycorax seemed to know that Alda was not honest.

So Alda only nodded.

Dreng looked from the distance where Caliban had disappeared below the rise of the hill and turned back to Sycorax. "Will our plan still work without him?"

Sycorax hesitated before she met his eyes. "It will work, it will still work, with only us."

Yes, Alda hoped that it would.

Chapter Thirteen: Horribly in Love

Dreng's thoughts were a net of worry since Caliban left. He stood alone on the clifftops with the miniature book, his hand shaking as he read and reread the spells' words in his mind. Again and again. And he finally looked out to sea, counting the whitecaps to clear his mind. Then he whispered the enchanted words in his internal voice, from memory.

Because he knew that when the time came, when he faced the witches that had destroyed his childhood dreams and left him alone and unloved, he might not have the book. But he would have his wits.

He was suddenly aware that Alda was at his side, likewise watching the sea. He glanced back toward the palace ruins, saw Sycorax pacing nervously, and returned his gaze to the ocean.

"Are you ready, Dreng?"

He only nodded. "What did Caliban say, before he left?"

"That you are a good man."

Dreng blushed. "I wish he had stayed. But love can make a man do strange things." He looked at her, but she remained unmoved.

Alda did not shift her gaze from the waves as she sighed, "Do you miss it?"

"No, I am done with her."

Alda's cheeks turned a sudden crimson. "I meant your ship. Your life on the ocean."

"Yes, sometimes, but..." He did not finish. He could not tell her of the horrors he had faced there, of the strength it had taken to overcome them. Of all he sacrificed to lead his crewmates, only to have them wrecked on the rocks below. She would not understand, so he held his tongue.

After a moment, Alda continued, "Before the flood, when we were in my cottage, you spoke of a name."

"Yes."

"What name?"

"Mine." He looked at her, set his jaw, and continued, "My father's ghost came to me and told me my name." He looked away, not wanting to see her reaction as he spun the signet ring on his finger.

Alda was silent for a moment as if waiting for him to speak. Finally, she asked, "What is your name?"

"What's in a name?"

She laughed unexpectedly. "You speak like Caliban."

"No, this is not jest. What does a name mean?"

She frowned. "It is us. Who we are. How others see us."

"Then I am Dreng." He tried to smile at her, but he sensed his expression was something else.

"So before you were called that, when you were called something else, you were *someone* else?"

"Yes." He wiped his hair from his eyes as he continued, "In a lifetime, we all play many parts."

Alda had a faraway look, as if lost in a memory. "All the world's a stage."

"Yes." Dreng hesitated. "The boy I was before is dead." He took a deep breath. "I should be, too."

"What do you mean?"

"I might have died before, long ago, in the hold after Prince Hamlet's escape, if not for you. And if I could have left this toil all behind, I would." He paused and corrected, "*Sometimes* I think I would."

Alda stepped back as if hit by a sudden wind. "Why?"

"I have done things since, experienced things, too, that make me wonder if this world would be better off without me."

"I do not —" Alda stopped, and Dreng could see her eyes search for words. But she composed herself and changed her tone, "If the witches have their way, there may be no world left for any of us."

"Something must remain, surely." He spoke with more optimism than he felt.

Alda studied his face, and her brow furrowed. "They drain magic, Dreng. What is left without that? Only chaos, like Caliban said." She met his eyes. "And we are all that is between them and a dark and joyless world."

"You will die to stop them?"

"Yes." She did not hesitate. "And you?"

"Of course. A thousand times, if I could."

Alda's shoulders slumped slightly at his response.

"Alda, I —" He stopped abruptly and stooped to his knees at her feet. His eyes searched the rocky ground, looking for something lost. He pushed aside her skirt and lifted her foot, retrieving something from beneath it.

She stood, bewilderment crossing her face, until he finally stood and met her eyes again. "Alda, when I was a boy, before I went to sea with my father, my mother gave me a token. A pebble from the shore, the last place where I stood on dry land." He held out his palm and revealed a black, smooth stone. "She said that it was my homeland and that it contained the love and power and knowledge of the generations that came before me."

His voice shook as he continued, "I lost that stone the night the witches killed my father. I always thought it protected me, somehow, and that is how I lived when he did not. And now, *you* need that protection." He placed it into her hand, his fingers covering hers for too many heartbeats as the waves crashed in the distance.

"Alda, all is about to change. The world. Our lives. But if we can bear this, we can bear all."

She nervously smoothed her hair behind her ears and started to speak, but stopped.

His heart sank.

So he stammered, pleading, "I only — I simply — I need you to know that from the moment I first saw you on *The Tempest*, from that, that moment — I only wish that I could have found you sooner, before — before all of this."

She remained silent. And in that moment, Dreng, who had forgotten so much over the years, somehow recalled Caliban's words: "Doubt thou, the stars are fire, doubt that the sun doth move, doubt truth to be a liar." He drew a deep breath. "But never doubt I love."

Alda took his hand but looked down. He could not read her face as his voice quivered, "Never doubt."

Her eyes finally met his, and his arms wrapped instinctively around her waist. Through their tears — tears of joy or something else — they kissed.

Despite their too-many separations, despite their dream-like embrace in Fairy Land, despite all that had come before, Dreng knew this was real. This was the kiss that mattered. And he felt that she knew it, too.

Finally, he took a deep breath, his forehead resting against hers, before he again looked into her eyes and waited for her to speak. To react. He hoped that she might say the words he wished to hear. Words from her and no one else, not now or ever again. But she only took in a deep, ragged breath, turned, and released it silently toward the sea.

A sudden thunderclap broke their reverie. Alda stepped away from him and held her whipping hair as she turned back toward the palace ruins. "I came here, Dreng, to tell you it is time. We must face the witches now. Together."

She walked slowly away.

He waited for her to reach the palace's crumbled perimeter before he dared glance at the secret held tight in his palm: Alda's half of the cauldron's bubble, which he had so deftly lifted from her sock when he took the stone from beneath her foot.

Chapter Fourteen: How to Curse

As Alda walked away from Dreng, something inside her wanted to scream. But was it joy? Terror? Dread? Some combination of strange emotions?

She felt fear, certainly. Hesitation. The witches were powerful, and they threatened to consume all that Alda knew. But that was not the root of her internal turmoil.

No, this was more. New. Startling. It was from Dreng's words. His tingling touch. Their kiss. This was something Alda could not understand. Something she could not articulate. Something that existed better as a guttural scream than as mere words.

Which was why Alda had remained mute. How could she tell him how she felt? How could she convey such, such... She couldn't. Her words were lost.

And now, as she approached Sycorax in the courtyard of the ruined palazzo, she glanced over her shoulder one more time at Dreng and the ocean, and her heart rose into her throat.

Yet again, she pressed it down.

Within seconds, Dreng was at her side. Sycorax turned toward them both, her eyes anxiously scanning the skies. "They told me we would meet again. In thunder, lightning, and in rain." As she spoke, droplets began to fall. "Call them now, Dreng. I am ready."

"We are ready," Alda added.

Dreng held the book tight in his palm and breathed the words to the "pricking thumb" spell: "Call all about me in the dark, and like the savage salt-sea shark, I beckon thee with my own blood until the charm is firm and good."

They all waited.

Alda listened. And as the wind whipped her hair and blood-stained dress, she a did not feel fear. Instead, she felt only disappointment.

This was not the ending she had wanted. As a child, she had imagined being an old spinster in her cottage — alone, yes, but reading and cooking and happy. No, not happy. Content. And safe.

Now, after so much had changed, she still wanted to be happy and content and safe in her cottage. But not alone.

She never asked to be ripped from her home, hurled into disconnected stories that wove through other times and faraway realms. Before all of this, she would have been happy to become the eccentric maid on the seventh island, a figure in a fairytale told by local children.

But here, now, she could not return to the life she once wanted. She was trapped in her own fate like some prisoner in a castle dungeon.

As was Sycorax. And Dreng.

Dreng.

After he spoke, once he completed the words of the spell, nothing happened. Silence.

Silence, and then wind.

Alda was about to lose hope when Dreng reached into his boot and produced a dagger. He held it expertly in his hand and placed the blade gently against his thumb.

Blood trickled from his fingertip as he replaced the weapon.

Then, lightning. Alda saw it strike between clouds before she heard the thunder. Another flash and thunder clap, closer. And then the ground heaved. Alda stood firmly, her feet slipping and shifting while she somehow remained upright. The earth seemed to rattle, its surface vibrating until the dirt fell away into tiny fissures, revealing a glittering, red granite stone beneath.

The shaking intensified, and Alda moved closer to Dreng as the stones and broken timber of the surrounding ruins shifted and tumbled down the mountainside. Soon the three were atop a smooth hill, thrust into creation by the powers of the magical storm, its crimson-granite surface reflecting the flashing lights above.

Alda looked to Sycorax, her fist clenched tightly around the pearl of wisdom. To Dreng at her side, now reciting the spell's words again and again and again, his voice booming above the noise of the storm. He was calm. In contrast, Alda shook with fear, her jaw clenched tightly and painfully.

Dreng, still repeating the words, touched her elbow reassuringly, and she realized this was not bravery. It was experience. This was not his first battle. And she would not let it be his last.

As they waited for the witches to appear, Alda knew that even though the forces were equally numbered, the odds were against her party. Her magic, her skills, were novice. Untested. Not like the centuries of power wielded by the wayward sisters.

Alda knew there would be death.

And she could not live in a world without — she could not live if, if her comrades did not. She would do what she must to protect him, no, them.

Sycorax turned toward Dreng and Alda, interrupting her fear, the blonde hair of her borrowed body whipping like a golden flag. "No matter what, stand your ground. We cannot give them an inch. If we do not retreat, the day will be ours."

Alda suppressed her apprehension, nodded, and again looked to Dreng. Sensing her dread, he smiled, took her hand, and squeezed her fingers.

The touch gave her some stirrings of bravery, or at least resolve, and she took a breath. "Dreng, I —"

More thunder. Lightning. Rain. The witches appeared, hovering in rising mist. Their black cloaks fluttered upward in an unnatural breeze, their hair curled and crazed, their faces shadowed with beards and hatred.

Dreng stopped his chant, and Alda expected them to charge, to attack, but they only laughed. Not a cry of mirth, but a cackle. Like angry geese on the Grand River. The sound gave Alda a chill, reminding her that they were less than human.

Or more than mortal.

Alda wondered aloud, "Should we speak to th—" The word stuck in her throat as Sycorax clenched her fists, hissed the secret words to an ancient spell, and loosed a burst of energy that flashed from her slight form in a white-blue light that pulsated in heated intensity.

Dreng turned his head away from the light, and Alda briefly shielded her eyes with her forearm. When she opened them, she saw the witches cowering, stunned, unable to move against the power of Sycorax's beam.

This was Alda's time to act. Her moment. And, for that moment, she had hope. The witches were held at bay easier than she expected. Or was it a trick?

She looked to Dreng, and each had something like relief in their eyes. She took a breath and readied to fight beside him.

But it was not as Alda expected. Instead of facing the witches, instead of muttering the words to bring the trouble fire spell, Dreng took Alda's shaking hand, and dropped something small and round into her palm.

As he closed her fist around it, Alda tried to scream out, but her voice was lost.

Before Alda vanished, before the cauldron's bubble whisked her away, she heard Dreng say, "I love nothing in the world so well as you."

But Alda had no time to respond.

Chapter Fifteen: Die to Live

"She is safe!" Dreng's voice was lost in the fury of the witches' storm. For a flash, he imagined himself again on *The Tempest*, commanding his men in the moments before he was washed overboard.

But Sycorax saw. The beam of light withered from her fingers as she wiped Miranda's golden hair from her eyes and held the pearl of wisdom to her forehead like a jewel in a crown. This was a spell Dreng did not know. One that was not in a book. This was deep magic. Instinctual. Something he could not understand.

As her fingers changed colors, turning from burnt orange to rusty red, Dreng braced himself for some impact. A whirring sound filled his ears. Then a scream, not from human lungs but like an injured bird. Then a boom like a cannon. And another. A third.

Wind whirled past him as the witches somehow took to flight.

The ground quaked, and Dreng lost his footing. As he pushed himself to his feet, scanning the dark skies for the weird sisters, a sudden fire filled the heavens. It was not the trouble fire, not a snare. This was new but familiar.

Sycorax had loosed St. Elmo's fire, the same flames that took his father's life and gave him painful scars.

But, strangely, he felt relief. This would be enough. This spell that could bring such awful fury would surely stop the witches.

He looked to Sycorax, slumped below the lights that emanated from her hands and head, their colors dancing in the clouds above. She was intent, focused, so he scanned the space between for the witches. Nothing. They were gone.

Had they vanished? He could not help but smile.

Yet Sycorax did not seem to share his joy. She turned sharply, her eyes filled with a wrath that Dreng could not have imagined from the woman he once thought he loved.

And as he watched her, helpless, she burned. The St. Elmo's fire did not consume her. She seemed unscathed. Instead, it surrounded her, leaping in tendrils like some terrible serpent, high into the thunderheads and deep into the granite earth, which erupted in a shrill chorus of whistles and moans.

And although he held the ragged book in his hand with the trouble fire spell, he did not read it. He knew the words, not in his mind but in his heart. "Come deadly flames to charm the air..." And as he spoke, an orb of fire rose at his feet and shot like a cannonball toward the witches. The trouble fire combined with the St. Elmo's blaze to create a raging wall, a column that burned into the sky and sucked the air from his lungs.

Again, Dreng thought this was the end, that they would be victorious. He felt his shoulders ease as his nostrils filled with the scent of burning pine.

But the battle was not yet decided. Sycorax erupted like the sun rising over a waveless ocean, her flames illuminating the mountaintop in fierce, red light.

In a heartbeat, the witches fell from the thundering heavens and hit the ground. Dreng hoped, wished they might lie still. But they rose again, the three holding hands as they formed an outward-facing circle, chanting and spinning until the red-green flames of the trouble fire leapt into the air in a funnel and dissipated.

All was eerily calm. Dreng felt like he was within a hurricane, winds and chaos all around but eerie silence in its center.

And then he looked to Sycorax, the flesh of Miranda's body gray and spent. Their eyes met for a too-brief moment, and Dreng wanted nothing more than to run to her side and support her as they faced the witches together.

Yet he could not move. He was frozen to the spot, either by fear or magic, as he had been so many years before aboard *The Tyger*.

For a flash, his mind returned to the ship. A helpless, terrified boy who cowered as disembodied voices sang a destructive chant in his memory. Voices. Four voices. The three witches, and...

Sycorax? But the thought was unwelcome here, now. Out of joint. Out of time. Too late.

So he could only watch helplessly as Sycorax collapsed, her clothes falling heavy on her sunken form as a puff of white smoke erupted from her body.

She was gone.

And Dreng was alone with the witches.

All he had were his words. So he spoke, again and again, the enchanted words for the trouble fire. Sparks erupted around him, but no more flames.

The witches stopped spinning, and all was still. But not silent. The mountain squealed louder, its rock grinding beneath his feet, wailing hymn-like chords into the heavy air.

And then the weird sisters were ever stronger, their eyes aflame in the murky darkness. Rainless clouds obliterated the sky. Thunder rumbled from unseen lightning. And the flames in the witches' eyes spit forth into a ruby sphere that hovered malevolently before them.

Dreng expected it to surge toward him, like some horrible shot, but it simply hovered. Then, laughter.

"He is but a mouse."

"Where is my Gray-Malkin?"

"No, we are the cats, sister."

"He is prey."

"Let him pray."

"Too late for that."

"But not to toy."

"A new one."

"Should we take him?"

"A fourth for us?"

"No, take him all."

"In part."

"Parts."

"Apart."

"And keep him for a spell?"

"Or more?"

"Aye, keep him."

"No, take him."

"Take from him."

They spoke quickly, their words overlapping as if they knew the replies before they again spoke. And with each word, Dreng felt a loss. Like grief, but more tangible. Something leaving from his soul. Something being torn from him. Joy. Hope. Courage. Love. All the world's invisible magic.

The witches were stealing his magic as they continued to speak, sucking it from him like a horrible whirlpool as the wicked orb before them grew. And he knew they would use it to spread their chaos. To harm Alda. Or worse.

But Dreng could not flee. He could not attack. He could only stand, rooted helplessly to a single spot as the mountain's squeals escalated into a discordant harmony.

And then he heard a sound. Not music, not exactly. But something deep and reverberating. Something both magical and grounded.

Something from below his feet.

The crimson, burning mountain sang, its hollow notes twisting into something like a tune.

And Dreng realized the witches were right, the prophecy was true. He would not leave this place, not alive.

He would die here. If by their hands, the witches would drain whatever powers he might have like some leech gorging on blood. They would use him and leave him to rot.

Or...

He could not stop death. But he could at least meet it smiling.

As the witches chortled, he bent toward the ground. His fingers touched Caliban's dagger, its blade too cold within his boot. Before the witches could finish him, he held the weapon in his fist and steered its blade with all his strength into his chest, into the scar they had given him so many years before.

And as he fell to the ground, he felt a rush leave his body. Magic? Life? Certainly something seeped out of him, something warm and wet. Perhaps only blood.

Dreng tried to lift his head, but its weight was too much. His breath shallow. A pain in his chest that only increased as he gasped like a fish on the deck.

He felt like he was drowning. Drowning on dry land, so far from the sea. And as he floundered and fought for air, the witches stood in a circle above him, their red eyes gazing down like the fires of stars.

At least, he thought, *Alda was safe.*

Chapter Sixteen: Sorceries Terrible

Alda found herself in Netherfeld, surrounded by nothing. In her palm was the cauldron's bubble, its two halves fused in a line of bright blue. She was alone. In a void. Devoid.

Why did the cauldron's bubble bring her here, of all places? This was not where she needed to be. It was not where she wanted to be.

She had to get back, and quickly. Dreng should not have done this. He should not have sent her away against her will. It was reckless.

And where did he get a cauldron's bubble?

Alda felt in her sock. Her half was gone. He must have taken it and joined her part with his.

How?

When?

Of course, atop the cliffs. The black pebble was a rouse. He had stolen the bubble when he reached near her foot. And the brief, electric shock she felt when his fingers touched her ankle was distraction enough for her to not notice the half-bubble's absence.

And now, he was in danger. She must help him. And Sycorax. Because despite everything — they needed her now. She could not abandon them, not leave them to battle the witches alone.

But Alda's hands were shaking with more than fear. Her palms were smeared with sweat. As she tried to close her fist around the cauldron's bubble, it fell to her feet and was lost beneath the folds of her stained skirt.

She bent over, searching, feeling, groping aimlessly in the darkness for her one shining piece of hope.

And after too many seconds of fruitless searching, her hope likewise faded as she fell to her knees, her breath coming in shallow pants as the vast nothing around her felt all too claustrophobic.

She let her head drop back, her face searching what should be the heavens, as she wailed simply, "Where?"

"Here." The word was both calm and calming.

Her grandmother. Alda stood, her mouth agape as she stared at the shadowy, ghostly form before her.

"Gramma? Where have you been? I've looked for you."

"And I am found."

"But now I'm lost!" Alda's voice rose in pitch until her voice broke on the final word.

"No, now you see."

"See what?"

"The truth."

"Yes, the truth." For a moment, Alda forgot about Dreng and Sycorax and the witches as other memories boiled to the surface. She remembered the encounter with her grandmother's ghost in the cottage, and her tone became bitter, the words souring in her mouth. "That Phillida was my mother. That you knew she was in Fairy Land and never told me she was alive."

"She was lost, too, and I could only save one. I chose to save you."

"You mean *control* me."

The shadow of the old woman laughed. "No, child. There is power in our family. Your mother, if taken by the witches, could become a weapon. She was safe with the fairies."

Alda spat, "She was a prisoner."

"We were safe while she was in Fairy Land."

"*We*?"

"Yes, the world." Her grandmother paused and added, "She knew this. And now you know, too."

"Why didn't you tell me before? In the beginning?"

"I told you that you had to discover it in time."

"But you left me!" Alda felt petty for harboring anger at someone who had died, but she still hurt. Deeply.

"I had to leave so you could find the way."

"But the witches — they said a witch cannot die."

"When I died, you became my heir. More of my magic became yours."

"You — you *chose* to die?"

"It was my time."

"No, no." Alda felt a thick knot in her throat. "How?"

"A spell."

"But you never asked. You never asked me what I wanted!"

"You were too young."

"I am just as young now!"

"No, you have lived a lifetime since."

Alda took a deep breath and exhaled, uncertain how to respond. After a moment, her grandmother continued, "You have the legacy of my magic, Alda. A part of the ancient, extinct magic that the witches cannot control. That they cannot understand. You cannot let them take you. You must fight."

"How?"

"With my help."

"Help? Then help me find the cauldron's bubble, and I'll take you —"

"No, Alda." The old woman sighed. "I am a shade. A shadow. A soul without a form. I am weak. Easily defeated if I leave here." She paused, her eyes studying Alda's. "No, you must have faith."

"Faith?"

"In yourself." As her grandmother spoke, a streak of green light whirled above. A spirit. It came into form above the old woman, hovering some feet above Alda.

A Luna moth.

"Phillida?"

It faltered and fell several inches before it recovered. Alda noticed one of its wings was broken. A piece missing.

"You are hurt?" Alda's voice cracked. Its injury likely happened because of her, when the spirits helped her escape the witches.

"Do not spend your worries on me, child, because there is more at stake now than..." Her voice trailed off as she perched atop Gramma's shoulder.

Alda's eyes searched the visions of her ancestors. She wanted to say so much. To ask so many questions. But there was no time. Not now. And, perhaps, she would not like the answers. So instead of the past, she turned her thoughts to the future. "Help me defeat the witches."

"Alda," her grandmother's voice was soothing. Like a forgotten lullaby. "You doubt yourself. You think yourself weak and slow and incapable."

"That's not —"

"Listen, child. You think you are like the governess in that old novel. But you are truly a princess. No, an empress. The heir of Hecate. Stand alone. Command the magic. It will do as you bid."

"But *how*?"

Her grandmother's cold shade squeezed her hand as the moth alighted above, flashing green across Alda's face.

"Words. Release the words you hold inside like some great deluge. The words will flow into magic. Flood them."

Alda remembered a poem that her grandmother often muttered late at night. "From out our bourne of time and place the flood may bear me far..."

But the final word was not spoken in Netherfeld.

Alda uttered "far" atop the crimson mountain, above the ruins of Prospero's palazzo on the enchanted island. In her hand was the cauldron's bubble, placed in her palm by her grandmother.

And before her was a scene of devastation.

The sky erupted in an unnatural storm. The ground reverberated with a strange music. Lights and rain and smoke and multicolored flames swirled like watercolors in a jar.

And the air smelled of an evergreen forest. No, a burning pine. Like the dead dryad.

Amid this turmoil were three hunched forms. The witches. Their faces illuminated from below with a pale, green light.

Alda braced herself to attack them, her fists shaking and her mind focused with the intensity she needed to — to what? To somehow channel the strength of her grandmother's ancient magic.

Alda shook her head, clearing her mind. Her attention felt like the tip of a needle, all thoughts narrowed to a single point, all else that did not matter pushed to the periphery and out of focus. She shifted the invisible beam of her thoughts to the witches.

Yet, her worries shifted. Where was Dreng? And Sycorax? Had the summoner abandoned them? And would Caliban return, with help from Miranda?

But Alda's heart sank when she saw him — Dreng — prostrate on the red earth, a strange glow emanating from his form. The witches above him. The culprits. She feared him dead but somehow knew he still breathed. She had to act quickly. To save him.

She wailed, the sound involuntary as her heart strained against her chest, and the witches saw her.

But, strangely and suddenly, Alda was not afraid. She smelled the familiar scent of rosemary as calm trickled from her fingertips to her toes. She moved mechanically as if remembering some old dance, her arms turning in ways that she did not understand as wind rushed between her fingers.

"He is dead." They laughed.

A lie. Alda did not believe the witches, their equivocation.

"Dead."

"And gone."

"No!" A flash. A rush of hot air. And a scream that Alda did not feel coming from her throat.

"You cannot save him!" The witches' words were a taunt. A distraction.

Words.

As Alda gripped the black pebble in her hand, her body remembered her family's ancient powers, the sensation she had felt when she was trapped in the pit so many months ago. As a white-hot aura enveloped her form, she let loose the secrets of her soul. "I am little and young and inexperienced, but I am still fierce. And I am worthy. Worthy not only of my family's powers but of love. And I had that, all too briefly."

Her voice cracked, but she continued as her limbs tingled and glowed. "When I met him on the ship, I knew that — I knew there would be more to our lives. And that we belonged together. And I would never say it, never breathe it, hardly dare to even hope it, but I still *knew* in the depth of my being that our lives would be as one. No, they *will* be as one yet. We share some strange destiny, some future in which we are together. To the end. To the end. No, beyond that. To some happy epilogue."

Hail fell. Its icy orbs stung Alda's cheeks and hands.

The witches cowered as the flames from the trouble fire went out, replaced by something far more terrifying.

White lightning, leaving Alda's hands in blinding streaks and flashes. Reverberating thunder. And Alda's words, her agonized words, released in torrents of emotion, "Dreng cannot be dead. He never will die. Because he is immortal. Not immortal to the rest of the world. Not some mythical god. But he is *mine*. As long as I live, as long as I breathe his name and whisper his life's story, he will live on."

Tears streamed down her cheeks as hot rain fell hard and strong from the heavens. "You cannot take him from me. And if what you tell me is true — if his earthly form is indeed dead, I know that is only his body. His soul lies elsewhere. Half in Heaven. Half intertwined with mine. You cannot tear him from me!"

Her face was drenched with tears and raindrops, red with anguish and hailstones. She closed her eyes, no longer caring about the witches or her imminent danger. Only Dreng. Only the words she could not say to him on the clifftop. "I love him. I love him. I love nothing so well as him! And I will save him yet! There is no power in all of nature or the heavens that will tear us apart."

Lights flashed behind her lids. Then a jolt of cold. She opened her eyes to darkness. Steam rose from the mountain. As the mist evaporated, Alda saw the silhouettes of the witches against the retreating lightning on the horizon.

No, not witches. Stones. They had turned to monoliths like those in the circle on the moor, three great boulders forming a triangle above Dreng's broken body.

Alda felt numb as she wiped her black hair from her face and reached his side, taking his hand as she knelt. Blood seeped through a deep wound beneath his torn shirt, spilling onto the granite at his side. His hands were limp and fallen, unmoving. His breath shallow, fast, as Alda wiped his dripping hair from his forehead.

The strange calm was still upon her as Alda realized his lung was injured. Perhaps at home, in her cottage, she could do something to help. At least something to ease his pain. But here, here she could not.

Yet, there was hope. She had the cauldron's bubble, whole, intact. She could use it, take him to safety, and —

No. It would tear them apart, as it had before. And she could not leave him, not like this, not now.

So she turned, looking once again for Caliban or for Sycorax, and saw a pile of clothes nearby, covered in a strange, white dust. Alda knew that the summoner, too, was gone.

Alone again. And helpless.

"Dreng, it worked. I —" She wiped a silent tear. "The trouble fire, you did it — I think the witches — they're gone!"

Dreng remained motionless. His features ashen and sunken. His lips, quivering, were blue.

All this, Alda realized, all of their toil, was for naught.

*   *   *

Dreng did not know exactly what happened next, after he thrust the dagger into his chest. No memory of falling or of pain. First, he had the sensation of light, of heat, but all turned to black behind his eyelids. Now, the ground was cold at his back, but he felt comforting warmth on his hand as he fell deeper and deeper into the enveloping darkness.

"Dreng, can you hear me?"

Alda's voice, calling him. He struggled against some oppressive, invisible weight, and opened his eyes.

"Alda." He forced the word out, willing his parched lips to move. His thoughts wanted to form more words, to whisper that he *knew* her, somehow, from the beginning. That they were to share a story. That their souls and their lives were intertwined, despite only meeting for fleeting moments.

But this was the end of their tale. The final act. No, the curtain.

He felt a wave of emotions. Not only sadness and fear, but disappointment. He had once imagined them living together, old and invalid, sharing a bed in some distant cottage as they dozed, listening through an open window to leaves rustle and birds sing and ocean waves crash. It was an impossible image, a fleeting hope of stability and warmth and all of the things that Dreng had never known.

A dream of home. Of love.

He tried again to speak, but the poetry of his soul was lost in a rattle. His eyes closed.

He sensed her crying, sobs wracking her body as she bent over him. He tried to open his eyes, to see her again, one last time, then to reach for her, to comfort her, but he could not will his worthless frame into motion.

Did she understand? Did she believe all that he had said before? Did she know all that he could not say now?

Did she feel how deeply he loved her?

With a rasping, final breath, he sighed, but no words escaped his lips.

Silence.

And he let the blanket of darkness fall over him, stifling his soul and comforting his shivering form.

His last thought came as a kind of instinct, a flash of consciousness: *If only he had more time.*

Chapter Seventeen: Dagger of the Mind

Alda felt Dreng's hand relax in hers. She leaned over his form, holding him, gasping, trying to coax him back into motion, into being. Into life. But her tears did not resuscitate him.

Yet she still held tight to his hand, as she had with Caliban. The black pebble from the clifftops pressed between their palms. She wiped Dreng's matted hair from his forehead, running her finger over the rough whiskers along his chin.

Her breath was shallow and fast as she held onto hope.

But his breath ceased.

Frantic, Alda whispered, "I am here, Dreng. I am here. We are safe now. Come back to me. Come back. I'm waiting. Please, please. Come back."

And then she felt for a pulse, wishing once more for his heartbeat against her skin. But his heart, too, was still.

He did not return to her.

Dreng was dead and gone. Past the bar, like in one of her grandmother's oft-quoted poems. His form cold and unmoving, his eyes closed to all.

Seconds passed. Minutes. Hours? She stayed by his side like one of the weeping women on a marble gravestone.

Finally, after what seemed an eternity, she straightened his shirt over his wounds, covering the scar and puncture from which his life seeped. And then she placed his arms across his chest like a medieval grave on a stereopticon card: a knight in repose.

But as she squeezed his palm one final time, she felt a fragment of parchment. Prospero's tiny book of spells. Covered in Dreng's blood. She wiped it on her skirt and stood, her eyes searching the horizon.

Now, what should she do?

The moon shifted, and she saw a glint near Dreng's feet. A dagger. Alda held it too tightly as she studied its metal. It lacked a sheath. For a moment, she held it before her, staring at the blood on its blade. She could fall beside him, now. And sleep, or something like it. She shifted the weapon in her hands, feeling its weight.

Wait. The word reverberated in her mind. That was not the way.

She dropped the bloody dagger before her and, trembling, stumbled to the broken form of Sycorax.

Only clothes and dust. No body, no blood. Like the discarded costume of a travelling actor.

There was no one left, not here. Caliban had abandoned them. Ariel, too. Dreng. Sycorax. Alda's hands shook, so she twisted her fingers into a knot and pressed it against her abdomen. But the shaking spread up and into her heart until it escaped in a sob.

She could return to Netherfeld. Yes, to her mother and grandmother. To — to what? Live in darkness? In a land of spirits? No.

Dreng would not be there. Death would be a better escape. Because then she would be with him.

Again, the dagger seemed to call her. To beckon. So Alda squeezed her fingers into fists and focused on the present.

After some time, her breaths became more even. Her mind less clouded. She remembered how to deal with death, what she did when her grandmother passed.

So she scanned the rubble around her, looking for something to mark the place where her friends had fallen. A memorial. A gravestone. The palazzo's stones were strewn near the perimeter of the mountain, thrown aside by earthquakes and the fires' force. Yes, one such stone would do.

As Alda walked toward the rubble, the moon reached its zenith and shown through parting clouds onto the red granite at her feet. And Alda saw a shadow.

She was not alone.

Near the three witches' monoliths was a silhouette. No, a shade. A figure flickering between gray and black. Like her grandmother in Netherfeld, yet different.

Sycorax. In her true semblance of the girl once called Ophelia, not the borrowed body of Miranda.

Alda stared at the being, afraid to speak first. Finally, she approached it with the trepidation of meeting a wild beast.

And the shadow rushed toward her with an expression mixing both fear and joy.

"Alda, you are returned unharmed!" Sycorax smiled, the expression out of joint with her surroundings.

"Are you, are you hurt?" The word was not right, but Alda knew not what else to say.

"I am as I am. I have been like this before, and —" Sycorax's expression sharply changed as her brow furrowed. "The pearl of wisdom, it was not enough. The witches, they — But you, you are safe. Yes, *you* are saved. Because Dreng sent you away — And Dreng — Where is Dreng?"

Alda mournfully turned her head, and Sycorax followed her gaze. The shade flitted toward his body and bent over him, her ghostly fingers flickering across his face.

"The witches, they, they killed him, and I —" Alda could not finish as another thought entered her mind. "Did you know of his plan?"

Several heartbeats of silence. Then, simply, "Yes. He wanted to save you, Alda —"

"And you, you let him stand with only you against the witches?"

"I thought — the pearl of wisdom, its powers — I thought we would be victorious."

"You let the witches murder him!" The words shook with anger.

Sycorax's eyes landed on the dagger, and she looked sorrowfully at Alda as she whispered, "No, no. They did not do this. They would use magic. A curse. A spell. Not a blade." She paused and added, her voice unsteady, "*He* did this."

"He wouldn't."

"He saw himself cornered. Outnumbered. This, his escape." Sycorax straightened, her form hovering above Dreng's corpse. "He was more an antique Roman than one of our time."

"No, no, he would never, never leave me like that."

"He saved you. Saved us all. If the witches had taken him, if they had used him, his powers..." Her voice faded as she examined the three stony monoliths.

Alda swallowed, her throat suddenly too dry. "Will the witches return?"

Sycorax reached a shadowy arm toward the stones. "No. We are safe from them. Your magic is elemental, natural, of the earth. And the earth transformed them." Her expression changed, and she added, "You are like Medusa."

But Alda did not respond.

The summoner's eyes fell once more to the ground, to Dreng, and her voice took on a hollow, distant tone. "My spell, my magic, my sacrifice... Alda, this was not meant to be."

"Yet... it is."

They stood in silence, Alda's bloodied, wet dress cold against her legs, her face expressionless and her mind vacillating between disbelief, anger, and helplessness.

Sycorax glanced again at Dreng and shook her head, her ashen features bent in sorrow. "We cannot leave him thus."

Alda nodded.

"We should mourn him. Honor him. Set him adrift on a raft. Like ancient sailors in their long boats." Again, Sycorax paused. "Return him to the sea."

"No, we cannot leave him alone, like, like that." Alda wiped a tear from her cheek as something between courage and regret stirred her heart. "He was yours in life. Let him be mine in death. Let me remember him. Alone."

Sycorax started to object, but the consonants stuck on her tongue. Finally, she tilted her head and relented, her shadowy shoulders falling, "As you like."

Silently, she vanished like rising fog, and Alda was the only living soul atop the crimson mountain.

Chapter Eighteen: Quintessence of Dust

Finally, the tears dried on Alda's cheeks as she stood atop the pale cliffs that fell into the sand below. The place where she last spoke alone with him, with —

But she knew that behind her, the green glow of the pyre's flames still flickered on the red mountaintop. Consuming the one thing she had wanted. And though she did not turn to watch it burn, and though she was too far to feel its heat, its flames were too close and too painful.

As the sun illuminated the sea before her, Alda sighed. She was alone, here. Sycorax had not yet returned. Caliban remained missing. But she had the cauldron's bubble secure in her sock, along with the miniature book.

And the signet ring that he had worn — worn until the last — spun in her fingers as she thought about her future.

A knot formed in Alda's throat, choking her. She coughed, but the sound came out as a laugh, a kind of giggle that was appropriate only for a lunatic. Alda tried to suppress it, but the more she did, the louder and more boisterous it became. It felt like someone else laughing, not her.

And suddenly a poem came to mind, one with a line she had spoken to her grandmother in Netherfeld, one that seemed too fitting now: "Such a tide as moving seems asleep... when that which drew... turns again home." No, she had lost those verses, those rhymes. Forgotten like a dream at dawn.

But she remembered a second poem, too well, one with words she could not fully comprehend until now.

"So we'll go no more a-roving, so late into the night." A pause. "Though the heart —" She inhaled, her ragged breath not sustaining her through the lines. She stared out at the sea, watching the white-topped waves, as she continued, "Though the heart be still as loving, and the moon be still as bright."

Her mind returned to the funeral fire that spit and crackled unheard in the distance behind her, the illumination that had once been Dreng, so she forced herself on, "For the sword outwears its sheath, and the soul —" She suppressed a sob. "The soul —"

Her voice stopped, and the final word echoed from the cliffs below.

"This is not the end."

Alda started at the voice and turned to see Sycorax returned, her shadowy form gray and transparent, but her blue eyes flashing with renewed energy.

Alda once more faced the sea, her tone dark. "He is burning."

Again, "This is *not* the end."

"It is."

"You will find happiness someday."

"I doubt I will." Alda's tone was bitter.

"Why?"

"Love is not for our world." Alda felt anger rise in her throat. "You and Hamlet. Caliban and Miranda. Phillida and Oberon. You and, and *him*. Me, and, and —" Alda wiped her flushed cheeks. "We are all the stuff of tragedy."

The two women stood in silent agreement for several heartbeats before Alda realized, "I could go to him." She spoke swiftly, excitedly, "I could take my cauldron's bubble and return to the time before he was killed. I could stop the witches and save him. And you." She looked at Sycorax, pleading, but the shade of the summoner lowered her eyes.

"You would risk the world for a single soul. The witches could capture you, Alda. They could steal your powers, become stronger. Invincible. They are dead *now*. If you go back into the past and interfere…" She was quiet for a moment, her brows furrowed. "I loved him, too, once, but the witches have been killed. Magic has been saved. The world is now protected. Do not jeopardize our victory."

Alda's heart raced and hands shook. Sycorax was right. She knew she was right, but still —

Finally, Alda steadied her voice and loosed accusatory words, "Why are you here, Sycorax? Why not go elsewhere? Anywhere? You are free. Like a spirit. Go as you will."

"I want to stay here." She paused. "With you."

Alda did not respond.

Sycorax continued, "Many years ago, my Hamlet told me to go to a nunnery. It was meant to be nonsense, yet there was sense behind it." She was silent for too long and finally added, "He must be dead now, too."

After a moment, she sighed and gently touched Alda's shoulder. "We have magic, you and I. We know something of its power, its spells. We can stay on this island, study our skills, record them, perhaps teach others. Begin something like a convent for women who are written out of their own stories. For outcasts like us." She took a shaky breath. "This is *my* island now, once again. Let's make it ours, my friend."

"I cannot — I am not your *friend*." Alda felt the lie in her words. Despite the hatred, the distrust, there was something between her and the summoner. Something akin to friendship, if not exactly such. "And I cannot stay here, not with, with —" Alda glanced at the flames atop the hill, and a piece inside her broke. She collapsed, sobbing, and Sycorax reached for her, but her shadowy form brought a chill like a winter wind.

Concern filled Sycorax's voice. "You are stronger than you know, Alda."

"But how do *you* know?"

"Because I am, too. Stay here, with me."

"I cannot."

"Why?"

Alda did not have an answer. But she knew this was not her place, not her time. She did not belong here. She belonged in Grand Ledge, on her island, surrounded by the memories of her grandmother. Of *him*.

The place seemed to call her.

"I must return to my cottage."

"What is there for you, now?"

"I don't know. Not yet. But I *will* know." Alda's voice cracked. "Or I won't. And I will die there, as I always imagined."

"You will learn to live in time."

"How?"

"Grief is like an ocean. You can sink, or swim, or learn to float on its surface. I float." The final word was too literal for a spectre.

"But I sink." Alda wiped hot tears from her neck.

"Then go." Sycorax's voice was firm, commanding. "But if you ever choose to return, I will be here."

So Alda forced herself up. All had seemed slow, since he died. Like walking underwater. And now that Alda finally moved, she wanted to do so quickly. She had to leave, to flee. So when her feet were steady, she faced her companion and opened her fist, revealing Dreng's signet ring in her palm.

"I was going to throw it into the sea," she explained. "So a piece of him could always be within the waves. But it was not his, not truly. It came from your Hamlet. So it should be yours, now." Alda set the golden circle on a rock at Sycorax's transparent feet.

To Alda's surprise, the shade stooped and placed it on her own shadowy finger. "You will find yourself again, but it will take time."

Alda bit her lip and wondered aloud, "Do you think we shall meet again?"

"We know not what this world holds. Or the next." Sycorax's lips curled into a forced smile, despite the sadness behind her eyes. "But I will find my way. As will you."

Alda nodded. "Farewell, Sycorax. Ophelia. Whoever you are."

She bowed her head. "Until we meet again, Alda, heir of Hecate."

As the summoner's shade spoke the final word, Alda stepped to the cliff's edge. She could use the cauldron's bubble on the island now, but Alda needed release. So she once again hurled herself from the dreadful summit and clasped her fingers around the orb. As she fell hopelessly toward death, Alda vanished.

*   *   *

When the too-familiar sensation of movement and comforting warmth passed, Alda found herself alone. And she was safe. An autumn breeze rapped at the windows of her cottage, blowing sunset-hued leaves against the cracked and broken panes.

She should sleep. She was exhausted. The witches, his death, her fall. Each had taken something from her, and she had little left to give. But all was not well. She could not rest. There was still much to do.

Her cottage was ruinous. When she had left, swept away in the flood with him and transported into Netherfeld by the cauldron's bubble, it had been late summer. Now, when she returned, months had passed. So before the autumn sunrays vanished, she gathered candles and set to work.

Mud caked the walls above her knees. Mold grew on soft surfaces, and its black veins traced unclean curves up the yellow wallpaper and onto the ceiling. Furniture was strewn about as if thrown by a giant.

Glass and ceramics broken. Yet somehow the stereoscope was safe above the fireplace, its warped cards faded but usable. At least she could yet escape in its images when her toil was complete.

This was not her only flood, not the first time waters had risen into the safety of her cottage. But it was the most severe.

Years earlier, Alda awoke to water pooled below the crib in which she slept. It was exciting, then. Something different and unexpected to pass the time. An adventure. And her grandmother had borne the burden, scrubbing and shining and moving their meager belongings into the center of the garden. "You are safe here, always. I will protect you on the island. And the rest is transitory. What we need, we will clean. Sunshine will make it like new," Gramma explained.

Alda wondered aloud, "How? It is only light."

Her grandmother smiled at the little girl. "No, it has powers. It can purify. And it can heal."

Now, after so many years, Alda worked alone in the moonlight, cleaning and scrubbing until her knees ached and knuckles bled.

As the sun rose the next morning, she stood in the garden and watched its beams creep through the swaying trees. She needed to heal.

In the new light, she took the cauldron's bubble from her sock and held it in the morning's glow.

It was empty, like a hollow soap bubble. Near weightless and practically imperceptible to the touch. It was empty. Without Dreng, she could not make another. She was here, alone. And trapped.

She sighed, helpless. But not useless.

Three days passed. Three days removing all traces of the flood. She saved the sofa and armchair, some dresses, her favorite mixing bowls, her grandmother's handwritten recipe cards. The black velvet cloak that had once concealed the cauldron's bubble.

Some parts of her past survived. The rest did not matter.

No, nothing mattered. Because no matter how much she cleaned and concentrated and stood in the sunshine, he was still gone. Not only him, but all of the life she had known before.

For fleeting moments, Alda regretted leaving Sycorax. Yet each time, she reminded herself that there was something here for her. Waiting. She simply had to discover it. In time.

So as the sun eased down toward the trees at the end of the third day, she stood beneath the orange and red foliage and allowed herself to feel for the first time since her return to her world and her time.

She knew, logically, that Dreng would have died much sooner, if not for her. That he may have even died in the hold of the ship, a lonely boy lost at sea, if not for her sudden appearance. And then again, in Fairy Land. So she assured herself that she had helped him live for a little while, at least. Longer than otherwise. And even a small moment of time with him was better than none.

But it was not, not truly. And, ironically, Alda had always expected more time. She delayed speaking to him, telling him how she felt. She had imagined some future in which to breathe, to rest, to finally and simply converse. She needed more time. But that was impossible.

Still, she tried to find comfort in one of her grandmother's favorite poems. "'Tis better to have loved and lost than never to have loved at all." The quote was spoken only in her mind, yet she choked on a sob on the final word.

It was nonsense. Surely the poet who had written that was old. Or had never truly loved. Or held onto false hope.

Alda had no hope. Not even false hope. Only memories. So she returned to them, first flitting over the earlier events on Prospero's island, of how she rediscovered Dreng in the palazzo courtyard. Then again, when they met so serendipitously in Fairy Land. And then once more, before the palazzo crashed around them.

And their encounter on the clifftops, when he gave her the pebble. How she wanted so much more then. More than a kiss. How she wanted to tell him so, so much. Words. Words — words that she should have spoken. Words of love.

For a moment, she felt she was there again. The salty air on her cheeks. Her hair wild in the wind. And in her mind, she told him all. The words she unleashed at the witches, and more. She told him of her dreams and fears and how he fit into all of the hollow places of her existence. How he would fill the void of her soul, if only — If only they had more time together.

Her thoughts lingered there, not wanting to return to the more recent pain.

But too quickly her memories enveloped her, not letting go. The smell entrapped her first: a piney scent atop the crimson mountain. Then the cold air of the storm. And Dreng. His hair or skin or some other odor belonging to a man. His hand on hers, for a brief flash. Then being ripped from that. Passing through time and place to the realm of nothing. Being helpless. Returning too late.

She should have stopped him from sending her away, somehow. He should have told her of his plan. They should have discussed it before the encounter, together. They should have talked. Then, maybe...

Alda felt tears drip down her neck and returned to the present. A beam of light broke through the trees and caught her eye. She squinted and turned away, suddenly too aware of where she was.

It was late evening. She was dizzy from so much time lost in her thoughts. Lost.

Yet there was hope. If only...

Alda closed her fists and focused her mind, as she had before. Her thoughts narrowed, and, and, and... nothing. No powers. No magic. No more hope.

Dreng was not all that was dead and gone.

And she remembered the stone, the black pebble that he had given to her on the clifftop. Clenched tightly in her fist.

Her grandmother had told her of worry stones, meant to absorb sorrow or fear. If this was such, then it was surely full. So Alda turned back toward her cottage, near the front door where Dreng had once passed, and knelt on the flagstones. She dug her fingers into the dark soil near the worn threshold and deposited the pebble next to the foundation.

As she smoothed the loam over it, she felt like she had at her grandmother's burial. Although it was only a rock, she mourned for it. No, not for it. For him.

She stood suddenly as she realized that she could not stay here. Not another moment. So she turned sharply and crossed the footbridge to the Ledge Path and clambered up the washed-out trail until she reached the mural of the three animals. "When shall we three meet again?" The words inscribed below it were unexpectedly hurtful because Alda knew the answer: Never.

She turned from the mural, so beloved in her childhood, and trod the worn path toward the long bridge and its electric lights, gathering wilting flowers and wiry evergreens from the steep ledges as she passed.

Chapter Nineteen: Fortune Brings in Some

The cemetery was at once familiar and foreign. The summer leaves Alda remembered had turned yellow against the dark greens and blues of the pines. But even though the sun was only a sliver on the horizon, Alda easily found her way toward her grandmother's earthly resting place.

Yet as she approached its simple flagstone, she felt as though she was being watched. It was an unnerving sensation, something she had not experienced during her so many previous visits since her grandmother's passing the prior winter. Alda turned in place, feeling more curiosity than dread in this garden of death.

Then Alda saw a ghostly form beneath a blue spruce: half a man, only a torso and arms. Its incomplete silhouette obscured in shadows and movement. Hesitant, Alda approached, doing her best to always have at least one headstone between herself and the phantom.

Ten paces. Twenty. Thirty. Alda was nearly upon the figure when it — no, he — laughed.

And she realized this was not some ghost or ghoul. It was a man holding a worn spade, standing in an open grave. A gravedigger. His eyes smiled as he again looked at her, but his mouth and nose were covered by a dusty bandana. Despite this mask, Alda recognized him as the same man who had buried her grandmother amid laughter and inappropriately jolly songs.

"Here again, after so long?"

"I visit less frequently than I did before..." Alda paused and added, as if apologizing, "I have been away."

"I envy you an' wish my visits were as seldom." He grunted as he continued to dig. His accent was strange, distant. He was not from Michigan.

After several heartbeats of silence, Alda felt a wave of recognition and wondered aloud, "Have we met, elsewhere?"

"I know you, yes, and your handiwork." He paused long enough to wink at the bundle of foliage in Alda's hand, and she understood. He added slyly, "You wreathe my hands' work."

"Well, plants were important to Gramma." More silence. "I should go." She turned once again toward her destination, but the jovial man cleared his throat as he dug.

"What's past is prologue."

Alda again faced him. "What do you mean?"

"That's what this grave will say. Or what it will read. Rather, what those who read it will say to themselves. It's a kind of poetry, no?" The man stopped digging and met her eyes, his mouth and nose still covered.

"I suppose." Alda hesitated. "And ironic."

"Why?"

"To think that life is prologue. For what? For death?" Despite herself, she choked on something like a laugh.

"For *whatever* comes next." He leaned on the spade and wiped his brow. "Poetic irony. The end is the beginning."

"That's nonsense."

"Spoken like one who knows sense. Or one who has lost it."

Alda shook her head and said, more seriously than she intended, "I doubt I ever had it. Not enough sense, at least. Or good."

"Bad sense."

She nodded.

"And now?"

"I have even less."

The man cleared his throat. "In what sense?"

Alda again suppressed a laugh, amused. "In every sense."

"But you can still smell and see and hear and taste. You have all five."

"You forgot feeling," Alda corrected.

"You may have lost that. It is easily deposited here, with the senseless."

Alda started to understand his word game, his equivocation. "Death is senseless."

The man nodded, his gaze fixed with hers. "Some times." There was an unusual pause between his words.

"No, always. Death is always senseless. Useless. For naught." An image of Dreng, unspoken words trembling on his lips, flashed into her mind. "It is deaf and mute and tasteless." Tears formed in her eyes. "But it reeks. And it touches, too much."

The man shifted and broke their gaze, his eyes turning to the empty grave in which he stood.

A sudden thought occurred to Alda, and her curiosity escaped her lips, "Have you ever buried someone whom you love?"

"I do not bury anyone."

"Well, have you ever dug a grave for anyone close to you?"

"The graves I dig make them far."

"No, I mean, have you dug a grave for anyone that you love?"

"I do not dig graves for anyone, nor do I bury anyone. Only any *body*." He chuckled on the final word.

Alda's frustration darkened her tone. "You know what I mean."

"My knowledge is mean," the man snorted.

"No, I, I was serious, and you —" Alda faltered. She should not have asked. The question was too personal. It was rude to prod a stranger thus. "I'm sorry. I —"

He held up a hand, stopping her. "Without my wit, I am nothing. All is jest, here. Laughter is what separates the living from the dead."

"And dirt. And decay." Alda sighed. "And time."

"Time is all they have now. And it is what we lack, what we are missing." He motioned to the surrounding graves. "But they all stood here, at one time or another, and looked at these stony faces as we look upon them now."

Alda wiped a tear from her cheek, and the man's tone changed to something softer as he continued, "Look there, at that red granite monument." He nodded toward a waist-height gravestone, its top arched and carved with two clasped hands. Alda walked closer to it, and the gravedigger prodded, "Read it."

The words were covered in moss, so Alda wiped it away as she squinted in the dim light and read, "Stranger pause as you pass by. As you are now, so once was I. As I am now, soon you shall be. So welcome death, and follow me."

She stood upright and rubbed her back as she once again faced the gravedigger. "It calls me to death. I have half a heart to follow."

"No, no." He shifted the spade in his hands. "It is a reminder. All here were once alive. In a different time. Some, in a different place. If we had lived at any other moment, we might have known them." His voice lowered with a serious gravity. "Our paths might have crossed."

"Yes, but they are dead. Now." And as Alda spoke the final word, she felt too keenly the absence of her cauldron's bubble. "Now is all that matters because now is where we are. Where I am."

The gravedigger snorted, "But it is not where you *may* be." He finally lowered his handkerchief, and his too familiar sneer curled into a toothy grin.

"Caliban?"

His face was lean and worn with age, lines etched above his cheekbones and at the corners of his mouth.

Alda stammered before she blurted, "How did you — Why are you here?"

"You told me to find you in the cemetery, witch."

"I did not."

"You will. Later."

"Why?"

He flashed his sarcastic smile, "To tell you what to do."

"You know I do not trust you, so I might not listen."

"But you will listen to *him*." Caliban held out his palm to reveal another cauldron's bubble, shining and purple in the twilight. "As you are now, so once was I."

Alda reached for the orb, but hesitated. "How did you get this?"

"I made it." He lowered his voice. "It can transport two people, together."

Alda looked at him questioningly. "How?"

"That is something you will learn in time." He awkwardly cleared his throat and continued, "But the bubble's power is nearly used up. One trip more, or two. I needed it, before I could give it to you, you see, for Miranda, and, and — that is a story for another day."

He sighed and changed to a more somber tone, "Dreng was not always Dreng. There was once a time when he was called Thomas Chatterton —"

"Is that his name?"

Caliban nodded. "His birth name."

Alda lowered her eyes. "He never told me his true name."

"When you knew him, he was someone else. He was Dreng. But before all of this, before the island and Sycorax and you and me and Miranda, he was a boy on a ship. And he still is, or was. Not now, but then."

Caliban again offered the bubble, and this time, Alda cupped it in her shaking palm.

"Then I must go." She set her jaw resolutely, feeling equal parts ecstasy and trepidation, as she thrust her flowers into Caliban's hand. "Take these. As thanks."

"But these flowers are for the dead."

"You will be, someday." But Alda realized she had another question, "Did you find Miranda?"

"Time will tell."

Alda understood. "But you cannot."

The gravedigger shook his head, entertained by her frustration.

Alda lowered her voice as she considered, "Yet you said that I told you to come here."

Caliban nodded and grinned, his eyes laughing.

Alda continued, "Then I *will* meet you again."

He lowered his gaze and kicked dirt from the spade, but did not respond.

Alda blurted, "When?"

"Tomorrow or tomorrow or tomorrow or the last syllable of recorded time."

"Well, until then..." Alda embraced the strange man in the grave and awkwardly pulled away, wiping his dirt from her faded blue dress. "Caliban, try to be kind."

"As always, my dear witch." He made an extravagant bow, and Alda likewise bent toward the ground, a smile crossing her lips.

When Alda stood, Caliban was gone, spade and all. Vanished.

She felt a kind of nervous excitement, a sense of both butterflies in her stomach and a boulder crushing her shoulders as she gently ran her fingertips over the smooth surface of the cauldron's bubble.

She knew what she might do, but should she? *Could* she? After all, this cauldron's bubble was not hers. It would take her where she needed to go, not where she wanted to be. Where might it take her?

As she wondered, she sat, shaking, on the edge of the grave, her feet dangling within its depths, and held her face in her hands and breathed until she felt something like calm.

When Alda finally raised her stinging eyes and sat upright on the grave's edge, she lost her orientation in the twilight. Her head spun, and she leaned awkwardly to try to regain equilibrium until she fell forward, head over heels, into the shallow pit.

The damp dirt clung to her hands and hair as she turned onto her back and looked up at the darkening sky, aware that death was inches away on all sides. She thought of the witches' words: *In the grave.* "The rest she'll know in the grave."

And Alda laughed, not only in her throat but in her spirit. Yes, this was her path. This is what she must do. The witches' strange words confirmed it. For a moment she steadied her breath as she examined the glimmering sphere of the cauldron's bubble in her fingertips. And Dreng's words echoed in her thoughts: "I only wish I could have found you sooner, before —"

So Alda clasped the purple orb in her fist and exhaled slowly as warmth washed over her. And she vanished.

A cold autumn breeze swept through the graveyard, rustling the dry leaves until they rattled.

*   *   *

"Take me with you!" The words hung on the dying boy's lips, their echo hovering in the damp air above him.

But the mysterious girl vanished. And the boy, bloodied and alone in the hold of *The Tempest*, lost his last, brief, shining hope of deliverance. And now, as he felt the warmth of his own blood pool under him on the warped planks, he knew he would prefer death to what might come.

The crewmen's feet thudded above and changed in pitch as they quickly descended the steep stairs. Two seconds, perhaps three, and they would be here, hovering above him. They would also find Ernesto's body, discover Prince Hamlet to be missing, and blame the survivor for both crimes.

Survivor. Dreng coughed. Not for long. And if he did live, somehow, if his body did not break from whatever punishment the crew saw fit, his spirit would surely die. He could not emerge from this ordeal whole, intact.

One second more, perhaps, before the crew found him. A breath. A heartbeat. But in this limbo, that second seemed too long, the wait an eternity. Death would be freeing. An escape.

He gripped the golden signet ring in his fist and awaited his fate.

Movement. Not the crewmen. Not Hamlet returned, nor Ernesto resurrected.

The scent of rosemary again filled the hold, and the girl appeared. No, a young woman. The same, but aged. Dressed in blue, her black hair cascading down her shoulders.

His eyes met hers, and though he could not speak, Dreng thought, *You are returned.*

She crouched at his side and brushed his damp hair from his forehead. "My name is Alda Reeding. And this time, I will not leave you."

His heart leapt as their fingers intertwined. And they vanished.

Chapter Twenty: What Dreams May Come

When Alda exhaled, she was once again within her cottage, the sky outside turning purple-blue in the approaching night. The bubble had returned her, here, now. This was where she needed to be.

And she was not alone.

The boy had lost consciousness, his limbs limp and heavy as she hoisted him onto the tapestried sofa.

The same sofa where Dreng had convalesced after their escape from Fairy Land.

But this time was not the same. That had been *her* experience, but not that of this boy. *She* remembered, but he would not.

And despite Sycorax's warning about returning to the past, Alda understood that — in her own lifeline, at least — the witches were yet gone, defeated. Sycorax was alone on her island. Caliban was elsewhere having his own adventure. All of that was real. And Alda remembered that it had happened. The knitting needle of her existence was still straight with a beginning and an end.

And Dreng was still dead.

This boy was not Dreng. This was Thomas. This was a different yarn. The old cut and discarded. This one tied anew.

This was a rebirth. A second chance. An opportunity to grow with him and, if fate was kind, grow old with him. And to love him, in a way. A different way.

Yet, now they had more time.

As Alda watched the boy sleep, she twisted her hands nervously and realized that the cauldron's bubble was clenched in her fist. Rather, its remains. It had shattered into tiny fragments, dust that fell to the floor like sand in an hourglass.

This had been her final trip, her final adventure.

And this boy did not know what Dreng had known. He could not read the spell to help her create another bubble. Thomas did not know magic.

Dreng's life before, what he had experienced with Sycorax and Caliban and the fairies and witches, and whatever happened before that, on his ship, all of that was now gone. Like a dream, once mistaken for reality, now not even a memory.

But although the past was gone, it was not entirely vanished.

She remembered. And from her memories, she could weave words. A story. She would tell him. She would tell him all that she knew.

She would give life to his imagination with words.

And she could show him, with the help of her stereopticon cards, which she stacked neatly on the table near him with trembling fingers. When he awoke, he could examine them. They could view the images of distant worlds together and live in their shared fantasy.

The boy could have two lives, one safe within her cottage, and one in the world of dreams and visions and the poetry of story.

That, Alda decided, should be enough. For now.

So she boiled water and gathered herbs to heal him. And as she prepared a tonic, she rooted her mind to the present, focusing on the details of this moment.

Now was all that mattered. And the future. Not the past.

*   *   *

The boy, who before he closed his eyes had been bleeding and dying, unloved and alone, opened his lids to a place of warmth and safety. *Home.* The word slipped into his mind, something foreign and unknown but so, so wanted. No, desired.

And there, across the small, strange, still room, was a girl. The girl from the beakhead. Alda. Aged from when he first beheld her, yet not significantly. Only some years his elder. But worn. And tired.

He watched her busy herself with something in a bowl, something that smelled of the scent he had remembered and then forgotten. *Rosemary.*

And though his side burned from his wound and his limbs were weak, he wanted to see her. No, help her. So he pushed himself upright, and his movement caught her attention.

"You're finally awake!" She dropped the bowl with a hollow thud on the table, rushed to his side, and knelt before him.

"How long have I —"

She took his hand. "The best part of four days."

The boy wiped his forehead, his fingers tingling. It felt like he had only blinked. "Where am I?"

Alda hesitated, her mouth opening and closing several times before she released a flood of words, "This is my cottage, on an island in the Grand River, near a town called Grand Ledge, that is in a state called Michigan..."

He barely listened as she explained the geography in some detail, her eyes beaming into his as her hands clasped his sweaty palm.

And when she was finally done, her eyes narrowed as she observed his confusion, so she added, "This is another time, centuries after you were on the ship."

He wiped his swimming head. Another time, in the future? Another place entirely? It was too much to comprehend.

Yet he was not afraid. He belonged here, somehow.

She seemed to sense his thoughts as she assured him, "You are safe, now. Dr —" Her tongue caught on a word, and she whispered, "Thomas."

"Thomas?"

"Your name is Thomas Chatterton."

He could not conceal his surprise. "You know my name? You know *me*?"

The girl nodded and removed one hand from his to wipe a tear. "Yes, yes! I know you."

"Who are you? An angel?"

She laughed. "No, of course not." She cleared her throat and confided, "I was once a witch."

"So you are magical?"

"I know a little magic."

"Teach me." He tried to sit but swooned, his head hitting the soft cushion behind him.

She sighed, "I cannot."

"Why?"

She stood and poured water from a flower-covered jug on the large table. He drank from a dainty, chipped cup, gulping its contents until not a drop remained.

Alda studied him, concern etching her features. "The magic is gone now." She paused a moment and added, "But while you convalesce, I will tell you a story, a tale of a life you might have lived."

Alda gave him a stack of images etched on parchment. Not paintings, something more clear. Small and detailed, colored pictures of ruined buildings and exotic landscapes and flora and beasts the boy had never before imagined.

She explained, "You can look at these through my stereoscope..." She handed him a quaint device of wood and metal. "And see the world. From here. From safety."

The boy nodded, and they sat for several silent heartbeats as he tried to understand.

Finally, he cleared his throat and asked, "Alda?" She waited patiently for him to continue. "Are we two alone here, in this place?"

"We are not alone because we are together. We will never be alone again."

The boy saw his joy reflected in her eyes, and they fell into a comfortable silence.

Alda stood and returned to the mixing bowl, and Thomas weakly eased himself upright and studied the fantastical images on the cards. As he carefully turned them in his hands and squinted at them in the dim light, a miniature book fell to the floor at his feet. He struggled to bend over and reach its worn pages, his healing wound still painful and swollen, but he finally collapsed victoriously into the cushions with the tiny book in his hand.

As he turned its leaves, the dark, mysterious shapes within its pages bent and transformed into words that he understood. He read.

And finally, Alda reached his side with a spoonful of dark green liquid, and he drank obediently, his throat closing momentarily on its bitterness. After another swig of water, he murmured, more to himself, "This is a strange book."

She seemed not to notice what was in his hand. "What book?"

He held it into the fire's light and suddenly saw that it was streaked with blood. A shiver shot up his neck, and his words shook. "It, it speaks nonsense. Lists of fantastical objects and absurd phrases that I do not understand. Are they riddles?"

He glanced at Alda's face and saw the color drain from her cheeks. "Riddles? You can read them?"

"Yes, but I do not understand. What are these things? What is..." he turned several pages. "A cauldron's bubble?"

Alda stumbled pack, dropping the spoon from her shaking fingers. She looked at him as one would stare at a ghost, as he had most likely beheld her when he saw her standing on the beakhead. And she leaned against the wooden table to steady herself as one might grasp for support during rough seas.

The boy began to speak, but words caught in his throat as he struggled to comprehend his companion's emotions.

And then she smiled.

Elation spread across her face as if some light radiated from within. He had never before seen such an expression, such ecstasy. She was the most beautiful, radiant thing he could imagine. And he, somehow, had given her this happy reaction.

So he asked again, "What is a cauldron's bubble?"

"A cauldron's bubble? I will show you — soon enough — after you are recovered and healed. In the spring, when the wildflowers bloom."

Alda wiped an unexpected tear from her eye and sat next to him on the long chair. She gently took his hand and covered his fingers with hers. "I have seen a lifetime of strife, as have you. But I suspect you and I — we still have great adventures before us, Thomas."

He suddenly felt older than his years and, for the first time, truly safe as he whispered, "Together?"

She nodded.

"I would not wish any companion in the world but you." He smiled, and the expression felt strange on his face. Unfamiliar, but delightful.

Alda laughed as she stood, the sound sweet and high, and struck a match above the fireplace. She lit a wax taper as she returned to his side, and he watched its light dance in her eyes.

"Let's have a story now. About the lives we might have lived." Alda took a deep breath and held firm to his hand. "I've heard that the past is prologue, so that is where we'll begin..."

When shall we three meet againe?
In Thunder, Lightning, or in Raine?

When the Hurley-burley's done,
When the Battaile's lost, and wonne.

That will be ere the set of Sunne.

~William Shakespeare (1564-1616), *Macbeth*
Witches' Conversation, Act 1, Scene 1
First Folio, 1623

Alda and Dreng will appear again

with Caliban in a new, stand-alone novel

Caliban and the Void

to be released on

October 10, 2022

About the Author

Amber Elby is the author of three fantasy novels based on Shakespeare's plays: *Cauldron's Bubble, Double Double Toil*, and *Trouble Fires Burn*. In the last millennium, she was born in Grand Ledge, Michigan but spent much of her childhood in the United Kingdom. When she was nine, she saw her first Shakespearean comedy, *Much Ado About Nothing*, in London. Many years later, she studied Creative Writing at Michigan State University's Honors College before earning her Master of Fine Arts degree in Screenwriting at the University of Texas at Austin. Amber enjoys watching Shakespearean performances — in person and on Zoom — with her husband and two daughters and divides her time between teaching at Austin Community College, traveling, and getting lost in imaginary worlds. She spent this year creating several virtual plays, hosting the *Jane Eyre* Readathon for Bring the Brontes Home, and also working on her upcoming novel to be released in 2022, *Caliban and the Void*.

Author's Note

In response to the *No Holds Bard* podcast's #CauldronsBardflies book club question, "What is magic?"

Magic isn't simply spells and wands. Magic happens every day in the improbability of the mundane. Ever since I was a child, I have adored O. Henry's short stories because their twists and turns are all possible, so their magic is in their coincidence. We see this in our lives, too, but we often take it for granted. My favorite magical experience, one that I could never transpose into a work of fiction because it is so unbelievable, is the story of my husband: we were born two days apart in the same hospital and were released on the same day, but we spent our early childhood in separate cities. When we were ten, our families moved a few miles apart, so we met in fifth grade. In middle school, our schedules were generated by computers, and we were the only two people to have the exact same schedule in seventh grade; he was assigned seats next to me in math and English and was in my history group when we learned about Medieval England — when we reenacted fiefdoms, I was the Lady, and he was my Knight. We were friends but didn't date until high school, and he only agreed to go to the movies with me due to an epic miscommunication in which he thought we were going with a group. Somehow, all of these little twists pushed us together. That is magic. And, coincidentally, we moved across the country a month after our wedding for me to attend graduate school at the University of Texas in Austin, which is a mile from O. Henry's house.

A Note About Grand Ledge

Grand Ledge, Michigan actually exists. It is a place of mystery and legend and the allure of what has been and what might still be.

Today, it is a quiet town where children ride their bicycles on traffic-free roads to get ice cream at Lick-ity Split, and adults leave their car windows rolled down, with their purses on the front seat, when they catch a $2 film at The Sun Theater.

Visitors can still go to what was once the Seven Islands Resort, but there are neither seven islands nor a resort. The only accessible landmass in the Grand River was constructed from the remains of the first two islands: a narrow stretch of grass with scattered trees and a meandering, paved trail. It is structureless, save for a large, open air gazebo. The resort itself is gone, lost. But it used to be very different.

In Alda's time, at the end of the nineteenth century, Grand Ledge was dubbed Michigan's Second City, behind only the capital in splendor and affluence. It was a center of commerce, with a bustling chair factory, clay pits, and kilns to fire bricks. There was a railroad depot and railyard, and it was the second city in the state to receive electric street lights, and the first to have a roller coaster and rollerskating rink.

Visitors flocked to the picturesque Ledge Path, where they etched their names and chipped off sandstone for souvenirs. They rented bicycles and canoes and even swimming garb to enjoy the natural tranquility along the river and creeks. Several hotels sprung up on the islands, and a glamorous Opera House was erected on the riverbank near the bridge. There was even a small zoo with exotic animals.

The town was picturesque and enchanting. And then there was a flood. And another. And another. And all was lost, eventually.

Many residents in Grand Ledge today do not know the city's past. Its colorful history was largely forgotten, shared only as oral histories with schoolchildren who walked from the Masonic Lodge to Fitzgerald Park, with scant visible reminders like the annual "Mudge's Follies" vaudeville style show, named after the ill-planned resort hotel. The Opera House stands, although now in a new location, and many of the old buildings lining Bridge Street exist as they once did. But they are out of context, in a way, without knowledge of their past.

Our history is forgotten, and people do not even realize that they have forgotten it.

Even a well-intentioned journalist questioned the validity of the historical details relating to my hometown, but all is true about Grand Ledge within these books, except that Alda's seventh island was in fact a wilderness with no cottage. Or at least not a cottage that anyone saw or recorded.

If you go to Grand Ledge today, explore Oak Park; walk between the Grand River and the ledges. Along the trail, you will first see a spiral etched into the cliff's sandstone face, created by a hand long since gone. Then farther along the trail, approximately fifteen feet from the ground, you will see a mermaid carving, created decades before I was born. Visit the library to see a painting of the "When Shall We Three Meet Again" mural, hanging above the children's books; another painting depicts the round and towering hotel. And on Lincoln Street, the Historical Society's Museum holds treasurers from the city's past for you to explore.

With Alda's story, maybe more people will remember Grand Ledge. Or discover it. Perhaps others will look into their own hometowns and uncover their cities' history. We are each the sum of our environment, and we must know its past in order to appreciate the present. Remember.

A Note About the Green Children of Woolpit

"I thought you knew about the Green Children, Amber?" My professor eyed me curiously from across his desk as I shook my head. "You should read about them."

I was in the final semester of my Bachelor of Arts program and had been sitting on a sofa in the basement office of my screenwriting professor, listening as other students chatted. I don't remember how the conversation turned to the Green Children, but I was suddenly reminded that my professor also taught history.

"What should I read?" I examined the books lining his wall.

"I don't know. Look online."

So I did.

And like all good legends, I discovered more questions than answers.

In short, the myth of the Green Children of Woolpit originated in the south of England in Suffolk during the twelfth century. The various versions differ, but they all involve a boy and a girl with unusual, green-hued skin who suddenly appeared in a wolf pit — a large hole for trapping wolves — speaking an unknown language and purportedly from a distant land. Perhaps Fairy Land. Perhaps Belgium. Perhaps Ireland.

At first, the children could not communicate and only ate green food. After many years, the children adapted to the local diet, lost their verdant tones, and learned English.

The children then shared the story of how they had been shepherds and followed their flock toward the sound of a great bell. They claimed to have been entranced, possibly stumbled into a cave, and suddenly awoke in the wolf pit.

It is likely the boy died before he reached adulthood. The girl was apparently named Agnes and went on to marry, having children of her own who were not green. And the rest is lost to history...

Except the story refuses to be forgotten. It is the foundation of theories, of fan fictions: perhaps the children were from a neighboring village, born of immigrants, orphaned or abandoned, suffering from malnutrition that led to delirium that led to their entrapment in the wolf pit.

Or perhaps they were from an underground realm, a place without sun, the land between humans and fairies and the supernatural.

Perhaps the children were from a different dimension altogether.

And in these conflicting fictions, the loose threads of plot began to weave themselves into a new pattern within my mind.

Alda, instead of Agnes. A dying boy. Fairies. A portal. A foreign language. Another world. Another time. Another story altogether.

Even though William Shakespeare is my primary inspiration for this series, his works are not my sole source.

I sometimes have the feeling that no ideas are truly mine, that I reach into the ether and pull at the coat strings of the past, unweaving and restitching as I write. And that somehow, in the end, I am left with something that looks only slightly like its original form.

In other words, "there be nothing new, but that which is, hath been before."

A Note About Thomas Chatterton

Unlike other characters in my books, Thomas Chatterton was a real person. My character who bears his name was not based on the actual Thomas, but I chose this appellation to pay tribute to a literary figure who deserves to be remembered.

Thomas Chatterton was an eighteenth century English poet born into poverty more than 100 years after Shakespeare's death. Despite its brevity, Thomas' tragic life story is worthy to stand alongside the Bard's plays. He spent his childhood among the gothic spires and flying buttresses of the St. Mary Redcliffe Church in Bristol, an orphan son of a sexton who had left him a treasure trove of medieval manuscripts.

These fantastical tales served as fuel for young Thomas' imagination and later became inspiration for his feats of forgery. You see, Thomas Chatterton was deemed too poor to be a "real" poet. And his style did not fit with the Enlightenment literature of his time. So he created a *nom de plume* — rather a complete, fictional persona — named Thomas Rowley, who wove epics about Bristol's romantic past. Thomas successfully sold these widely praised "Rowley" poems as legitimate manuscripts from the Middle Ages, until he had the audacity to share his identity as the true author with the popular novelist Horace Walpole, who then decried the poems as immature and immaterial.

Thomas was devastated. He had dreamed of a life as a writer in London and had spent his savings to acquire lodgings, but with little reliable income from his writing and a black spot on his name, his options were dire. After weeks of living off scraps, too proud to accept handouts from friends and neighbors, Thomas drank poison and died alone in his cramped attic lodgings, the torn fragments of his poems strewn across the cold floor. He was seventeen years old.

And, like something in a tale by Shakespeare, his death was mistimed. Four days after Thomas' suicide, a would-be patron named Dr. Thomas Fry arrived at the poet's attic room, searching for the talented writer, only to find that his offer of employment came too late. But Dr. Fry diligently pieced together Thomas' poems and helped preserve them for future generations.

Now, Thomas Chatterton is widely regarded as the originator of English Romanticism, his poems having inspired the works of William Wordsworth, Lord Byron, Percy Shelley, John Keats, Dante Gabriel Rossetti, and scores of other literary innovators and dreamers.

So Thomas Chatterton's name appears in my book not because I directly based a character on him but because he lived out of joint with his world. Had Thomas been born in the time of his medieval epics, his narrative genius would have been lauded. Had he lived in the age of the later Romantics, his poems would have been appreciated. But he lived in the middle, not fitting into his own century. This is why he shares a name with Dreng: both were interlopers in their times, out of place. And both struggled to overcome their disjointed fates. Dreng's birth name is an homage to this young man who exited our world too soon but who still left an irrevocable mark.

Yet the name of Thomas Chatterton serves another purpose. It is a reminder to appreciate those who create, to raise up artists and dreamers and support them however and whenever possible. His name is intended to encourage readers to search for forgotten and undiscovered authors — silenced or marginalized voices — writers from the past and the present who continue to challenge and inspire but who might otherwise be overlooked.

Yes, Shakespeare is instrumental in all fiction. But others need to be heard as well. Listen.

Shakespearean Character Allusions Within this Text

Ariel, from *The Tempest*

Boatswain, from *The Tempest*

Bottom and the Rude Mechanicals, from *A Midsummer Night's Dream*

Caliban, from *The Tempest*

Celia, from *As You Like It*

Chestnut munching woman, from *Macbeth*, offstage

Cobweb, from *A Midsummer Night's Dream*

Egyptian Sorceress, from backstory of *Othello*

Gravedigger, from *Hamlet*

Hamlet, from *Hamlet*

Hamnet, William Shakespeare's son

Indian Boy, from backstory of *A Midsummer Night's Dream*

Ferdinand, from *The Tempest* and also *Love's Labour's Lost*

Ghost, from *Hamlet*

Hecate, from *Macbeth*

King/Claudius, from *Hamlet*

Master/Captain of *The Tyger*, from *Macbeth*, offstage

Miranda, from *The Tempest*

Moth/Mote, from *Love's Labour's Lost* and *A Midsummer Night's Dream*

Oberon, from *A Midsummer Night's Dream*

Ophelia, from *Hamlet*

Phillida, from backstory of *A Midsummer Night's Dream* and also *Galatea* by John Lyly

Polonius, from *Hamlet*

Prospero, from *The Tempest*

Puck/Robin Goodfellow, from *A Midsummer Night's Dream*

Queen/Gertrude, from *Hamlet*

Queen Mab, referenced in *Romeo and Juliet*

Sea-maid, from backstory of *A Midsummer Night's Dream*

Sycorax, from backstory of *The Tempest*

Titania, from *A Midsummer Night's Dream*

Wall/Tom Snout, from *A Midsummer Night's Dream*

Will/Billy, based on William Shakespeare, character in *As You Like It*

Witches, from *Macbeth*

An Excerpt from Caliban and the Void
Chapter Twelve: What's Past is Prologue

Caliban hesitated with his fist above the door. Should he pound or gently knock? With a huff, he kicked the footplate instead and nearly slipped into the mud at his feet.

Silence within. Then hurried steps, moving away. Then closer. Finally, the door creaked open, revealing at first an eye. A wider crevice. A face, slack-jawed. Then the door was thrown open, its hinges whining in protest.

Alda stood in the threshold, a wooden rolling pin held above her shoulder, ready to strike. Behind her, a warm glow emanated from the cottage, its yellowed walls dancing with shadows. Plush furnishings. Hanging images in grays and browns. Herbs drying above an oaken table. A rumbling fire below a mantle with some sort of spherical candle.

It did not appear like a witch's abode. "I expected more in you than in the ordinary." Caliban started to step inside, but she blocked his entrance.

"You? How did you find me? Now?" Alda's voice was low. Hoarse, or threatening.

"I told you I would return, witch."

She crossed her arms. "How did you get here?"

"Magic."

"What kind?"

"Does it matter?"

"I thought I was safe, here. Protected." Alda glanced nervously behind her and shifted her weight.

So Caliban seized his advantage and skirted around her, his muddy footprints staining her neat floor. "Did you not think, that you were safe everywhere?"

"No. Of course not."

"Why not? Mother — Sycorax — told me you three had defeated the witches. And their chaos."

Alda turned her back to him and quickly crossed the room. She nervously tapped her foot for a moment before she lowered the rolling pin onto the table beneath the drying herbs.

As she moved, Caliban smelled rosemary.

"There is more evil in this world, Caliban, than only the witches."

"And in other worlds."

Alda nodded. "So I remain vigilant." She paused. "Why are you here?"

Caliban hesitated, aiming to conceal his quest. "I am in need of a reader."

"What do you want me to read?"

"Not you, Alda. Dreng. I came here because — I came here to find him."

A sigh. But it was not from Alda's lips, and her form became rigid.

Caliban finally scanned the room. His gaze fell on a figure reclining on a long chair, asleep near the fireplace.

Caliban's eyes met Alda's, and she grabbed his arm. "Caliban, don't, he —"

But her warning was not enough to slow his eager stride. He crossed the room in three steps, but stopped at the sleeping figure's side.

It was a boy, barely a teen. Disheveled, dark hair plastered in sweat against his forehead. His lips parted, breathing unsteadily. Scars on his cheeks and hands. Caliban pushed away the woolen blanket covering the boy and saw a wound on his side, dressed with white linens. The skin surrounding it was clean, yet the boy slept as if battling some fever.

And for a moment, Caliban felt a strange wave of nostalgia. Like a child discovering a lost plaything. Or a starving man acquiring a meal. Or a faithless sinner witnessing a miracle.

But, no, this boy did not belong here. Time was out of joint. This was Dreng, yet from the past. Some distant version of himself ripped and torn and thrust into this globe.

Alda finished her phrase, "— he's not Dreng."

"What did you do, Alda?" Caliban hoped Alda did not see the tears welling in his eyes.

She set her jaw and responded, "This is Thomas."

"Thomas Chatterton?"

Alda nodded meekly.

"That was Dreng's name. His birth name."

"I know. You told me."

"I did not."

Alda moved closer to Caliban's side, and her voice became softer. "You will."

"When?"

"In the graveyard."

Caliban repeated, urgently, "When?"

"Several days ago." She paused. "But you were older." Alda started toward the long table and, without turning, asked, "Would you like some tea?"

Caliban hesitated as Alda pumped a lever that shot water into a copper kettle. She passed behind him, securing the kettle to an iron hook above the fire. As the water on the kettle's surface hissed in the heat, Alda silently joined Caliban as he watched the sleeping boy.

After a moment, Alda lamented, "He's not the same, you know."

"I do know." This boy was some poor duplicate, like the hollow of a carved image pressed into sand.

"Whatever magic he learned before, whatever skills he had with his enchanted words, that knowledge is gone now."

Caliban realized that sweat had pooled on his brow and wiped it away.

Alda continued, "As are his memories of that life." Alda sighed and checked the kettle. She continued without meeting Caliban's gaze, "This is the boy from the ship. He never grew into the man —"

"Man?"

Alda relented, "Boy — that you and I knew. Our Dreng was of a different timeline, a different yarn in the tapestry of time. This boy, Thomas, knows nothing of magic and spirits and witches. And, if — no, when — he recovers from his wound, I'll ensure that he never learns of such things."

Caliban caught something like a sob in his throat. He had hoped to find Dreng, in some form. Alive, somehow. Resurrected. Caliban had assumed that the cauldron's bubble would lead him to his lost companion. But this sleeping boy was a stranger.

Thomas would never know of the mermaids, of Fairy Land, of Miranda, or the enchanted island. He would not remember the stars.

Dreng was dead.

Alda busied herself with the kettle, carrying it with her faded skirt to the table, retrieving mismatched cups from a shelf above a window. She appeared not to notice the tears streaming down Caliban's cheeks. Yet he did nothing to hide them.

After too many minutes, Caliban took a ragged breath and joined Alda at the table, a three-legged stool creaking beneath his weight as he collapsed into it.

He blew into the hot contents of his mug, hesitated, and mused, "Yet, something may be in his memory, locked. What has Thomas told you?"

"Nothing. He has been in a delirium since I retrieved him from the ship." Alda sipped and added, "He has not yet awoken, not fully."

"So he may know these things, these remembrances from his other life?"

"How?"

Caliban glanced at the boy before gulping his drink. He choked, spat, and forced his voice into a harsh whisper despite the desire to bellow. "What is this damned liquid?"

"Tea." Alda suppressed a laugh.

"Poison?"

"It's made of dried leaves."

"How can leaves be fermented?"

"It's not alcohol." Alda laughed outright. "It is meant to be soothing."

Caliban sipped, cautiously, the warm liquid unpleasant and earthy.

Alda stood. "Try some sugar." She sprinkled white crystals atop the drink and stirred it with her finger.

Caliban drank again, and the bitter was replaced by something sweet. He drained the cup. "I would have preferred ale."

"They say you can see your fortune in the leaves." She tilted the cup before him, revealing a jumble of something that resembled seaweed upon the beach.

Caliban scoffed, "That is impossible. Who says such things?"

"The spiritualists. They camp upriver this time every year."

"Spiritualists?"

"Fortune tellers."

"Frauds."

"Psychics."

"Charlatans."

"Mystics."

"Mere mortals."

"Would you like to visit them, Caliban?"

"Of course not." Yet Caliban examined the leaves, hoping to see something of what may come. After a moment of desperate inspection, Caliban prodded, "You said that I saw you in a graveyard?"

"Yes, twice."

"Twice?"

Alda folded her hands and stared at a wall, breathing steadily, until she looked down at her jittering fingers and began, "You buried my grandmother."

"What?" He lowered his voice, mocking, "Did I kill her?"

"Caliban, please. Listen. You buried her, years ago. When I was alone. Before I found the cauldron's bubble, tucked within a hidden pocket of her cloak. You sang, then. And laughed. And it was, well, uncomfortable."

Caliban nodded. He would jest at death. But he did not speak as she continued.

"When I met you then, it was inconsequential. Before I knew of witches, and Miranda, and you. And my parents."

"Parents?"

"Oberon and Phillida."

Caliban shifted uncomfortably. He had encountered them briefly in Fairy Land.

"And after all of that, after our grand adventures. After you left. And Dreng — after Dreng faced the witches — I returned here. Alone."

"Why?"

Alda sighed, "I don't know. I could have stayed on the island, with Sycorax. But I knew I had to come here." She uncrossed her fingers and tapped nervously on her teacup. "Have you ever had a feeling, like something was lost, but you did not know what was lost?"

Caliban thought of Ina. Of Miranda. Of Dreng. The stars. And he nodded.

"I felt that about this place. That if I returned here, then somehow I could find the part of me that was missing. And, once here, the graveyard called me. And that is how I found you."

She silently sipped her tea, holding the cup to her lips for too long.

"What happened then, in the graveyard?"

"I cannot say."

"Why not?"

Alda faced him, her eyes steely. "I cannot tell your future."

"But you must."

"I have already, already done something terrible — torn a hole in time, or worse — by bringing Thomas here. I cannot cause further damage."

Caliban considered, "Perhaps you are here with me now, and with him, because you told me what to do in the graveyard. Perhaps my future self only knew, or rather knows, what to say then because you shared that secret with me, now."

Alda bit her lip and pressed her fingernails into the tabletop. She looked first to the ceiling, then to a yellow wall, and then to the boy near the fireplace. She set her jaw and relented, "Fine, Caliban. Fine. But if something horrific happens because you know —"

"It will be fine, as you say, Alda."

She cleared her throat, again glanced at the ceiling, and whispered, "You were there, digging a grave. And your face was covered, so I did not know it was you, at first. But I recognized you from before, from when you buried my grandmother. Your voice — you are not from here, from Michigan, so I remembered that you had dug her grave. And you said that what's past is prologue."

"Past is prologue?"

"It was written on a gravestone. And you, you made some jokes." Alda seemed to laugh, but the sound was awkward. "And then you showed me another gravestone, one that read — I memorized it — it read, 'Stranger pause as you pass by. As you are now, so once was I. As I am now, soon you shall be. So welcome death, and follow me.' You, you said that it was a reminder that all those who are now dead were once alive. And, and I thought of Dreng. Then you revealed yourself. And gave me a cauldron's bubble. Wait, wait, I have it here, or rather part of it."

Alda stood and eyed Caliban suspiciously as she retrieved a small, metal box from the shelf above the window. She placed it before him and again sunk onto her stool, her foot convulsing with impatience.

Caliban pried the lid open. Nestled within, atop scraps of floral fabric, was a mound of dust, fine and purple.

"What is this?"

"A cauldron's bubble. Its remains."

"Have you attempted to repair it?"

Alda shifted, avoiding an answer. Caliban considered further. "Yet it, it's purple. How else is it — was it — different?"

Alda shrugged. "You told me it could transport two people."

"Could it?"

"That is how I saved Thomas."

"I gave it to you? Freely?" Caliban closed the lid and slid the box across the table.

"Yes. How did you make it?"

"I made it?"

"So you said."

"I do not know. I have not made it, yet." He rubbed his chin. "How did you make your bubble, the one before this?"

"With his help." Alda nodded toward the boy. "Before, when he was

Dreng. When he knew how to read the spell properly."

Caliban understood. She did not hold this magic. "And prior to that, you used your grandmother's bubble? That you found in her cloak?"

Again, Alda nodded. "She was called Hecate. A witch. A powerful witch. She knew much more than I ever will."

Worry flooded Caliban's mind. He had come to this place, to this island, to find Dreng, to seek his aid. To read the spell. And Dreng was gone. Not simply dead. Gone. And Alda raised new questions, new problems. "What else happened in the graveyard?"

"I fell into an open grave."

"Why?"

Alda scowled, "It was an accident. And then the bubble took me to Dreng, dying in the belly of his ship. And then back to my cottage, with him. With Thomas."

As Caliban pondered, the fire's spits and crackles filled the silence. Alda stood and poured more liquid into Caliban's cup, dashing crystals again across its surface. He watched them dissolve as he wondered aloud, "But can Thomas read?"

"How could he? Thomas is from before the island. Before he met you or me or magic."

"Can we wake him, now, and ask?"

"No."

"But —"

Alda frowned. "I said, no."

Caliban drained his cup and tried again. "I need his words, Alda."

"And I need him."

Caliban laughed, hollow and dry. "You are the witch from the old stories, are you not? You steal a boy and keep him as your captive and, what, roast him in your fire? Devour him?"

Alda stood, bending threateningly over the table. "I saved him. I won't let you destroy him." She again sunk onto the stool, her hands trembling. "You or anyone else. He is innocent now. You cannot corrupt him."

For a flash, Caliban saw his mother in Alda. Protective to the verge of destruction. She could suffocate this boy, here in the confines of her little cottage. The walls could crush him alive — if not physically, then spiritually. She could kill his soul. And whatever was left of Dreng.

And Caliban could not abide such a death for his friend. "I will return, then, later."

"When?"

"Tomorrow."

"No."

"Next week?"

"Next year."

Caliban shook his head. "That will be too long."

"For you, or for him?"

"In a month."

"Three years."

"Alda —"

"Five years."

"Alda, that is too much time. I —"

"You came here with a cauldron's bubble, did you not?"

Caliban was silent.

Alda continued, "Then what is time to you? It is a blink. You can make a year seem like a second."

"Yes, but the rest of the world — time does not stand still for others."

Alda stood, and Caliban followed her lead.

"Come back in five years. Let this boy have his childhood in peace.

When you return, you may see if Thomas can help you then."

As if on cue, Thomas groaned and stirred, tossing onto his side and throwing the blanket toward the fire. Alda glanced nervously at the boy as Caliban stepped toward him. But the witch circled around and blocked his path.

"Caliban, if you truly need his help, then come back in five years. Seek your answers then." Alda placed her hand on his chest, as if pleading. But her touch quickly became rigid, icy, as she pushed him back toward the threshold.

Caliban slipped on his muddy boots and tumbled toward the door. Alda opened it with one hand and shoved Caliban with the other. She narrowed her eyes and repeated, "Five years, Caliban. Not a moment sooner."

The door closed, and Caliban realized that he was without, in the cold and dark. The air heavy and wet around him. Predawn sunlight streaming through the trees. He thought briefly of Miranda, of where she might be. Of Prospero. Of what might change in the years he would lose. No, in the years they would lose. If the others were in a place of years, of time, as he was here. And he thought of Alda. Of the powers he knew her to have. Of the harm she might do to him. Or to Thomas.

Five years. That was too long. Far too long. Yet, yet, Caliban had to consider more than himself. To think of others. He was no longer alone in the world, in his cave. He had friends now. He could not simply stomp and steal and curse as he once did, as a child, secluded on his island.

So despite wanting to knock on the door again, to dash it down, to rush within and wake the wounded boy, safe and warm by the fire, Caliban instead closed his palm around the cauldron's bubble. And blinked.

*   *   *

The rising sun was warm on Caliban's shoulders, its light filtering through the thin leaves on the horizon. The ground was hard and dry. Birds sang, distantly. Voices, even farther away.

The door to Alda's cottage was still before him, marred with scuffs and scrapes. Years had passed for this door and the inhabitants beyond it, but not for him.

This time, Caliban knocked softly, his fingers trembling within his fist. Silence. A second knock. More silence. Finally, he tried the knob, and the door opened with a rusty whine.

The cottage was different now. Dim and dark. The only light from the windows. The furniture was worn, unkempt, dirty. The walls a deeper shade of yellow, smudged with mud and soot, their patterned surface peeling and torn.

And scattered about were clumps of red dirt. No, not dirt. Clay. Salted, fired clay. In forms of things fantastic. A reclining lion above the fireplace. A flowered tree trunk by the hearth. Above the window, birds. And upon the wooden table, a winged figure, bird-like, with the torso and head of a human.

It was Ariel, cast in clay.

Caliban stepped to examine the sculpture closer, but movement from the long chair near the fireplace caught his eye.

Alda sat upright, her feet bare and dirty beneath a veined blue-gray dress. Her hair unkempt and ragged. Her eyes unfocused, as if looking into the distance. "You are here. Precisely to the minute. They told me you would be late, or that you would not return, but I did not believe them."

She sunk again into the chair. Caliban knelt at her side. The strong, defiant witch he had known was gone. This was a wreck. A shell. A shadow of Alda.

"Who told you?"

"The women. They whisper to me."

"Women?" He stood. "Other witches?"

Alda turned on her side and propped her head on her arm. "But we are safe. I trapped them in my walls." She nodded across the room, and Caliban followed her gaze.

Painted onto the wall in thick, red mud was a spiral. A witch-trap.

"So we are safe," Alda continued. "For now. But he is not. Not tonight."

"Thomas?"

She nodded.

"Where is he?"

"Away." Alda laughed, the sound high and shrill. "He does not believe me. About the women. About their danger. About, about, it all. He thinks me mad." She grinned, and Caliban saw something like madness in her countenance. "But he can read, Caliban. You were right. You were right. You are right. I learned the next day, after you left, I learned that he could read. And I have waited for all of these years to tell you. But I have not told him about his reading, not what it means. Not what his words can do. But he remembers, yet, still, somehow."

"Remembers?" Caliban stumbled into a chair behind him. What had happened here, to Alda, in the time between?

This was her cave, he realized. She had been trapped, not only the boy. She had been suffocating here, alone, unfriended, and forgotten.

Caliban had abandoned her. Like Ina had abandoned him. Like Miranda — That was unforgiveable.

"Yes, he knows what we know. Somehow. A part of him does. A part of him remembers." Alda stood suddenly, her arms moving in wide arcs as she pointed at the clay figures around the room. "He made these, Caliban. He created them." She lifted the lion from the mantle and thrust it onto his lap.

Caliban studied it. Its fired surface was smooth, well-hewn. Its underside rough and angled. The proportions and features were all correct, even the tuft on its tail. On its side were initials: AMR.

"He might have seen a lion in a painting. Or a statue. This, this is not proof of memories." Yet Caliban felt the doubt behind his words.

"The lion was the first he created. Look, Caliban, look. Those are my initials. He knows them. He knows them. Thomas knows them. Alda Midsummer Reeding. I didn't have a middle name before, when I met Dreng. Thomas gave me that name. Because of my birthday. So Thomas carved those initials." She took a deep, shaking breath. "But Dreng molded the lion."

Caliban ran his finger over the letters, musing. He understood time, well enough, and magic. But what of memory, the warder of the brain?

Alda crossed the room and pointed to the birds. "And Dreng made these birds. The birds from the enchanted island. From your island. And, and Ariel. Look, he made Ariel! Just yesterday, he gave me this figure. How could he know Ariel, Caliban? How could Thomas know about a harpy?"

Caliban replaced the lion above the mantle and walked cautiously to the table. There was no doubt that the figure was Ariel.

"Did you tell him, Alda? Did you tell him about his other timeline?"

"Yes, yes, of course. How could I not? But I did not tell him everything. Not everything. Not about Miranda or Sycorax, no, not about his wife. Not about Ariel. And not about you."

Caliban scowled, started to speak, but bit his tongue. There was more here, more than time alone. There was some strange magic at play.

"But they were fairytales, Caliban. Myths. Legends. No 'you' or 'I' or 'us.' They were stories of far, far away lands. Of lost people, of characters. Not biographies. Only, only tall tales."

"Where is he now?"

Alda shifted nervously.

"Alda, where is Thomas?"

"At the clay pit."

"The what?"

"The clay pit. Across the river. He mines clay."

"Why?"

"Because he needed occupation. And that is safe. Honest. It is what men do here, in Grand Ledge. They build chairs or fire bricks or dig clay. That, or attend on those at the resort. But that is not safe. That is where the women are from." She ran her fingers over her hair as tears formed in her eyes. "And I thought, I thought — I thought that Thomas could not think if he dug clay. That he would be safe from his thoughts. Yet, yet he makes these things." Again, she waved her arms. "He must dream these figures. Because he sneaks into the pipe kilns and fires them and brings them home. I, I only wanted him to be safe, you see. Safe."

"You wanted him to be ignorant."

Alda laughed, "Ignorance is bliss."

"Who would say such a thing?"

Alda's heavy breaths suddenly transformed into a sob, and then a wail. She plunged onto the stool, and it crumbled beneath her force.

Caliban rushed to her side and lifted her shoulders, cradling her shaking form in his arms. It would have been comical if not for her complete dismay.

After several heartbeats, her breathing calmed. He half-carried her back to the long chair and sat beside her, his arm still around her shoulders as she leaned into him.

"I waited for you, Caliban, to tell you. I waited and waited and waited. And I wanted nothing more than to tell you. To share my secrets. To have you help me. And him. But the waiting, it was too, too much."

"You told me to return in five years. Not a moment sooner."

"When have you ever listened to me?"

She was right, Caliban knew. He could have returned at an earlier point, to check on the boy. To see if he was safe. To see if Alda was safe. But he instead was cautious. No, honest. He was honest to a fault. Absolute. A moral fool.

And Alda's current state was the cost of his honesty.

A thud. A crack. A scream.

Alda jumped to her feet, and Caliban followed her gaze.

The wall opposite, the wall with the muddy witch-trap, bulged. Something behind it stirred. As Caliban froze, Alda leaped into action. She plunged her fist into the cold hearth and flew across the room, muttering curses beneath her breath as she drew a larger spiral in soot, expanding the mud's curves.

The noise stopped, and the wall reformed its plane.

Caliban gasped, "The wall, it —"

"I told you. It was one of the women. I trapped her. And others."

"Yes, but —"

"You thought me mad as well?" Alda smiled coyly. "Like Thomas." She wiped her soiled fingers on her skirt, and Caliban realized that the gray he had thought was a pattern above the blue of her dress was truly a series of soot marks.

How many women were caught in spiral sigils behind the cottage walls?

Alda calmed herself, smoothed her skirt, and attempted to straighten her hair, adjusting several pins. "Come, friend, we will go to him. We will see Thomas. Or Dreng. Or whomever he may be. And I will tell you of the other women."

She left the cottage hastily, and Caliban knew not what to do, but follow.

Caliban and the Void

will be released

by Verdopolis Press

on October 10, 2022.

The author would like to thank and acknowledge...

My husband, who — thanks to our Shakespeare friends and his own drive for self-improvement — finally understands my books. Welcome to the dork club, my love! Keep quoting Hamlet as much as possible.

My Zoom friends and reading companions, Beers & Bard. "What, HO?"

Alice and Victoria, who do so much more than they ever take credit for.

My two girls, who became the best little pandemic hermits they could be.

Finally, this trilogy edition would not exist without Liam Milner. Thank you.

CAULDRON'S BUBBLE

The Grand Ledge Public Library, who lent me all of their books about Joan of Arc, and whose paintings of the city's past helped inspire my childhood imagination.

My teachers, including those not listed here. Teachers never know how much they are truly appreciated, so I want to especially thank (in order of appearance) Mrs. Goering, who made us explore; Jenny Deja, who gave me many years; Richard Knopp, who asked the right questions; Larry Sanders, who let me read *Ivanhoe*; Larry Livingston, who sang to us at Interlochen; Diane Wakoski, who told me that there are too many people in my head for poetry; Tess Tavormina, who cannot be given enough thanks; Bill Vincent, who let us imagine in his underground office; Stuart Kelban, who made me appreciate cold opens; Richard Lewis, who complimented my action lines and gave me confidence; and Sam Baker, who patiently tolerated my obsession with Lord Byron's *Don Juan*.

My draft-readers and critiquers, who gave so much time and thought in exchange for these few words. Thank you (in mostly alphabetical order) Jill Dickinson, who was so generous with her help; Anali Gonzalez, who got this out of the blue; Ben Gross, who probably likes Tolkien too much; Nori Hubert, who shares my passion for Joan of Arc; Katelyn Patterson, who reads more than anyone I know; Tina Risinger, who has the patience of a saint; Erin Risinger, who deserves extra credit (show this to your teacher); Eric and Emily Risinger, who both missed out at Starbucks; and Christina Potter Swan, who deserves credit for the word "Hamlety."

Brandi Harrison of Typejar Studio for her beautiful cover art.

My late grandparents, Bob and Arleta, who told me stories about the past.

My parents, who showed me the world and made me question reality. My late father, who taught me that Jane Eyre is beautiful, Hamlet is sane, and that the cook is the most powerful man on a pirate ship. My mother, who let me watch *The Twilight Zone* when I was too young, introduced me to William Sydney Porter and H. H. Munro, and took me to The Sun in my pajamas.

And especially Tony, for everything. Thank you.

DOUBLE DOUBLE TOIL

My publisher, Verdopolis Press, and all of the people involved with the publication, who gave me enough freedom, the right dose of advice, and a constant stream of reassurance.

Malvern Books of Austin, Texas, a bookseller that propagates the "weird" in our city and was kind enough to host my launch.

The #BookBloggers who took the time to review my books, especially those who participated in my blog tour. You are more appreciated than you know.

My teachers, especially Jen Deja, who always shows up; Bill Vincent, who told me of the Green Children of Woolpit; and Tess Tavorimina, who let me argue that Ophelia is a witch because she floats before she drowns. Also Stuart Kelban and Richard Lewis, whose ears were probably both ringing for several years as I reread notes from their classes, and Amanda Ferrari, my teaching friend.

My new friends, Dan Beaulieu and Kevin Condardo of the podcast *No Holds Bard*, as well as the entire #Bardflies community. I wish I had found you all sooner because I wrote my first novel within the bubble of academia, not knowing that there are others in the world who share my strange visions and passions and loving irreverence of Shakespeare. I may have only discovered you all this past spring, but our shared community seems to run so much deeper. #BardfliesUnite

My perennial friends, Adam Gobeski and Charlie Wallace, who continue to tolerate me on their podcasts, *The Gobeski/Wallace Report* and *Cinematic Respect*, and who literally stood up for me while graciously wearing cravats.

My draft-readers and critiquers, who sort through the grit of early versions and somehow find diamonds: Patti Briggs, who gave time she didn't have; Susan Gebhard, who runs on enthusiasm and mocha; and Jill Dickinson, who is the embodiment of kindness and patience and friendship.

Brandi Harrison of TypeJar Studio, who once again collaborated to create the beautiful cover art.

My mother, who wears a *Cauldron's Bubble* Tshirt and tells strangers about my books.

My two daughters: the youngest, who befriends fairies and understands the magic of the natural world; the eldest, who is fierce and confident and makes her own magic.

My husband, who somehow still puts up with me when I have one foot in reality and the other in a fantasy that only exists in my head. You are my compass, the most perfect person in the world for me, my companion and inspiration. I am so grateful for you, and these words are insufficient.

I realized, too, that there was an omission in the *Cauldron's Bubble* acknowledgements: William Shakespeare, who wrote the stories that are still reworked and rewritten in nearly every piece of fiction, whether consciously or subconsciously, and the players in his lifetime and since who have cultivated his words and made his worlds and characters relevant throughout the centuries. Thank you...

TROUBLE FIRES BURN

My publisher, Verdopolis Press, who continues to support and encourage me.

Malvern Books of Austin, Texas, which is still the best kind of "weird" and was once again kind enough to host my launch.

Mixtape Marketing for offering sound advice.

The #Bookbloggers on Twitter and elsewhere, who help connect readers with authors, with a special shout-out to Rosie Threakall for catching up outside of the blogosphere (aka in real life).

Literature Lady herself, Twitter thread extraordinaire @Literature_Lady, who talked with me about my books on her podcast.

Charlie Wallace and Adam Gobeski, who still put up with me after all these years and who, for some incomprehensible reason, allow me to occasionally join them on *Cinematic Respect*.

The #Bardflies and their fearless leaders, Kevin Condardo and Dan Beaulieu of the acclaimed podcast *No Holds Bard*. This community is the epitome of acceptance, open-mindedness, and appreciation of all things Shakespeare. I give you my hands.

Montgomery Sutton of the Rude Grooms for lending me his words.

The self-proclaimed "biggest fans" of my books: Alice Bloomer, who has seen more plays than anyone I know, and Liam Milner, who creates amazing fan art.

Susan Gebhard for being my source of enthusiasm and a companion for playground chats.

Andy Bates for carefully reading and catching my "mettle."

Jill Dickinson, who has been my rock(star) since Book One, and who is the most giving and selfless person I know. And Jill even gave me my beloved *Hamlet* pillow, which has quite literally had my back for Book Three.

Brandi Harrison of TypeJar Studio, who reworks my scribbles into beautiful cover art.

My mom, Pam, who is a fighter and the best Bubby to her granddaughters. Thank you.

Finally, the people behind Dreng and Alda: my husband, Tony, and our fierce little girls, Alix and Annie. You give voices to my characters and inspiration to me. Thank you, so very much.

And, of course, Bill the Bard, always and forever.

CPSIA information can be obtained
at www.ICGtesting.com
Printed in the USA
BVHW071238120821
614282BV00001B/48

9 781732 314283